STRAY SOULS

"A shaman? A shaman is the knower of the path, the seer of truth, the wanderer of the hidden ways. The dude who is in the know, the one who sees what the kids are too dumb to look at. To put it in little words so as you'll understand – your half-decent shaman always knows where the nearest public bog is, and if it's worth legging it for the bus"

Samuel the Elbow, *How to Be a Shaman –*
a Beginner's Guide

"They say that the soul of the city is being ripped apart.

I've never had much time for 'them' and the things 'they' say but, for once, I find myself forced to agree. It begins with a rusting, a place where new foundations were laid and which are now turned to orange-brown. Then a cracking, the road beneath your feet splitting though the tarmac is fresh. Then a dripping, the water coming through from the pipes overhead, then a creaking; wood splinters against wood, glass breaks and someone may leave a bin bag behind the pane to keep out the draught but that is all, and it is forgotten, and it withers, and it dies. People don't understand how a city dwindles like a living thing, but that is what it is and, like all things that live, it too can die.

And this shaking, this crumbling, this death by little silences falling in busy streets, this hollowness of all things – I am powerless to prevent"

M. Swift, 127th Midnight Mayor of London

STRAY SOULS

KATE GRIFFIN

Orbit
An imprint of
Little, Brown Book Group
100 Victoria Embankment
London EC4Y 0DY

An Hachette UK Company
www.hachette.co.uk

www.orbitbooks.net

ORBIT

First published in Great Britain in 2012 by Orbit
Reprinted 2014

Copyright © 2012 by Catherine Webb

Excerpt from *The Troupe* by Robert Jackson Bennett
Copyright © 2012 by Robert Jackson Bennett

The moral right of the author has been asserted.

A CIP catalogue record for this book
is available from the British Library.

ISBN 978-0-356-50064-5

Typeset in Weiss by M Rules
Printed and bound in Great Britain by
Clays Ltd, St Ives plc

Papers used by Orbit are from well-managed forests
and other responsible sources.

Chapter 1

How to Become One with Everything

It was raining when Sharon Li became one with the city.

The rain may have had nothing to do with her moment of profound spiritual revelation but is worth mentioning just in case. The kebab she was eating definitely had nothing to do with it but will prove relevant in the sense that if she hadn't dropped it onto her trousers, she might have stood in the rain a little longer marvelling at the majesty of the universe, which could have had a long-term medical impact and thus affected the course of events yet to come. As it was, the sensation of orange goo oozing into the fabric of her jeans would provoke her to take practical action where other minds might simply have dissolved in mystical wonder.

Meanwhile she stood, bits of salad falling from their plastic box, her body temporarily forgotten. The rain rolled down her face, glued her black hair to her pine-coloured skin, deepened her orange top to sodden brown and seeped through the soles of her shoes. On a nearby railway line a goods train clanked by at ten miles an hour, its wheels screaming like golems being beaten to death. Two streets away the night bus threw up a sheet of dirty water from a blocked drain over a drunken group from a stag party wrapped in cling film and not much else. A car alarm wailed as a trainee thief smashed a window and made a grab for the mobile phone left on a seat. A door quietly closed as a husband, heading off for the flight to his conference in Spain, tried not to disturb his wife; she, entirely awake, lay sensing the warmth he had left behind. A fox stopped on its walk through the night and turned its head towards the sky as if wondering which star tonight shone for it behind the bank of sodium cloud. Paint dripped down the metal shutter of an off-licence from an amateur attempt at graffiti. A lorry laden with tomorrow's milk skipped a red light because it could, and just tonight, just this once, the speed camera forgot to flash.

And for a moment, just one brilliant, burning, unbearable moment, Sharon Li knew everything there was to know about the city, every street and every stone; and her thoughts were in the wheels of the cars splashing through the puddles and her breath was in the gasps of air drawn through the railway tunnels and her heart beat with the turning of the river.

Then, because the human mind is only capable of comprehending so much, she forgot.

Chapter 2

One Door Closes, Another Opens

Later, in circumstances that Sharon Li would certainly have frowned upon, the entire balance of reality is about to be pushed off the bungee.

Soft cloth drags on carpet.

A door closes in the night.

Flicker of shadow across a door.

Sound of falling.

She says, "They'll find you they'll find you you have to get out now!"

Her voice is a gabble of forced breath, sandpaper in the throat, glass in the lungs.

A finger of wind commanding silence.

"Oh God."

A brush of something soft against rapidly cooling skin, a whisper of sound that has no words, nor has ever felt the need.

"Let me live."

Paper stirs across the floor.

Something . . .

. . . changes.

She says, "No. That isn't what I—"

And she dies.

Chapter 3

Time Is Only a Perception

That was then.

This is now.

He snuck in the back way as always, hoping that today his PA would get bored of trying to catch him. But there she was, as always, waiting at the bottom of the lift, papers in one hand, half-eaten egg and cress sandwich in the other.

He puts his face into neutral-yet-resilient and summons the lift. She slips in beside him, as if she'd casually been waiting at this place, at this time, a fortunate coincidence, two professionals having a chance encounter. And says, "Have you read it?"

"Good morning Mr Mayor, how are you? Why, isn't it lovely if surprising to see you, I just happened to be passing!" he intones.

"Good morning, Mr Mayor. How are you?"

"I'm very well, thank you, Kelly, and yourself?"

"Absolutely topping, Mr Mayor, completely the best. Would you like a foot massage and a cup of tea before commencing the business of the day?"

He sighs. Every day they have this encounter, and every day it ends the same way. "What was the first question?"

"Have you read it?"

"Vague as that is, let's play safe and go with no."

"Mr Mayor—"

"Kelly, I've got things to do, people to see ..."

"I really feel it's important."

"You said that last week, with the white paper on basilisk activity in the Barking sewage works."

"Well, it is important – you can't think it's not."

"I'm sure it's important. I just wish you hadn't tried to prove your point by sending me on a field trip."

"Mr Mayor," she tries again, at once wheedling and determined, "just take a look at *this*."

She hands him a paper. Since she's been his PA, Kelly has got good at knowing just how much paper to give him at any time. Only one sheet of A4 and he feels patronised; an entire folder and he won't bother reading. Five to seven pages of essential notes have become the standard, with the really important stuff, the absolutely *vital* stuff, tucked in around page 3.

He reads page 1 and huffs. Flicks to page 2 and sighs. Gets to page 3, shows no reaction, turns to page 4 and ...

... turns right back.

She watches his eyes dance over the words as the lift slows to a halt on the top floor. The doors open but he doesn't move. His lips move silently as if the portion of his brain usually dedicated to absorbing this kind of information is crying out for assistance from any other interested lobes.

He says, "No but what?"

"You've found the ..."

"Too bloody right, and no, but seriously, *what*?"

"I told you it was important!"

"Yes but no but I mean sure, I get where this is coming from, but actually—"

"I'm told they get a lot of interest from Facebook."

"Facebook! *Facebook?!* I've got a city infested with horrors of the night crawling from nether darkness; I've got monsters and demons and missing fucking goddesses and creatures whose footsteps burn the night and wards failing and meetings – bloody hell, I've got bloody fucking fiscal meetings with the directors' board – and they're doing this with *Facebook?!*"

"That's how I understand it, Mr Mayor."

"Couldn't someone tell them to stop?"

"I'm not sure that would be a good idea."

"But it's ridiculous!"

"I think it's rather sweet."

He looks up from the paper, and now there's no attempt to keep the horror off his face.

"'Sweet'?"

"Well, in its way . . ."

"Kelly, you're a guardian of the night, a magician who wears black and not for its slimming properties; you've been trained in how to kill people in many different ways and when you're not giving me bad news, you're in theory running around the city hunting down all the things too nasty to be named, and you think this is *sweet*?"

She thinks about it. "Beats blood-drenched midnight orgies."

Chapter 4

Good Preparation Is the Key to Success

The hall was hung with dusty red velour curtains. There were orange plastic chairs stacked against the wall, and a trestle table bearing an unwashed coffee mug, a free newspaper from yesterday afternoon, a ruptured tennis ball and a discarded umbrella with its workings mangled by a strong wind. One door led into the church next door; the other said FIRE ESCAPE and led into the mite-filled alley between the hall and the neighbouring barber's shop.

The barber, Antonio Anthonis, born in Athens, raised on Eurovision, described the hall as "a nice enough place for the kids, yes?"

The vicar's wife, who handled all the hiring and scheduling of events, described St Christopher's Hall as "a friendly community venue where people of every age and disposition can come together in celebration of each other and their local area."

The vicar, the Reverend Adam Weir, with a more liberal understanding of most things than his missus, described it as "twenty-five an hour and you'll wonder why you're forking out so much, but, believe me, when you see the other places you'll just be thrilled. Price goes down to twenty pounds an hour if you can convince me you're doing something moral or pious, and fifteen an hour if there's free tea and biscuits. Church reserves the right to take leftovers and I don't drink Earl Grey."

Sharon explained what they did.

The vicar listened. His eyes had run politely but thoroughly over Sharon as she'd talked, taking in her ankle-high purple boots, cropped jeans with the tattiness left in, orange tank top and the streaks of electric blue dyed into the front of her hair. He nodded appreciatively at the key bits, though his eyes did eventually start to glaze over.

"So," she concluded, "I think, yeah, that it's . . . it's moral *and* has biscuits."

"Tell you what," he said. "Throw in an extra packet of Jammie Dodgers and we'll call it a tenner."

That was five weeks ago.

She'd had to wait two weeks for Gospel Singing (Level 2) to finish their rehearsal period in the hall, and also, Power Dance (Dance Your Way to the New You!) had got in first to the slot she'd wanted, forcing her to push things back another three weeks. Following her posting of time and place on Facebook and Twitter, the feedback was generally good, though some people did ask if there was a discreet way in.

It had of course been one of the things she'd checked in advance.

She arrived early, while the hall was still occupied by Youth Judo (Discipline, Fitness and Safety for Your Children), and waited outside until the mums had collected their small robed warriors. The instructor was the last to leave. He was a short man with dreads down to his hip and a white duelling shirt that warped under pressure from within. His face was the brown of soil after rain, and his smile was dazzling.

"Dan," he said, gripping Sharon's hand with fingers that could have squashed coconuts like a wet sponge. "You must be . . . What do you guys do?"

"Support group," Sharon explained.

"First time here, yeah? Where were you before?"

"Nowhere. This is our first meeting ever."

"Wow, that's great. Hope it goes well for you." Another flash of teeth, brilliant in the fading light of evening. "Have a good one, yeah?"

And he too left.

For a moment Sharon stood alone in the hall.

Outside, the sky was a cloud-scudded grey-blue, sliced with falling autumn leaves. From the pub on the corner she could hear students from the local hall of residence discovering just what the deal was with cider and, importantly, what happened after. The smell of paprika drifted in from the restaurant two doors down. Someone dinged their bell as they cycled by. In Exmouth Market, lined with cafés, bars and boutiques, darkness was an invitation to raise the volume. The church and its community hall was a box of silence against the rising sounds of laughter and the clatter of glasses.

She put down her plastic bags on the table. They contained five packets of custard creams, six of Jammie Dodgers, two of chocolate fingers (milk) and two of chocolate fingers (white). A bag of apples to make up for the sweetness of all that had gone before and a bunch of bananas for those who didn't like apples because, frankly, who didn't like bananas? A large box of builder's teabags, a smaller box of Earl Grey. Another small box – of herbal teas (mixed) for those who didn't like tea – a litre of milk, a box of white sugar, a packet of plastic teaspoons, a packet of plastic cups, a packet of foam cups (heat resistant) and a bundle of paper plates. Two packs of bright red napkins because you never knew, one bottle of instant coffee in case no one drank tea, two litres of orange juice from concentrate, one litre of apple. A kettle. Small, white, plastic. Just in case.

Turned out, the hall had its own kettle. After all, the leaflet did say "amenities provided".

Chapter 5

Keep Your Eye on the Goal

Approximately half a mile from St Christopher's Hall, and Gavin McGafferty is about to die.

He doesn't know it right now; in fact, right now he's having a hard time thinking of anything through the red haze of contempt clouding his better judgement. He walks, and doesn't fully grasp where he's walking, and under his breath he mutters, "Fuck fuck fuck fuck fuck fucking . . ."

A bus sweeps by. It's his bus. He was waiting for it at the stop outside the chemist, but when it didn't come fast enough, he started walking to the next, and now there it is, passing by at that perfect point where he's too far to run, and he knows, he just *knows*, that it, like everything else, is out to get him.

"Fuck fuck fuck SHIT . . ."

It is perhaps unfortunate, in a strictly humanitarian sense, that in less than fifty yards Gavin McGafferty will have his throat torn out with a single swipe of a fist-sized claw, his left ear ripped from the side of his face and his pelvis fractured by the sheer weight of creature bowling him to the ground. Nevertheless, his co-workers, when informed of the unfortunate event some twenty-two hours later, will pause a fraction too long as they consider his departure. There may even be some who, going to the bathroom afterwards to compose their faces in an appropriate mask of grief, find themselves looking in the mirror and breathing out a slow sigh of guilty relief. Gavin McGafferty is not a man who endears himself to the universe, and it is in this vein that he understands that the driver of the 159 bus that overtook him on the corner has waited – absolutely waited – just outside his line of sight for the right moment to screw him, personally, over.

The world has been conspiring against Gavin McGafferty from the start. He knows his co-workers talk about him behind his back; he knows that his work – which is fucking good fucking work, FUCK! – has been made to look shit by the apathy and personal hatred of his peers. He knows that no man can achieve perfection against such a world of inadequacy, but most of all he knows, more than anything else, that he is right and everyone else is wrong, and if he looks shit it's only because the rest of them are out to get him.

"Fucking stupid fucking arsehole . . . "

He turns onto St John Street and sees the bus stop. The 159 is pulling away, two kids visible in the back seat, framed by the bus's internal white lights, laughing, probably at him. There's no one at the bus stop, no one on the road. They're all on the bus, or inside the last fucking taxi in EC fucking 1, not that they even need it, lazy pricks, because they're probably not going far, to a wine bar or something, whereas Gavin is going – *Gavin* is going to—

A motorbike grumbles into life behind him, distracting him from his train of thought. Its engine rumbles, a low throaty growl, then keeps turning over. He crosses the quiet street. The bike is still revving, but now there is something wrong with the sound: a potency, a thickness, a thing within it that . . .

"Fucking stupid fuck fuck fuck . . . "

. . . that pauses for breath?

He hesitates on the edge of the yellow light that frames the empty bus shelter. Something soft presses on a loose cobble stone, which sings a hollow note as it bumps against its neighbours. Other men might have looked back. Other men might have wondered. Gavin McGafferty knows better than to look. Only an idiot looks.

He steps up to the shelter and looks at the timetable. At this time of night, the 159 runs every twenty to twenty-five minutes, which he knows means at least half an hour. And it'll be full of weirdo druggies and stupid kids, and he'll be late, which is fucking fine because they can all fucking wait for him anyway but shit shit shit shit . . .

A ripple in the sound behind him, and it's louder, and it's closer, and that ripple – for that is the word – could almost be defined as the sound a soft leathery lip might make as it rubs its way across protruding fanged teeth, while a deep rumble inside a ribcage pressed within a hundred pounds of taut black flesh might yet prove the source of this persistent grumbling.

Idiots look.

Idiots look.

He's not an idiot. Jesus, he's Gavin McGafferty, he's the shit, he's the stuff, he's the guy on the up, and all those fucking idiots around him who talk behind his back and try to bring him down because of their envy, their *envy* for Christ's sake, they don't understand. They'll never get it, they're the kind of guys who'd look, they'd look and he wouldn't he wouldn't he . . .

Looks.

The start of the scream doesn't make it all the way to his voice box before it finds itself some three feet away from the air that should have supplied it. The teeth that remove his left ear dig deep enough to crack the solid sphere of his skull like a pistachio. Arguably, it's the combined weight of Gavin and his attacker hitting the ground that causes the fractured pelvis. But frankly, given the time the paramedics spend trying to identify the body afterwards, no one really bothers to check.

Chapter 6

In the Friendship of Others, I Find Myself

The first one arrived on time, at 9.05 p.m. exactly.

The next at 9.07. There was a lull at 9.08 and then, as if an infrequent and much-denounced train had finally pulled up, at 9.11 they all started to tumble through the door of St Christopher's Hall, with sideways glances as if to say, and you are *who*? Some smiled nervously and offered to shake hands – or whatever limb seemed suitable. Others kept their eyes on the floor, or clasped the shoulder of a more approachable companion come along to give support. One or two sneaked in under the mantle of their own very special disguises or glamours: there was the ever-reliable yellow fluorescent jacket that nearly guaranteed invisibility to all who wore it, through to a full-blown burka, rather let down by the hint of talon protruding beneath as the wearer folded herself uncomfortably into a plastic chair.

"Tea, coffee?" Sharon asked the gathering assembly as they shuffled their seats into place. A chorus of grunted affirmations came back, no one wanting to acknowledge that they were so difficult as to *need* tea or coffee but, that said, if someone else was having one anyway, they didn't see the harm ….

One or two braver guests tried talking to each other, stop-start conversations that fell into a lull as they gathered into a communal circle. Watching from the corner of her eye, by the time the door to the alley finished banging shut Sharon had counted fourteen individuals of various shapes and sizes.

Not a bad number, she decided as steam began spouting from the kettle. And considering how limited her biscuit budget was, it was probably for the best. Not that anyone was going for the biscuits, though many eyes were upon them. Sensing this might be just the incentive to socialise that everyone needed, she grabbed two from a paper plate and munched loudly.

A voice said, "I've got ginger nuts."

Sharon looked round. A freckled face peeked from beneath spear-straight hair that his mother probably told him was rich auburn but which no one else could deny was carrot from its pudding-bowl line up to its thick roots. The accent was Welsh, tinged with an apology for same, the height was average with an inclination towards short, the frame needed an extra ration of chicken soup, and the clothes were pure nerd. From the ends of the battered leather jacket one size too large, black fading to green where time had done its damage, to the ends of his never-run-in running shoes; from the beige trousers that sagged around the middle to the unironed tartan-pattern shirt with its mismatched buttons, this was a man who understood that he should care about fashion, but couldn't quite make fashion care back.

She must have stared, because he swallowed, Adam's apple rising and falling hugely, and said, "I suppose some people might be allergic to ginger nuts? I'm sorry, I didn't really know what kind of thing you were supposed to bring to this sort of meeting, see?" He tried a grin, dazzling as a squally shower on an overcast day. "I suppose next time I'll bring some fruit salad."

"What?"

"Fruit salad? Although some people don't like pineapple, which I don't understand because I really like pineapple but everyone is different aren't they? I mean of course they are that's why we're here I suppose, even though actually," a laugh designed to be rich found itself on hard times, "we're not really!"

He pushed the packet of biscuits among the rest, and mumbled, "Would you like a hand with the tea?"

Sharon said, "Uh, thanks, I mean . . . yeah. That'd be great, cheers."

"I'm Rhys," the man explained brightly, occupying himself over the tea with the dedication of the truly relieved. "Rhys Ellis." Then, in a lower, conspiratorial voice, "I'm a druid."

"Really?" exclaimed Sharon, and now she too found that the mugs of tea were the most interesting things she'd ever handled. "That's very uh ... that's very ..."

"Welsh?"

"Kind of, yeah."

"I learned druiding in Birmingham."

"That's less Welsh."

"Yes, but my second teacher was from Swansea. Actually, my first was from Bangkok and he smoked these nasty cigarettes all the time. At first I thought they were some kind of herbal thing, see, to enhance his communing with the primal forces of the city, but in fact they were just cheap." He laughed, so Sharon dutifully laughed as well. Before the laughter could end and words could muscle back in with disastrous consequence, she grabbed a handful of mugs and turned to the other people there.

"Tea!" she shrilled. "Who'd like a nice cuppa?"

Chapter 7

Rhys

So my name's Rhys, and I'm a druid, see?

Well, I suppose I'm a druid, I don't know, it all depends. According to the exam board I'm not actually a druid yet, I'm still an apprentice, but I was only one paper away from passing and if they won't let me try again then I don't see how they can be so ... well ... Anyway, yes. What else should you know about me? I work in IT – actually in IT support so it's like when your system goes down at the office then I get called up and I go in and fix it and tell your people how to fix it see and that's really interesting because I meet lots of people and every day is different and I quite like it. I mean, I like being a druid too, but it's not like there's much money in being a druid these days. Druid magic is all slow magic, all about being patient and letting the city's rhythms take their natural course at a proper pace and everyone is all "No, we want it now" and they go to sorcerers and wizards and people like that even though actually sometimes the quick fix isn't the right one, see?

Anyway, the problem ... I mean, I wouldn't say it's like a massive problem, I mean, it's not like I've got a disease, see, and it's nothing criminal or anything like that! It's more how ... how everyone said I was going to be a druid and I was going to be the leader of my circle and all the lads in Birmingham were very excited and I was very excited too, but then when the season comes I just can't . . . And also if I get nervous then sometimes it comes out too, and the doctor says it's just psychosomatic now as how there's actually nothing in the environment to set it off but it really does get in the way when you're trying to summon a pipe dragonling or something, and so you see I don't really want to I don't exactly like to and it's not a problem but it's . . . well, it's rather ruined my life, actually. There. I said it. I was supposed to be . . . and now I can't. And I don't know what anyone can do to make it better.

Chapter 8

Cast Off Your Chains and Soar

"Before we begin," said a voice, "I totally have a question?"

All eyes turned to the speaker. If he'd had the vascular capability, he might have blushed. Peroxide-blond hair on a bone-white face, skinny blue jeans, leather shoes and a tight-fitting white T-shirt all proclaimed the owner, a man of probably no more than twenty-five years old, to be comfortable with his sexuality, even if the rest of the world wasn't. "So yeah, hi there. I'm just wondering, with this meeting – are we going to change the hours for daylight saving? Only my complexion really takes some looking after and I can't be having too much sun, if you know what I mean."

Silence in the hall.

Eyes turned inexorably to Sharon. She rose to her feet. This moment was something she'd been preparing for.

She said, "Uh . . ."

And stopped. Somehow, in all those hours spent in front of the mirror practising being open-minded and understanding, with help from books carrying titles like *Everything I Ever Needed to Know Was Inside Me Already*, the rallying cry of "Uh" hadn't been mentioned.

" . . . these are issues," she added hastily, because you couldn't go wrong with a good "issue" or maybe even a "challenge", "which we can all address. If anyone has any concerns about the set-up of this group then of course please do say so, and we'll try to, like, address that."

It had been going so well.

"Excuse me?" The voice wasn't loud or aggressive or even particularly projected but there was something in it, an indefinable thickness of sound, that cut through every conversation. The speaker was hard to focus on. There was a sensation of bulk, aided by the fact that the speaker's chair seemed to be warping under pressure. But as Sharon looked and tried to gain an exact sense of weight or height or skin, or even gender, such information seemed to slip just out of her grasp, like wet soap in a hot bath.

"Excuse me," he, or maybe she, or perhaps – yes and without wanting to be judgemental – perhaps *it* said, "May I have another biscuit?"

Several gazes flickered back to Sharon. "What? I mean of course. The biscuits are here for everyone to enjoy. Please, help yourself."

"Thank you," he/she/it replied, rising with the majesty of a sunken submarine from beneath raging depths. All eyes watched it go to the bar. All eyes watched it pick up a biscuit with a grace and care that surely came from having fingertips larger than a lion's paw, and all eyes watched it return to its chair, which groaned under the imposition. It ate and, for a moment, there was an impression of teeth in that not-quite-face, teeth indeed that no wishful thinking could deny.

"Well, I think that's just the kind of thing we should talk about," said a voice at last, and Sharon nearly shuddered with relief as she turned to the new speaker. This was a man, mid-fifties, with demarcated strands of mouse-grey hair combed across his spotted, massy skull. He wore a navy-blue suit and a red club tie, complemented by a thick leather belt done up several notches too tight. But his face ... Somewhere the gods of grease and the gods of time had drawn up their battle lines, and as their wars had raged the mercenaries of wart and spot had joined the foray, fighting to a standstill entrenched in the bags beneath his eyes, under his wattled chin and all around the remnants of his frayed hairline. At the gaze of the others, he bristled, and with petulant pride he declared, "You don't see *me* coming here in a chameleon spell, and a cheap one at that, do you? I may see the appeal of an occasional glamour, the odd protective enchantment, when in more refined social circles. But here, surely, we must by definition wear our true colours!"

"There won't be nudity?" queried someone. This was a question which Sharon had been hoping to posit herself, and so dismiss before the evening could get out of hand.

"I don't think we should rush into things . . ."

"How does this work then?" asked a third.

This time Sharon was ready. She coughed, pushed her chair back, stood up with arms folded in front of her, and said, "Uh, yes, so I guess, uh, I should explain." She took a deep breath and launched, far too fast, into her prepared speech. "Thank you all for coming to this very first meeting of Magicals Anonymous. I'm pleased to see what a good response we got from the Facebook campaign and on Twitter and I'm sure as the weeks go by we can come to help each other and . . . and stuff. Here we aim to support and assist each other with all our . . . our . . ." the eyes of everyone in the room, so carefully avoided, were beginning to burn into her " . . . our issues and things, and as this is the first time we've met I guess we should say a bit about ourselves and why we're here. So, yeah. My name's Sharon . . ."

"Hello, Sharon," sang out a cheerful voice, into a silence. "What?" asked the speaker. "Isn't that what we're supposed to say?"

" . . . and I can walk through walls."

Chapter 9

Pride Is Only the Self-Knowing of Great Men

He is the second greatest shaman who's ever lived.

At least he thinks he's the second greatest shaman who's ever lived, but actually the matter is open to debate. He's definitely in the top three, but it's undecided as to whether he, or Blistering Steve, late of Streatham Common, is the true claimant to second place. The argument arises thus: did Blistering Steve succeed, in a moment of transcendent magical brilliance, in crossing the boundary between spirit and flesh and become, in a veritable flash of blinding light, a creature entirely of smoke and air; or, less impressively, did he merely contrive his own spontaneous combustion in an experiment gone tragically wrong? The evidence is vague either way, but as Blistering Steve's rival to the title would point out, if his experiment had gone so well, surely he'd have been back, albeit in ethereal form, to let someone know?

Academic magicians are nothing if not prone to rivalries.

Laying all this aside, for now it is important to note the following:

Firstly, that the second – possibly third – greatest shaman who's ever lived, has not today got his fix of peppermint super-strength tooth-paste, and this has undeniably dented his mood.

Secondly, as he walks in that place between what *is* and what is merely *perceived to be*, with that special walk that only shamans know how to do, he looks down, sees something smoking beneath his feet, and is worried.

Chapter 10

Respect Others and Respect Yourself

His name was Kevin and he was saying,

" . . . so yeah I mean it's like so totally uncool what's happening with modern hygiene. I mean, chlamydia, gonorrhoea, hepatitis, herpes, HIV, and that's just like the stuff they pick up at the routine screening! You know how hard it is to find decent, drinkable blood these days? Alcohol, drugs, fatty diets, not enough green leaf vegetables and I'm like *hello*?! I'm not even going to drink your good stuff so I don't see how you're planning on living if that's the best your cardiovascular system can produce!"

Sharon leaned a little further forward. This was, she'd concluded after the first ten minutes, the safest look to go with. The act of resting elbows on knees forced her into a position that showed interest, while resting her chin on her hand provided good head support and stopped her mouth from dropping open.

"Anyway," concluded Kevin, trying not to twiddle his bright blond hair, "I was having some issues with the, you know, the . . . " He made a whistling sound and with two fingers twiddling in front of his face somehow managed to indicate the place where fangs might be. "So I went to the doctor and she was all like 'So you've got a syndrome' and I was like 'Are you fucking kidding me? I'm like the bane of the immortal fucking night or whatever what the fuck do you mean I've got a syndrome?' and she was all like 'Yeah but it's a cool syndrome' and I was like 'Lady, don't give me this it's a cool syndrome stuff, because I've gotta tell you I've got some real issues with personal hygiene anyway and if you're about to tell me that my body is now, like, out to get me, well I honestly can't tell you what I'm gonna do.' And she gave me this leaflet and was all like 'It's called Seah's syndrome and you've probably had it for a while. So when you were living your blood group was O negative and now you're dead' – and you know she said 'dead' which I thought was just *so* prejudiced – 'and now you're dead your blood group is still O negative, so that's like the only blood group you can drink.'"

"Is that a popular one?" asked Mrs Rafaat. She was resplendent in a bright orange sari, with greying hair and a collection of thin silver rings on the fingers of her left hand.

"Like fucking no!" moaned Kevin, throwing his hands up in the air. "Only like fucking eight per cent of the population or whatever! And turns out a lotta the guys got this, only it's not cool to talk about it, which again I think is so like, so stupid? But if you're AB positive or something like that well then you're really okay because you can drink like anything but O negative and that's all you can fucking have, and I don't know if there's like, any scientific reason to think this but I really think these O negative fuckers don't live clean. I have to bring a questionnaire along now and everything. I mean, really, it's like a fucking dis-as-ter."

Silence as the room waited for a little of his indignation to clear. Then someone applauded, and the others joined in. Kevin shifted in his chair uncomfortably, flashing the lightly fanged grin of the rarely appreciated, not quite able to believe this moment would last.

"I'm sure we'd all like to thank Kevin for his uh ... personal story," Sharon recited, forcing a rictus smile.

"Thank you, Kevin!" intoned the room. It was curious, Sharon noted, how it only took two or three people to feel the urge to chant their greetings or their praise in harmony, and suddenly everyone else was joining in, just in case their neighbour felt the urge, and then their neighbour's neighbour felt the urge and, before they knew it, they were being left out or worse being *rude*. It had almost become a competition to respond faster than others, so as not to be last and caught demonstrating a lack of appreciation.

"Does anyone have something they'd like to add?"

Everybody avoided each other's stare. Then one hand – the strange hand belonging to the strange creature whose features no one could entirely perceive – went up, and that voice that was not he nor she but therefore had to be it and more of an it than the average something dared to be, asked, "What kind of questions?"

"Oh, the questionnaire!" exclaimed Kevin, face lighting up at a chance to explore his problem further. "Well . . ." A big black sports bag was pulled out from under his chair and opened to reveal, just for a moment, a box of latex gloves, a pack of sterile wipes, a tube of expensive-looking toothpaste and a spindle of dental floss, all floating on a sea of sterile packaging, before from all this a plastic folder containing several sheets of A4 was revealed, neatly typed up and laid out with tick boxes. "Dietary standards *obviously*, sexual history *obviously*, foreign travel of course, visits to malaria sites, iron content, recent hospital investigations, history of needle abuse, history of drug abuse, history of alcohol abuse, history of jaundice . . . In fact if anyone wants to take one I've got plenty of spares."

"I really don't think that's gonna be a great idea," blurted Sharon. As Kevin's face fell she added, "But if anyone is interested in helping Kevin out I'm sure they can speak to him after the session."

"What if we don't know our blood type?" asked a small woman with mousy blonde hair who'd introduced herself as Jess (Hello, Jess) "and I turn into pigeons".

"Well, I'd say you should like get yourselves tested and signed up to the donor register," exclaimed Kevin. "And I hope you've all got donor cards too because there's like thousands of people on the organ donor register who die every year because they can't get a part and I'm like, guys, charity begins at home, you know?"

The next response came from a woman sitting hunched up, who wore with all the ease and familiarity of a polar bear in a bikini a full-length brown abaya that couldn't quite disguise knee joints which bent the wrong way. From beneath her robe she produced a small whiteboard and a green marker pen. With her gloved hand – only three fingers in the glove, Sharon couldn't help noticing, and two of them distinctly curved in a way which might well have been claws – she wrote carefully on the board and turned it to face the group.

Does the blood have to be human?

"Uh, *yeah*," withered Kevin. "I mean, no offence, I'm sure your blood is like, totally amazing. But if I can't fucking drink anything except O rhesus fucking negative, then banshee blood is probably like, way out there."

"Can I quickly ask," Sharon interrupted, before the conversation could get much more organic, "do you want a stool or something, because you don't look very uh ... very comfortable on the chair?"

The creature in the awkwardly worn robe turned its head slowly and Sharon could have sworn she saw a hint of amber-yellow in the tiny slit across the eyes. The marker pen slipped busily across the board.

Thank you, that is very kind, but I am happy to sit however everyone else sits.

"This is a place for everyone, regardless of their um ... their situation ... to be comfortable. If arrangements can't be made for the comfort of our members here, then, uh ... I think we can agree we've uh ... kind of screwed up?"

The woman – if that was the term – hesitated. Sharon sensed that somewhere beneath the fabric a set of mighty teeth longed to chew on the end of the much-gnawed marker pen. Then:

Would anyone mind if I hung from the rafters for a while?

"Uh ... that sounds fine to me. Anyone got any problems if ..."

Sally.

"If Sally hangs from the rafters?"

There was a chorus of "Sure, whatever" from around the room.

The creature called Sally nodded in what might have been gratitude, slipped her board and marker under one arm, and unfolded. Standing on the rickety chair she unfolded first from the knees, which bent backwards beneath her robe like the hind legs of a horse; a hint of talon curled round the seat of the chair for support. She straightened her back, which may have been long and spindly, and unfolded a pair of arms that may well, to judge by the stretching of the robe from finger to shoulder, or by the hint of protruding greyish-blue leather, have been connected to wings. She threw herself upwards in a single motion, not so much an act of strength against gravity, as a moment of pure intimidation in which the forces of nature considered their adversary and decided it wasn't worth kicking up a fuss. There was a flap of black and grey, and a flash of red, and then three claws, each jointed three ways, locked onto one of the horizontal rafters under the sloping triangular roof. The robe flopped backwards, revealing stick-thin grey calves and boney thighs, clad, for the sake of decency, in bright red and white leggings.

Dangling upside down, Sally the banshee removed the whiteboard from its resting place in the crook of her arm, unpopped the marker pen with a flick of her thumb and carefully wrote:

Thank you for your patience and understanding.

Chapter 11

Learning Is the Path to Self-Knowledge

The four greatest killers the world has ever seen have come to town.

Sharon Li doesn't realise this and, frankly, why should she? There's a lot of stuff out there for one girl to know, especially a shaman who's expected to know so much stuff it's a miracle she can remember any one thing at a given moment. And would she really want to know about this? Because Derek doesn't.

Derek, high social secretary, and quite possibly high priest, of the Friendlies, servant of the Lonely Lady, watchman of 4 a.m. and, as if that wasn't enough, moderately successful owner of a tool hire business operating out of Balham (third off the price if all items are returned on the same working day) says, "Who's there?"

And then he sees.

"How'd you get here?" he asks, already knowing the answer but feeling he ought to keep the conversation going just in case. "What do you want?"

These are redundant questions, as he knows perfectly well what they want and, more to the point, that he'll be unable to give it to them. Not through lack of trying, but because truly he does not know the answer to the question, the inevitable question:

"Where is she?"

He hopes the honesty shows in his face as he answers, backing towards the furthest wall. "I don't know."

The four greatest killers in the world didn't knock, didn't jingle, didn't rattle, didn't crash, didn't jar, didn't crunch on their way in, and now, as they move, they make no sound except the quiet mantra that is their murderous chant.

"Come on, pal . . ."

"Mate . . ."

"Mucker . . ."

"Where's the lady hiding?"

"Are you going to kill me?" Derek asks, or rather, the part of him that desperately wants to live and which, regardless of everything that common sense predicts for the next five minutes, still hopes to explore this receding option.

"Kill you?" one asks.

"Us?" one exclaims.

"Wanker," offers a third.

"Tosser," agrees the fourth.

"Why'd we do that, mate? You think we're that kinda guys?"

"Gotta look out for that, mate."

"Just give us what we want . . ."

"Tits!"

Derek's eyes dance to the one who makes this rather incongruous contribution to the conversation and see him smile. His smile is lecherous, his smile is the ogling grin of a man who's spent too much time in high places observing the things that pass below, his smile is the smile God would have worn when enjoying a dirty joke with Satan, just you and me, hate the attitude, love the wit. Then his eyes move to the other three in the room. How they entered he does not know, but how they will leave he can fairly guess, and he sees that they too are smiling.

Four faces . . .

. . . but all the same smile.

A whimper escapes him before he can prevent it, his fingers scratch into the brick wall at his back. "Please . . ." he whines. "Please, I don't know. She's just vanished, that's all, she just disappeared!"

"How'd she do that then?" asks one.

"Magic!" suggests another.

"Poof – farts – poof!" cackles a third.

"Right stinker," concurs the fourth.

"If you can't help us . . ."

" . . . then we'll have to find someone else . . ."

" . . . because our guvnor . . ."

" . . . he wants her so bad . . ."

" . . . so bad I mean it's like he's got this massive thing . . ."

"Wanker!"

"Arse."

"Lovely pair of knockers."

"So you see . . ."

Four faces fill his world, four faces and they are all the same face, the same smile, the same eyes, the same voice, whispering their words as the floor cracks beneath his feet and the walls grow fingers of mortar and dust to wrap around his throat and dig into his skin.

" . . . we ain't never gonna stop . . ."

"Overtime, yeah."

"Payday!"

" . . . until you give us Greydawn."

He tries to scream, but the concrete is already giving way beneath him, sucking him down, and the walls have curled their ragged fingers around his face, stopping his mouth with mortar and dirt, filling his throat, his lungs, with thick grey sludge, and still he tries, and no sound can emerge until he is bursting from the inside out with the weight of it and his eyes dribble tar and his face is red, then scarlet, then purple, then the orange-brown of sandstone and clay, and at the very, very last a tiny puff of air escapes his lips, the very last puff that he shall ever breathe, and if you listen closely, if you crane your ear right up next to his face, before it is pulled down into the foundations at his feet, you might hear this one word:

Howl.

Before he is sucked down beneath the street.

Chapter 12

A Dog Will Love You More Than Any Man

She said, "I get so lonely sometimes.".

She said it so softly, so gently, that for a moment the gathered members of Magicals Anonymous exchanged glances, just to check that they'd heard it aright; but yes, that was the sentiment, that was the word.

"It's not something I can really explain," she sighed. "But these last few years I've just known that I don't belong, and people won't understand."

The room lapsed into silence. The speaker was Mrs Rafaat (Hello, Mrs Rafaat).

"And I'm not really magical at all, you know. I mean, I've been tested because I was having these experiences, but they weren't so much experiences as things that happened around me but actually I don't know any wizarding or witching or anything and apparently if I tried to cast a spell it would probably just go *puft*, but the thing is I do seem to know things, and really things do seem to happen and I suppose I'm actually a bit of an intruder here so I really hope you don't mind, but you all seem like lovely people and I am very interested and really yes – but yes, really actually quite worried. I've been feeling that way for a while, something I can't quite put my finger on but I'm rambling. I'm rambling aren't I? So yes, that's me. Would anyone mind if I had another cup of tea?"

In her mid-fifties, she spoke with the faintest remnant of an Indian accent, softened by many years of life in Wembley. Her orange sari, threaded with blue and purchased in Bethnal Green some ten years ago, was getting a bit tatty round the hem.

"But I don't mind, I mean some people say it's silly to wear a sari in Wembley, but actually I think it's very comfortable, and modest, and allows you to have some strong colour in your life without making a fool of yourself because it's so easy with fashion these days to make a fool of yourself, I'd say it's a safety thing, isn't it, wearing what you're comfortable with not to make a point. I'm rambling again, aren't I? I'm sorry, I do that.

"Um, excuse me?" The bone-white, wrinkle-ridden, spot-stained hand of Mr Roding (Necromancy is such a misunderstood discipline) was raised in polite enquiry. "I don't mean to complain, and I'm sure you're a very lovely woman, Mrs Rafaat, but feeling 'quite worried' isn't what we're here for. I mean, we all feel worried, don't we?"

A chorus of consent.

"But our worries stem from very specific causes. I, for one, can halt the passage of degrading time upon my body through the use of ancient lore studied over many a sagely lifetime, but I still haven't found a solution for the skin-sloughing issue. The books recommend aloe vera, fat lot of use that was. But, the thing is, Mrs Rafaat, I'm not sure your problems really compare."

Mrs Rafaat's face sank. Seemingly each muscle contracted one at a time until only a pair of wide, sorrowful eyes protruded. "I'm very sorry," she mumbled, unable to meet Mr Roding's watery-green gaze flecked with shattered capillaries. "I just didn't know where else to go and when I saw that this group was organising I thought . . . it seemed so right. I can't explain it, but I know . . . I don't know what I know I just know . . . there's something terribly important I've forgotten. But I don't know what it is."

One or two dirty looks were shot at Mr Roding, who had the good manners to stare in shame at his shiny black shoes.

Sharon cleared her throat. "It's okay, Mrs Rafaat. We're completely on board with where you're coming from. In fact, I've personally experienced something similar to what you describe. I uh . . . I know things. I don't know how, but . . . there was this moment. A moment when I knew I knew everything about the city, everything that was, and has been, and will be again and then . . . then I didn't. So I guess I'm saying that's cool, you know?"

Was that a helpful response, she wondered? Did senior citizens appreciate the multi-faceted aspects of that well-worn "That's cool, you know?" "We're all glad to have you in this group, aren't we?" she added, shooting a glare around at any possible dissenters.

A mumble of assent arose from the gathering, and Mrs Rafaat's head lifted in cautious optimism.

"That's very nice of you, but if you really don't—"

"We do," insisted Sharon. "We absolutely all do." She had a very stubborn chin when she needed one. Somewhere in the lineage of the Li family several generations of well-bred Manchurian ladies had each married a well-educated young man, only to discover that while a charming smile went a long way, a sharp heel and well-kept nails might get you further.

"They say," stammered Mrs Rafaat, "they say . . . something is missing. Places where there should have been noise are . . . Is this something people are worried about because I find it very worrying? They say that the spirits of things, I mean, not the spirits, not the fairies or anything fluffy, but the . . . the heart of things, the soul behind the walls the . . . the things with the ears, if that makes sense to you, they say they're vanishing. One night they're there – you walk alone but you are not alone – and then the next they're . . . they're gone."

Someone coughed. The cough belonged to Rhys I'm-a-druid-well-sort-of-well-I-tried-but-you-know-how-it-is (Hello, Rhys). It was followed by a shuffling of feet, a twitching of elbow, a shivering of one shoulder and a slow look round the room just to make sure that no one really, really minded that he was about to speak.

No one seemed to mind.

"Uh, what do you mean 'gone'?"

"I don't know," said Mrs Rafaat. "That's the trouble with just knowing things; it never really comes with all the details."

"When you say 'spirits'," interjected Mr Roding, "are we talking benevolent small essences or the malign unleashed power of a blue electric angel?"

"I'm very sorry," Mrs Rafaat said, "it's terribly vague."

Ms Somchit (It's not about the black, it's about how you wear it) cleared her throat. At five foot two, with curly black hair falling to her shoulders and skin the colour of fresh almonds, she had the cheerful look of someone who had seen the worst that the world could offer and had actually expected it to be much, much worse. Her black clothes had a priest-like aura, and a small white badge in the shape of a shield bearing a red cross through the centre and a red sword in the top left-hand corner added to the ecclesiastical vibe.

"So . . . you're experiencing hollowness, emptiness, doubt, despair and a great sense of wrongness," she clarified, "but you can't exactly say what it is. Have you tried acupuncture?"

"Oh God, acupuncture is like the most amazing thing ever," agreed Kevin, brightening at the mention of medical intervention. "I had like, this utterly amazing craving for the blood of the innocent babe and then two sessions, acupuncture, me, and I was like, wow totally yuck with that virginal blood."

"Can you get it on the NHS?" asked Mr Roding. "Acupuncture, I mean."

"You'd probably need a referral," offered Ms Somchit.

"How about counselling?" suggested Chris Hi-I'm-an-exorcist-but-you-know-I-don't-think-a-confrontational-approach-is-helping-anyone. "It's great that you've taken this first step, love, but actually talking things through with a professional can be so liberating."

"Are there counsellors who understand the . . . the um . . . the magical thing?" asked Mrs Rafaat.

All eyes turned to Sharon. "I'll look it up," she promised.

Chapter 13

Kindness to Others Nurtures the Soul

The meeting melted away.

After, Sharon couldn't remember the details of what happened at the end. It could have been the excitement of the moment. Or it could have been all the glamours and concealment spells clashing in bursts of steel-silver and emergency-blue light as their owners drew too near each other.

Someone had suggested that they all join hands and give thanks for the spirit of companionship. Someone else – probably Mr Roding – said that was the most ridiculous thing he'd ever heard. Then someone else suggested that if they were going to link hands in a circle they should sing "Auld Lang Syne" – until Mrs Rafaat pointed out that singing in the presence of Sally might be considered crass.

I don't mind, replied Sally. I enjoy the vocal range of humans.

Eventually, they'd just shaken hands and promised to contribute to the Facebook page and come back next week. Sally had detached herself from the ceiling in a single flop that somehow landed her without a sound and nervously offered a three-clawed talon from beneath her robe for Sharon to shake. The skin was arctic cold and, as Sally carefully wound her claws round Sharon's hand, struggling not to break anything as she did, Sharon heard the rustle of wings, heard a crunching just behind her ears and tasted a thing that could only be the feather-coated splat of raw pigeon bursting in her mouth. She turned green and locked her smile into place before Sally could notice. There was a hint of a smile behind Sally's mask and, having succeeded with what was quite possibly the first handshake of her adult life, she spun brightly on the spot and, once she'd stabilised and got her wings back under control, carefully wrote:

Thank you for your understanding and support.

Then she was in the alley round the side of the building, there was an impression of blackness against the night and the beating of wings, and she was gone.

One person remained after the meeting filed out, and while this individual was trying to be inconspicuous, there was no denying its bulk and weight as it loomed over the biscuit table.

It had waited for the last one to leave, then said, "My name is Gretel."

Sharon looked up and then, because Gretel was standing so close, she looked up a bit further. Features blurred before her eyes, not so much through a twisting of the light, but from a twisting of the brain, as if it couldn't process what it was trying to see. She smelled old garbage dump and chilli sauce cutting through even the muddling power of Gretel's cloaking spell. Resolutely Sharon thrust out her hand, palm open, and exclaimed, "It's a pleasure to meet you, Gretel. I'm so glad you could come to our meeting."

The thing called Gretel hesitated, then reached out one hand, wide enough to pick Sharon up by the skull, strong enough to crush any living thing it held. Sharon's fingers brushed a palm of grey hairs bordering on soft quills or spikes, sticky with some orange stuff. For a moment she looked and there was . . .

Troll didn't do it justice.

Troll wasn't the word.

Sure, troll was what this was: undeniably, irrefutably troll, beneath the spell. But the mere word failed to capture the breadth of back, and the thickness of black quills covering face, shoulders, arms, hands, bare feet with yellow nails inclining to claws; elbows wider than Sharon's waist, face rounder than a blown-up beach ball, and teeth stained the colour of the rubbish dump and sharpened on a diet of ground glass. Troll didn't capture the stink of it, the head-spinning stench of it; troll didn't capture . . .

Her eyes roamed across the creature and, no, the idea of "troll" had never extended to the extra extra *extra* large nightgown, patterned with garlands and puppy-dogs and doubtless the last in the shop that would stretch over Gretel's prickly form. Sharon heard herself stammer, somewhere between the haze and the smell, "I really ... hope to see you next week and that you'll find the meetings ... productive and helpful."

Their palms parted and Sharon staggered back against the table, gasping down air.

Gretel the troll shifted uneasily. The floorboards creaked underfoot as she transferred her bulk from one foot to another, like a bus driver testing his suspension before a difficult hill. Then all at once, as if there'd only be one chance to speak and this was it, Gretel said, "I really enjoyed the food that you provided, Ms Li. That was very nice of you. I like human food but no one ever serves me not even the takeaway and I try to get the leftovers but people don't seem to like it if I hang around their restaurants so I was wondering, Ms Li, and obviously I could pay, but I was wondering if you could maybe and you don't even need to keep the receipts but I was wondering if anyone would mind if next time you or not even you or just someone someone in the group and I should have asked but I feel so ashamed but maybe if someone in the group could bring some pizza?"

Chapter 14

Friendship Comes From Unexpected Places

It is forty minutes later.

Sharon walks.

The smell of refuse has diminished now, overwritten by the smell of Thai Panang curry and prawn crackers. She'd got a takeaway from the restaurant down the street, and the two of them, Gretel and Sharon, had sat in busy, munching silence on a bench in Spa Fields, a crafted park of unnatural dips and swells, and eaten. Sharon had used chopsticks, and Gretel had tried but couldn't get them between her fingers, eventually knocking the two sticks together and using them as a very small shovel to push food directly into her mouth. Gretel had offered to share the prawn crackers, but the bag was already stained with the grease from beneath the troll's fingers where they had smeared the plastic, and Sharon had said she was full up.

Getting into the park hadn't been a problem. There was a rusty chain on the gate, held together with a thick padlock. Gretel had snapped the lock between her fingertips and tucked a five-pound note into a link of the chain by way of apology. When they were done, Gretel had smoothed out the dent she'd made in the bench where they'd sat by kicking it from below until once again it formed, more or less, a flat surface. Sharon, not wanting to add to Gretel's modest vandalism, had taken a deep breath and walked straight through the fence. She found fences easier than walls. Less mortar, more air.

"Can you smell the fish oil?" Gretel sighed. "And the tiniest hint of cumin?"

"It's very nice," mumbled Sharon.

"There are so many people who don't appreciate coconut in their cooking, but I think it's just amazing. It balances the chilli, absorbs the ginger, softens the garlic, infuses the meat . . . but you must know all of this, being human."

"Uh . . . not really. I kind of live outta the chippy."

"Oh." Gretel struggled to hide her disappointment. "Well, that's very nice too. Do you cook?"

"Me? Not really. Well, my mum taught me a bit, like, Chinese cooking and that, but you have to go miles to get the proper ingredients and actually beansprouts aren't the world's greatest vegetable. I know it disappoints her that I don't really try, because apparently I'm not going to get myself a nice young man like this."

It had all come out rather fast. Gretel absorbed this information before coming up with the obvious question. "A nice young man?"

"Well, you know. The whole turning-invisible, walking-through-walls, not-cooking-beansprouts thing is really bad for relationships."

"Is it? Why?"

"I guess . . . I *think* . . ." Sharon paused. "Actually, I have no idea."

When they were done she collected the wrappings and recycled the cardboard boxes in the cardboard bin and the foil boxes in the foil bin; and with surprising speed and litheness for such a large creature, Gretel was gone.

Sharon walks.

Somehow, unnoticed, the hour had crept over the city when the moderately drunk called it a night, and the seriously drunk settled down because it wouldn't really hurt, for one last pint. The bus stops along Rosebery Avenue were crowded with the two extremes of late-night humanity: those who suspected you were out to get them, and those who knew that you were their best, best friend in all the world. Exmouth Market stood at an unusual crossroads within central London, at a place with Underground stations all around, representing nearly every line to every place, yet where none was quite within convenient reach.

Sharon waited at the bus stop. Sadler's Wells was emptying for the night, an audience of ballet lovers in pearls and expensive clothes thronging onto the street. Several examined the machine selling bus tickets, anxious to master it but careful not to let their ignorance look foolish.

The countdown on the bus shelter said the bus was seven minutes away.

Sharon walked to the next stop.

It took her three minutes.

Here the bus was still seven minutes away.

This stop was less heavily populated, partly due to a drunk woman, her skin blue-grey, eyes wide, trousers torn and a smell radiating off her that was much more than beer. She was harmless now, sat in the white fluorescent light of the shelter with her mouth open and a dried sheen of spit tracked down the side of her chin. But those few others at the bus stop kept their distance in case of worse to come.

Sharon walked on by.

Angel lay ahead, brilliantly lit, yellow and red, brake lights and outdoor café tables, pubs and restaurants. No matter what the time of year, crowds of drinkers here spilled onto the street, glass in hand among the ATMs, estate agents and mobile-phone shops, to down a pint or two after their curry, or sushi, or Afghan stew, or Thai platter, or chilli wrap or . . . almost any cuisine of choice.

The wealth of Islington was almost untouched by its status as a social hub, which pulled in every level of society to mingle opposite the antiques mall or by windows advertising LUXURY TERRACED HOUSE, BARNSBURY, only half a million quid per room. Class wasn't dead; it had just learned to look the other way when queueing at the bar.

As Sharon rounded the corner onto City Road, her bus went by. The next stop was a hundred yards, beyond a set of lights. She considered running, chose not and oddly didn't feel the spike of rage so common when missing a bus that only ran every twenty minutes.

Hugging the bus route nonetheless in the hope of transport, she headed on down City Road. A small rise created an almost-bridge above an old canal basin; canoes were stacked in neat racks on its far side, and converted brick warehouses jostled with new glass-fronted apartments that offered studio living to the sound of wavelets slapping against the bollarded waterfront and the rumble of traffic. A square metal shed bore a sign shyly declaring it an electricity substation and hoped no one minded this vital service being so inelegantly sited amid prime real estate. A garage offered twenty-four-hour conveniences and doughnuts of every kind; a bit of graffiti on its wall reminded onlookers to ‼PANK‼

Somehow the next bus was still seven minutes away, and would probably remain so until the instant of its arrival. The air smelt of rain to come.

Sharon thought without thinking. Distance passed unnoticed, as if she stood still while the city turned, and all because her mind was full of unstoppable, incomprehensible sounds ...

So yeah, I turn into pigeons ...

Dental hygiene is like so important when you're a vampire!

There's surprisingly little meat on a pigeon.

The one time I tried tea tree oil my skin actually just fell off!

He howled, and he howled.

Then they were gone.

She flinched, and didn't know why.

There had been a moment ...

A searing moment, an instant, in which everything had been, the whole city, the world, everything, had been so ... *so* ...

But now it hurt to remember.

And if anyone had been looking, which would itself have been remarkable, they may have observed as Sharon walked a certain ... fuzziness about her, a certain ... indescribable vagueness, not so much a fading or a vanishing, not exactly an attainment of nothingness, but more a sense that here was a thing ...

... which did not merit the observing?

A manner in the walk, a briskness of pace, head down but chin forward, arms swinging but in no sense power-walking off that extra chocolate bar; rather a walk that could only be described as *belonging*. The walk of her who belonged, and if they'd looked ...

Or rather, if they'd not looked ...

Since not looking was the inevitable next step ...

They might have seen Sharon Li begin to disappear.

But by then something would have made them look away altogether.

She rounded the bend towards Moorfields eye hospital, opposite a pub bearing the golden figure of an eagle and the words of a song:

"Up and down the City Road, in and out the Eagle . . ."

As a kid, the song had always bothered her. "That's the way the money goes – pop goes the weasel!" She'd pictured a small twitchy-nosed furry creature exploding in the claws of a bird of prey, and when they'd sung it in nursery school, she'd cried.

All that had been long before the moment, before it had all gone wrong, before everything had changed and the fabric of reality had seemed a little . . . just a little . . .

Her pocket was buzzing.

Sharon struggled to free her head of thoughts, or not-thoughts, of this mess of unspoken ideas rattling around inside her brain like a penny in a washing machine. Her mobile phone was a grey brick, given to her when she left home by her dad, even though she already had a phone whose number he could never remember. He'd set himself up as the first number of her speed dial, and added to her contacts list a local doctor, police station, solicitor and sexual health clinic, folding her hand around it and telling her that she didn't need worry about phoning home too much.

He'd made it all of forty minutes before calling her once she was out of the door, which, by her father's standards, wasn't bad.

Now, though, as her phone rang, no number appeared, and when she thumbed it on, it felt cold to the touch.

"Hello?"

A man's voice answered, conversational, light, friendly. It said, "We're the one with the flaming wings."

"What?"

"By the traffic lights."

She looked up. There were several sets of traffic lights ahead, by the ugly mess that was the Old Street roundabout, a rumbling grey-white place where three boroughs collided like hungover fighting bulls. There were always people waiting at the traffic lights, or walking up a ramp from the tangle of subways below, and at any one moment any number of them could be making a call.

But there was one leaning against the pedestrian-crossing sign beneath the symbol of the walking green man. He looked like someone bored with waiting for a taxi, but he had a phone pressed to his ear and even in the settling night she could see he was looking at her – and there were ... there *were* ...

"Come on if you're coming," he said and hung up.

For a moment Sharon stood still and did nothing.

She was confident her father wouldn't have approved of her following strange men, but then, without actually forbidding anything, her father had never really approved of much. He'd just quietly hoped that his daughter, in her own sensible way, would come round to understanding *why* he wasn't happy on her account.

To the left lay the road home, back to Trish (the loud one) and Ayesha (the quiet one) and yesterday's washing-up and bed and sleep, and tomorrow she would go to work in the coffee shop for Mike (the short-sighted one), and nothing that happened tonight would seem real and Magicals Anonymous would be just another Facebook group until the next meeting, and she'd begin to doubt if it had happened, if she'd shaken the hand of a banshee and had dinner with a troll and received a phone call from a man who'd said, "Come on if you're coming" and ...

... and he was already crossing the street, heading towards Goswell Road. Which seemed, Sharon thought with a momentary flash of pride, pretty damned arrogant, like he knew she was going to follow, whereas he really couldn't because that was kind of psychopathic, and what the hell kind of girl did he think she was anyway? Besides, she could look after herself ...

She *could* look after herself.

She followed.

Chapter 15

The Body Is But a Vessel For the Soul

Sammy the Elbow, second (maybe third?) greatest shaman the world has ever seen, once listed all the walks of the city. They went like this:

Tourist amble with bumbag bouncing and gormless face so that people know you wanna get mugged; rush-hour scamper of the tossers in suits who are way too busy to be late and so you'd better get out of their way; lovers' sidle, hand in hand, the city nothing to them, movement just a way of getting closer together for snogging, yuck; copper's stride of "I own this so bring it on if you dare"; traffic warden's prowl, three in a gang, slow down the parking bay, quick to the next target and a cuppa tea; old lady's waddle and fat man's stagger, schoolkid's skip and Mum's ramble with the heavy buggy; jogger's pain, late man's breathless run, early man's easy lope. Way you walk says everything about you in this city, says who you are, where you're from, what you're doing, what you want, what you'll get. There's only two walks what are any different from any of these, only two walks what matter for shit.

First one is the shaman's walk, which moves at the perfect rhythm of the city, not too fast, not too slow, not owning nothing but not scared neither, the walk of them that belong, with nothing more and nothing less than that, them that are a part of something bigger, the walk which you can't see, because you fools don't know how to look. Beggar King gets it, knows it's not just about the way you move, but the way you think, understands how to walk on the surface of the earth and leave no mark beneath your shoes, but then he's the fucking Beggar King, if he doesn't get it then what the crap does he think he's doing wearing a crown?

Only one other walk worth the business, and only one dude gets it. It's the walk that closes up the gate, it's the wall that pulls the shadows along behind it, and you spot it by the way the pigeons fly, by the turning of the water in the overflowing grate, by the stretching of the light from the lanterns overhead, and by that tingling at the back of your teeth where all your fillings are starting to hurt. Only one guy does it, but it has been done for a thousand years, and that, you ignorant piece of piss, is the walk of the Midnight Mayor.

Chapter 16

Tread Softly Upon the Earth

There was something funny, Sharon decided, in the way the man walked.

Not too quick and not too slow. Not idling but not in a hurry either. He didn't limp or stagger, didn't hesitate about the turns he made but neither did he flap, nor did he walk head down, uninterested in a destination he had reached a thousand times, but seemed to look around constantly as if absorbing a place he'd known as a child, familiar but distant, beloved and suspected all at once. It was a walk which she would have to run to match, yet if she equalled his pace and remained some easy distance behind, it was the precise speed at which *it* happened.

She hadn't noticed the first few times, which she reasoned must be the point – no one else had noticed either. If you weren't ready for it, then noticing that you'd accidentally turned invisible wasn't as simple as it sounded. Nor was it invisibility as such. It was more ... a lack of perception. She walked and, at a certain speed, with a certain movement, a certain state of mind, it was as if she was so much a part of the city – or perhaps ...

... the city was so much a part of her?

... that passers-by no longer bothered to make the distinction.

This was that walk now, she realised, played pitch-perfect. But the man walking the walk in front of her wasn't vanishing from sight, as she might have done; rather he seemed to move as if this was his natural state, utterly comfortable and entirely on edge.

She wasn't sure she wanted to catch him up.

They walked, the three towers of the Barbican rising up on the left. Traffic in this part of town longed to use rat-run streets, little cut-throughs and byways, and to discourage such a notion, the council had closed off most of these, or put up bollards, or turned them into one-way routes so that now only the occasional well-read cyclist dared stray from the traffic-clogged beaten track.

It was therefore inevitable that off the traffic-clogged beaten track was precisely where they went.

They turned into Whitecross Street, by day a market selling hand-made soaps, hand-reared meats, hand-fermented cheeses and watches that must have fallen off the back of a lorry. By night the shops were shut, and the pavements seemed too narrow for the empty tarmac road. With a policy of, if you can't beat 'em, join 'em, street artists had been invited in to work on the walls of the old houses, or make their mark on the shutters pulled down in front of the pharmacy or stationer, leaving splashes of colour, jagged lines or tag marks, or the image of a fat bulldog with a lugubrious face, three storeys high and unimpressed by all it surveyed.

The man turned again, walking faster now that they were practically alone, daring Sharon to run after him, get too close. She matched his speed and felt the air around her begin to strain as the fine balance between what was seen and what was perceived struggled to know what to make of her stride. She caught glimpses of

fire at the end of an alley still not burned out

  gaslight green in sodium glass

               smell of frying

  sound of the street vendor's call incomprehensible numbers at impossible speed ...
for a pound!

and looked away, deliberately, from all the things that lurked, as out of sight as she was now. That was the major drawback about becoming invisible: all the other invisible things in the city wanted to know if they could join in too.

The man passed a tiny chapel, barely a cabin with a spike on its head, swung south towards the underpass beneath the Barbican, a place where expensive gyms clashed with convenience stores specialising in plantain and cheap fags, then turned again and was slipping through a galvanised steel gate, barbs on the top and a sign on the front that read: 24-HOUR MONITORING IS IN USE ON THIS SITE. Sharon heard his feet clatter on a metal stair as she hesitated, then took a deep breath and pushed on in. A rectangular yard, barely large enough to hold a lonely man's car, was hidden from daylight by high brick walls. A single iron staircase led up to a fire escape whose door was drifting shut behind the man, and there was something here, something . . .

Missing.

. . . which she had no better name for.

She stood on the cracked concrete of the yard, and looked up at broken windows, at walls with crumbling mortar, where even the graffiti artists couldn't be bothered to paint. She saw the yellow lichen flaking off the bricks behind the stair, smelt raw sewage from a neglected gutter, saw purple buddleias sprouting from a crack in the wall.

Missing.

A thing missing here.

She put her hand on the stair rail and felt rust, sensed the metal warp and hum beneath her step, thought she heard voices a long way off, and bit her lip and climbed. At the top a yellow sign hung crookedly by only one nail. It read, VISITORS PLEASE RING RECEPTION.

Sharon pushed the door back and the hinges groaned like a mountain trying to move. Inside, thin night-time light bounced off the shattered glass in the windows and formed a pattern of razored illumination across the floor. Among a vista of concrete pillars stood the remnants of machines that no one had bothered to sell, or wanted to buy. Some she couldn't recognise; others hinted at their purpose: great pipes cracked in two, old pedals snapped in the middle, fat rusted wheels where once an engine strap had run, and all now silent. Even the beggars had fled, leaving the odd trace: a burned-out mattress, a crumpled beer can, a torn shopping bag and a note written in charcoal on the walls: DON'T FORGET TO TURN OUT THE LIGHT.

She saw straggling ends of cable suspended where once bulbs might have hung, and listened to the *drip drip drip* of a shattered something at the other end of the floor, and wondered if there were rats here. She thought perhaps there weren't.

"There used to be, you know," said a voice, enormous in the silence, and yet, she suspected, not that loud.

She jumped, holding her bag in front of her like a shield, and shouted, "I know karate!"

A silence ate up her words, like a whale swallowing plankton. Then the voice answered, "Seriously?"

Sharon hesitated. It occurred to her to run, to vanish through the walls, to go back into the city, where, invisible, she would be safe, to walk the walk of all things unperceived, not that she'd ever tried it in an emergency, if this was that, if that was what this turned out to be. But despite its scepticism, the voice – male, young without being innocent – sounded almost impressed.

So, "Yeah," she called into the dark, "I know karate and I kick and bite and scream and all sorts of mega-shit and you wouldn't like to screw with me, okay?"

A shadow moved against the blackness, then crossed into the faint light cast through a shattered window. She saw a hint of dirty coat, a mess of dark hair and, somehow, a flash of too-bright blue eyes, impossible in the gloom. "There used to be something here," he murmured. "When you came in here in the dark, it was the thing that guided your hand to the switch. When the machines failed, it was the tick before the bang that told you to get out of the way. When men said, 'Wasn't that lucky?' the thing, whatever it was, laughed and knew there was no luck. It used to be here, and when all else failed, it kept the beggars warm by the fire and made sure the ashes didn't quite go out and the wind through the window didn't reach every corner. Do you understand what I'm talking about?"

"No," blurted Sharon, still holding her bag to her, tense as a samurai ready to fight. "Sorry, no."

The shadow sighed, ran a gloved hand under a badly shaven chin – and there it was: a tingling at the back of her teeth, a sensation on the air, a smell like metal trying to burn, just for a second, before it too became lost behind that blue-eyed stare.

"You have to find out what happened to the dog," he said. "It's important."

The words took a while to digest. Then, *"What?"*

"I'd do it for you," he went on, "but there's . . . things. Politics, mostly, but also . . . it's not really my field, you see? I mean, fire, flood, electrical damage, earth splitting in two, no worries, but this . . . And there aren't many of you, there never have been, it requires such a special state of mind. And I imagine you've got a lot to do, so please believe me when I say it's important. It's more than important. It's the single most important thing you'll do. I mean, I'm told that childbirth is considered kind of the big thing in a woman's life, something we're probably not going to understand, but otherwise, please believe me when I say that there is nothing you can possibly do more vital to the well-being of the city than finding out what happened to the dog."

Silence.

Then, "You don't know many women, do you?"

If it was possible for a facial expression to speak, then even in the darkness his face was a fluent conversationalist. Finally, "Okay, so the childbirth thing maybe wasn't—"

"Also," she said, "there's this thing called email? If you wanted to talk to me about death and destruction and stuff, then you could've tried that. Or even buying me a cup of coffee or lunch or something. I mean, it could've been professional, but all this . . . kind of blows it. Who are you? You weren't at the meeting."

"No," he admitted. "But I had someone keep an eye out. And actually, while my initial instinct was rather . . . Well, perhaps on reflection I can see what you're trying to achieve. And I'm sorry about the lunch thing, I really am, but there's people watching and emails are monitored, and I do respect what you're trying to do, although . . ." His voice rose in indignation. "Although starting a Facebook group called Weird Shit Keeps Happening to Me and I Don't Know Why But Figure I Need Help is not, may I just say, the best way to go about making friends. And did you have to call it Magicals Anonymous? Couldn't you have started a group called something like . . . I don't know . . . Self Help for the Polymorphically Dubious? or No Chanting Please or something a little less . . . in your face? Is that too much to ask?"

Sharon thought, then exclaimed, "Yes! Yes, it is too much to ask. Because I'm sorry, I know I keep coming back to this point, but who the hell are you and what the bloody hell is going on?"

The man sighed again. "Did I mention the politics?"

"Yeah, but that sounded to me like something you say whenever you just want to blame other guys for you being crap."

"I do not; that is totally ..." He hesitated, mid-indignate. Then, "Okay, so you may have something there. But seriously, this treading softly thing isn't our style, and while I'm generally an open and honest kind of guy, and I know you may have a hard time believing this, in my experience all that this open, honest groove has led to is serious cleaning bills and writs for damages. So, sorry if I haven't just jumped in there with 'Yo Sharon, there's shit going down, please fix it.'"

Sharon felt herself swallow without meaning to, and murmured, "You know my name?"

"Sure I do," he replied. "You're Sharon Li. You're twenty-two years old. You work in a coffee shop as what I believe we're now meant to call a barista, and you are, Christ knows why, the founder of Magicals Anonymous, a self-help group of the mystically buggered. You're also, in case you're wondering, so far in over your head that I imagine you're soon going to have a hard time working out which way up is anyhow, *and* you've probably got enough brains to realise it, *and* though you're a shaman you're clearly not practised enough to recognise the hollow shell of a place, like this building here, where a spirit should once have been, so I'd work on that, if I were you." She thought she saw the flash of a grin in the darkness, then he asked, "Have you considered evening classes?"

"Have I—"

"You seem like you're big on self-improvement, and anyway ..." He stopped, his head turning with pigeon speed towards some unseen shadow. Sharon shifted, listening for something more, and thought she heard ... maybe just a train passing below?

"The question you have to ask is this." His voice sounded far-off, distracted, his blue eyes were turned elsewhere. "Where did they go? I've done all I can but I'm no shaman. I don't know how to walk down the hidden paths. The spirits of the city are missing and it's not natural and it's not evolution and it's not right and—"

And she heard it and so did he, somewhere outside in the settled gloom, a sound which you hoped would be an engine starting, the slow winding-up of oversized gears and which, as you listened, the more you listened, truth intruded on hope and it became ...

"Don't look back," he said. "It wants you to look."

It became . . .

"Time to go now," he added. "Time to run."

Starting at the very bottom of the register, almost too low to almost too high, it grew and grew and it became from the floor to the sky: *bbbbhoooowwwwwwlllll!!!!*

She looked up at the man in the window and there was light in his hands, light on his skin, a brilliant electric blue and he wasn't human – nothing human looked like that – he was a thing wearing human flesh, he was a face pretending, a body bursting from something else inside, and as he looked round at her his eyes burned and in them were a million million voices all shouting all as one and she . . .

. . . ran.

Chapter 17

Movement Is Freedom

Sharon ran.

She didn't know why and she didn't know what from, but the man in the darkness had said run, and from his back had grown a pair of burning angel wings and she knew they weren't real, of course they weren't real, but they were real to her eyes, which was all the reality she felt she could cope with right now and

and she'd had supper with a troll

and shaken hands with a banshee

and heard a creature howl

So now she ran.

She ran straight through the shaman's walk, that place where she became invisible and all the invisible things began to crawl out for her to see. She ran straight through it and out the other side, unseen footsteps running through the night, a gasp of breath heard where there was nothing to be seen; and as she ran, the shadows dragged behind her and the whispers of the things buried just beneath began to creep and clutch their way out from beneath the paving stones, tangle their memories around her legs and tell of

Drip drip drip on the cobble stone

Spring-heeled Jack jumping over the rafters

Ten for a pound, ten for a pound, get 'em 'ere!

Howl!

Howl!!

Howl!!!

And as she ran she felt lighter, thinner, as if she wasn't merely becoming invisible to the eye that saw, but growing invisible in herself, her very matter melting about her, and on the streets there were creatures clinging to the walls, there were finger bones scratching their way out from between the lines of mortar, and a smell of . . . wet dog?

Something was sticking to her feet. She glanced down and there was a viscous goo on the pavement, coming up from below the pavement, thick and black and not black

thick and red and seeping through her shoes, and it wasn't real, of course it wasn't real, she knew it wasn't real, but the streets were bleeding, seeping blood upwards, and the stench! She gagged and nearly fell, briefly flickering into visibility before picking up the pace again and forcing herself on, running, and she thought she could hear

something running with her.

In the darkness behind.

A great heaving of lungs.

A great falling of paws.

A great gasping of breath.

A great running monster whose breath stank and whose bellow-lungs pushed out air like

She wanted to look but then

"Don't look back," he'd said. "It wants you to look."

Traffic surged past Old Street roundabout, but it was far, far away, horses pulling against the reins of the man in the Ford Mondeo who drove them, scuttling thief-boys spilling their Starbucks coffee, time mixing as past and present clashed in silent explosions around her, and she could taste blood in her mouth and knew it wasn't her blood, and see the howling of the thing, of the whatever-it-was behind her, as movement in the air, like heat haze disturbing the sky, but this haze was all around, rippling against the street light and sucking the colour from it and

Don't look back. It wants you to look.

Her heart was racing and her mouth was parched and crusted around the lips where blood was drying, and she wanted to laugh and throw her hands up to the sky and scream at the moon – which was not there – and tear at the silent traffic that stop-started against the lights and could not see her, nor even perceive itself, the drivers oblivious as the black fog of their engines melted with the black fog that had hung over London for a hundred, two hundred years and

She ran across the street and felt something move beneath her.

It was a jolt, a shock, an almost physical force that threatened to trip her, knocked the breath from her and sent her staggering, hands out to support herself against the nearest wall.

Her hands passed straight through and so did she, tumbling head first, through the wall of a private dental clinic and its posters of patients who reported their immaculate smiles to be the most important thing in their life, onto a scrubbed tile floor. She lay there gasping as the blood thundered in her ears and the world outside seeped back into place, reasserting the sodium colours of the night, the busy crawl of the buses and the weary honking of horns by irritated drivers.

Some lingering tracery of that shadow vision, the shaman's vision that came with the shaman's walk, was still settled over her eyes. She crawled to her hands and knees, then got up, keeping her back turned to the wall through which she had stumbled.

She listened but heard no howl.

There was, however, a breathing, a slow rise-fall, a steady drawing in and pushing out of breath, like a huge motorbike engine made of muscle, waiting to start.

She tightened her fingers around the strap of her bag, closed her eyes and prayed to who-cared-what-for-anything-good and slowly, stomach spinning faster than her step, turned.

No one there.

Just the slow thump-thump of breath that wasn't her own. Her lungs were heaving, grabbing down air, but this sound, this breathing, this steady roar – it could circle the globe and still have oxygen left for resuscitating an elephant.

She told herself she was being ridiculous and knew she wasn't.

She told herself that this was absurd, that she was standing inside a dental surgery on City Road and she'd get in trouble with the police if they found her and soon an alarm would go and she should really move.

And did not move.

She thought about Gretel the troll and Sally the banshee, about Kevin the vampire and the man with electric-blue wings, and wondered what they would do.

Stand here paralysed, she concluded. Frozen with fear at an unknown something waiting in the night.

She told herself she was a shaman.

She thought she heard a voice, tiny and far off. "Tonight, on who wants to be a shaman, will Sharon take the challenge or will she give up her dreams?"

It seemed an unlikely voice to hear in the dead of night, and she concluded she must be going mad.

Having proposed madness, she considered it further and decided yes, all things considered, that probably made the most sense.

And that being mad, there was probably no escape from madness so, hell, she might as well go outside and dance the dance.

She took a deep breath and stepped back through the wall.

A woman at a bus stop with a violin case on her back glanced up and furrowed her brow as she tried to work out if she really had just seen a girl appear out of nowhere, or if she was joining in some universal process and going insane.

Then she shrugged and chose not to think about it.

Sharon looked around her: red brake lights heading in one direction, and white headlights streaming in the other. Old Street roundabout wasn't big on sleep.

No trolls lurched, no monsters stirred, no men with blazing eyes and burning wings appeared to offer cryptic messages.

As an experiment, she walked back towards the Angel, until she hit that perfect stride where invisibility began to seep over her skin, where she was so much a part of the city that no one bothered to notice her any more, and she heard it again.

The slow rumbling of breath.

Further off now.

Perhaps an illusion.

Perhaps a plane passing overhead.

Don't look. It wants you to look.

She walked away and then, in a single swift moment, moving too fast to have second thoughts, she turned and looked.

There was a wall across the street. It towered above the houses, it blocked out the sky, it was black and ancient and its stones were sea-smoothed-round and the mortar dripped blood and whispers, and fingers beckoned from the shadows of every indentation, and in the centre of this wall, this giant, impossible wall that spanned City Road like an urban overpass, this wall that traffic drove through like it was nothing at all when it was clearly everything that ever mattered, there was a gate. Black wood soaked through with blood and corseted with bone and, above the gate, a shield of white from which red blood flowed, running down from a giant cross, while another bleeding sword set in the top left segment of the shield dribbled its liquor down to the ground, the whole thing encased in silver-black claws.

Claws which rippled.

Sharon looked up and there it was, metal skin and twisting lizard-tongue, wings folded back and knees bent, eyes spinning and wild, a dragon holding its bloody shield above the gate, just like all the little dragons around the city carved from stone: the symbol of the City of London. But unlike those stone dragons, this one was alive. And it was staring straight at her, and it wasn't pleased.

She backed away as the dragon flexed its wings, droplets of blood shimmering on their spiked tips. It opened its mouth to hiss and its throat was a yawning pit and its eyes were spinning red flame.

Then something moved beneath it, and its head snapped round towards the gate. And it occurred to Sharon that, in this giant black wall that no one else seemed able to see, that traffic passed through like it wasn't even there, it didn't seem natural for someone to have left the gate open.

The dragon screeched its indignation and snarled at the gate, and its voice was the sound of untuned brakes and its breath stank of the hot dust of the Underground.

Sharon peered at what it could see, and thought she made out something beyond the open crack of the gate; and she knew, *knew* that it stood where the old city wall of London had run. Through the gate that shouldn't be open something was looking at her that ought not to be there. Its eyes were yellow, its jaw was wide, its fangs dripped black venom and, as its shoulders rose and fell, it made a *whumph whumph*

whumph sound like a steam engine beginning to move. It looked at her, then raised its head and howled.

The dragon screamed and launched itself from its perch above the gate, throwing itself down at the thing in the gap. Fang met claw and Sharon put her hands over her ears as the two forces met and tumbled, gashing each other until their blood began to flow and burn the tarmac beneath their feet and she . . .

. . . turned and ran.

Chapter 18

What We Do Defines Us

It was called Coffee Unlimited and its tag line was SIMPLY AMAZING COFFEE!!

Its best price was £1.80 for a cardboard cup of thin brown slime which the blackboard behind the counter declared to be *Classic Americano — made from finest hand-picked coffee beans and crafted to perfection by our trained staff, this is the classic beverage on which COFFEE UNLIMITED forged its reputation.*

People came and people went, and weren't particularly happy about either action, yet somehow, impossibly, Coffee Unlimited had found a tiny part of Pentonville Road where there wasn't something better on offer.

Pentonville Road was not a glamorous place to spend a lunch break. Traffic roared east from King's Cross to the Angel with the recklessness of bored drivers who've spent too much time at a red light and are determined to make it into fourth gear if it kills them — or anyone who gets in their way. In the opposite direction, traffic slouched round a one-way system where oversized lorries drove through undersized streets in search of that elusive sign that pointed, in all its cryptic glory, to THE WEST.

Shielded from these geographical misdemeanours by a grubby sheet of glass, worked the staff of Coffee Unlimited — *Happy to Help!* —

creating alchemical concoctions on whose mysteries they were sworn to secrecy and, frankly, did anyone really want to know? Greg, twenty-seven, Polish, studied stage management and worked towards his visa with relentless good humour and a wry resignation at the impossibility of anyone pronouncing his surname correctly. Gina, half Indian, half Greek, entirely stunning, apologised for other people's mistakes until the day Robin, American, brash and utterly unimaginative, finally went too far and blamed her workmates for the incident with the exploding pot of pressurised cream, when a new aspect of Gina struck down all before it in hitherto pent-up rage. And Sharon, who kept her head down and did her very best not to turn invisible before the customers' eyes or forget to open the storeroom door when fetching another litre of on-the-turn milk.

Above them all, ruling from afar, was—

"Were you late this morning, Sharon?"

Mike Pentlace, five foot five of carrot-crowned lechery, iPhone fused to the palm of his hand, perpetually trying to make its voice activation recognise his drawling tones, forever failing.

"Uh . . . yes, Mr Pentlace, I was, a little."

This is the voice of Sharon Li, after four hours sleep, three of those spent in nightmare, who staggered out of bed forty minutes before her shift began and opened the door half expecting to find blood outside. This is the bleary look of Sharon Li as she hangs her head before the wrath of her employer, wondering whether her life is real or if in fact she hasn't made a terrible mistake to think so.

"Yeah, but you should just tell me these things."

"I'm sorry, but there was this meeting last night and it overran . . ."

"Yeah, but I get that, yeah, but you have a responsibility to be fit for work. I mean, I'm not angry, yeah, but you've got to come in here fit to work and I mean I didn't want to say nothing because, yeah, but it's not really something I usually care about but actually you're just kinda . . . You don't have a good attitude, you know what I'm saying?"

"A good attitude?" echoed Sharon, the milk in her hand gently turning.

"Which I don't get," added Mike Pentlace, thumbing his iPhone just to make sure there wasn't an app which could get it for him. "Because, yeah, but this job is important, yeah? But you seem to think that you're not so much one of the team and I'm saying, yeah, but you're not going to get better than this. I mean I don't want to sound ... but you're not so you've gotta have a positive attitude, yeah, and that doesn't just mean turning up on time, it means smiling more and looking happy and being, yeah, but being more ... I don't know ... more less weird."

Sharon tried it.

"Yeah, but okay," concluded Pentlace, disappointed with her wretched attempt. "Well, just go back to work, okay, and we won't say anything more, yeah?"

She went back to work.

Robin exclaimed in her best head-turning whisper, "Wow, he is like totally an ass!"

Gina added, "You okay, hun?"

Sharon smiled gamely and topped up the espresso machine one bean at a time, placing each one into the grinder with a murmur under her breath of "I am beautiful."

Pop the bean inside.

"I am wonderful."

Pop another bean inside.

"I have a secret."

Push it down into the blade.

"The secret is—"

"Fucking service!" shrilled a voice behind her.

She turned.

There was no one there.

"Are you all like, deaf or what?" added the voice. It was male in that its highest register was still below the normal female range, but so bubbling with indignation that it had nearly cracked on through to a whole linguistic realm of its own.

Sharon looked around. Gina was putting out slightly stale muffins in a row on the cake counter. She liked laying out the cakes, and was continually adjusting them so that whenever someone took a muffin, the display was instantly restored to maximum mathematical neatness, for the next customer's aesthetic delight.

She didn't seem to have noticed the furious voice.

"What the fuck does it mean 'medio'?" ranted the voice, its indignation rising to a new pitch. "Where's tea?"

Sharon edged towards the sound just as a hand, grey-brown and all knuckle, gestured above the lip of the bar in lurid contempt at the available options. She leaned over and looked down.

A pair of gum-yellow eyes stared back, and a plume of black nasal hair quivered in indignation at the end of a flattened nose the colour of dirty slate. "About fucking time! I want tea. I want it in a mug *this* big." A pair of four-fingered hands, fingers too long, skin too leathery, made a gesture that was nearly the same size as the creature's head. "And I want the bag left in to soak. No point having fucking weak tea!"

Carefully, with a nonchalance that she'd cultivated with great care over many years, Sharon examined the rest of the café. If anyone else was aware that a three-foot goblin in a bright green hoodie which proclaimed SKATE OR DIE! across its back was attempting to order tea, they weren't showing it.

"Milk, sugar?" she asked.

"Both, lots!"

"Biscuit?"

"Do I look like I want a fucking biscuit? Why do you people always try to sell me shit I don't want?"

"I'll be a few moments."

She made the tea on automatic, staring vacantly ahead, waiting for the moment when Robin came back from wherever it was Robin went when she got bored, and saw the goblin, and screamed. Or for the clash of Greg dropping the tray as he surveyed the bare-footed three-toed little creature quivering with rage against caffeinated consumerism and all its follies, or for – oh God – for the moment Mike Pentlace swanned back in while trying to make a Very Important Phone Call, only to be stopped in his tracks by the bodily odour of a creature who had heard of this showering thing but thought it was for nonces.

She poured in too much milk and the cup nearly overflowed, its contents held in by surface tension alone. She tipped some away, then remembered the size of the goblin's gesture when he'd ordered his tea. A thin line of brown now dripped down, sullying the clean white cardboard with the trickle of shame.

Still no screaming.

She turned back to the counter and pushed the tea towards the questing fingertips of the goblin.

"Two twenty, please."

The fingers stopped mid-curl around the mug. "Two fucking twenty? For a cup of fucking tea!"

"A very large tea," corrected Sharon, and flinched even as she spoke. "In the mornings we do tea free with sandwiches between 8 and 10 a.m., or in the evenings sometimes we knock down the price on the muffins because if we don't then we have to throw them away or sell them the next day at the very front and hope no one notices."

"Where do you think I'm going to get two twenty from?"

Sharon considered. "Aren't there charities?"

"For goblins?"

"Um ... I didn't know people were allowed to discriminate on grounds of ... you know, ethnicity."

"Are you calling me ethnic?"

"No sir," blurted Sharon. "I'm just saying you're uh ... you're probably a minority group and that's maybe good because you know when you get those forms and it says 'Do you consider yourself disabled?' and you say 'Yes' because then they have to give you an interview in order to fulfil their quota, well, you being like, you know, a goblin and stuff, you could probably say you're disabled and discriminated against and that's really good for these access questionnaires and—"

"What the hell are you talking about?" demanded Sammy the goblin, so loud that Sharon knew, she *knew* someone had to hear, someone was going to look, they were going to see her talking to a goblin and that would be it, another ignoble end to another ignoble job, sacked for a reason no one could quite name but everyone accepted, because they could have sworn they saw her turn invisible but weren't completely sure.

"Discrimination," she babbled. "I mean I know there's people who say that positive discrimination is still discrimination just like unpositive discrimination, I mean like negative discrimination but you gotta look at things and go 'Shit, there are way more rich white dudes than rich black dudes' but then I guess it's all proportional and really I don't know much about it so—"

"Which are you? White or black?"

"What?"

"You?" demanded the goblin. "What 'ethnicity' or whatever are you?"

"I'm ... well, I suppose I'm ethnically Chinese but I was born in Barnet."

"Barnet, Barnet, shitty shitty Barnet!" sang out the goblin, and Sharon closed her eyes, waited for the shout, the gasp of horror, the cry of amazement, and it was ...

... nowhere.

She opened her eyes and looked – really looked – and saw the world as if through a broken magnifying glass, or a TV screen set to interfere. Someone had sprayed a settling mist over all things, but rather than cause the world to thicken, it seemed to make all things that it touched a little more translucent. The glass shimmered in the shop front like a caged liquid trying to break free, and at the empty tables sat the shadows of those who had sat there before, their features shifting in busy silence. The light from outside made each mote of dust visible, rippling away from her fingers as she moved them through the air. And looking round at the people, she saw ...

She saw not one but many, a many that was one ...

She saw

Pallid features of the man reading the newspaper, hair growing thin before her eyes, falling away, skin turns white and retracts into bone and he glances up and wonders why she stares and

She saw

Another shyly holding hands with Greg as he speaks words in another language, which she knows though she has never before heard these sounds and

Above Gina's head, in Gina's head, the sound of music, a song half heard, half remembered, what and where, and the what is

Sung by her sister

And the where is

Richmond Park as a child, barely able to walk, a deer came by and she laughed and her mother was afraid and that made her laugh harder

And she heard

Tick tick tick beneath the streets

And smelt

Burning on the earth

And she felt

Burning in the palm of my hand our hand our hand burning in the palm ours is mine is

And she looked down at the grinning face of the goblin and there was an infinity between her and him, an infinity before and an infinity behind and a world of dust between his toes and she held on to the counter for support but it was barely there, barely real, she was gasping for air, gasping for breath, and he said, the words too far off:

"Do you have any toothpaste?"

She rocked back to normality, the real world asserting itself like a slap on a choking man's back. The shadows were gone, the sounds were gone, the goblin was gone and he was

No, not quite gone. There was a faint something in the air, a shimmering of movement, a clattering of change and a sulkily paid two pounds twenty was there in front of her where it hadn't been before and a little voice, far off, was saying:

"We'll start at Seven Dials, eleven tonight. Don't be fucking late."

If she scrunched her eyes up, she thought she could see the walk of the goblin as he waddled towards the door, and trace his passage by the splatter of tea as it slopped over the edge of his cup. Then he was gone, out through the door and into the street.

Although, she noticed, as he left he didn't bother to open the door.

Chapter 19

Lonely Is the Burden of Command

Some four and a half hours before a goblin walked into Sharon Li's life and demanded extra large tea with milk and sugar, Sammy the Elbow, second (possibly third, really, who could say?) greatest shaman who'd ever lived, was annoyed if unsurprised to receive a visitor to his den.

The den was in Camden, and had been advertised as a "studio flat", which was far too small for Sammy with his bed of cardboard, soft beds being for losers, and his extensive collection of tinned food and toothpaste.

This visitor, from whose back blazed wings of blue fire that might have been those of an angel, or perhaps of a dragon, and whose eyes were two endless pits at the bottom of which burned unending madness, said, "Wotcha."

Sammy had replied, "Oi oi, you look shit, don't you?"

His visitor considered this proposition. Since it came from a three-foot-nothing goblin whose body had clearly interpreted the genetic command to sprout hair as relating more to ears, nose and belly button than any real growth on the surface of his skull, he wasn't sure if he was ready to accept Sammy's diagnosis without querying the perspective from which it was made. Then again, what Sammy lacked in outward presentation, he more than made up for with a certain unstoppable grasp of the situation. So the visitor gave a shrug and said:

"Rough couple of . . . well . . . everything."

"You know about Dog?"

"I love the way you do that."

"Do what?"

"Just *know* stuff."

"I *am* the second greatest shaman ever to walk the earth, ain't I; how thick would it make me if I didn't know shit? It's not like you get to be as talented as me without picking up some stuff."

"It's killed again."

"Some prat in Clerkenwell, I know."

"It—"

"Tore his throat out, ripped off his ear. I know, I know!"

"And last night I went to the place where the spirits were and heard—"

"Its howl, of course you fucking did, it's been howling for weeks now and you're just too fucking 'boom' to do anything about it, aren't you?"

"Its footsteps—"

"Burn the earth, I know, I know!"

Silence. Then the man whose blood was fire and whose eyes were an endless storm, said, "Sammy, in all the many things you know, and I get that there's a lot, has it occurred to you that sometimes it's just plain good manners to let the other guy finish?"

"I'm a busy goblin, I can't sit around for everyone else to catch up. Besides, you're the Midnight Mayor – what you going to do about it?"

The man addressed as the Midnight Mayor sighed. "I'm trying. It's hard."

"Fucking lame."

"I've found someone I think you should meet."

"You wanting favours now? Bad habit to get into, needing favours."

"She's a shaman."

"Any good?"

"Maybe. Maybe very. But she needs training."

Sammy spat, a single globe of green-tinted spit flying across the floor. Where it hit concrete, it began to smoke, giving off a thin acrid white vapour. "Can't be handling kids."

"It's important."

Sammy's eyes narrowed in suspicion, a finger waggling towards the other's face. "You ... *scheming*, Midnight Mayor?" he asked.

"Me? Scheme?"

"Don't get me wrong, I think you look like a thicko in a bin bag just like everyone else, but then that got me thinking, maybe you *want* to look like a thicko in a bin bag, maybe that's all part of the game, pretend to be a thicko so that when you stop being a thicko everyone's so surprised that no one notices you're not that bright anyway."

"I can see you've thought this through."

"Too right."

A silence stretched like the screech of chalk across a blackboard.

Then, "She's founded this thing, this society. It's called Magicals Anonymous."

"Shit name."

"Dog's killings aren't random."

"Course they ain't."

"He's targeting a very specific group of people, all connected to a very specific operation."

"Course he is! But you're too tied up with the cash thing to do nothin' 'bout it!"

"The four greatest killers the world has ever seen are in town."

"What's new?"

The man addressed as the Midnight Mayor said, "I think they were hired by a wendigo."

Silence again.

Then, "You pillock."

The man called the Midnight Mayor grinned. "Thought you might say that."

Chapter 20

To Understand Others Is to Comprehend Yourself

There were a lot of messages waiting for Sharon when she got home. Her shift had been long, occasionally stressful and frequently dull, all beneath the shadow of her boss, judging his employees without raising a finger to contribute. Three months she'd worked in the coffee shop, and that was two and a half months too long. But where else was she to go?

She sat down in front of a tiny laptop, her leaving-school present to herself, and flicked through the logs. Most of the messages were via Facebook, and nearly all were from members of Weird Shit Keeps Happening to Me And I Don't Know Why But Figure I Need Help. Some were nice. Sally the banshee wished to thank Sharon for her initiative and enthusiasm in chairing last night's meeting; Gretel the troll had attempted to express her delight at Thai food and wondered if maybe next week they could try Mexican, but unfortunately the size of her fingers had crunched the keys and most of what emerged was an unintelligible medley of letters. Chris the exorcist had attempted to post an ad on Facebook for Exorminator – Exorcism With Love – which Sharon removed with a firm little note requesting that all promotional material be kept off the group page.

One was from a stranger, requesting permission to join the group. There was a message attached, which read:

Sorry to run off last night, but there was a bloodthirsty hound prowling through the spreading shadows. Asked a friend to pop by and see you at work. He's cranky but okay. Bring toothpaste.

It wasn't signed. The name of the sender was one MS. She clicked through to his profile page. It was almost entirely empty. In the "About me" section someone had written: Protector of the City, Defender of the Night, Guardian of the Mystic Walls. Like you believe a word of it.

Only one other person seemed to have ever looked at the site of MS.

KS: This is not what I meant when I suggested we raised your public profile.

MS : Bite me.

KS : How do you feel about Twitter?

MS made no reply, but two days later KS was back again.

KS : Did you have to hex the backup servers too?

After that the conversation lagged.

Sharon sat back, drumming her fingers along the edge of the desk. It wasn't every day, she concluded, that a goblin demanded you met for purposes unknown at 11 p.m. in the middle of town. But then it wasn't every day you had curry with a troll or got patronised by a guy with invisible burning wings at his back. So perhaps she should just write off the entire week as being a bit odd and go with it.

The man in the empty factory had said she was a shaman.

He'd said a lot of other things too, most of them in haste and with an infuriating lack of detail, but that had been the part that stuck. That had been the bit she knew was right, as she had spent so much of her life *knowing* without knowing how.

She googled shaman.

Her laptop chugged through the search, chewing every byte like an old cat on dry biscuits.

Pictures populated her screen, one pixel at a time. Shamanism didn't look like a profession with great fashion sense. Feathers she could handle, though less so through her nose. Pages of ravaged faces, men and women with lives etched canyon deep into their features, stared out of the screen with the reproachful gaze of the too wise wishing for ignorance. She tried reading a few articles, and the words blurred before her. Vegetarianism seemed in, especially mushroom dishes. Drumming seemed likely. Leadership was an absolute must, but nowhere did it say exactly *how*, or give any useful pointers like whether to bring a clean pair of trousers. The implication was that if you were a shaman, then you probably knew already what you were doing.

She looked at the clock on the wall: 9.45 p.m.

A pile of books stood on the wobbly fake-wood table by the bed. They were much thumbed and well annotated, and featured such helpful titles as *Believe in Yourself* and *You Are the Best*. They offered a variety of guidelines on how to live your life in this uncertain age, ranging from five minutes of meditation every two hours – which Sharon had calculated to mean at least five hours a week of sitting on her behind trying to breathe through her nose – through to a healthy diet of celery and beetroot juice. She felt rather guilty about her collection of self-help books, not least because she couldn't shake the feeling that much of their wisdom was the stuff her grandmother would have spouted when tipsy on too much rice wine. None of the books advised on what to do when you accidentally turned invisible, or walked through walls; nor, above all else, whether either of these had dangerous medical implications. Having no real information on such conditions and being largely unable to control them, Sharon had tried instead to manage her concern at the situation through helpful mantras, extensive lists and, during particularly difficult times, multicolour highlighted charts entitled "My Aims" pinned to the inside of her cupboard door. These proclaimed things such as I will get a proper job and I will learn how to use the self-assessment tax service and of course, above all else, I will take control of my own magical nature. This last point she'd highlighted in both blue and pink, creating a smudged, rather unintelligible note of good intent.

10.10 p.m.

Downstairs Trish was watching TV, loudly, with the living-room door open. It wasn't much of a living room, mostly dominated by one grubby sofa and a coffee table supported on books, yet for all its lack of space somehow they could never find the remote. She loitered in the bedroom doorway, listening to a merry male voice proclaiming, "What a stunning performance! She really gave it everything she's got, and here's her mother, looking so proud . . ."

Ayesha was out for the night. When they'd moved in together, Ayesha had told them she liked to study late in her university library. Trish had laughed and made a joke about a line of boys; Sharon had laughed too, until she'd seen how deeply Ayesha had blushed and caught the smell of old paper clinging to her hands. Sharon didn't like touching old books; it annoyed her to hear the scratching of the pen and the rippling of the thousand microscopic bugs that lived in the spine. Certain things, it seemed, wanted her attention whether she was invisible or not; books and blood being right up there.

She put her satchel over her shoulder, pulled on a pair of thick socks and her purple boots, and went downstairs to the living room.

"Hey, Trish," mumbled Sharon.

"Hey, babe!" replied Trish, eyes not turning from the screen. "Good day?"

"No," admitted Sharon. "I got told off by my boss, and a goblin came into the shop and ordered tea, and last night a guy with these wings told me that I had to find a dog and then there was a howling and I ran away."

"Sounds good, babe, sounds good!"

"I think I'm meant to do something, something important, and I don't know what it is."

"I get that all the time, babes," sighed Trish. "It's like, I'm looking at myself in the mirror and I can't work out what's wrong and it takes like, for ever to realise I forgot my earrings!"

Sharon smiled meekly, the only response she could find, while Trish suddenly leapt forward on the sofa and screamed at the TV, "What the fuck? You can't vote for him – he was fucking shit! Jesus!"

On the screen a boy, barely seventeen or eighteen, was hugging a woman in a white dress and crying with joy while around him bright lights flashed and portly ladies of an age to know better screamed like chemically maladjusted schoolgirls.

"Trish?" asked Sharon.

"Yeah, babes?"

"If I'm not . . . If you don't hear from me tomorrow, will you tell someone?"

"Yeah, yeah, babes, of course, whatever."

"I'll text you."

"Cool, babes. Fucking hell, what is she wearing? Slag!" screamed Sharon's flatmate at the TV.

Sharon drifted back down the hall, feet barely touching the thin carpet, head bowed and mind scarcely there, took her coat off the hook by the door and let herself out.

Chapter 21

Trish

You wanna know about Sharon? Uh, like, why? I mean, she's my friend of course, you know, like my sister and that, but she's like ... I mean, okay, so, I'll just say what I think here, yeah? She's like, really nice and that, and I really respect her and everything, but I'm just like ... She's weird, you know? And I'm like, Jesus, can't you just stop being weird already? Like, you've only got yourself to blame. She doesn't even watch *X-Factor*, what the fuck?

Chapter 22

Seek and You Shall Find

These were the words Sharon whispered as she stood hugging herself by the central pillar at Seven Dials, alone and impatient:

"I am beautiful, I am wonderful, I have a secret."

The theatres were emptied and shut, the lights still burning above their padlocked doors, and the traffic was thin, with a distant bubble of sound towards Cambridge Circus and St Martin's Lane. But the pubs were still open and nearby restaurants were serving their finest dessert wine, one thumb-sized glass at £12.80 a sip, excluding service.

Seven Dials was, as the name suggests, a place where seven roads met. There they made a small circle around a pillar, from which blue clock faces dressed in gold looked down at the neighbourhood's narrow lanes like a warning to mind your seconds and watch your step. According to some local businesses, this geographical anomaly in the larger street plan of London was a *village*, a corner of Covent Garden that featured not mere purveyors of goods but boutiques offering the ultimate in handbags, shoes and hair for the truly tasteful and shockingly rich.

Sharon knew she was neither of these. Her purple boots clomped on the smoothed stone below the pillar as she walked round and round, murmuring, "I am beautiful, I am wonderful, I have a secret . . ."

A cab crawled round one corner, driven with the caution of

somebody who suspects he's made a mistake but hopes no one will notice.

"I am floating calmly beneath the surface of the river ..."

A paramedics' car paused at the bottom of Monmouth Street, its blue lights silently flashing. It did a circuit of the pillar, then another. On the third attempt the driver made a wrong decision, leaving him with not enough room to turn. The passenger door opened and a medic got out, green bag slung over his shoulder, and began jogging back the way the car had came, while the driver circled again in search of a way through.

Sharon paced, circling the pillar like the second hand on a lethargic clock. In summer tourists sat huddled here while scanning their maps for Trafalgar Square, where they could huddle beneath a larger pillar in greater numbers. By day shoppers not only went in search of high fashion, but sought quirks, strange hold-outs in a sea of universal trend. A shop selling nothing but beads for the enthusiastic craftsman; a theatrical bookshop with a love of musicals and high tragedy; the model shop featuring stormtroopers in all sizes from keyring to lifelike with added comics for the true enthusiast.

"I am beautiful, I am wonderful, I have a secret, the secret is—"

"You got toothpaste?"

The voice was loud, belligerent and unmistakable. Sharon turned, just in case the universe was about to pull another, unwelcome surprise and, sure enough, there was the goblin in his oversized green hoodie which drooped down to his knees, SKATE OR DIE! blazoned across his back and the image of what looked like a cool penguin in shades performing a trick on his front.

The recollection that this was real and this was happening – or at the very least that this was something she was perceiving to be real and if she was mad she might as well go with it – held her back for a moment, and a default answer of "What?" issued from her like notes from a run-down stereo.

"Toothpaste, toothpaste!" shrilled the goblin, hopping from one foot to the other. "You got the mark of the Midnight Mayor on you so he must've talked to you so he must've told you to bring toothpaste!"

Sharon looked down at herself, saw no mark, craned to see over her shoulder, and felt down her spine for what she could only assume was the mystic equivalent of a KICK ME sign. The goblin rolled his eyes. "You are as sharp as a bag of boiled potatoes, ain't you?" Gleefully he bounded forward and before she could object grabbed Sharon's right hand in his. His skin was leathery, dry, thick, given a rougher edge by a thin coating of black bristles almost invisible against the skin.

"Here!" he snapped, waving Sharon's hand up and down in front of her face. "Look here!"

She looked.

There was nothing.

"You gotta stop trying," the goblin exclaimed. "It's about seeing a thing in the corner of your eye when you is walking down the street and thinking, 'Fuck me I didn't see that' and then when you think you should go back to check you're running late for a meeting so you don't and you never know – it's that, that's what you gotta see, them things that don't want you to see them at all!"

Sharon swallowed, thought about Gretel the troll, her face lost behind an ever-changing mask of don't-quite-want-to-look. She looked away from her hand, then swept it quickly in front of her vision in a single dismissive gesture, pulling free of the goblin's grip, and, for a moment,

there was something on her hand.

Something red and bright and hot, a pair of crosses that vanished the second she stared, agape. "There's a bloody—"

"I know!"

"But I didn't—"

"I know, I know!"

"How did—"

"I know!"

Sharon hesitated, eyes swinging back to the goblin. "Hold on!" she said. "That one was a question."

"I know!"

"And that isn't an answer."

"I know, I know, I'm getting there," fumed the goblin. "Midnight Mayor's watching out for you. There's them that say one guy's watching out is another guy's manipulating like a pot of play-dough, but with this one it's kind of hard to call, like, is he really that pig stupid or is he playing like some fucking long game? Most punters are too thick to tell but I know where I'm gonna stand at the apocalypse, just saying."

Sharon stared at the goblin, and the goblin had, perhaps, the good grace to look embarrassed. She felt in her pocket and handed over the tube of toothpaste. The goblin snatched it merrily, leaping with surprising vigour into the air and spinning away. The lid was off in a single twist and his head tilted right back as, with every sign of satisfaction, he squirted a fat stream of blue-white goo into his mouth, rolled it around inside and swallowed.

Sharon's face was a picture of distaste, the goblin's of delight. "Not too fucking bad," he concluded, wiping his foaming lips with the back of his hand. "Next time get whitening."

"Who's the Midnight Mayor?" demanded Sharon.

"Protector of the city, guardian of the night and all that crap," sang out Sammy, slipping the toothpaste inside his hoodie for later. "I'm all like 'You can't say you're the protector of the city and not have a big hat' and he's like 'Screw your big hat' and I'm like 'It's your fucking style sense, whatever.'"

"But that doesn't mean anything! 'Protector of the city' is the world's stupidest job description ever! And besides who are *you*?" demanded Sharon, her hands slamming onto her hips as if by force of gesture alone the conversation could judder to a halt.

"Sammy!" replied the goblin, giving her a look which implied that if she hadn't worked this out already or, more, been somehow attuned to the very nature of this mystery, she wasn't worth his time. "I'm Sammy the Elbow, second greatest – *second* greatest, wankers! –" he shouted at some unknown academic audience "– shaman to ever fucking live. I've seen the path and walked the walk, I know the secrets of the sodium night and when I say jump toot sweet you jump toot sweet yeah?"

"What do you mean 'the Elbow'?"

"You really are ignorant as a cheeseburger, ain't you? Didn't you learn nothing at school about goblin tribes?"

"No," she replied, a glare of defiance seeping into her face. "I know this is like, way out there, but at school we learned about chemistry and geography and how to put a condom on a banana. We did not learn about goblin tribes, because until, like, two minutes ago I didn't fucking know there were goblin tribes, so cut me a break, okay?"

To her surprise Sammy grinned, revealing a small collection of very large brown teeth. 'There'd have been this thing," he explained. "You'd have been walking along, probably by yourself, only you weren't by yourself because you weren't never by yourself but you were probably too dense to know that, and there would have been this thing, this sort of 'Oh what the fuck' thing."

"'Oh what the fuck thing'?"

"Yeah. And you'd have been like 'Something is happening' only like I said, you'd be too dense to know what it was and then there'd be this second, and in that second you'd know everything. Everything that is and was and will be in the city, every brick and stone and piece of squished chewing gum, every secret and every dirty party, you'd know it all and then," his grin widened, "you forgot."

Sharon stared down at her feet and remembered the feeling of rain on her face, the taste of kebab in her mouth. And something else, something bigger, that she hadn't been able to bring back.

"Okay," she said at last. "So what do you want?"

Sammy the Elbow, second (?) greatest shaman to walk the earth, spread his arms wide in delight. "What do you think, carrot-brains? I'm your new teacher!"

Chapter 23

Salvation Is Within Your Grasp

Howl!

    Howl!!

        Howl!!!

He hears and he runs.

His name is Scott, his mum raised him Catholic, his dad raised him wizard, and now he's beginning to wonder if maybe his mum wasn't on to a better thing. Usually he combs his hair back over his scalp to hide the premature bald spot that was another unwelcome genetic inheritance. Now his hair stands up like the quills of a hedgehog facing down a cement truck, and if he has any time to interact with it, it's to pull it out, strand by strand.

He runs until he can't breathe, and pauses on a street corner to fumble with his phone.

"Help me!" he shouts into it. "Help me!"

"The secret," replies the voice on the other end of the line, "is not to look back."

"It's coming for me!"

"It wants you to be afraid."

"You said you'd protect me!"

"I also told you to run, and here we are."

"Help me!"

"I'm coming. Keep your phone on. *Run.*"

He runs, shaking with fear; his body become his new worst enemy. At times like this, he feels, his legs should grow wings, his back should become light, his stomach full of helium and he should fly along, every muscle feeding off the urgency of his mind and making it easier for him, blocking out the pain. That doesn't seem to be how it works. He's never been so tired, nor so far from home. He runs, not knowing or caring about the direction any more, just straight, in a straight line until he reaches the edge, and he hears behind him – so much worse than the howling in the night – he hears a silence. The thick impenetrable silence that comes when the traffic stops, the deafening roar of a silent fan, the impossible nothing of a non-dripping pipe. His is the only noise in these sleeping streets, his the only movement, a firework at a funeral. Don't look back.

He realises that he repents.

Fear can do that when guilt fails. And he has plenty of fear.

Lights ahead, a main road – no one dies on the main road, the idea is ridiculous – he runs towards it, a night bus swoops by at the end of the street fulfilling its role of perpetually never being quite where you want it. He staggers onto Fleet Street, a road too narrow for the daytime traffic that clogs it, too wide for this night-time emptiness. The tall shops and offices are clustered in recognition of their sometime medieval ground plan, inconsistent grandeur mixing with modern slabs of concrete, old porticos bearing stone faces that guard the way to the latest sushi bar. Not 400 yards away he can see the back of a black dragon on a stone plinth, its head turned outwards towards the place where the City of London meets the City of Westminster, its spiked wings as tall and sheer as the Gothic ornamentation on the Royal Courts sat right by it. He gasps down a shuddering breath and staggers towards it down the middle of the street, feet flapping on the tarmac, head tilting forward, ready to fall. He can see a figure waiting just the other side of the dragon, a man dressed in a tatty coat, a flash of blue from his eyes – impossible at this distance, a thing imagined – and from the phone in his hand he hears a faint voice proclaim, "You're nearly there. Don't look back."

His mouth opens in an unstoppable grimace, he wants to laugh even though the dragon is still so far, and hears behind him, so close:

hhhhhooooooooooowwwwwwwwwwwwllllllll!!!!

hunting cry

a snuffling, a shuffling, a thing that becomes the bounding rhythm of a gallop, soft paws on the ground that wouldn't make any noise but that the thing above them is so heavy, a thump of unstoppable force beating against the street and a bellowing of breath through tight black nostrils and it's here, it's here so close now and must be this second, must be now and

"Don't look!" shouts the man at the end of the street. "Don't look!" he can feel its heat, smell the blood and dog stench in its fur and "Don't!"

he knows this is how the others died but they couldn't stop it either and

he looks.

He didn't realise jaws could be so wide.

Chapter 24

Respect Your Teacher As You Respect Their Learning

Sharon thought she heard...

...but it was nothing.

She trailed behind Sammy the Elbow, falling into step automatically, and half-listened as he explained.

"In the good old days we got treated with proper respect, it was all like 'You know shit, wow!' and we were all like 'Yeah so give us your virgins' only virgin has always been this really dodgy term, especially, I gotta tell you, especially in north London. Then there was this thing with the Tower and everyone was a bit like 'Wow, we should've done something' and that kind of didn't do the rep any favours, which is crap because I was in Derby so didn't have nothing to do with all that shit but by the time I come back to London you've got amateur magicians, you've got shit mystics talking like they know shit, you've got untidied hexes everywhere and the Midnight Mayor is some bloke who isn't even totally dead yet. I mean amateurs! Shoddy spellcraft everywhere and when people come running 'Oh, Sammy, there's unbound shades on the loose in Kennington' I'm like 'You've only got yourself to blame' but do they listen do they?"

"I don't know, do they?"

"No!"

"And uh . . . is that . . . for any particular reason?"

"What's that meaning?"

"Well, I'm just saying – I mean, it's nothing to do with you as a person, I'm sure you're really cool and that – but I'm just saying . . ." She hesitated. "You're not really giving off positive vibes and I'm guessing people do like that, especially when, and I know this is going to sound really bad and I don't mean it in a discriminating way, yeah, but especially when you're three foot tall and a goblin."

Contemplative silence.

Then, "Is you saying it's cos I'm short?"

"The height . . . may be a thing, yeah."

"Is it you're saying it's because of my . . . *ethnicity*?" Sammy savoured the word as a food taster might enjoy the professional satisfaction of that first tinge of cyanide.

"My sociology tutor told me how ethnicity was only a social construct," she announced. "It's like as how, it's not just about your race and that, it's about your culture and your social identity."

"What social identity?"

"I guess what I'm saying is that it's not because you're a goblin, it's because you're . . . kind of negative about everyone else. Sir." The "sir" was thrown in as an afterthought, as Sharon's brain offered up the view that, sure, even though Sammy barely came up to her waist, that didn't mean he couldn't bite.

"You ain't met many goblins, squishy-brains." It was a statement delivered with the certainty of someone who not only knows the answer to his own question, but can see the wretched consequences of it right before his eyes. "*I'm* fucking civil."

"Why are you teaching me?" demanded Sharon, the words dropping before she could stop them.

Sammy shot a glare at her. Even at this hour St Martin's Lane was busy with people wondering how they were going to get home, as clubs and bars began disgorging the tipsy, the sozzled and the truly smashed into an ear-wringing night. Sharon and the goblin scurried past a tapas bar where the bouncers wore badges on their sleeves, and on a wall by the door a motley collection of mojito-fuelled revellers sat enjoying a quick fag. No one seemed to notice Sammy and, as Sharon realised with a faint jolt, nor did anyone seem to see her. It was the walk, that very special walk where all eyes fell straight through them, an invisibility by default usually known only to security guards and cleaners. Sammy was doing it on automatic.

"I am trying to tell you about the way things are," he shrilled, "and you just keep asking stupid questions!"

"It's not a stupid question," she insisted, moderating her voice to keep it level as they turned up Long Acre. Mannequins stared out from behind sheet glass; the local council were again drilling in the middle of the street just in case they'd missed a deposit of famed Soho crude. "A lot of shit has been happening the last few days and I thought it was because of Magicals Anonymous and how people might get interested in that, but now I don't think it's about that, I mean, not just about that, because sure it's weird but this is a whole different level of weird."

"First you called me short, and now call me weird?" demanded Sammy.

"No! I'm saying that weird, like ethnicity, is like . . . in the eye of the beholder, you know? So there's probably guys out there who are like 'Wow, I'm talking with a goblin' and that's completely cool but, like I've been trying to say, this is my first time and so yeah, I'm allowed to say it's a bit weird and in fact –" she puffed up with sudden, revelatory pride "– in fact, yeah! This is something difficult I'm going through and I think you should be fucking supportive about it and not give all me this grief, which isn't to say I'm not grateful for the teaching thing if it happens because I am yeah, but this is exactly why I used to get into trouble because people weren't understanding when things were weird and exactly why we need Magicals Anonymous, so yeah!"

She stopped so suddenly that the air seemed to bend around her as reality tried to work out what the game was. Sammy paused, looking back at her with his oversized, over-round eyes, and for a moment Sharon wondered how he did that, how he stayed unseen and stationary at the same time and if he'd ever got it wrong; then the rising tide of her indignation brought another burst of defiance.

"I've got a job to do, you know!"

"What job?"

"I'm . . . I'm a barista!"

Sammy snickered.

Sharon felt small and rather alone.

There was a flicker of something in Sammy's face that might almost have been him relenting. If perhaps he'd spent a happier youth among the garbage heaps of whichever big city, he might have held out a trembling hand in support. If he hadn't learned at a tender age that emotional intelligence had nothing on good athletic skills over a 400-yard sprint, he might even have ventured a word of consolation. As it was, he had, so he didn't, but kept on striding invisibly through the night, tutting under his breath. Sharon hesitated, then moved to catch up, swinging back into that rhythm where all things became a little bit thin, and a little bit soft around the edges, and the world went out of its way not to perceive.

Then he said, "This is the shaman's walk. You're crap at it but what's a goblin to expect?"

Sharon swallowed more than just air and ventured, "Are there like . . . medical implications and things? Like, am I going to wake up one day with, you know, cancer in my brain or that, because I noticed how sometimes I turn invisible and can walk through walls and things, but they say mobile phones have been linked with cancer and you don't know do you? Because I've seen those movies where wizards throw fire from their hands, and I think they must have like, really bad internal problems for that to work, like they must have horrible skin or like, be allergic to lactose or something, but it's not something they talk about on NHS Direct."

Sammy's mouth opened to say something rude before Sammy's eyes caught the earnest look on Sharon's face. He closed his mouth, took a steadying breath and declared, "I ain't never met a shaman what's died of cancer *never!*"

Sharon looked relieved.

"Dragon, yes. Met a shaman what died of a dragon," added Sammy, eyes drifting into some recollecting place. "Drowning, once. Being impaled on a tribal spear; crushed by an Underground train; electrocuted in a substation; eaten by a cockatrice although I think that weren't what dunnit, I think it was the manticore's sting what was the problem; spontaneously fucking combusted; shot at close range by a killer from the Order; and pneumonia, sure, all of that! But never, not once, not never, cancer."

"Oh," murmured Sharon. Seeing that this was Sammy's best shot at comfort, she added, "Good." Then a thought hit and she gestured furiously at the empty air. "I am not sticking feathers through my nose!" she exclaimed. "I don't mean to be ungrateful or whatever, but I'm not having any of that! My mum would do her nut!"

"Feathers in your nose?" shrilled Sammy as they rounded the Royal Opera House and headed east towards the imperial architecture and health-aspiring coffee shops of Kingsway. "Why the hell should you stick a feather up your nose?"

"I googled shamans," she explained weakly. "And mystic dancing – I mean, I'll give it a go if it's like, really important, but last time I went to the disco my mate Sue was all like, 'Hun, it's nice that you're trying' which meant I had two left feet and everyone else was way sexier and, like, knew what they were doing but if it's absolutely essential then I guess I can try."

"Dancing?" Once more Sammy's indignation rose towards its default level of fever pitch. "Feathers?!"

"Wikipedia said—"

"Wikipedia! Wikipedia!" He threw up his hands, and there was a change to his walk, faster, slightly too fast for the world around him, invisibility straining against the righteousness of his anger. "Wikipedia is what's wrong with modern wizardry!" he shouted. "Everyone's like 'Wow, I can do that' and then what do they do? They cross their secondary summoning circle with the shield line, and they invoke with sodium instead of fluorescent and they're all like 'Wow we're so good at what we do' and then who has to clean up the bits of brain splattered up the walls? Experts! Experts have to fucking do it and I'll tell you what, I'll tell you!" His whole body trembled with outrage and as he walked, Sharon couldn't help but notice. The air seemed to shimmer around him, lights flickering in the street as if the universe yearned to help him endure his heightened emotional trauma, but couldn't quite work out how. "It's always the goblins that get blamed! Racist, that is! Racist discriminatory ethnic social fucking whatsit!"

Sharon glanced around to see if anybody had noticed. There was no one around, which was lucky considering that Sammy wasn't just verging on visible, he was heading for inflamed. But there was something watching: shapes in the darkness, shadows that hid *between* the light of the street lamps, figures that turned away when she raised her head to examine them, the passing image of a cleaner sweeping away the dirt before Sam's bare three-toed feet, the flicker of a head turning in a window above to see what all the fuss was about, the scuttle of a fox pausing in its passage across the street to marvel and disappear. None of it real, and yet all watching.

And even as she watched back, Sammy's pace slowed again, and they all began to fade, receding into the same shadow world through which the goblin moved. "Mr Elbow sir?" murmured Sharon, once the tide of Sammy's indignation had retreated, to reveal a little pool of potential calm. "Do you ... I mean, you probably don't but have you ever ... There's this webpage I run, okay, it's called Weird Shit Keeps Happening to Me—"

"Sounds crap."

"We've got this help group going."

"Bollocks!"

"You say that," pressed Sharon, warming to her theme, "but I don't think you're the only one who feels discriminated against because of your ... your appearance and your ... well, your smell and stuff, which is fine. I mean it's totally cool, and my mum always said that collective action was the only way to achieve lasting change and I always thought that sounded a bit ... But if you feel like you need to talk about anything then we hold meetings once a week and the first one went really well I think and you know you're ... you're not alone is what I'm saying. I guess."

To her surprise, Sammy's silence was almost thoughtful. Then, "You got a tribe?"

"What? Uh, no. I mean, I used to hang out with the girls down the shopping centre, after school and that, but security said we had to move on, which I was so angry about, yeah, because we weren't any trouble to no one and I actually wrote a letter!"

"You're a shaman – you gotta have a tribe."

"Well, uh ... I don't think I do. Sorry. Is that a fail?"

Sammy grunted. "There's almost no shamans never. I mean, people always talk about how there's never many sorcerers, but there's less shamans. Sorcerers are just wankers who get that life is magic, like that's a big deal. They're all into their special effects, their boom bang boom shit – any old tit can be a sorcerer once they learn how to feel the city beneath their feet. And there's the shamans of *the* Tribe, the guys who get all bonded on self-mutilation and that, but they're only shamans because they lead, not because they *know*, and half of them are dead anyways. But proper shamans, *real* shamans – you and me – we got the other thing. The deeper thing. We don't feed on the city like sorcerers do, we don't use it for our power. Us and the city, we're the same. We're one. You gotta get used to two things when that happens."

"What things?" asked Sharon, almost in a whisper.

"First thing is that you ain't never gonna be alone. Wherever you go, it'll be with you, in you, you in it. No one's never alone in a city."

"And the second thing?"

"You're always gonna be alone," he replied with a little shrug. "Cos no one else will ever get it, and cos you'll always know how much bigger everything is. You can try and explain it, but you can't, because you're a shaman and they ain't. Now, you may be into your self-help shit but, as a goblin who is like pretty fucking good at what I do, and I'm not just saying that because I am, I'm gonna give you the best ever advice ever. Deal with it."

Sharon deflated.

They walked on together in silence. The gate was shut across the entrance to Lincoln's Inn. Sammy swaggered through its black wood without breaking stride. Not noticing what she did, Sharon followed him. Lincoln's Inn was a place of grass (not for walking on) and stone terraced mansions (not for cluttering) scarred with shrapnel from one of the very few bombs to fall on London in the First World War. And there it was again, the sense of eyes watching though nothing living stirred: a figure running up the steps to the high red-brick chapel, the rattle of a trolley, laden with paper, on the paving stones, though nothing moved to make such a sound, the hiss of gas from a wrought-iron lamp long since extinguished. There were shadows here trying to be seen, but afraid to go that final step and be perceived.

"It's not about power," explained Sammy. "Leave power to wizards and sorcerers and that. It's about knowing the things beneath. Stop!"

He stopped so suddenly, Sharon walked into him. He staggered forward, cursing, recovered himself, spun around, and then there he was in his full three-dimensional glory. A goblin, an actual goblin, stood in the middle of Lincoln's Inn with his hands on his hips like an angry aunt. For a moment the sheer absurdity of it overcame Sharon and a single giggle escaped her before she pressed both hands over her mouth as if to deny the merest squeak.

Sammy's eyes narrowed, and beneath her hands Sharon tried to fix her features in what she imagined shaman apprentice after shaman apprentice had attempted as their "Really, that mushroom?" expression in the face of their aged, possibly feather-touting, probably mystic-dancing shaman master's ire.

Sammy, looking like someone who'd seen it all before, let it pass. With a finger punctuating every vital word, he exclaimed, "There's lotsa walks you gotta learn! The walk you've figured is the piss-easy walk and if you hadn't figured it, you wouldn't be worth the bother. It's the shadow walk, cos you are part of the city and the city is part of you so why should them that look see you cos all they can see is the fucking city, get it?"

Sharon nodded energetically, and risked easing her hands away from her mouth.

"That's what they see when they see you, cos they are seeing you when you do the shadow walk, but they ain't seeing you, they're just seeing the city and who bothers to fucking look at that? No one!" he answered before Sharon could offer a response. "No one bothers to look because the old skills are dead and the younger generation are all like 'I've got an app for that' or whatever. It's a disgrace."

Sharon went with nodding again, as her safest option.

"There's the other walks too," he went on. "There's the spirit walk, which is deeper than the shadows. It's the walk where you can see what really is but you gotta remember," wagging the finger, "them things what you can see are gonna look straight back at you and that can freak out the incompetent wankers but –" another stab with a quivering, many-knuckled joint " – you'll be okay because your teacher is just that bloody good!"

Nod, nod went Sharon. It really seemed the best way to avoid trouble.

"There's the dream walk. Like the title kind of bloody suggests, you've gotta be dreaming to do the walk but don't think it ain't as real as any of the others because what the fuck is a body without a mind, yeah? You walk through the dreams of others and they're gonna dream some freaky shit so you just be fucking careful when you walk. Your spirit guide will protect you a bit, but again it's just a product of your brain so don't treat it like it's gonna pull anything special any time soon."

Sharon raised a querying hand.

"What?" demanded Sammy, stamping a foot at the interruption.

"My spirit guide?"

"You ain't met your spirit guide yet?"

"Um . . . I dunno. Would I know if I had?"

"Course you'd fucking know! It's a fucking spirit guide!"

"What does it look like?"

"Different for everyone. It's a part of you, it comes from you. Like me," Sammy puffed up a little, "*my* spirit guide is no less than a psycho-mystic representation of Benjamin the Eye – I don't expect an ignorant pink thing like you to know 'bout him – but Benjamin the Eye was only one of the greatest shamans *ever* and I see him because that's the level I'm playing on! You're probably gonna see like . . . rabbits or some-thing."

"Rabbits?"

"Or something!"

"My spirit guide looks like rabbits?"

"How the hell should I know – do I look like I waste my talents on shit like that?"

"I thought you said a shaman was supposed to know things."

"Important things! Important fucking things!"

"Okay then, okay," replied Sharon, her indignation rising in the face of Sammy's. "So tell me something knowy."

"Blue is a stupid colour for hair."

"That's not knowy, that's an opinion and it's a rubbish opinion too," she retorted. "You can't just come up to me and go like 'I'm your teacher' and not have an Ofsted file or nothing, or a CV or those little cards with quotes on it saying things like 'I used to walk among the living dead but then Sammy taught me how to control my necroman-tic powers and now I do yoga' and all that shit – so you convince me that you're all you're talking about."

Sammy hesitated, looking about the street. They'd emerged from the Inns of Court onto High Holborn, an arterial road with delusions of grandeur unsupported by its tendency to sell mostly stationery, and now as Sharon folded her arms and waited beneath the glare of the red traffic lights commanding stop to the absent traffic, Sammy the Elbow cast around for inspiration.

"Right," he declared and, grabbing Sharon by the hem of her jumper, dragged her towards a nearby stone wall.

"Hey, you can't just—" she began. But, without slowing down for the wall's thickness, Sammy walked straight on through, pulling Sharon after him.

Chapter 25

Follow Your Heart

They'd passed through into a camping shop. The lights there were out, a glow from the street slipping in past mannequins in woolly hats, sensible boots and rugged rucksacks. Passing one particular shelf, Sammy sniffed in derision.

"Thermal underwear. Stupid bloody humans can't take a bit of cold."

Sharon averted her eyes from Sammy's knobbly knees. "What are we doing here?"

"Gonna summon a spirit, innit."

"Are we?"

"If you're gonna be a flipping shaman, you gotta get used to spirits and their shit."

"No drumming?" asked Sharon nervously.

"No drumming," he replied. "Drumming is only ever for amateurs. I want you to look round at this place and tell me about it."

Sharon surveyed where they were. She made a point of being slow and deliberate. "Okay," she said. "If I told you it was a camping store and we're trespassing, you'd probably say something like . . ."

"Bollocks!"

" . . . which isn't really fair, if you think about it," she went on, "because you gotta know I wasn't gonna be able to say much more about this place than that so you were all geared up to put me down even when you asked the question, which again, I think, is totally frowned on by Ofsted."

Sammy scowled. It was an impressive scowl, making unnatural-looking folds in his face as his lips curled back to reveal his oversized yellow teeth. "You gotta think about all the stuff people don't usually see," he chided. "Look proper like!"

Sharon sighed and looked again.

The shop was silent.

Posters of snowcapped peaks lined a wall of ski boots; folded tents were laid out beneath one larger construct of fabric and poles with a sign proclaiming DELUXE 7000 – TAKE YOUR HOME ON AN ADVENTURE!! There was a faint smell of cleaning fluids and the slow red glare of a security alarm confused by the absence of broken glass or splintered doors in the wake of the two shamans.

She looked, and for no evident reason a shudder ran through to her bones at the sight of a thermal jacket padded almost as thick as the human frame it was designed to protect; as her eyes wandered over the balaclavas something silky brushed her cheek. Turning, she heard a till slam shut, coins jingling in its plastic drawers, and she spun round again, staring towards the checkout counter with its discount offer on dripping water bottles and keyring compasses whose points couldn't find north.

She hesitated.

Something wrong with this picture.

Stepped towards the counter, reached out for the plastic bottles lined up by the till. They were nipple-lidded, garishly bright, their price reduced from ridiculously high to merely silly for a one-time-only twice-monthly sale. She could hear the rubbing of the fat red felt-tip pen as it struck off the old price hanging round their necks; and from the top of each bottle water tumbled, silent and clean, a slow fountain that barely rose up before it tumbled back down, pooling on the counter, then a rippling down onto the floor. The compasses in their boxes were spinning, the needles racing round and round. As the water spread across the tile floor towards Sharon's feet she thought she heard the whisper of the sea, tasted salt, felt icy air press against her cheek. Hesitantly, she picked up a bottle, and heard the crash of crates as they were loaded into an iron container, smelt oil on deck and voices crying out in a foreign tongue, turned and saw a man in a top hat and walking cane, papers rolled up before him, sat at the table where knitted hats and scarves were sold, waiting for his meeting,

and she dropped the bottle, which rolled away across the floor.

The flow of water stopped, had never been there, but the man remained.

"Sammy?" she hissed. "There's a dead Victorian dude sat by winter headgear."

The goblin tutted. "So?"

Sharon edged closer to the figure, its head bowed, face lost in shadow. She could feel . . . a contracting around her, the walls not so much closing in as bending, craning to watch, and when she glanced up she saw the snow billowing off the posters of mountainsides in far-flung places, ice crystallising on the plastic soles of the ski boots, and knew that though it wasn't real, it was nonetheless true. A thin mist filled the air, blue-grey, the stink of it made her nose itch and tightened her throat. As she neared the man in his black top hat, she felt something sticky beneath her foot and saw a piece of yellow gum on the floor, carrying the imprint of her boot. A few paces from the man, now only one. She stood before him, trying to inspect him, but his features were lost beneath the top hat. She glanced at Sammy for advice, and saw for an instant in the goblin

Blistered feet

Endless road

Never come back

before he said, "Go on, look!"

She turned back to the man on the headgear table, reached out gingerly and prised the hat from his head. His eyes flashed up at her, two ochre-stained balls swivelling in a hollow skull, a tongue rattled between his lips of rotted grey-black leather, and his nose was hollowed down to two great holes and a thin piece of bone. She dropped the hat and scrambled away – away from him and away from the stinking mist, staggering back into the cool darkness elsewhere in the store.

Sammy grabbed her by the sleeve as she leaned against a wall and gasped for breath, coughing out the taste of smoke. "What'd you see?" he demanded.

"Dead dude," she replied, trying not to shrill the answer. "Very much ... dead dude. Am I going to start projectile vomiting? Only seeing dead people isn't something I'm really big on and really not something I signed up for."

"You gotta learn how to see the things what are there! All the stuff underneath, all the things just outta sight – even the dead things! It's all part of the shaman thing!"

"Really? Only I was hoping it'd be ... nicer than that."

"Nice? *Nice?* Magic ain't supposed to be *nice.* You want nice, go look after baby penguins at the zoo!"

As career advice went, Sharon had heard worse. "Okay," she grumbled, forcing her breathing to slow down. "Tell me about the dead dude."

"This place was a merchant's office," explained Sammy. "Company what sold opium out to China and that. Now course they buy all their stuff from China, which I guess is kind of funny, 'cept the stuff they get from China's all like, plastic drinking bottles and that and not so many drugs, not here anyways."

"So dead dude was a drug dealer?"

"Nah, he was a merchant!"

"Who sold drugs?"

"Yep."

"Kind of then," said Sharon in the tone of someone puzzling out a great problem, "like a drug dealer. Why'd I see him?"

"Time," Sammy replied. "Time and secrets – people try an' bury 'em both, stick 'em down beneath bigger roads and brighter lights, pretend that they aren't there. You get it sometimes when you touch people, or things – that feeling when you know all the things that are true about them, all the things they don't want you to know. You taste it, the bitterness in their mouths, the worries in their heads, hidden away. But it's always there, stuck just beneath the surface, making this world what it is, and you, bein' a shaman an' all, you see it. An' sometimes it sees you."

Sharon blanched. "No way am I talking to dead dudes," she insisted. "I mean, I'm sure it's groovy in its way, but there's some serious God questions raised there and I can't be having it right now, thank you."

Sammy mimed exasperation. "You're at one with the city now," he explained. "You don't really get no more havin' it than that. Come on."

He marched out into the street through a wall of T-shirts carrying such life-affirming messages as TO THE END AND BEYOND! and CONQUEST IS VICTORY, designed to inspire bold camping adventurers to look to their navels in search of inspiration.

Outside was chilly, damp, the traffic a sullen stop-start of odd cars and buses by the lights of Holborn Circus infuriated at how few pedestrians were crossing. They passed Hatton Garden, a street of goldsmiths selling rings and other jewellery to the naive, and pawnbrokers buying them back. East lay Smithfield Market, whose long aisles, beneath its Victorian wrought-iron roof, were built to take deliveries of meat by the cow and blood by the bucket. Sharon shivered and thrust her hands deeper into her pockets as Sammy strode past shuttered shops with warning signs informing would-be thieves that they'd be prosecuted to the limits of the law if they so much as considered breaking into these properties, within which no money was kept overnight, so there.

"Every building's got its history," explained Sammy as they marched up the office-shadowed street of Snow Hill. "Even the new ones, cos they've been built on something. They've got secrets and stories – it's like the sorcerers say! Where there's life, there's magic and that, and all a shaman does is notice. Every street, every stone, they've all got something inside 'em, scratching to be heard. Trick is knowing which bits to listen to and which to ignore, cos let's face it, if you listened to all of it, your brain would go dribbling out of your ears." Sammy seemed to relish this idea. Then with a stamp of his foot he declared, "Only some silly bugger's gone and buggered about with it and muggins 'ere has to bloody fix it!"

A seed of suspicion stirred in Sharon's mind.

"What do you mean, buggering about?"

"Buggerin' about!" he retorted, as if that should be explanation enough. "Playing silly buggers, tampering with the forces of nature and that! 'Ere!"

He led the way to a little side road and stabbed a finger towards a squat round building that sat on the corner. The street was barely wide enough for its one-way traffic, with iron bollards unevenly spaced down its length as if, one at a time, a century of accidents and disasters had been removing them.

"Like that 'un there."

Sharon followed where he was pointing to the darkened windows of the building. A white banner over the door proclaimed, COMING SOON!!! It didn't say what was coming soon, but that hadn't stopped the maker getting very excited. Plywood covered its shopfront windows, and above, on the smaller windows in the building's rounded corners, someone had written in the dust, **Expect no mercy**.

"Was this one owned by a slave trader?" asked Sharon.

In reply Sammy just waggled his eyebrows, which were of the same magnificent thickness and colour as the black hair that quivered beneath his broad grey nostrils. He waited until, with a puff of exasperation, she marched towards the locked door and straight through to the other side. She sensed a moment of pressure, a flash of darkness, then she stood in a wide empty room with a central pillar supporting the ceiling and heaped dust sheets kicked against a chipped plasterboard wall. Thin street light drifted through cracks in the plywood window covering; even so, it took a while before her eyes adjusted to the settled gloom. The last occupants had left few signs of their purpose: a bright green fire exit sign, some leaflets spilled on the floor and a blackboard still chalked with the words, EVERYTHING MUST GO.

She felt, rather than heard, Sammy step through behind her, his yellow eyes glinting a little too bright in the darkness.

"Whatcha see?" he asked.

"Nothing. I mean . . . you know, some stuff, but nothing."

"Whatcha hear?"

She listened.

The nothing she heard was almost deeper than the nothing she saw, a great dead heartbeat that had forgotten how to pulse.

"Nothing."

"There's signs you can look for," he explained. "The shop that opens and six months later shuts again – might just be the economy or shit, might be a shop trying to sell smelly candles by a football stadium or whatever – but then the shop after that shuts in six months, and the one after that in three and you gotta start asking yourself, is it cursed? And the answer is of course it's fucking cursed – I mean how dense are you?" He kicked at a can of solidified paint. "You're a shaman," he explained. "You're at one with the city – which ain't great for the city, I gotta tell you, cos if you're the best it can do then it's so stuffed – but anyway you're meant to see the things that ain't there. Hear the things no one else can hear. Whatcha hear?"

"I said, nothing."

"Whatcha see?"

"Nothing. Is this some new teaching method or what, because I'm pretty sure I've seen Channel Four make documentaries about this kind of abuse."

Sammy clapped his hands in busy command. "Nothing!" he repeated. "You're dense as lead in a treacle pie but you ain't that dense. You ain't seeing nothing, you ain't hearing nothing cos in this place there ain't nothing left to be seen." His voice was suddenly soft and loud all at once, the clearest she had ever heard him speak. "Someone's been stealing the souls of things. Been plucking them right out, a building here, a building there, sucking them dry. The spirits in the statues, the dryads hiding in the traffic lights, the ghosts in the graveyards, the shadows that walk beside you in the night – they're what you hear, they're what you see, even the stupid bloody people what haven't got two brain cells to rub together, they don't know it's them they're looking at but they *feel* it, they feel the things just the other side of the dark. There was something here, there *should* be something here, and it's gone. Someone took it. Someone's been taking them all, all the shadows of the city. It ain't a good death; it ain't fire or flood or any of that Midnight Mayor shit. It's a slow, declining death that don't bother to say hello or bye bye and you don't even notice you're dying until you're already dead. That's what this nothing is. Only a shaman knows to fix that."

Sharon found herself turning, staring right at him, the little angular shape of grey goblin in the dark. "Okay, then," she said. "How'd you fix it?"

"You gotta find them, the lost ones. All the spirits and all the shadows that got stolen away. You gotta bring them back – you gotta bring . . . " He hesitated. Then, "You gotta bring *her* back. The oldest of them all, her what keeps the city walls shut, what keeps out the dark. The Lady Who Walks Beside, our Keeper of the Lamp, the Silent Friend, the Lady of 4 a.m. She's not just some building spirit or some imp at the end of a lane, she's . . . she's the one who keeps you safe from the thing you don't dare look at in the night. Greydawn, they call her, and like everything else in this city, she's . . . missing."

"'Missing'," echoed Sharon, then, with a surge of realisation, "Oh, bloody hell, is this what all this cryptic crap has been about? The guy yesterday who didn't buy me lunch, you turning up demanding tooth-paste, 'missing spirits' and all that? You know, Sammy, it could've been great. I was open to it, I really was, I thought, yeah, sure, he's a goblin, but I'll be open-minded and try and learn from him, but really, *really* all this is about, at the end of the day, is some missing . . . person . . . with a lot of daft names." She quivered with an outrage worthy almost of her master.

"Course it is, stupid!" he exclaimed. "But you think I'd be bloody wasting my time on some cabbage-for-sense baby shaman if the fate of the whole fucking city weren't at stake? You think the Midnight bloody Mayor would give two farts about you if he wasn't shit scared that this time he can't find a big enough shovel! Course you gotta do something about it and course you should be pleased!"

"Why?"

"Cos now you've bloody met me!" Sammy threw up his arms in exul-tant affirmation.

Sharon hesitated. Somehow, it seemed, she was on the brink of being told about all those unnamed things of which she'd known so little, but up to now she couldn't have asked the right questions.

"But . . ." she said, struggling, "and . . . I mean, I can totally see how I'm not gonna like the answer here, but I'll be really pissed if I don't ask . . . why can't you just fix it?"

Sammy raised his eyes in despair. "I may be the second best shaman ever to walk the earth," he explained, "but people just don't respect my height."

"Your—"

"And I . . . I kinda have differences with a few of the powers that be, you know, which isn't my fucking fault because the Beggar King had it coming and the Bag Lady shouldn't have said what she said and the Seven Sisters did look stupid in that dress so what I'm saying is I'm just completely fine, I'm totally great at fixing this shit but there might be a few tossers what get in my way."

"And . . . they won't get in mine?"

"Stupid, innit?"

"I gotta say, if the fate of the city is on the line, then I kinda figured you'd be a bit more on it, Beggar Lady and that besides."

"It's . . . There's things, okay? Stuff that I did that was . . . Besides, this is human shit and you're never gonna learn nothing if you just sit on your arse, so can it, okay!"

"But what am I supposed to do?" wailed Sharon. "I don't know nothing about anything; I work in a coffee shop! If you're all so shaman special then you should fix it despite being . . . a minority group. Or get this Midnight Mayor bloke to deal with it, because all I can do is walk through walls and turn invisible, and from everything you've said, that doesn't sound like it's gonna be any use to anyone."

"Ain't you listening?" demanded Sammy. "You're a shaman! You can do the shadow walk sure – I say *do*; it's kinda like watching a shark trying to swim backwards up a waterfall, but at least you've got the idea – but you've got the dream walk and the spirit walk and you can see the city and it can see you and that makes you . . . it makes you almost kinda . . . " Sammy's hands flapped as he sought to express an idea. "It makes you almost kinda okay!"

Sharon put her head in her hands. Sammy hesitated, then waddled to his feet and padded over to her. He patted her uncertainly on her knee, that being the easiest part to reach without standing on tiptoe and embarrassing himself, and added, "Chin up, squishy-skin. What's the worst that can happen?"

Chapter 26

Do Not Invite Calamity Into Your Home

There is, in accordance with the universal law of balances, a worst that can indeed happen. Currently the worst that can happen is sat on the steps of St Christopher's Hall in the darkest part of the night and considering its next move. There is a hint of overweight belly within the sensible shirt, a suggestion of buttock peering out behind the drooping blue jeans, a protrusion of sensible boot and, of course, the ubiquitous yellow fluorescent jacket. The worst that the world has to offer, the greatest killers that man has ever seen, sit and drink builder's tea from polystyrene cups, and the night is silent in their presence.

One says, "Hey!"

One says, "Whatcha?"

One says, "You smell that?"

One says, "Heard it barking."

One says, "Knockers!"

One says, "Lovely pair . . ."

One says, "She was here . . . but then she went."

One says, "If the Friendlies don't know . . . "

One says, "Is she hot?"

One says, "Great arse."

One says, "What kind of name is that?"

One says, "Wankers."

One says, and there is a certain relish in his voice as he reaches this conclusion, "Bloody stupid name."

One says, "What's she do?"

One says, "'Divides the night from the day', whatever the hell that bloody means."

"Keeper of the Gate."

"Our Lady of 4 a.m."

"She Who Walks Beside."

All four pause, and consider these words, and find in them nothing that impresses.

One says, "Let's get her."

One says, "Bacon fucking sarnie!"

One says, "Greydawn shit."

And they smile.

Four faces – but all the same smile.

Chapter 27

Dreams Are the Story of the Soul

It was three in the morning.

Sharon walked home.

Sammy had muttered something about him staying late into the night. She'd thought she'd heard a dog bark in the distance, and when she looked again Sammy was, briefly, afraid. Gotta go, he'd said. Gotta feed the imps yesterday's recycling. This whole city shit – you fix it for your homework, okay?

Then he was gone.

She walked and had never felt so alone.

She walked the shadow walk, the walk just-out-of-seeing, and sometimes, when her mind wandered, she thought she walked the spirit walk too, and the forgotten things came crawling out between the cracks in the paving stones, and pawed at her, and asked her to remember them.

She collapsed on her bed in the silent house, where once

family of five rowing – go on bit me do it then do it – how dare you talk to me like that I am your mother – I hate you! I hate you I'm not your brother!

had argued, voices singing in the pipes out of the creaking boiler cupboard, and she pressed her head into the pillow where once

a mother rolled over in her sleep, dreaming of flying above the sea, before the memory faded with waking

and swore and cursed and finally, fully dressed, she slept.

Even in her sleep, she walked.

She walked in a place where there was no light, and no need for light, seeing without sight, hearing without sound.

She walked through a city, and it was bright, and burning, and behind every light there were faces watching and beneath her feet was the place where other steps had fallen, and then between it all there were a few places, just a few but growing more, where the light had gone out. An emptiness where something else should have been. Here a girder turned to rust, there a bulb that could not be replaced, or a water main cracked beneath the street, gushing up silent and unplugged.

She walked the dream walk, passing through the thoughts of the child who lived two doors over and who dreamed of

you're never on time never on time never on time for class

while below the old woman slumbered, her mind giddy on blood thinners, who dreamed of

smell of paper in a place forgotten long ago.

She walked, and the dreams and half-dreams and downright nightmares of the city scattered before her, the half-heard thoughts of the slumbering streets, and as she walked she felt tiny, and alone, and heard the silence all the more when she passed by the building with the boarded-up door coated in dreamtime mists.

She thought she heard the rustling of spiders crawling into open mouths, chitinous legs on soft lips.

She wondered if she was naked on her first day at work, and decided she probably wasn't but that it would be best not to look.

She heard the crackle of electric wings, far off.

She wanted to go home, and couldn't quite remember where home was. She was in the street, and it was familiar and unknown, the physical reality lost behind the dream walk, her body one place, her mind another, and all around behind the darkened windows the dreamers dreamed of

flying glorious free! wonder of wonders up and up and up and nothing I ever dream will ever be so ecstatic

her lips on my neck

paper drowning in paper did I did I did I do it did I get it done?

email email writing email in my sleep email to him and email to her tap tap tap dancing on the screen and it's still not right!

Sharon put her head in her hands, burdened by all the sound, and still it came, the rising whisper of a thousand dreaming minds, a million dreaming minds, the city dreaming, united in sleep, all of it rising up around her and

there were footsteps on the earth.

No, not quite right.

Not feet.

Paws.

Each the size of a woman's shoe, splayed out into three points with a sharp claw at each end. The creature's, every stride was longer than Sharon's reach, and where its paws pressed down, whether on the thin floor of reality or the fiction of a dream, they burned the earth.

. . . didn't mean to make it happen didn't mean to leave . . .

falling out of the bunk falling out of the bed falling so far so far so long so fast but I tried I tried so hard sir

something under the sheets oh god don't let it be a snake please god not a snake in the bed a snake crawling up my leg I can't move I can't move god please

She threw her head back, opening her mouth to scream, silent screaming in the silent, roaring night. And there was a voice, louder, more real than anything which had come before and it said, to the sound of scampering feet:

"Good evening, ladies and gentlemen, and welcome to tonight's episode of – *Dream Walking!* I am your spirit guide for tonight, Dez Cliff Junior, as today we ask ourselves, Shamans? What are they like?"

Sharon thought she saw a figure. He was stepping through a grey-blue mist. There was a flash of white teeth, a suggestion of curly blond hair, a flare of orange-tanned skin, and a voice that whispered:

I am with you.

Then nothing.

Chapter 28

Sally

Hello, my name is Sally, I am a banshee. Forgive me not shaking your hand, but my touch turns the blood of mortals to ice within their veins, and at the sound of my voice men writhe and scream. I prefer letter-writing. Email is useful too, but I spent so long learning how to hold a fountain pen in my talons and I struggle with keyboards. I also believe that the art of letter-writing is one which should be preserved, as it creates a more personal, thoughtful missive than many of these modern communication media.

I do not believe I have a problem as such. I am a banshee and being a banshee is all I know, so to suggest that I struggle with this identity is to imply that I either do not know myself or that I have awareness of another way of being, neither of which I believe to be the case. Problem is therefore a negative understanding; rather I am attending Magicals Anonymous for its opportunities and positive effects.

I wish to broaden my mind. Specifically, I am looking for evening classes that are friendly to my particular situation. I considered t'ai chi, but my wings get in the way. Cooking seems very interesting, but there are very few cuisines which cater for the pigeon lover. I would love to do pottery, but my talons ruin the clay on the wheel. But I think now I have found what I want to do, what I really want. I sleep, you see, in the cooling tower at Tate Modern. A lot of banshees use these sorts of perches – good view, decent air flow and the food tends to come to you, although the family of peregrine falcons I have to share my lair with does rather put off the average seagull. But I digress. A few months ago I was having a dream, and in my dream there was a howling and a screaming and a falling, and I woke and I too was falling, and in my confusion, by mischance, I fell through a window and into the gallery itself. (I'm most terribly sorry for the damage.) The gallery was empty, deserted, but I had never been inside before, and as I tried to sweep up the worst of the glass and remove any shards from between my claws, I saw for the first time the wonders that it held. I don't understand art. I have never been introduced to it, never inducted fully, as you might say. And at first this made the experience the more frightening for, looking at the paintings on the walls, the sculptures on their plinths, the installations and the films inside that empty place, I felt feelings that I could not explain. Why should some splashes of oil on canvas induce fear, or grief? Why would a tin can make one smile? What is it in a jagged shard of metal that cries danger, or of a daub of colour on the wall that expresses longing? I do not know, and neither the peregrine falcons nor the banshees of my kin seemed to understand my concern.

So you see I am not here so much to express a problem, as to enquire into the possibilities of evening classes in Impressionist painting.

Chapter 29

Tardiness Is the Parent of Sloth

She woke at 11.26 a.m. to find her alarm clock had finished wailing four hours ago, and there were three missed calls on her mobile phone.

She fell back asleep for another ten minutes, then woke with a jolt that sent every capillary in her body into overdrive.

11.39 a.m.

And her shift had begun at eight.

Sharon fell out of bed, her bright blue hair sticking upright, yesterday's clothes hot against her skin. She crawled across the floor, grabbed her phone and recognised with horror Mike Pentlace's number, then Gina's number, then Pentlace's again. The house was empty, Trish and Ayesha having both gone out. As she staggered towards the bathroom and pulled back the shower curtain with its images of yellow ducks, her mobile played back its dirge of messages.

"Hi, Sharon, it's Mike. Yeah, but I know we talked yesterday, but you're late again and, yeah, but I want to be nice about this but actually, yeah, this is getting unacceptable. Call me, okay?"

"Hi, Sharon, it's Gina here. Just calling to make sure you're okay. So uh ... give me a call, okay, babes?"

"Sharon, it's Mike. You haven't called. Call me now."

Toothpaste foaming in her mouth, Sharon's gaze cleared enough for her to look blearily up at the mirror. The toothbrush stopped moving.

A stranger looked back at her. Sure, the eyes were brown and the skin was almond, the hair was black streaked with blue, but the back-combed look of dull-eyed exhaustion that stared out from the dirty glass belonged to some other woman, some older, possibly mushroom-munching woman who had seen such things as no words could recreate. The events of the night replayed slowly through her mind. Sammy the Elbow, the walk through Covent Garden, the empty shop with its too-quiet corners, EVERYTHING MUST GO, learning the names of the walks – the shadow walk, the spirit walk, the dream walk and of course somewhere just on the edge of recollection a merry male voice proclaiming, "I am your spirit guide for tonight!"

She half closed her eyes, toothpaste rolling down her chin, and tried to steady her racing heart. She was tired, she was beat, her feet ached, her legs ached, her neck ached, her brain ached. She put down her toothbrush in the jar and spat out the toothpaste. Slowly, methodically, she washed her hands and her face, and dabbed off with a towel. Then she picked up her mobile phone and, for the first time in her life, pulled a sicky.

"Hi, Mike," she intoned when he didn't pick up. "Sorry I didn't call but this major family crisis came up and I've gotta take today off. Sorry. Bye."

The lie, thin as winter sunlight through dusty air, settled over her with a strange unexpected ease.

Then she called Gina.

"Hey, Gina, it's me. I'm just letting you know I'm okay. Something's come up and I'm really sorry I can't be there today. I'll try not to do it again; call me if you want to and I'll try to make it up soon."

Then she switched her phone to silent, swept her hair back from her face and began to run herself a very hot, very slow bubble bath.

Chapter 30

To Strive for Perfection in Your Endeavours Is to Achieve Perfection in Yourself

Lunch was pizza.

A whole pizza, with pepperoni and extra tabasco sauce.

Sharon ate it in her dressing gown and rabbit slippers, and sat by her computer typing with one hand, feeding herself with the other. The view outside her small window seemed bright and still and friendly. There was a sense in the air of a different world. That strange, unknown world of 9 a.m. to 5 p.m. when during daylight hours people moved around the city freely, not trapped in an office or a glass cage. A curious time, which belonged to pensioners going to the butcher, to nannies taking their charges to the park in the holidays, to students wandering between classes, and that strange social stratum known as the self-employed, who felt no need to set their alarms or count the seconds down to the sweaty surge of rush hour, so long as the work was done someday, somehow, somewhere. Sharon wanted to giggle, and the urge to go and do her weekly shopping nearly compelled her out of the house, just to see what the market was like in the middle of a weekday, without men in suits coming back from work or parents with yowling children. She tried to imagine a world without weekend queues and not having to run for the bus. The wrath of Mike Pentlace seemed tiny, the coffee shop far off. She was a shaman and could walk through walls and, dammit, the art of whisking soya milk to a fine froth would have to wait. There was a city to save!

A city to save.

In the excitement, she'd almost forgotten.

How did you go about saving a city?

She googled it.

It seemed as good a place to start as any.

Recycle more, build less, bicycle more, drive less, build skyscrapers, build terraces, preserve historical housing, demolish unused stock, more parks, fewer car parks, more car parks, fewer bins – the answers seemed numerous and diverse, and not one of them seemed to deal with what she had in mind.

Her good humour was deteriorating, as she logged into Weird Shit Keeps Happening to Me, and posted on the wall.

Sharon Li: Hey guys, does anyone know anything about the spirits of the city all disappearing or nothing? Drop me a line if you've got any ideas! ☺

Well, it was progress of a sort.

She drummed her fingers and waited for a reply.

None came.

It seemed surprising that Sammy the Elbow hadn't recommended any proactive policy in her quest to save the city – whatever it was that it needed saving from. He hadn't even suggested she try meditation, which was surely a likely thing for someone supposedly in touch with the spirits.

Sharon sat on her bed and tried to adopt the lotus position.

She could get one foot on top of her thigh, but not the other. She swapped legs and, sure enough, the previously recalcitrant foot rested easily in place, while her other leg got stuck in a frustratingly un-karmic pose. She tried breathing slowly through her nose and on the fourth breath got bored.

She went back to the computer and googled spirit.

Frustratingly, her first few hits seemed to relate to computer software and airlines, and it was a while before pictures of swirling lights, innocent fairies and, to her slight confusion, galloping horses began to populate her screen.

The Internet, she concluded, wasn't getting her anywhere.

This revelation took a little processing since, in nearly all of her education, she'd been reliant on it to get even a C grade. To be so badly let down at the last would, she concluded, be one of the hardest parts of becoming a shaman.

She tried to think about becoming a shaman, and her mind drew a blank. Don't go there, it proclaimed. Be smart.

She thought about the empty building in Holborn where Sammy had held forth.

She thought about a man called the Midnight Mayor who'd stood with his back to the light in an empty place in Clerkenwell and murmured, "Don't look back. Run."

She thought about the silence, the too-thick silence that had set her teeth on edge. A thought drifted in from the outer edges of her awareness, raised one hand and politely asked if it could get a word in edgeways.

It was a good thought.

It involved more walking.

Sharon reached for her shoes.

Chapter 31

Do Not Judge by Appearance

His name was Bryan with a y. The y was important – the y marked him out as an individualist. His suit marked him out as one of the crowd, and his work as a letting agent absolutely confirmed him to be a sheep in human form. But still, whenever the darkest doubts crept into his mind and whispered that he'd sold his soul for £39,000 a year before tax and a flat in Fulham, he reminded himself that he was Bryan with a y and thus maintained some integrity.

He said, "So, what do you guys do?"

The woman to whom this question was addressed smiled what he couldn't help but feel was an overly brilliant smile. She was young – too young to be looking at this particular (very fine) property off High Holborn (rich with potential), and her straight black hair was streaked at the front with brilliant blue. Though she'd clearly tried to dress up for the meeting – arranged with all of twenty-five minutes notice – beneath the hem of her slightly too-short black trousers she wore purple boots, and on her shoulder bag were pinned nearly a hundred badges proclaiming, to Bryan's growing alarm, messages in favour of peace, brotherhood and social equality.

"Coffee shop," she replied briskly, looking around the empty hall of the office. "Coffee Unlimited is the company name – we make simply amazing coffee." Then, as if it had been bugging her for a while, "It says 'Coming Soon' above the door to this place – what's coming?"

"Well, that depends, Ms Li," replied Bryan, tugging at his individualistic, borderline-racey blue-and-white-striped tie. "I think you'll find the price per square foot of floor is very reasonable, considering the superb location—"

Sharon cut in, "So . . . nothing's coming?"

"Hopefully, you are! The development potential of this site is absolutely wonderful and I think you'll find that among its many attractions are –" his voice deteriorated briefly into a jumble of misplaced syllables and grunts as, in his enthusiasm to demonstrate the attractiveness of the space, he stumbled backwards into an overturned paint can, the nearly solid liquid still clinging to the lip and a smell in the air, an odd . . . almost refuse-like aroma clinging on from the recent past "– are its uh . . . its . . ." His voice trailed off. Really, was this what coffee executives looked like these days? But he'd looked up Coffee Unlimited and it had seemed reputable enough, and if they were looking to expand – but her hair was *blue*, and the look on her face as she examined the open-plan floor of this (excellent for the asking price) retail space was . . .

. . . disturbing.

But then he'd found this place disturbing for a while.

There was something in it, a muffled quality to the street noises outside, a thinness to the light creeping through the plywood over the windows, a loudness to his step on the dust-covered floor that was disproportionate to the force that made it. A hollowness in the air that made him want to run.

"What was the last business here?" she asked almost too casually.

"Uh . . . a herbal remedy outlet."

"And how long did they last?"

"I believe that they moved on for internal administrative reasons."

"Yeah, but how long?"

"About four months."

Sharon nodded and didn't look surprised. "And before that?"

"Before the herbal remedies?"

"Uh-huh. I'm asking cos of the important business data stuff," she added to assuage his reluctance.

"I believe it was an optician's."

"And how long was that here for?"

He hesitated, then blurted, "Coffee shops do very well round here, very well indeed; you're in the perfect place for the lunchtime crowds and there are so many offices—"

"Yeah, and how long?" she pressed.

Bryan sagged. "Six months."

He felt hot round the back of his collar. He hated coming here, hated trying to sell this place and hated, above all, hated the fact that in the last three months not one, not *one* customer, regardless of how low he pushed the price, had been remotely interested. He didn't understand. He was offering prime real estate at a rock-bottom price in a central part of town – a deal which under any other circumstances would have got him fired – and yet people left nervously, as if someone had died and there was a bloodstain on the floor that hadn't been cleaned up.

He realised Sharon was taking notes meticulously on a flip-up notepad under a heading which looked for all the world, from this angle, like <u>Saving The City</u>. Nor did he miss the emphatic double underlining with a ruler.

"Anything . . . odd happen here, ten months ago?" suggested Sharon. "Any complaints from the neighbours? Chanting? Dancing? Like, did anyone repaint the walls or anything in a way that made you think 'Yeah, animal sacrifice' or something like that?"

Bryan swallowed. This was getting a bit *too* individualistic for his taste. He thought about his sales figures and the flat in Fulham and replied, "Uh . . . not that I'm aware of. The property's only been on my portfolio for ten months, so maybe the previous management company might know something about that? But they can't offer you the same deal," he added, "which is, I must say, absolutely incredible for the—"

"How about uncontrollable screaming? Possession? Like, girls in pyjamas climbing off the walls and their heads doing this thing . . ." Sharon tried to turn her head all the way round to demonstrate the thing in question, tongue sticking out between her teeth, before returning to a rather more normal manner. "Anything like that?"

"You'd have to speak to the previous management company."

Her eyes narrowed in suspicion, pen poised over the largely empty notebook page. "Is this freaking you out?" she asked. "I'm okay with subterfuge when you need it, but a lot of the time I figure a direct approach, combined with a sort of doe-eyed charm, probably hacks it. My mate Tom says it's hypocritical to play the dumb blonde, not that I'm blonde, in order to get what I want *and* be angry about it at the same time, but Tom has had issues ever since the incident with the pogo stick so I'm not so sure if . . . Are you sure you're okay?"

"Uh . . ." It was the long syllable of a man for whom language will no longer suffice.

"I've got several management techniques for when things freak me out," she went on. "I used to get panic attacks back at school, owing to the fact I really wasn't fitting in. Breathing through your nose helps, and so does counting from ten backwards. I was taught this saying too – 'I am beautiful, I am wonderful, I have a secret, the secret is—'"

"I'm not freaked out," insisted Bryan with near-asthmatic intensity. "I'm happy to help in any way I can."

"There are support groups," offered Sharon. "Just saying."

Bryan's glassy-eyed look suggested that, even if a support group had walked up to him right then and offered the secret of eternal happiness, all he could have done was try to sell it a condo. Sharon sighed and went back to her notebook. "So . . . you come along ten months ago and take over this place, and since then it's been silent? I mean like . . . you haven't been able to rent it?"

"The economic climate," he replied, recovering himself a little. "The recession. People are so reluctant to take courageous decisions, to see a great opportunity even when it's laid out before them."

"Why'd the last lot get rid of it, then? I mean, why'd your company get involved?"

He was sweating now; he could feel a slow stain seeping out beneath his armpits. And, oh God, had he remembered to put on deodorant this morning? "New buyer," he blurted, though he really wasn't sure why he felt the urge to be so honest. "A new company bought it but they didn't really want the place, they were only here for a few days then they moved out but they own it outright so we were brought on board to try and let it but they don't really seem to care and I'm just saying it's a wonderful opportunity for ... a wonderful opportunity ... a ... "

Something in Sharon's smile, her fixed, radiant smile, was making the sweat prickle down his spine. "This company," she sang out sweetly, "what's its name?"

Chapter 32

Do Unto Others As You Would Have Done Unto Yourself

He said, "But they—"

She said, "Now Mr Mayor . . ."

He said, "They're a bunch of total—"

She said, "Now really, Mr Mayor, may I suggest, just suggest, that before you suggest the sponsors of the biannual Aldermen's dinner, stakeholders – and serious ones at that – in our very own Harlun and Phelps, suppliers of half our weaponry, and the gentlemen who pay for the golf memberships of senior staff – may I suggest you think before suggesting that these gentlemen engage, as a universal collective, in acts of a socially untoward sexual nature?"

He seethed, fingers drumming on the edge of his desk. A *desk*, how he *hated* having a desk; it reminded him every day of how easy it was to fall, how quickly you could forget the things that matter and throw them into the trash can to eternity that lay tucked beneath his damn desk. "Okay," he said. "Okay, Kelly. Leaving aside, for a moment, the sponsorship and the dinner and the shares and the golf; leaving aside, in fact, any reference to sex or death, can I just say this: they are *evil*."

"Mr Mayor—"

"And before you say anything, may I just add, I didn't call them tossers or wankers or festering warts on the arse-end of the devil's rotting behind. I didn't say that they were irredeemable gits, blaggards no less, nor the sewer that lies beneath the nether pit. Oh no! I kept it simple, I kept it pure, I kept it almost polite; you could have tweeted my views and still had characters to spare! Burns and Stoke," he concluded, with his arms flailing in their grubby coat, "are evil bloody bankers!"

Chapter 33

Let Your Surroundings Reflect Yourself

There had been some time spent on the Internet.

Then there had been some time spent on the phone.

Sharon discovered, to her annoyance, that by being flappy and vapid she got much better results than if she phoned up and just asked a simple question.

It took three hours, but the answers began to come through.

Retail space, High Holborn, unoccupied. Owner – Burns and Stoke.

Industrial unit, Clerkenwell, unoccupied. Owner – Burns and Stoke.

Brownfield site, Bromley; empty residential estate, Kentish Town; abandoned sixth-form college, Deptford; rotting community hall, Mitcham – the more she looked, now she knew what she was looking for, the more they began to emerge. All across the city Burns and Stoke owned properties with nothing much in common except that they were all empty, all abandoned, and no one seemed to want to do anything with them.

What had Sammy said?

"It ain't a good death; it ain't fire or flood; it's a declining death that don't bother to say hello or bye bye and you don't even notice you're dying until you're already dead."

Sharon sat back in her chair in a small Internet café off Holborn Viaduct – *We Repair Computers & Sell Fresh Smoothies!* – and considered. She was feeling, it has to be said, remarkably on-it. She hadn't felt this on-it, in fact, since that time during sociology AS level when the teacher asked the class what social construct meant and she hadn't only given an answer, it had been a good answer, and everyone had seemed very surprised. Was this, she wondered, what having a fulfilling career was like?

There only really seemed one thing for it.

She googled Burns and Stoke.

The Internet and Sharon Li had had good times and bad times, but if there was one truth about their relationship, it was that they had had a lot of times. There was nothing html could hide from her for long.

Burns and Stoke – three years ago, a small investment company struggling with the fact that the debt it had bought in London and sold in Hong Kong to be sold to Shanghai to be sold to Paris to be sold to New York to be sold to New Delhi to be sold to Washington to be sold to Tokyo . . . had turned out not such a solid debt after all.

She flicked through articles warning of closure, whispering of redundancies and, ultimate sin, no Christmas bonuses. The imminent demise of this company didn't seem to have attracted much more attention from the press than as another sob story waiting to happen in a time of crisis until, at the very last moment . . .

New Faces at Burns & Stoke

Shares recover on the news of a new management team taking over at the beleaguered investment firm Burns and Stoke. The new chair of the board, Mr Ruislip, promised to overhaul every aspect of the company's portfolio in an attempt to see where interests may be broadened in these difficult times . . .

And without any real warning or explanation, without any deal or bail-out or tangible change at all, from what Sharon could see, suddenly it seemed as if Christmas was back on the menu for Burns and Stoke.

It occurred to her that she knew nothing about banking.

She wondered if this would be a problem.

Hell, no, after all . . .

"I am beautiful, I am wonderful, I have a secret," she muttered.

She wrote down the address of the head office, picked up her bag, her notebook and Travelcard, and went in search of trouble.

Two Underground changes and forty minutes later, and Sharon stood on the street opposite the front door of Burns and Stoke and wondered if she hadn't made a mistake.

"Door" was in itself inaccurate. "Door" implied a nicely made pair of tall wooden panels that swung out on hinges, with maybe a matching frame and a brass knocker. This wasn't a door. This was a gateway, made of glass, all of it, not a single steel support in sight. It was a doorway for the king of the giraffes to parade through, flanked by his minions the overweight elephant and the portly bear. It was a spinning blade of a door, a perpetual swishing entrance to wonders, guarded by a man in white gloves and a bowler hat. Visible beyond him at a reception desk sat two women more beautiful than anything Sharon thought she had ever seen, who flashed smiles brighter than a full moon on a cloudless night. Their perfect nails clattered over keyboards as they noted your name, visiting office, date of birth, present address, National Insurance number, retinal pattern and political intent. A palm tree hung over a pool of pebble-lapping water, fed by a silver waterfall that fell from three storeys up with the same impossible silence as that of the opening door. The wall beyond the reception desk was also glass, revealing a hint of private pavement that led straight out onto the river, though, Sharon noted, no one seemed to have felt the urge to install tables or chairs for any workers wanting to admire this view. Clearly all they needed they already had within these crystal walls.

She felt tiny standing outside this monument to wealth, a gnome in purple boots. She hugged her bag to her chest and waited for the man with white gloves to look at her and call security, who were doubtless discreetly scattered around the half-hearted rock garden that ran down the centre of the square outside. The offices of Burns and Stoke felt no need to vaunt their presence on the building itself, but signs quietly pointed, with an old-fashioned innocence, from around the former docks of Canary Wharf, indicating which silver-clad embodiment of wealth lay above which private gym or behind what exclusive wine bar. Overhead, the Docklands Light Railway was as politely subdued as the signs themselves; underneath, subways bustled and hummed with shops full of the swish of silk on leather, the buzz of men buying expensive ties and women searching for designer handbags. It was a paradise, a testimony to wealth, health and clean living – bright, brilliant and utterly soulless.

Look and see, as only a shaman can.

There are shadows here, memories of things that went before, but they are crushed, buried beneath the reflective surface of the streets. When as a shaman she moves, when she walks and the boundaries grow thin between what is seen and what is perceived, the shapes of the creatures burrowing just beneath the surface become visible, like the shadows of fish beneath murky water. It is a place for cold zephyrs, for the spirits of the icy wind. Beneath the underground tunnels a greedy-eyed minotaur lurks, chewing on gold watches and playing the markets, while in the warm server rooms fire salamanders with flickering tongues warm themselves on the mother boards; all unseen, unknown, but no less real for that. Torn sheets from the daily newspapers swirl across the ground and sometimes, as the wind catches them and throws them up, they have a shape, form and limbs.

Sharon took a deep breath and walked towards the building. The man with white gloves eyed her, polite but doubtful, as she stepped into the revolving doors. They spun at precisely the speed to knock little old ladies off their feet, but not fast enough for the raging impatience of anyone late for a meeting. Inside, Sharon looked up, then up a bit further, through a shaft of glass: glass walkways linking glass offices which looked out onto elaborate glass sculptures. She shuffled up to the desk where the most beautiful receptionists in the world smiled their lighthouse smiles and felt, if possible, even smaller and possibly a bit spotty.

"Uh . . ." she began.

"Hi, how can we help you?"

"Well I . . ."

"Do you have an appointment?"

"Um, no."

"Who are you visiting today?" The voice was sparkling, the smile was blinding, everything about them was sensory overload, the words hardly registering.

"Well, I, uh . . . I'm . . . I'm writing an article on urban . . . urban redevelopment and I was wondering if I could uh . . . like talk to someone in Burns and Stoke about their uh . . . their stuff. Yeah."

The smile shimmered like a mirage.

"And who would you like to talk to?"

"Um. The development guy?" she hazarded.

"Do you have his private extension?"

"No."

"An appointment – oh no, you already said. How about press credentials?"

It occurred to Sharon that for a smile to stay that fixed and that brilliant must have taken months of training and possibly surgery. "Are you fulfilled by your job?" she demanded, and couldn't quite believe the words had come out.

The smile stayed fixed, the eyes unnaturally wide.

"Pardon me?"

"Your job," she repeated. "Are you fulfilled by it?"

"I love my job!" sang out the receptionist in a voice worthy of the worst automated lifts. "I am completely fulfilled by my career and the life choices I have made. My life coach tells me so!"

"Your . . . life coach?"

"I'm sorry, if you don't have an appointment then I really must ask you to leave."

Sharon wondered if she was being insulted. The sheer quality of the smile, the beauty of the face, the perfection of the uniform and brightness of the long painted nails, made it hard to focus on the details of what was actually being said. "I'll come back later, shall I?" she mumbled, feeling her face flush bright red, and before the receptionist could charmingly wish her the best or perhaps invite her to have a truly splendid day, she gripped her bag more tightly and nearly ran out of the building.

Sharon Li sat by herself in a fake garden composed of fake concrete rocks between which rolled a fake gleaming stream and fumed.

She fumed at the receptionists of Burns and Stoke for making her feel like an idiot, at Sammy for making her look like an idiot, at Mike Pentlace for being an idiot yet to come, at the man with blue electric wings for talking to her like an idiot, and most of all at herself for being, above all else, a complete and utter plonker. What the hell did she think she was going to achieve? What the hell did she think she could do?

"Hi there!" sang out a chipper voice.

She spun round on her seat.

No one there.

"In this week's episode," the merry voice went on, "we discuss the fate of the city. Sharon's problem or not?"

She turned again – the voice was right beside her, filling her world, yet no one was speaking. Beneath her she felt the rumble of the Jubilee Line crawling out towards the bubble of the Millennium Dome and heard the slow electric whistle of the Docklands Light Railway overhead. She stood up, peering into a border of thick spiny bushes mulched with fake wood chippings, just in case it hid the owner of the voice.

"In this groundbreaking exposé of the weakness of the human psyche, we take you on a voyage to the deepest parts of the unconscious and ask – shamans, what are they good for really?"

She straightened up sharply, and barked, "Right, you! Wherever you are, whatever you are, stop mucking around or I'll do you! I know bloody tae kwon do and this is like your fair and legal warning!"

Silence from the shrubbery.

A woman dressed for jogging, music player strapped to her arm, smiled nervously at Sharon from across the path. Sharon flushed scarlet and stepped further from the border. Overhead a twin-engined plane whirred as it approached the runway of London City Airport; cars circled in concrete tunnels beneath her feet. She walked, slipping unconsciously into invisibility, fingers clenching and unclenching with growing rage. Rage at Sammy, at the world, at herself, and at the voice which she couldn't get out of her head, the faceless voice which proclaimed:

"A little bit further and you could win a piece of your very own understanding!"

She snarled silently at the words, then her expression changed in response to a flicker of thought. A little deeper, she told herself. She raised her head, looked around at the glass-walled streets, where even the twee signposts mimicked American style in a celebration of London's wannabe-New-York and all its riches, and walked, and looked deeper.

A little deeper, a little bit further through the glass, and if you look and if you listen there is ...

pop of lid being pulled off pills
argument in the office
    telephone rings
  fireworks victory at solitaire!
   woman alone in the toilet who weeps at the mistake that others shall soon know
      flick out the grime from beneath his teeth with a piece of peppermint floss,
date tonight, date with the chick gotta look good
   unlock the strip club behind the curry house, because some truths are true even in
this place.

She pressed her hands against her head but it was there, just beneath the surface the

      crunch of wasabi beans god I hate this stuff gotta be healthy
coffee stinks!
   pop! champagne
(pop! paracetamol)
      gotta get high gotta get high gotta get high so much — but it's not a problem
  Hi there!
stink of armpit on the train
    I wasn't jumping the fare I just didn't notice
  Hi there!

Her head hurt, God but her head hurt, look too deep and all you could do was look, see the things you weren't meant to see, hear the things that weren't meant to be heard, and the world was buzzing, heaving, churning, roaring, the glass melting off the walls, the leaves falling off the trees to reveal the bare truth underneath, the mists parting between what was, what is, what will be and through the mists she saw

fake suntan?

All that could be and had been: the swaying of masts in the dock the roaring of exhaust from the engine of the van the *snap snap* of leather shoes on freshly laid earth the swinging of girders on the end of the crane and

"Hello, there!"

No, but really, fake suntan?

"Welcome back from the break, everybody!"

She looked up and there he was, brighter than the decaying silver surroundings, standing out in the uncertain, changing world like an iceberg at the equator. He clapped his vivid orange hands together, straightened the oversized lapels of his bright white suit, slicked his dyed black hair back from his carrot-coloured face, flashed his brilliant grin and proclaimed, "Welcome, Sharon Li, to the lowest depths of your spirit walk, where all that is and all that may be become one with each other! I'm Dez Cliff Junior and I will be your spirit guide for today!"

Chapter 34

Within Yourself, You Will Find the Answer

She stood in a fake rock garden as, all around her, the shadows of past and future swung through the empty air, and exclaimed, "You're my *what?*"

Dez Cliff Junior, resplendent in the finest garb forty-five pounds could buy, flashed another brilliant smile. "You, Sharon Li, are the lucky winner of today's prize draw for not just any ordinary spirit guide, not just some knock-off ghostly replacement, but me! Your very own manifestation of the subconscious, guardian angel ghost of everything you've always known but never been able to handle! So tell me, Sharon . . . " an oversized red microphone appeared out of nowhere in Dez's hand and was thrust towards Sharon's face " . . . how are you feeling about becoming a fully fledged shaman?"

She stared from the microphone to Dez, and back to the microphone. "What?"

"Come on, Sharon," urged Dez, "for all the viewers at home."

"What viewers at home?"

"It's a phrase."

"No, but really, what viewers at home?"

A flicker of frustration passed over Dez's face. "Just say something profound, okay; we'll edit it at Judgement Day."

"Who the fuck are you again?"

The microphone vanished from whence it had come and Dez stuck his hands on his hips like someone, Sharon couldn't help feeling, she kept meeting in the mirror. "Now look," he exclaimed, "I didn't ask to be manifested like this; it's your fault for watching too much daytime TV. But I'm here now, and you summoned me, so why don't you just—"

"I summoned you?"

"I merely follow viewer demand!" he protested.

"I didn't summon you."

"Uh – sorry, but you did. You thought, 'I feel crap and I need direction,' and what do you know, you flick over to spirit guide Channel 101 and here I am, so you really should start playing ball." The microphone reappeared and, with a more optimistic expression, Dez thrust it once again at Sharon. "So," he suggested, "how's saving the city going?"

"Shouldn't you be a rabbit?" Sharon's disappointed voice dripped scepticism.

"Why should I be a rabbit?"

"Sammy said—"

"You think your brain would manufacture rabbits as a spirit guide?"

"Okay, okay," she conceded. "So maybe not a rabbit, but how about something else? Something . . . I don't know, spiritual or something? Like maybe a giant deer or unicorn? Why do I have to get a cheap chat show host?"

"Cheap!" fumed Dez. "Cheap! Do I look cheap to you? Do you think this skin just *happens*? Do you think my hair is spray-on? I've had to fight long and hard to get where I am in this industry, and you know how I've succeeded where others failed? I'll tell you! It's my charming smile –" a charming smile was duly rendered "– and the willingness to crush the testicles of my enemies in my fists like garlic in a fucking press!"

Sharon realised her mouth was hanging open. "Okay then," she mumbled. "I guess this is a revelation into my psyche which I should be grateful for."

Dez still stood poised, microphone thrust towards her, waiting for the quote of the day. She turned away from his gleaming features and forced herself to look at her surroundings.

Still here, still Canary Wharf, but not Canary Wharf. The real world was a mirage: the people moving through it were shadows, and each shadow left an ever thinner echo of itself trailing in the air, and each echo was slightly distorted: here a shadow that wept, here a shadow that laughed. To look too long at anything was to see straight through it, around it: the sculpted rocks of the garden grew liquid and unstable as they were poured into their mould; the water surged back and forth like blood through a living body as an underground pump laboured to keep its silver surface trickling; the air from the vents politely tucked away in the bushes was soot-black and smelt of the tunnels. And look harder, deeper, longer, and there was still more to see, an infinity of layers peeling back before her eyes, if she only dared to stare, and . . .

And a white suit interposed itself, jolting her with its brightness against that shadow-tangled world.

"Uh, so, this is me putting myself between you and the camera, which I know is highly unprofessional," exclaimed Dez. "But as your spirit guide it's my job to stop you making a fool of yourself on the silver screen and getting lost in the oneness of the universe. Now . . ." He took a step back, opening his arms wide to the world. "Remember at all times this great truth! You are *beautiful*! You are wonderful! You have a secret! The secret is—"

"How the hell do you know that?" snapped Sharon.

"I am you!"

"I'm nothing like you! I've got bloody fashion sense, for a start."

"I am your subconscious given manifest form by your being at one with creation!"

"I am not at fucking one with fucking creation!"

"Sharon," chided Dez, "we are not looking for a 10 p.m. broadcast slot here. Of course you're at one with creation; you're just not handling it very well. But that's all right, because . . ." He swelled again with pride and vocal projection and claimed, "Here, tonight, I am going to take you on a journey of discovery, joy, tragedy, jubilation—"

"Tragedy?"

"Well, maybe not tragedy; not on purpose."

"What are you doing here?"

Dez folded his arms. "I'm here to encourage, to provoke, to inspire—"

"Cut the crap, what are *you* doing *here*?"

"You've got to go back into Burns and Stoke."

"Why?"

"I don't know why – how should I know? I'm just a psychological manifestation of your own subconscious!" wailed Dez. "You know you have to go back in there, so you're telling yourself to do it the only way you know."

"I don't need some . . . some . . . some orange dude to tell me what to do!"

Dez raised his eyebrows and said nothing.

"Fine," she said. "I get that you're only a manifestation of my subconscious mind, which, by the way, sucks, because I think spirit guides really ought to be bigger on the wonders of creation, but okay. So I totally get that you're only telling me something I already know, and in that sense I guess I really should listen to you because, in my experience, my instincts are usually right and thinking about things too hard is usually wrong, but none of this changes the fact that I've had a really bad couple of days and getting cheap advice from an over-tanned corner of my inner psyche is totally uncalled for. So you can just . . . just puff off or whatever it is spirit guides do."

"Back after this commercial break!" sang out Dez, and, indeed, with the slightest crackle of static, he vanished.

Sharon turned and marched straight back towards Burns and Stoke, her face scrunched up in wilful determination. She walked straight through the wall this time, not bothering to slow down for that slight pressure of the world parting around her, and all eyes kept impossibly, but firmly, turned away.

The tiles beneath her feet had been scrubbed to the point where they were almost frictionless; women in high-heeled shoes strode across them, but gingerly. Security men in navy-blue trousers and smart ties scrutinised anyone whose suit was less than 100 per cent silk with a professional eye grown used to a certain standard. Sharon considered the lifts, then rejected them. To take the lift was to stand still and, though she'd seen Sammy do it, she wasn't sure she herself could stop moving and remain unseen. Instead she passed straight through the glass barriers between her and the nearest emergency stairs and headed up.

Burns and Stoke was on the eleventh floor.

By the sixth she was gasping for breath.

At the ninth floor she looked for the nearest CCTV camera, then paused underneath, out of its line of sight, to bend over and catch a little air. It wasn't, she reflected, that she was unfit. It was merely that her fitness didn't extend all the way to her knees. Several self-help books had suggested that a healthy body led to a healthy mind, but as none of them had offered any advice on what to do if both mind and body kept on slipping into the nether reaches of perceived reality, she'd taken any recommendation towards thirty minutes a day of "muscle training" with a heavy pinch of salt. After all, what did these people really know?

She thought:

this is so stupid this is so stupid this is so so stupid why the hell would anyone do this so stupid

And what the hell kind of stupid name was Dez? Why couldn't her spirit guide wear long flowing robes and say things like "Ah, though confused you are, yet comfort you will find" or other more . . . spirity things? She'd been exposed for less than two days to the idea of being a shaman and already she was unimpressed.

As if to add to the moment, her phone rang in her pocket. She grabbed it faster than she had ever moved in her life and slammed it against her ear, not pausing to check the number.

"Hello?" she whispered.

"Hello?" roared a voice back. "Hello, are you there?"

She flinched, certain that the CCTV camera would perceive the vibration in the air of the voice on the other end of the line. "Who is this?" she murmured.

"Hello? *Hello?!*"

"Hi?" she queried, a little louder.

"Oh, you are there," exclaimed the voice. Then, suspicious, "Why are you whispering?"

"I'm uh . . . in a library."

If the caller believed her, he clearly didn't care. "Okay, yeah, so, basically I'm wondering if you, like, know a late-night solicitor or something?"

"What?"

"A late-night solicitor? Like, a twenty-four-hour Citizens Advice Bureau?"

"Who is this?" demanded Sharon, instinctively straightening up.

"It's Kevin," explained the caller, countering her with his own, less certain indignation. "Remember, like, Magicals Anonymous?"

A mental picture. A pasty-faced vampire with complex dietary requirements. Sharon pinched the skin between her eyebrows, trying to block one pain with another. "Kevin, yes, sure. Hi. I don't remember giving you this number ..."

"Uh ... Facebook, duh?"

Oh yes. Some part of Sharon's mind, the part that still knew that it knew everything there was to know and, more importantly, that everything was out to get it, made a note to start hiding personal details.

If Kevin had had any idea of feasting on shaman blood, at the moment he was clearly too indignant to consider it. "So listen, I went to see my dentist and he was all like 'Man, I can't be treating you' and I was all like 'Why the fuck not?' and he was like 'Honestly, you scare the shit out of me' and I'm like 'That's discrimination' and he's like 'Dude, I'm scared you're going to drink my blood' and I'm like 'Darling, I've seen what you eat for lunch and I'm telling you, I wouldn't drink your blood if it was the last pint on the planet' and he was—"

"You want to sue your dentist?" whimpered Sharon.

"Totally!"

"You don't think that might be a little ... aggressive?"

"I'm being discriminated against!"

"On the grounds of your fangs."

"Fangs is such a judgemental word—"

"I'm just saying—"

"Until attitudes in this country change," Kevin barked, "there can be no social progress!"

"And you're calling me because ...?"

"You're the shaman, right? Like, the one in charge?"

"Okay, so now I think that sounds like discrimination too. Since when did 'shaman' mean 'one in charge'?"

"Uh, so," she could almost hear Kevin's wrists flick with each word, "only like, for ever."

A door opened somewhere beneath her; there were voices on the stairs. "Look, Kevin," she said, scurrying upwards, the air twisting around her as again she began to fade from sight, "I like, get the community support thing here and I'm really sorry you had a problem with

your dentist and I'm sure we can work something out and that Magicals
Anonymous is completely behind you on this one but I've got this
really important thing I need to do now."

"Hey, like, you okay? You sound kind of ... I dunno ... breathy."

"How about I call you back?"

"Hey, I don't wanna kick up a fuss, but I'm like 'What the fuck?' with
this guy and teeth are really important so—"

"Bye!" she sang out, flicking her phone off and rounding the corner
onto the tenth floor.

At the eleventh she paused, hauled in a breath and glanced down
the staircase. Below – not very far – a triad of men and one woman
were jogging up and down the stairs. She managed to stop her mouth
drooping open. Bloody bankers taking their physical fitness so bloody
seriously they were running up and down the stairs ... *because they could.*
Some things, she decided, couldn't be learned from self-help books.

She tried the door. It was locked, so she walked straight on through.

The office was beautiful and wrong.

It was long and narrow, butted up against a great glass window overlooking a foyer full of more glass and polished tiles, and a bank of lifts
with panels that lit up to let you know you'd arrived. Someone had
conducted a study and decided that the best way to ensure integration
between staff and senior management was to arrange long ranks of
desks at which, in posture-fixing chairs, bosses and staff could sit
pressed forward against their screens, each cut off by nothing from
nobody, accessible, observable, their every deed remarked on by
passers-by. No space was given over on these pristine desks for the
usual distracting detritus of office life – gone were pictures of loved
ones, vanished were panels on which to stick magnetic images of Dr
Who or the Pink Panther. Post-it notes were for remembering vital
thoughts, not sticking on the backs of workmates; computers were for
emailing, not playing pinball; and if you felt the need to get up and
move, there were designated areas furnished with lime-green sofas for
you to perch on, each sofa no wider than a woman's shin and con-
structed to ensure maximum discomfort within a minimum time.
Meetings happened while walking; coffee was served only in the community area, from the sleek espresso machine behind the bowls of fruit.

The fruit was provided by the staff of each department, and while it wasn't obligatory to meet a quota, nor was it playing ball if you didn't achieve your weekly delivery of nectarines for the good of the company. The infrastructure of the office operated discreetly behind unmarked doors, and the single message board maintained for this purpose carried only two notices: an invitation to attend team Pilates at 7 a.m. on Tuesdays and Thursdays, and a request to all staff to please observe the new recycling policy.

Sharon gave up counting the people when she got to sixty. It was hard to do anyway, given the near-uniform of tie and suit. Even the women wore the same shades of black and grey, the same shoes, the same sheer tights; and all sat hunched at their desks with the same expression of determination. Numbers rolled down the screens, coded in red or green. The youngest employees toiled across the office pulling trolleys loaded with paper; the eldest leaned back in their chairs, hands behind their heads and phones tucked beneath their chins, and talked.

It was hard to tell what the company did, much less why it should own so many properties across the city from which the very soul had been plucked. Worse, as Sharon moved through the office, whenever she slowed down to examine someone closely, the world began to shift back out of the shadows in which she lurked. If she stood still she could feel the veil that hid her from sight begin to tear. Lingering to peer past one man at his flat-screen computer, she almost grew visible again, and a woman nearby looked up with a cry of "Oh, are you . . ." before Sharon darted back into the refuge of invisibility. As she made her way through the shadows that had to serve her for privacy, she looked in vain for anything out of the ordinary, the shimmers of illusion which had shrouded members of Magicals Anonymous or the smell of magic trailing after them.

Not only did she have to keep moving; it was harder here. The walk of the city streets no longer protected her, so that she had to adjust her pace, perfectly pitched between urgent stride and easy shuffle, at the exact speed that matched with invisibility within these walls. Sammy hadn't warned her about this, hadn't mentioned the changing nature of invisibility as her environment changed, and she cursed under her breath as she struggled to stay unperceived.

"And, back from our commercial break, we ask – what tips are there on staying invisible?"

"Shut up," she growled as the half-shadow of Dez the spirit guide shimmered into existence beside her.

"If only I wasn't a manifestation of your subconscious mind, I would be deeply insulted. As it is, this documentary programme only knows as much as you do, so however you look at it, you're in trouble!" sang out Dez before vanishing once more.

Sharon looked around as a shaman looked and saw . . . .

. . . nothing of much interest to anyone.

She drifted on through a meeting, where one man slammed his fist onto the table and proclaimed, "I'm not talking about the fucking Italians, screw the fucking Italians, I'm talking about the Hungarian bonds!"

The assembled table cringed from their boss's wrath. Papers were shuffled – another reason, Sharon noted, for the documents lying all around – it just wasn't as easy to doodle on a laptop as it was with pen and paper. Even here, it seemed, where productivity was king, the employees found a few small ways to rebel against their working life. She passed through into another meeting room.

"Uh, yeah, so the exposure is seventeen for now, but there's another two on the table once we get the figures through . . ."

These people talked, Sharon realised, almost entirely in numbers and acronyms. Fifteen – it took her a while to mentally add the million to the number in question – was being transferred via API through to the PCLL account while the HKL report was going to be converted into a LLI for application to another thirty-two on the move to MNB. She stared hard at the purveyors of this mystical information, and there it was, the truth of the thing, the shadow that lay at their backs and whispered of

bastard's bonus was fucking bigger than mine fucking arsehole how dare he look at me like that, like he's laughing fucking bastard

they mustn't know what I did

will this day never end?

waiting for me she's waiting for me so sweet . . .

Jesus, did he just ask me something? Was that something he asked me was that a question I wasn't listening I was . . .

"Uh, yeah, I can do that, Tim."

just play ball, play ball and in four years you'll have enough to get out four
years at full pay then into the account interest 12.1 per cent no tax that's enough that's
enough don't need more really do I? Do I need more no of course I don't . . . unless I
do . . .

Sharon's nose wrinkled in displeasure as the magical shadows each
danced behind their master's back. She turned and looked directly at
a wizard.

Of course he was a wizard.

She knew this, even though she'd never actually met any wizards,
unless you counted Mr Roding the necromancer, but then, who did?
No, this man was a wizard, she concluded, because no one walked
around with two faces. There was his real face, a perfectly well made
thing with a round, curving chin that showed no sign of bone, and
slightly deep-set eyes; and there was the artificial face, crafted from
whispers and power, stitched into his skin with little tendrils of power.
The artificial face, the one the world could see, was beautiful.
Unearthly, intimidating, unnaturally beautiful.

There was a word Mr Roding had used for that too – glamour. The
wizard wore a glamour, and for a moment Sharon's fear was subdued
beneath the question of what the self-help books would have to say
about that. Was it proactive (good) or self-deceiving (bad)? Was it a
tool for surviving the hurly-burly of modern life (respectable) or an
exercise in shaping yourself to society's prejudices (unforgivable, the
books exclaimed – be yourself)? Perhaps it was all of them at once.
Perhaps that was the problem.

She stared at the wizard, and he stared straight back, or rather
through her, slamming his fists on the table and proclaiming, "When
you lads have finished playing with your dicks, come and do some real
work with the big boys, yeah?"

Sharon's dismay deepened. The others laughed, as if something
funny had been said, and she watched his artificial face flicker with the
sound of the laughter, as if feeding on its environment, taking strength.
His real face, beneath the glamour, was set hard, contemptuous of
those who admired his so-called wit. It occurred to her that she need
only reach out and tug, and the true him would be revealed.

Then he turned and marched into the main office, barely acknowl-
edging the others behind him, like a departing royal personage. He

waved his hand at a lock on an electric door, which clicked open, and stepped through. Sharon slipped through after him, feeling something tug at her as she moved through the door, a weight and a pressure that she hadn't sensed elsewhere in the building. The office beyond was more of the same – uncomfortable furniture, beautifully displayed; desks with no privacy; people staring at screens; but this time there was a smell on the air, and it smelt of magic. She looked and . . .

There, in that woman's tattoo just visible above the line of her shirt, a vein had been drawn above her own; and as the blood flowed beneath her skin, so the tattoo itself pulsed with life and . . .

There a man stretched his fingers, and as they clicked like castanets thin grey fur tried to push its way out through the wrinkles in the joints, before he frowned and wrung his hands and the greyness retreated.

Sharon passed through the office, now fearing all the more that someone might look up and see her. She came to a stretch of wall on which a notice proclaimed, ACQUISITIONS, and, oh yes but at last, she recognised the pictures stuck to the whiteboard with little magnetic tabs. Here were the properties bought up by Burns and Stoke which, oddly enough, no one else seemed able to buy or sell. The places where even their history had gone quiet.

Then she heard someone say " . . . because he's dead!" and things got more interesting.

Chapter 35

Chris

Hi, I'm Chris (Hello, Chris). I'm an exorcist. I'm from Melbourne. Being from Melbourne isn't actually a part of my job, but the accent, the tan, the blond hair, the physique, you're going to be looking at me and going "Damn, he's no Brit" and so, sure, yeah, I'll get it out of the way right now and say I'm Australian and proud. And an exorcist. Australian first, then an exorcist, then a green belt in aikido, and I know that's not like a black belt, but I think that by green you're kind of getting the hang of things, anyway, what was I talking about?

Yeah, exorcism. I like my job, like I really do get a sense of satisfaction from a job well done, from knowing that the dead are finally at rest and the living can get on with their lives in peaceful, uninterrupted bliss. I also do curses, bedevilments and compulsions, for an extra thirty-five pounds including expenses but excluding VAT, just in case any of you guys have any metamystical baggage.

The problem – cos we're here to go through our problems, right, that's the whole point – the problem is this whole twelfth-century attitude you guys have towards the exorcism thing. I mean, it's not just you guys, it's everyone in the industry, and personally I blame the Italians more than the Brits, but you know, Brit-bashing, it's a great hobby. But everyone is all so "book bell candle" and "I banish you!" and there's shouting and flickering lights and ranting, and while I've never personally actually seen anyone crawl up the walls, projectile-vomit or turn their heads 180 degrees, there's all these guys out there who swear to it, which I actually think gives the industry a bad name. I mean, we're professionals, and if at the end of an exorcism for which you've paid a decent fee, you know, with your loved ones screaming and writhing and all that, if after forking out all this dosh you've still got to get blood out of the carpets, well then I think something's gone wrong, don't you? And being dead is traumatic! People never think of it from the other guy's point of view, but I'm just saying, if you're haunting somewhere it's probably because you were brutally murdered or all that so just take a moment to think about that when dealing with the projectile vomiting.

This is my card. I'm Exorminator – like Terminator only kind of without the guns. I believe in a holistic approach to the echoes of the violently departed. I think you should work through your issues, talk it through, reach a sense of harmony where actually both the living and the dead can move on in a groovy, non-pukey way. I mean, just because you're dead doesn't mean psychoanalysis can't help you out.

I don't get many commissions.

Chapter 36

Patience Shall Be Rewarded

There were two of them.

They were huddled in the "library". It was called the library because it had two bookshelves containing publications with catchy titles like *Accounting Practice 2009–2011, Vols XXIV–XXVI*. Despite containing all the most recent rulings on advanced accounting practice, whoever printed the books still felt the need to bind them like the Victorians did, and emboss the titles in gold, so they created a rather old-fashioned feel on the Ikea-style shelves.

The two arguing were a man and a woman. The man wore ... a suit; the woman wore ... a suit, and in that was all that could really be said. Not a pink tie nor a brass cufflink flashed to suggest any mark of individuality. Their voices were tuned down low and urgent except for the occasional flare, which was immediately hushed by the other. The woman was in her mid-thirties, the man in his late twenties, and if they could have huddled any more in the corner they'd chosen, they would have had to develop triangular spines. Had she the chance to inspect their wallets, Sharon might have learned that her name was Camilla; his Eddie. As it was, when she looked, the only thing she could see about them was ...

... *a single slipper soaked with the rain* ...

... *child's mitten left on the railing* ...

. . . greasy chicken wrapping in a dirty old box . . .

Blood on the carpet. It crackles underfoot. You have to lift your shoes clear of it and it sticks like gum, sticky gum and . . .

Sharon looked away, the taste of greasy chicken suddenly mixing with something far, far worse in her mouth. She swallowed the urge to gag right back down to the pit of her stomach and edged closer.

The man said, "I didn't believe it either, but now Gavin too?"

As Sharon felt the walls of reality try to press in against her, she shuffled this way and that against the shelves until finally she discovered a movement, slowly circling the edge of their conversation, which maintained invisibility without crippling her at the knees. She made a mental note to shake Sammy by the throat until he told her how to stay invisible without movement.

"It's a myth," spat the woman. "It wouldn't; it can't."

"I'm not saying I disagree with you, but you saw the reports. They were torn apart!"

"So you are disagreeing with me, Eddie?"

"No, no, I'm just . . . Well, yeah, I am. We took away its mistress."

"Did we?" she snapped, and aware that her voice was once again rising above civilised levels, leaned in tight and rapidly hissed, "Did we though, did we? Because I thought we did, but then when you look again what did we actually do, because we don't have her, do we? We don't have her and I'm looking at the figures from the last quarter and I'm telling you it's not enough, so if we did then we didn't, but anyway why would it? Why would it come through now? Not that I'm saying it did, because it can't!"

"Then how do you explain it? First Gavin, then Scott, and last night Christian thought he heard howling. How many does it have to get?"

"It might be something else."

"You don't believe that," snapped the man known as Eddie.

"The Midnight Mayor?"

"The Midnight Mayor doesn't tear the fucking heads off the people he kills; he doesn't play cat's cradle with their intestines!"

"Just because it came for them doesn't mean it'll come for us."

"Of course it'll come for us!" wailed Eddie, then pressed his hands over his mouth as if by holding back the words, he could hold back the thought. The woman flinched, waited for his breathing to slow as through his fingers he whispered, "It'll come for us and it'll keep coming and how do you stop it? We did this, we let it out and it killed them both, and now it's going to howl and keep on howling until we get her back. We have to get her back."

"We can't."

"We must!"

"You're not listening! We can't, we can't, not while—"

Coffee in hand, someone passed by so close to Sharon she felt the breeze from his passage on the back of her neck. She shuddered, straining to stay unseen, relaxed. The man and the woman smiled at him uneasily; the woman gave a mechanical little wave. Their colleague waved back, kept on going. The two huddled deeper, their bodies pressing almost into each other in an urgency to stay apart from everything else.

"What if we just tell him?" whispered the man.

"You want to? You really want to do that?"

"Maybe he'll understand?"

"Maybe he'll wear you for wallpaper, and anyway . . ." The woman paused, her head snapping round. For a moment she looked straight at Sharon, and her face flickered in doubt. Then her eyes slipped away; but it was there, an instant, a single moment. She had looked and, more importantly, she had *perceived*. "Did you . . . ?" she murmured.

"Did I what?"

"Did you see . . . ?"

"See what? Jesus, I can't handle this."

"Stop it! Stop it, it'll be . . ." Again the woman's head turned, searching the empty air. "Listen."

"What?"

"I said, listen!"

"I don't hear . . ." Then he too trailed off. "Footsteps?" he murmured. "Do you think it's *him*?"

"Listen!"

He listened.

But by now the footsteps were gone.

Chapter 37

Still Body, Focused Mind

Sharon walked into the single, small, women's toilet, all stainless steel and polished surfaces, turned the lock on the door behind her and breathed.

StupidstupidstupidstupidstupidstupidstupidstupidstupidstupidSTUPID!

What kind of stupid bloody idiot thought they could just swan into some stranger's office, what kind of pig-headed fool decided they were going to save the bloody city? It was insane! It was bloody stupid insane, and now she'd missed a whole day at work and why? Because a goblin – a *goblin*, which wasn't exactly a great recommendation to begin with – had popped out of nowhere and told her it was her responsibility. Like *shit*.

She pressed her back against the door and forced herself to breathe, whispering to herself, "I am beautiful, I am wonderful, I have a secret, I am beautiful, I am wonderful, I have a secret, I am beautiful, I am—" She slammed her fist into the door. "I am beautiful and wonderful and have a bloody secret!"

She hit the door again, hard enough to hurt, and felt a bit better.

Closed her eyes.

Breathed.

She was a shaman.

Think shaman.

She half-thought she heard Dez's voice whispering in the back of her brain and raised a single imperious finger and whispered, "Zip it."

He – or it – or possibly she, if he really was just another part of herself – zipped it.

She breathed through her nose until she felt confident enough to breathe through her mouth without hyperventilating. She turned to face the door and tried to remember the feeling of being unseen, the cool casualness of it. It wasn't a conscious will, there was no intoning or furrowing of brow; it was something deeper than that. An invisibility that came from the overfamiliar, a sense that she was a part of something so big that no one could really understand it, and, as no one could understand it, no one really tried to look.

She thought she could hear Sammy, see him gesturing furiously at the vacant air, proclaiming, *You can see the city and it can see you . . .*

She opened her eyes, and there it was again, that tinge overlaid on reality, the smell of things that had come before, the whisper of

> *God I need more coffee*

did he see me do that?

> *#myinsanity tweets what a fucking waste of time*

"Shut up," she whispered under her breath. "Shut up shut up!"

> *Jesus Christ what does she want now?*
> *if you could just flag the issues here*
> *concerned client, I'll give you concerned fucking client!*
> *Help us*

"Stop it!" she hissed at the twisting shadows hanging off the walls. "Stop it stop it now!"

> *What will he do if he finds out?*

oh God, Prozac

> *Help us*
> *don't want to tell don't wanna don't wanna*
> *Help us*
> *he'll kill me Jesus he'll kill me*
> *howl? howl? I didn't mean it. Didn't mean it didn't mean*
> *HELP US, SHAMAN!!*

The words cut through so loud and hard that Sharon yelped, jumping against the door of the toilet and slamming her elbow into the handle. She grabbed at the nearest stable object, which turned out to be a hand dryer that whirred into instant and obedient life, yelped again, and jumped back against the door one more time.

Being a shaman, she was beginning to suspect, was not necessarily a dignified career move.

Help us, whispered the walls. *Help us.*

She pinched the skin on the back of her hand until it hurt, then rubbed her hand until it didn't, took a steadying breath and walked out through the shut toilet door.

A second later she walked back in and undid the lock, just in case someone needed to use it later.

Help us, and the voice that whispered it in her head wasn't male, wasn't female, wasn't loud, wasn't quiet, wasn't soft, wasn't hard, wasn't furious, wasn't breathy; it was just . . . a sense without sound, meaning without words, pictures with no colour, a collection of certainties that assembled in her consciousness to proclaim, simply, truly and with no respect for the boundaries of language, *Help us, shaman, help us.*

Papers billowed gently in the draught from her passage, and deskbound eyes flickered up at the faint thud of her boots on the carpet, only for heads to turn back down as people failed to perceive the source of distraction, this moving unease on the air. Sharon walked without quite knowing where she was bound, confident and brisk, with the office stride of a busy worker, invisible to all. And now that she looked, really looked, there were echoes of other things, of truths unperceived. The taste of pills, dry on her tongue, dissolving to a sticky slime before swallowing; the feel of sweat sticking to the cotton shirt on her back, not that she wore such a thing; and, perhaps, hanging over it all, clinging like cobwebs to the fluorescent lights in the ceiling, the bitter adrenaline taste of fear.

Help us, whispered the walls, *help us.*

She thought she caught a glimpse of Dez moving beside her, his reflection layered over hers in the great panes of internal glass wall. He seemed to be slightly ahead of her, his face fixed towards a door at the end of the open office on which a yellow sign proclaimed, AUTHORISED PERSONNEL ONLY. DANGER – ELECTRICITY. There was a greyish shimmer to the door, a thickness in the air about it, but Sharon put her best foot forward and her head down and, like a bull faced with a bright red flag, marched straight towards it. She swung her arms from the elbows, took a deep breath, heard, *Help us, shaman, help us,* strode into the door and, like a bumble bee bouncing off cold glass, slammed straight back and fell on her arse.

The world seemed to freeze. She sat there as Dez faded, along with the whispers of the office walls, the magical tastes and senses of the place, the dirty secrets left scratched into the air, receding all at once as reality reasserted itself. Her bum smarted, her ears rang, and the door remained resolutely (a) a door and (b) in front of her rather than behind, as she sat on the floor, legs splayed out, mouth open. And she was visible.

A voice behind her said, "Um . . . Ms Li?"

The words took a few seconds to register. Then she was on her feet in a single movement and already proclaiming, "Yeah, but see I'm here to deliver the coffee yeah, Coffee Unlimited, the best coffee ever and . . . How do you know who I am?"

She turned and looked at her unlikely accoster. Straight carrot-coloured hair, a face frazzled with freckles, a striped shirt that someone may have told him was smart as a practical joke, and a blue tie covered in big white spots. He stood holding a coffee in one hand and a visitor's badge in the other. His face was set in a grin of apology and hope; his voice was Welsh, and his tone was the urgent tone of a man who doesn't understand how he could be in trouble but feels sure he is anyway.

A name surfaced from the marshland of memory.

"Rhys?" she hazarded.

Rhys, the not-quite-qualified druid and sometime IT consultant, grinned with his teeth and cowered with his lips, a strange battle working across his face. Sharon looked left, looked right, saw no one else who might have witnessed the less-than-shaman-like incident with the insufferably solid door and added very carefully, "You're not here serving forces of darkness and destruction, are you? Only that'd be a mega-problem."

"Um, I don't think so," mumbled Rhys. "I'm serving the servers, in fact." He almost laughed at his own joke, then thought better of it and hung his head. Across his features hope and shame fought their long-running battle, and the favourite took the prize.

Sharon looked from the druid to the door and back again, then grabbed Rhys by the sleeve. "You! Toilet! Now!"

"Oh, but I . . ." he began. But he was already being frogmarched away, his grin of unease and confusion stretching almost to his ears. He found himself, to his surprise, pushed bodily into the nearest women's toilet and the door slammed behind him.

Rhys cowered as Sharon smacked one palm against the wall by his left ear and, with her other hand, snatched the coffee cup from his grasp and deftly threw it in the bin.

"Oh, but see . . ." he began as the liquid seeped away.

"What the bloody hell are you doing in this bloody place and what the hell is wrong with that bloody door and you'd better tell me because I know bloody kung fu and am the knower of the hidden bloody path!"

A finger capped with a carefully trimmed nail, which had been painted blue until Sharon got bored with the maintenance work, quavered before the tip of Rhys's nose.

"I um . . . Well, see, it's, uh . . . We're in the ladies' loo," muttered Rhys, "which is fine, because it's, uh . . . but I've never been in a ladies' loo, see, and it's not that it's not nice to see you, because it is, it's very nice indeed, but—"

"Rhys!" barked Sharon. "Doors! Walls! Voices! You! Spill!"

"Ah, now, yes, I see, I, uh . . ." He paused, his chest swelled, his shoulders drew back and, with a sudden dread of what was to come, Sharon found herself leaning away as Rhys spluttered, "I uh . . . I . . . I . . . aaaaahhh . . ."

He sneezed.

The first sneeze was merely a shriek from the back of the throat, punctuated by an "I'm so sorry, it's just that . . ." The second was a great heaving from the shoulders. "When I get nervous, see, it's this . . ." By the third sneeze, Sharon was taking cover as far away as she could in the tiny space. Rhys's eyes dribbled, his nose turned red, and he rummaged frantically in his pocket for a much-used tissue. "Had it all my life, see, and it's . . . it's . . . it's . . ."

"Allergies?"

"Allergies," he agreed. "Though they say it's also psycho . . . psycho . . . pssyycchho – atchoo! – somatic, a stress thing."

"I wasn't judging."

"That's very nice of you, it's very nice, only I . . . I . . . aaahhhh . . ."

She waited as Rhys's body shook and his nose ran and his eyes seemed to swell in their sockets and his ears turned pink. "I don't want to be any trouble, see?" he managed to whimper.

"What are you doing here?" Her words, in the confined space of the toilet, should have been a furious hiss. Yet somehow Rhys's look of abject allergy-racked desperation made it dissolve into a gentler, more consoling enquiry.

"I maintain the servers," he explained. "I'm an IT consultant. I came to consult." Then, nervously dabbing the sweat and snot off his top lip with the sodden end of his tissue, "Are you . . . are you really delivering the coffee, Ms Li?"

"No, of course I'm not bloody delivering the bloody coffee, do I look like I'm bloody delivering the coffee? I'm here to save the city, ain't I?"

The words, once said out loud, seemed silly. But, concluding attack to be the best form of defence, she stabbed one finger, quivering with urgency, towards Rhys's inflamed nose, producing quite a satisfying cringe. "What do you know about missing spirits?"

"Um . . . only what Mrs Rafaat said at the meeting. And obviously what you see as a druid, see, but I'm not really meant to see that sort of thing, not without my certificate. That there are . . . are things going missing from the city?"

"What sort of druid things do you know?"

Rhys cringed again. It seemed to be his default setting. "Well, I'm not really supposed to talk about the sacred secrets of the druids, see, owing to how I never actually qualified—"

"This: ladies' lav," pointed out Sharon. "Me: angry shaman."

The argument, succinct as it was, had some effect. "They say," responded Rhys, "that the ley lines have been weakening, their power growing thin. The city wall is crumbling, and all the creatures that live just outside the . . . the . . . *atchoo!* – the veil of perception, they're fleeing the stones for fairer climes. Like Birmingham," he added, surprised to note that, by his own logic, this city fitted such a description. "The selkies have fled the Bermondsey sewer, and wishes made on the waters of the Fleet are no longer granted. The wyvern nest at Battersea Power Station withered, and they say the statues are crying blood, but I think that sounds a bit far-fetched, in fact quite Roman Catholic. But whatever's going on, it's got everyone very worried, even the druids, and they tend to think long term." Then, in a more conspiratorial tone, "You won't tell anyone I said so, will you?"

Sharon drummed her fingers against the wall beside Rhys's head. "Okay, what do you know about this place?"

"Uh . . . the ladies' loo?"

"Burns and bloody Stoke!"

"Well, I, uh . . . I know they run Windows 7, which keeps on crashing, and they use Internet Explorer not Mozilla, which I think is maybe a little . . . and that there's a script running in their main email server which routes all correspondence straight to the manager's—"

"Magic stuff!" snapped Sharon. "I need to know about the bloody magic stuff here that goes down!"

"Oh, I, um. I didn't know they did any magic or . . . stuff, either, actually. I just look after the machines."

Sharon pointed an angry finger at him once more and loomed. This was none too easy for a woman of only five foot five, but Rhys shrank back nonetheless and tried to become one with the nearest wall.

"You just told me that the city is withering up, and all you do is the computers?"

"Um . . . yes. I mean, it's like when the prime minister says it's a broken society and I think, 'Well, that doesn't sound very good but I feel all right.' What I think I want to say, is I'm not sure what I can do about it personally, myself."

Sharon opened her mouth to say something pithy and found nothing leapt to mind. "Okay," she admitted. "So maybe you've got a point. But this place – this place – Burns and Stoke . . ." She told him of abandoned shops, broken houses, empty factories. "If there's an unnatural hollowness there, they own it, yeah? Like there's nothing, the soul of the place ripped out? Are you gonna tell me it's a coincidence that wherever there's emptiness, there's them?"

"Um . . . no?"

Sharon relaxed a little. "Glad you said that. I mean, just to make sure my logic wasn't flawed or nothing."

"Oh, no!" he exclaimed. "It all makes sense now! Burns and Stoke – evil bankers – empty buildings – property rights – absolutely! Was this, uh . . . why you were being invisible?"

"I was being invisible because the receptionist was bloody rude!"

Punctuating each word with a finger jabbed into his chest, Sharon added, "What. The. Hell. With. The. Bloody. Door?"

"Which door, Ms Li?"

"The one I didn't walk through!"

"Could you narrow it down?" he asked, and at once regretted it. "What I meant is that you, and doors, and . . . and . . . aaaahh . . ." His face crinkled up ready to sneeze again. Sharon reached out and pinched Rhys's nose shut. His face turned purple as if he was going to explode from internal pressure. Then his eyebrows crumpled and he took on a look of sheer disbelief at the surprise of a strange woman pinching his nose. The sneeze died down. Sharon carefully let go.

"This happen to you a lot?"

"Yes, Ms Li. Sorry, Ms Li. This door you were . . . uh . . . not going through. Did you try knocking?"

She fixed him with a look that could have frozen a polar bear.

He gestured incoherently. "Well, okay, not knocking because of your, uh . . . secret mission to, um, save the city, yes, so um . . . was it warded?"

"Warded?"

"Yes. Like, with magic?"

"What does that look like?"

"Look like? I dunno. It doesn't look like anything. You don't see a ward, unless it's a really big one, I suppose, in which case there might be like, bits of wire sticking out or mystic runes or that kinda thing. Don't you know what a ward looks like, being a shaman?"

She scowled. "People keep saying 'being a shaman' like it comes with a job manual."

"Course you don't need a manual, Ms Li! Being a shaman, you just know!" His eyes met hers, and the start of a grin began to fade. "Unless, uh . . . I mean, I say you just 'know', but then I'm not a shaman, am I?"

"What *are* you exactly?"

"Well, I was trying to be a druid, see," he replied. "But I get these allergies and sometimes there's all this lavender, and after I had a really bad attack they said they didn't think I was right for advancement."

"Could you get through a ward? I mean, if I wanted to get through a warded door, could you open it for me?"

"Me? Do magic?" Snot began to bubble at the end of Rhys's nose, his eyes pushed against their lids, his body shook. "Oh, no, I don't think that'd be a good idea. Because I'd love to of course – I was actually meant to be the chosen one – but ..."

Sharon pinched his nose shut again, hard enough to silence him, and they stood there, in the ladies' toilet, while around them office life progressed in busy apathy. At length Sharon eased her fingers away from his nose and murmured, "Now, Rhys, this is important. Possibly it's the most important thing you'll do in your life, so don't balls it up. Who do you know who can beat wards?"

Chapter 38

Mr Roding

Necromancy is such a misunderstood art.

Personally I blame the media. They're obsessed with reporting bad news; they never give people the right idea about all the things we have achieved. Turn on any of these crap TV channels nowadays and all you get are zombies, virgin sacrifices, vampiric killing sprees and the walking undead. It genuinely makes me angry whenever I see necromancers portrayed in popular culture as cowardly, bloodthirsty or with a funny limp, as if ligature failure is something to be mocked! In point of fact the training is *extremely* long and taxing, and most necromancers I personally know – and I like to keep my finger on the pulse – are very hard-working individuals with an advanced understanding of organic chemistry. Decay is important. Death is important! Society needs undertakers and butchers and men who pull the guts out from fish, and in the same way I believe society needs its necromancers, to study the mystical aspects of decay and death. Because, frankly, this is a shockingly underfunded area of research, and someone needs to take responsibility for it.

Naturally, in such a poorly regulated area, accidents do happen, and I'm not pretending they don't. But consider the sacrifices we have to make in order to achieve results! I've been practising necromancy for a hundred and ten years and I'm not even eligible for a pension. Benefit fraud, they said down the local office. Benefit fraud! I had to get the birth certificate of a younger man to avoid the authorities, and keep his head in my freezer so that when they asked awkward questions I could just whip it out and pop a fifty-pence piece under the tongue and peel off the masking tape from the eyes and get it to . . .

Well, never mind what I got it to do, but you have to remember! With a severed head in the freezer, that's no frozen peas in your diet. You're not keeping ice cream, there's no handy loaf of bread to come back to after a long holiday in hot weather. And of course there's the odours. I have such trouble keeping up appearances. Dinner parties have become impossible. Ever since I used the bile of the basilisk to slow my metabolic rates I've had fantastic bone density but a terrible problem with these pustules underneath the crook of my . . .

What I'm saying is, it's hard to be a necromancer.

People never think these things through.

Chapter 39

Language Is God's Gift to Man

He looks and he sees and he says, "Oh."

The members of the board shift in their seats. They wear matching suits, matching ties, matching shoes and matching faces. It's not that they've been told to, it's not a conscious decision; it's simply that for the senior management of Burns and Stoke this is who they are. Or possibly just who they feel they have to be.

At the head of the table sits a man. Though the chairs run the length of the table, nevertheless without anyone shuffling their chairs or leaning away, there is a distance between him and the assembled board. And though he is dressed as they are, and sits as they do, and though some are sure they have seen him take a sip from his still, volcanic water in its perfect crystal glass, there is no denying that he who sits at the head of the table is different. Other. Apart.

"Oh," he repeats, his voice a breeze that wafts down the table as gently as floating silk. "This is disappointing."

On the wall behind him a film runs in grainy black and white. The camera looks at a door which proclaims AUTHORISED PERSONNEL ONLY. DANGER – ELECTRICITY. It runs on a loop of nearly fifteen seconds, its gazed fixed. It films nothing, nothing, nothing; then out of nowhere a woman appears and rebounds off the door. She is young, and her hair is black streaked with blue, and she is surprised.

A moment later she rises to her feet, grabs the hand of someone not quite in shot and pulls the person away.

The man at the head of the table turns off the image with a remote, swings back round in his swivel chair, which is gross and black and bigger than himself, and softly repeats, "Oh." Then his face twitches. His thin eyebrows contract over almost impossible pale blue eyes.

"Is disappointed the word I am looking for here? Does disappointed, as an adjective, carry enough weight to describe the sentiments I should express?" He turns to his nearest neighbour. "How does one express due concern and rage at the failure of an institution to protect its secrets? What do you think?"

"I think . . . disappointed is good?" she declares, eyes flickering across the table in search of something, anything to hold her gaze, that isn't his eyes.

"You don't feel it's a little . . . weak? As in, how one might say – he is disappointed, she is upset, you are angry, and I am going to rip your head off and suck on your spinal fluids? Is that not the definition we are aiming for?"

"Maybe?" she stutters, gripping the edge of the table.

If the man at the head of the meeting notices her response, he doesn't seem to care. "Disappointed," he echoes, turning the word over in his mouth. "Frustrated? Concerned. I am concerned that this woman," gesturing at the screen, "this woman who, from what I can see, has no significance whatsoever in the grand scheme of things, is interesting herself in our affairs. I am concerned that the Midnight Mayor continues to probe us despite the three-month golf membership we offered, which, I was assured, would be more than enough to guide him away from our affairs."

"He doesn't . . ." began one man, then wished he could swallow the words back down.

"He doesn't . . . ?"

"He . . . the Midnight Mayor doesn't like golf."

Silence. Then, "But everyone likes golf. People smile while they play it. They walk across well trimmed grass with their friends and they say, 'Isn't this nice?' How does the Midnight Mayor not like golf?"

"He said it was . . . it was . . . it . . ." The unfortunate executive was breathing hard. "He said it was a stupid wanky game for lazy tossers and we could take our golf clubs and stick them."

"Stick them?" queried the man at the head of the table. "Stick them where?"

"He seemed to think we'd know the answer to that, Mr Ruislip, sir."

The man addressed as Mr Ruislip sir leaned back in his chair. He wrapped his long fingers around the back of his thin shell-like head and considered the ceiling. Then he said, "The Midnight Mayor is being difficult, but he can be contained. However, this business with Dog is . . . may one say unfortunate?"

"Unfortunate is good, sir," stammered the woman nearest him.

"Unfortunate," he repeated. "It is unfortunate that Gavin was dis-embowelled – yes, unfortunate is accurate, isn't it, for it implies a negative attribute of fortune, so yes! And so it is indeed unfortunate that Gavin was disembowelled. Likewise it is regrettable," he savoured the word, warming to his theme, *"regrettable* that Scott was decapitated, and most . . . most *concerning* that Christian has started hearing the howling in the night. But, ladies and gentlemen!" He straightened, pleased at his own conclusion. "Ladies and gentlemen, let us remem-ber! The fact that you are all being dismembered, one at a time, only indicates how close we are to success! Indeed, the break-in of this unwelcome visitor, this woman, could also be taken as a sign that we are achieving our aims! Greydawn will be ours, and then we may all get our wishes and live . . . how is the phrase – happily ever after?" He sat back in his chair, beaming with delight. "And of course nothing shall stand in our way. Should we put that in a memo?"

Chapter 40

There Is Always a Solution

The house was in Walthamstow.

Sharon had never understood Walthamstow. Was it a posh suburb or a squalid dump at the end of the Victoria Line? She didn't know if it was big or small, where its centre was or how to measure it, for Walthamstow had this odd way of stretching out in unexpected directions, its lower end brushing the Olympic site, its topmost edge blending into forests, and motorways that suddenly found themselves amid greenery, as if an invisible limit had been thrown around the city, proclaiming STOP. On the one hand, she knew Walthamstow had an Underground station – possibly several – but the buses were the rat-route runners of the suburban city, single-deckers or ancient beat-up red monsters with the stuffing falling out of their seats. Bored youth, busy mums and old ladies pulling their shopping behind them on wheels mingled in the shabby little shops of its narrow streets, while over all fell the shadow of the area's new mega-markets. It was an unknown quantity of a place whose quality changed with every turn of the street.

This street was no exception. A mixture of shops and houses jostling each other as if the designer had dropped his plans on the way to work and not got them back in order before building began. An Albanian restaurant shared kitchens with a curry house; an off-licence sold Polish beer by the six-pack and French wine by the litre; notices in the window of the newsagent offered hatha yoga for women and cheap calls to Ghana for everyone. Amidst it all, small, quaint and defiant, was Mr Roding's house.

A path of chipped beige tiles led past a rubbish dump disguised as a front garden to a small red-brick porch. A ceramic family of ducks took flight across the bricks surrounding the front door; the flat plastic image of a teddy bear hugged a sign proclaiming this lone two-storey home, between the wine warehouse and the tyre yard, to be SUNSHINE COTTAGE. The curtains were drawn across every window of the house. The sun was setting on the world outside, the sky turning green-grey, the traffic faint and far off.

Sharon knocked.

Behind her Rhys fidgeted. He didn't quite know how he'd ended up in Walthamstow, though he had this memory of Sharon grabbing him by the sleeve and pulling him out of the toilet. He had this sense that she'd walked at a speed which didn't really have anything to do with distance covered or time taken, this special speed at which all things had begun to blur. And then. *Then* he couldn't shake the feeling, imagined or not, that as she dragged him out of Burns and Stoke with a cry of, "Come on, druid, make yourself useful!" she hadn't bothered to open any doors. Which was unfortunate, because he hadn't logged out of the servers at Burns and Stoke before shutting down, and if refusing to obey the laws of matter was disconcerting, failure to observe proper security procedures was just bad IT.

The door opened a cautious inch on a brass chain. A single pale eye regarded Sharon. "Yeah?"

"Mr Roding?"

The eye narrowed. "I know you," grumbled the voice. "You're that shaman."

Sharon beamed. "That's me, Mr Roding sir! I'm Sharon and this is Rhys."

"Hello," quavered Rhys.

The door stayed on the chain. "What you doing here?" demanded Mr Roding. "What you want?"

"Well now, Mr Roding," trilled Sharon, her voice rising like the call of an alarmed blackbird, "I was wondering if you knew anything about wards."

Mr Roding responded with the deep silence of a man running through, in his mind, the myriad ways in which he is not going to enjoy this conversation.

"Wards," he repeated. "As in hospitals or mystic?"

"The magical kind?"

"I do know about wards," came his voice through the door. "But then I did my own research, didn't I?"

Sharon hesitated. "I'm sensing a slightly negative attitude from you, Mr Roding . . ."

A grunt was the only answer.

"If I told you, Mr Roding sir, that the fate of the city was in the balance, would you be more positive?"

Mr Roding considered. "Nah," he said and began to close the door.

Sharon stuck her foot in the gap.

There was a moment of silence as shaman and necromancer wondered where things could go from here. Then Rhys leaned forward, raising one hand like a schoolboy at the back of the class and said, "Um, excuse me? I don't know much about this sort of thing, but have you thought about lavender oil?"

After a pause there came a cautious "What?" from Mr Roding.

"Well," gabbled Rhys, "I couldn't help but notice that, what with you being into the whole metabolic thing, which is fine, by the way, I'm not to judge, but I couldn't help but notice how you've got some, um, some dermatological issues, see? And I didn't get very far in the potions training because I get these allergies, but I am a druid and actually I think I could be really good and I was wondering have you thought about lavender oil? I know this amazing recipe for acne, you know. You don't even have to ceremonially strangle a cat."

Silence again.

Sharon removed her foot from the door. The door drifted shut; there was the sound of the chain being pulled off its track, and the door opened all the way. "You can come in," grumbled Mr Roding. "But I only got Earl Grey."

Chapter 41

Reflect But Do Not Dwell Upon the Past

A picture of the house of Mr Roding.

He lives alone and has done for some time. Japanese prints – flowers, wading birds, the fall of water between the trees – line a corridor painted a dubious lime green. Pale cracks line the ceiling where the pipes have begun to weigh a little too heavily. And everywhere there is the smell of air freshener. It's an almost visible cloud, overwhelming but still not enough to cut through the unmistakable odour of rot.

No, not just rot.

Something worse.

Meat.

Rotting meat.

The kitchen is maintained to almost surgical standards of cleanliness: a box of latex gloves by the sink and a dozen kinds of antiseptic with lemon-fragrance washing-up liquid lined up on white-tiled shelves. Two small windows swing open at the top to let cold air in and the smell of—

best not to think

—out into a back garden which to a four-year-old with a plastic truck would be a full-size jungle and which Mr Roding was evidently developing to the same ambition.

"I got no milk neither," he barked as the kettle began to boil. He snapped on a pair of rubber gloves before pulling matching mugs from a pristine cupboard. "It's barbaric to have milk with Earl Grey. I can do you a slice of lemon."

Sharon grinned a little too wide. "That'd be cool."

Rhys had turned a curious grey-green, his eyes watering under the weight of chemicals in the air. "I-I-I-I-I'm fine, thank you, sir," he gasped between pulses of histamine-laden blood.

The urge to call Mr Roding "sir" had overcome Sharon and Rhys almost as swiftly as the stench-disguising stench of the house he lived in. It wasn't that Mr Roding looked old – he could have passed for late fifties if he'd wanted to, despite a crook to his back that pushed his neck down and head forward. It wasn't the clothes he wore – black shirt and black slacks and a pair of brown loafers pinched up around the seams like an apple pie. Or even the way he talked. It was more in self-defence, through offering respect against adversity, though neither Sharon nor Rhys could quite say what that adversity might be.

Perhaps it was the slick sheen to Mr Roding's skin, the almost plastic quality about his face as if, between each layer of flesh, someone had stretched a sheet of grease-coated cling film. Or maybe it was the way he'd superglued some of his nails back on, with one or two of them crooked, or his mismatching false teeth, which protruded too far from beneath his top lip. Or, just perhaps, it was the unmistakable odour of a body whose internal organs had long since given up trying to understand their neighbours and settled for doing the best job they could under difficult circumstances. Mr Roding wasn't dead – definitely not. He was simply going through the process, and had been for nearly forty-five years.

None of them spoke while the kettle boiled.

None of them spoke as Mr Roding made three careful cups of tea. He dunked each tea bag individually, each one going in and out precisely twenty-five times. Then a single slice of lemon was carefully added to the mix and a tiny silver teaspoon dropped into the bottom of each cup. He handed them to Rhys and Sharon. Rhys quaked; Sharon's grin stretched a little thinner. The three eyed each other up, murderers at a poisoners' ball, and then, at an unspoken signal, sipped all together. A pause to observe effect. No one transformed into a specimen of the living dead, so all three began to sip more freely, in their own time. When a suitable quantity had been consumed to establish some kind of trust, Mr Roding pulled off his latex gloves, dropped them in an orange bag marked BIOLOGICAL WASTE -- INCINERATE ONLY and said:

"So you want to commit a crime, is that what this is about?"

"Oh, no!" exclaimed Rhys, only to be silenced by Sharon.

"Why d'you think that?"

He shrugged. "Youth these days, smashing things, breaking up wards ..."

Sharon bristled. "Because the youth of the 1950s were all rosemary and sunshine?"

"At least we knew how to respect our elders."

"Respect your ... what about the 1960s? What about the sex, the drugs, the rock and roll?"

Mr Roding sniffed, a dangerous thing for any man whose nasal hair was attached only by inertia.

"Besides!" Sharon felt her indignation rising. "You're the one who wasn't motivated by the concept of saving the city!"

"Saving the city – what do you know about that? Why do you even get to say those words?"

She hesitated. Rhys was staring at her too. It seemed he too hadn't received an answer to this question.

"Because a goblin shaman told me that the city is dying, the soul of the city is being ripped away; and because wherever this happens there's this firm called Burns and Stoke. And when I went to their office I heard the walls whispering, *Help us, help us*, and they were talking to me. And I couldn't see anything bad, but there was this locked door, and when I tried to go through it I couldn't because it was warded. And people there were scared, and Greydawn is missing, whoever that is, but everyone seems kind of worried 'bout that so I figured yeah, it's like, the fate of the city. You gonna help or what?"

The only sound came from Mr Roding, dinging his silver spoon against the rim of his cup. He laid the spoon down with a tiny clink and sipped his tea.

"What do you know about Greydawn?" he asked.

"Uh ... nothing," confessed Sharon. "Only what this goblin said."

"I've heard of her," offered Rhys. Two pairs of eyes turned to stare.

Under their semi-disbelieving gaze, he sensed sneezing soon to come, and babbled as fast as he could. "She's Our Lady of 4 a.m., the One Who Walks Beside, the Keeper of the Gate, the ... the ... aaaaahhh ... "

"You might wanna stand back," offered Sharon.

Mr Roding raised his eyebrows and took a step back just as Rhys erupted in a sneeze that sent clouds of air freshener gusting across the room.

"I'm so sorry, it's just that I ... aaahh ... aaaahhhh ... "

"He does this a lot?" asked Mr Roding.

"Dunno," replied Sharon. "Don't really know him. But yeah, so far I'd say it's like, a serious thing."

"I don't mean to, it's just I ... I ... I ... "

"You tried anti-histamines?" asked Mr Roding.

"They make me dro ... drow ... sleepy."

"What's so special about this Greydawn?" asked Sharon as Rhys turned his back to dab his streaming eyes. "Why's everyone worked up?"

Mr Roding put his cup down and leaned against the padlocked fridge. "Been a shaman long?"

"I'm learning," she replied, sharper than she'd meant.

"Then you might want some pointers on the city's major powers. Seven Sisters, Bag Lady, Fat Rat, Greydawn, Midnight Mayor, Beggar King ... "

"I think I've met the Midnight Mayor."

Mr Roding looked surprised. "You met him?"

"Yeah, sure. Dark hair, blue eyes, bit of a twat, that him?"

"I don't know," murmured the necromancer, a thoughtful expression spreading over his face. "Very few know him personally. He's rumoured to be incredibly powerful and extremely dangerous."

"He looked kind of ... scruffy."

"'Scruffy'?"

"Yeah. You know. A bit ... crap."

"You're certain it was him?"

"Well ... he did grow these blue electric wings, and had blood on his hands and, like, Sammy – he's my goblin – was all like 'Yo, Midnight Mayor' and that. So, yeah, I'm guessing he was the guy. He important?"

Mr Roding scratched thoughtfully at his chin, tracks of white skin flaking off beneath his nails. "Midnight Mayor only comes out for bad things," he murmured. "His involvement never bodes well. Did he tell you anything?"

"Um ... he told me to find the dog. Which, I gotta admit, even though I'm supposed to be a shaman and know all sorts of crap, I found majorly unhelpful."

"And you say Greydawn is 'missing'?"

"Yeah. Like vanished, only in a spooky mystic way that no one is telling me about. And, actually," Sharon demanded, "what the hell is the point of going 'You've gotta do shit' and then not telling me what the shit is I've gotta do?"

"I can see your problem. But then Greydawn is of the spirit realm, and only the shamans can understand that."

"D ... druids are also ... interested ... in spirits ..." tried Rhys, his shoulders shaking with the effort of suppressing the latest allergic reaction.

"Druids!" groaned Mr Roding. "Preserving the urban lore is all very well, but what do they do with it? Not even bingo nights!"

"Bingo nights!" exclaimed Rhys with a sudden enthusiasm that briefly overcame even his endocrine system. "We should have bingo nights for Magicals Anonymous! Or those social nights with a band?"

"I'm not sure we're kinda there yet."

"Or maybe trips to Margate? Although," Rhys said, deflating at the thought, "I guess it'd have to be night-time trips for Kevin and Sally."

"Have you been to Margate, young man?" demanded Mr Roding.

"No ..."

"That must be why you consider this a good idea."

"Can we just focus on the fate of the city?" said Sharon. "Like, who the hell is this Greydawn and why is everyone so like 'Whoa' about her?"

"She divides the day from the night," sighed Mr Roding, the patient teacher faced with a particularly dense student. "Which, in more practical terms, is to say that she is the gatekeeper between what *is*, and what is *underneath*."

"That's practical terms?" asked Sharon.

Mr Roding's lips curled in annoyance, revealing a hint of purple gums and yellowing tongue. "There are layers to the city," he proclaimed. "There's what people see – cars and buses and windows and all the rather more superficial aspects of our existence. Then there is what people choose not to perceive – runes in the graffiti, spells woven from telephone wires, wards cut out of pieces of scrap paper, those who walk under glamours and enchantments, or those who have mastered the shaman's walk – at which all eyes look away and don't know why. And beggars, of course. Beggars and shamans both know the way to move in the city, and be seen without ever being perceived.

"Then there are the things that lurk just beneath perception, a thing that is neither seen nor perceived, but is sensed in the deepest part of the soul. They are the shadows at the ends of alleys, the urge to run down an empty street in the middle of the night, the fear of the thing that falls on the floor upstairs when the house should be sleeping, the creak of a door that should not be open – the thing, if you like, in the cupboard, the nightmare that has no name.

"Everyone knows it's superstition, that none of it is real, and for the most part it isn't. But there are some truths, some buried truths, that lurk just the other side of the dark, in the place where the dream walkers go, in the corners where the darkness is a little too thick; and they are always watching, looking for a way to crawl from the night into the day. Shadows and ghosts, spectres and wendigos, the death of cities and the memory of a blackout, they probe continually, looking for weaknesses. Greydawn keeps them at bay. She is the Keeper of the Gate, the One Who Walks Beside. She keeps the unreal things unreal. And now, you say, she is missing, and the Midnight Mayor is talking to the shamans, and you want my help."

In the silence that followed Rhys even stopped sneezing.

Then Sharon said, "Mr Roding, may I shake your hand?"

Surprise flickered over the necromancer's face. He examined his own hand curiously, just in case he'd misremembered the decaying nails and the shedding skin. Then, to make sure Sharon wasn't just embarking on a joke too rude to be borne, he held it out to her, and she clasped it in her own and warmly shook the clammy flesh. "That," she explained, "is exactly the kinda thing people should just straight up tell me. What the hell is it with this cryptic crap?"

"It's curious," added Mr Roding, reclaiming his hand and turning it over a few times in surprise, "that the Midnight Mayor should make mention of a dog."

"It is?"

"In traditional images of Our Lady of 4 a.m. she is sometimes depicted as having a dog at her side. But if you really want to know about Greydawn," offered Mr Roding, "I'd try talking to the Friendlies."

"Who are they?"

"They're her followers. Worshippers, if you will."

"Um . . . do you mind if I ask my standard questions when someone tells me something like that?"

"Your standard questions?"

On her fingers Sharon ticked off the by-now regular list of enquiries. "No nudity? No drumming? No animal sacrifice?"

"Not when I last enquired. Why, is that something you've encountered a lot in your work?"

"Just playing safe. What about this ward?"

Mr Roding examined his crooked flaking fingernails. Then, "You think that this . . . Burns and Stoke is connected to Greydawn's disappearance?"

"I think they're connected to all the other spirits going missing. And Greydawn sounds like a spirit, and she's missing. So, yeah, you know what, as I'm a shaman and supposed to just know shit, then yeah, I'd say it's probably not gonna be a coincidence."

"In that case, if you can get me into Burns and Stoke without causing any unwanted questions, I will dismantle their wards for you."

"Seriously?"

"Necromancers have an unjustifiably bad reputation," complained Mr Roding. "And," he turned to Rhys, "do you really think lavender oil will work?"

Rhys brightened. "Oh yes. All I need is some lavender, a saucepan, some polenta, a tub of half-fat yoghurt, three cinnamon sticks and some water from the stagnant puddle that grows above a three-days-blocked drain, and I can do marvellous things for your skin!" He hesitated. "And maybe some rubber gloves."

Mr Roding, in as much as his facial muscles were animated, looked almost pleased.

"These Friendlies," asked Sharon, putting down her cup of tea. "You got their number?"

"No," he admitted. "But you can probably find them in the Yellow Pages."

Chapter 42

Sammy

Oi oi.

Name's Sammy.

Sammy the Elbow.

Only gonna say this once so you get it.

Head of the tribe is the head, council is neck, warriors is arms, scavengers is belly, hunters is feet, and me – I'm elbow. Cos I'm sharp and pointy and you don't wanna get me mad.

One other thing we gotta get clear here, while we're at it.

Second greatest shaman ever! *Second!* Not third, not bloody third, because Blistering Steve was a bloody moron and it was bloody spontaneous combustion what he did, not transcending to a higher plane or that! There were scorch marks on the ceiling! There was a carbonised shoe on the floor. I'm seriously pissed that you wankers would think that Blistering Steve, that incompetent prat who wouldn't know a subduction spell if it went off under his frickin' bed, is remotely on the same level as me! I'm good at my job! It's not just me being modest or anything, I *am* that good and that's the truth of it and I don't see why I should say anything other.

The problem – the only problem I have, because when you're as on it as me there ain't many things what can drag you down – the problem is people. Human people, as you're asking. They just don't get me.

I can walk up to your average Joe and tell him everything about his life, because I've seen it, I've seen all the echoes and all the stories you people carry around with you in your shadow, and I'll be right, and what'll Joe do? He'll scream and point and go "Goblin, goblin!" and call pest control and a wizard and I'll be like, "Oi, bozo! I'm frickin' telling you a frickin' smart thing here so don't give me this goblin crap because I am on it like mussels on the side of a polluted pier!"

Everyone's all like "It's not discrimination, you're a goblin" and I'm like "That is discriminatory whatsit or whatever" but they don't listen because, like they said, I'm a goblin! It is so frustrating having to deal with all these morons!

I'm not how you'd say a people person.

Chapter 43

Always Offer Friendship in Adversity

They are the Friendlies.

Technically, they are the Association of Friendly Members and Concerned Interests but, since none of their members really remember that and "afmaci" sounds like a dangerous Italian drink, they are, by unspoken consent, the Friendlies.

They are the union of late-night workers, of lonely beggars and the widows who sit alone looking out of darkened windows into the lost hours of the night. Their members are the cleaners who leave work at 5 a.m., the men with dirty faces slipping through the midnight tunnels beneath the city streets when the trains have stopped. Night bus drivers and street cleaners whose beat is five square miles of untended turf where the rubbish collects faster than they can clear it; security men who sit in cabins by closed gates watching TV that is meant only for gamblers and the lonely.

The Friendlies is where the lonely may be lonely together and, perhaps more importantly, where they may be told that for all the streets may be empty and the skies may be dark, no one who walks by themself in the dead of night is truly alone.

They have many shrines around the city. Usually these are discreet things at the back of community halls or tokens tied to park railings. A message scratched into the bark of a plane tree; the bicycle wheel left chained to a fence, though all other parts have been removed; the lifeless string of fairy lights that hang from a lamp post, though no one can quite work out why. But they only have one temple and it is . . .

"Here?" exclaimed Sharon, as they looked up at the sign Sellotaped to the door. "What kind of lame crappy temple is this?"

The sign taped to the glass front read, *Association of Friendlies — no flyers please.*

A much larger sign remained, faded and cracked, on the hoarding overhead. Its original orange letters had long since been pulled off, with only their pale outline still visible on a black background. This read, EDNA'S TANNING AND BEAUTY SALON.

"How about pinnacles?" demanded Sharon. "How about red carpets, the smell of incense, chanting and all that? I've only been doing this magic thing for a while, but no one has chanted at me once! What the hell is that about?"

Rhys hoped his shrug had a degree of consolation about it.

Sharon scowled. She glared around the street they'd come to and her scowl deepened. Since leaving Walthamstow they'd gone from full daylight to darkness, but then, in urban terms, they'd gone from the end of the earth in one direction to the end of the earth in the other.

"Tooting," she growled. "What kind of stupid religion builds its temple in Tooting?"

"There's a Hindu *mandir* in Neasden," offered Rhys.

"Yeah, but there's an Ikea near Neasden!"

"Is there a connection between Brahma and Ikea?"

"What I'm saying," grumbled Sharon, "is you can sort of get Neasden. It's a dump, stuck between more dumps on the end of a dumpy line which people only use to go from London Bridge to the Dome anyway, but! Even if there's nothing else about Neasden, at least you know that there you can always find a flat-pack table and an air cooler in the shape of a sunflower. But . . ." her face fell further yet as she surveyed the entrance to the temple " . . . Tooting?"

Rhys found he had no comfort to offer. Sharon rolled her eyes, strode forward and knocked on the door, grumbling under her breath, "Tanning salon my arse."

Whatever the Friendlies had done to Edna's Tanning and Beauty Salon, it wasn't for public display. Thick brown blinds hung in the former shop window and, as they waited, a single weak bulb came on over the door.

A woman opened the door. She was . . . Sharon and Rhys each took a moment to consider exactly what she was. She wore purple. Back in her early fifties this woman had considered her approaching old age, read up the available literature, studied peers and older colleagues, and resolved that not only would she not take being pensioned lying down, she wasn't going to take it at all. A giant purple cardigan sank almost to her knees; her legs were encased in huge pale blue trousers like a pair of spinnakers; a giant mess of gold and bead necklaces hung intertwined down her chest, while her silver-white hair had been crafted into a balloon style inviting the eye to soar upwards. Her throat was framed by a pair of dewlaps, and her earlobes, aided over time by the clunky gold and shell jewellery pricked into them, had grown so low they nearly flapped against her jaw. Above a superb set of false teeth, a radiant smile fixed itself on Sharon like a searchlight at a prison camp. She was . . .

"Sorry, sweetie, we're closed."

Magnificent?

Was that the word?

Whatever she was, she began at once to close the door. Sharon opened her mouth to say, "Oh no, but wait there's a—" and the door thudded shut as the woman retreated into the gloom beyond. Behind her the light went off.

Sharon looked at Rhys, who shrugged. Behind them traffic crawled through the blinking traffic lights of Tooting, little farting cars seeking a better place in the narrow backstreets.

"Rhys," she said, then paused, groping for the right words. "I'm just wondering – and I'd like you to be kind of honest on this one, because it's gonna be important – do I look . . . *spiritual* to you?"

"Spiritual?"

"Do I look . . . " she ventured, "sagely? When you see me, do you think 'There is a woman replete with the mystic wisdom of the ages' and stuff? Do you get a mental picture of ancestors who did drumming, and men who went 'Aaaah' whenever asked a question, and not in a sore-throat way? Do I give off . . . an aura of enlightenment?"

"Um." Rhys had meant to say this as the opening of something good. Somehow, the rest of the sentence didn't follow.

Sharon sighed. "No," she murmured, deflating. "Didn't think so."

"Maybe we should try later?"

"I am not trekking all the way to Tooting, to fucking *Tooting*, to try again later! Do I look like I'm made of Travelcard? Besides!" An angry flap of her arms demonstrated just how besides this besides would be. "Fate of the city, remember? Come on."

Before Rhys could protest that, actually, he wasn't a walking-through-walls kinda guy, Sharon grabbed him by the sleeve and pulled him after her.

There was a moment of doubt, a sensation of being sucked on like the human equivalent of a boiled sweet, and when Rhys opened his eyes, he and Sharon stood in the one-time Edna's Tanning Salon, with the woman in purple turning to face them with an expression of horror and dismay.

"How did you . . . ?"

"It's okay, we're here to save the city. Nobody panic!" replied Sharon.

"You're . . . saving the city?"

Sharon hesitated for no more than a second, then proclaimed, "Yep! That's me, totally on it, saving the city. Me, a goblin, a necromancer and a bloke called Rhys."

"Hello," offered Rhys.

"You just walked through my wall!" exclaimed the woman. Not in anger, but in a tone of social embarrassment, as if years of good breeding and experience hadn't quite informed her of an appropriate response.

"I do that," explained Sharon. "I was worried about it for a while – I really thought there'd be implications. I mean, not just with my health, but maybe with God and Satan and that, because, actually, how's a girl to know? But everyone seems to say it's okay and I'm thinking I should just go with it."

"Well, dear," exclaimed the white-haired woman, "that's all very well, but we really are closed."

Sharon looked around the room. All apparatus from its previous, commercial life had been removed save for two reclining chairs and a wall of grubby mirrors. The floor had been cleared and re-covered with dirty mattresses, battered cushions and stained pillows. Bits of cardboard were lined up in what might have been pews to face a table converted to what could only be an altar.

It wasn't just the £1.99 aromatic candles lining the table's back edge, nor the bunting of cheap plastic flowers Sellotaped around its top. It wasn't only the neatness of the offerings assembled on its surface, laid out as votives to some god, nor yet the locked donations box tucked away below. All of these were suggestive of themselves. But what clinched it was the sign stuck up with Blu-tack on the wall beyond. In blue felt-tip pen someone had attempted to draw an open hand reaching out to an eager congregation. With the same instrument they had also inscribed the words She Is With You.

It was an altar, inescapable and true, an altar in the shop floor of a Tanning Salon in Tooting.

With the expression of the tactful atheist entering a hushed church, Sharon examined the offerings. None seemed to be dripping blood or glinting with gold, which gave some reassurance. Indeed, however tidily they'd been presented, this collection, laid out for the unknown *She* of the altar, was more an assemblage of knick-knacks and hand-me-down souvenirs, odd bits of scrap and strange story-weighed mementos of trivial events. There was a plastic sandwich wrapping on which someone had painstakingly written, 3.20 a.m. with thanks, a clean Thermos flask missing its screw-in seal, a pair of old shoes worn through at the toes, an orange fluorescent jacket carefully folded, a navy-blue flat cap with its faded badge buffed up as bright as the metal could go, a megaphone with a hole where the batteries should have been, an old tin whistle and a meticulously stacked collection of train tickets, assembled over the years and held together with a rubber band.

Displayed on this crooked table, they looked more like rejects from a car boot sale than objects of worship, yet the *Mona Lisa* could not have received more care and attention.

"Can a temple close?" Sharon ventured.

"St Paul's Cathedral closes," murmured Rhys.

"Shut up, Rhys."

"I'm afraid business hours are between 11 p.m. and 5.30 a.m. So if you don't mind ..."

"Business? I thought you were like ... religious and that."

"Religious? Good grief no!" exclaimed the woman. "We're more of ... of a mutual appreciation society, you might say. We appreciate the world around us, the *hidden* world around us, if you like: the world

of the spirits that watch over us in the night. It's not worship at all —
that would be so crude. It's more . . . a fan club. A fan club for the spir-
itually appreciative!"

"You're Greydawn's fan club?"

A flicker passed over the woman's face and Sharon saw it: the
shadow that twisted at her back. Sharon shared the clenching in her
stomach and *knew*, without even needing to sense it as a shaman, that
the woman was afraid.

Then, louder and brighter than she needed to be, "Well, yes, of
course, Greydawn! Our Lady of 4 a.m. is a generous and kind spirit, a
protector of the night — vital, in fact, for the well-being of the city!
Naturally we like to express our appreciation to her."

"Excuse me?" Rhys had one hand raised in polite enquiry. "There's
no, uh . . . human sacrifice in your appreciation, is there? Only I feel I
ought to ask, see, because sometimes people say 'appreciation' and it
means all sorts of sticky practices."

"Good grief, no! Why on earth would we?"

"How about initiation rituals involving two long sticks and an ice
bucket?"

"Sweetie, at my age?"

"Orgies?" he asked with the tiniest glimmer of hope.

"Do you know what that would do for our relationship with the
local council?"

"No," replied Rhys earnestly. "Would it be good?"

"You have to fill out enough risk assessments just to hold a prayer
meeting, let alone budget for condoms."

"Do you?"

"Now look," barked the woman, and it was an imperious bark when
she needed it, "it's very nice of you to drop by and I do wish you good
luck in your future endeavours to save the city and all of that business,
but really, I have a lot of things to get on with."

"Yeah, but," Sharon shifted uneasily before coming out with it,
"Greydawn is, like, missing, yeah?"

A movement over the woman's face. Not recognition, but perhaps
a well-practised substitute.

"Oh, yeah," confirmed Sharon. "She's missing. And there's spirits
vanishing from the walls of the buildings and the stones of the street.

And you – your name is Edna Long and you used to be a hairdresser here, and I know that because I can hear the snipping of the scissors and, though you can't see it, your floor is covered in a carpet of human hair. But then, but then . . . " Sharon grimaced in concentration " . . . you were going home late one night and you heard these footsteps behind you and there were two men and you thought, 'They're gonna mug me, they're going to rough me up,' but you didn't dare run because that'd make them run and they'd outrun you and then . . . " a certain thinness was apparent around Sharon's hands and face, a certain fading-into-nothing as she spoke " . . . and then you felt something move in the air beside you, a hand slipped into yours, though there was no one there, and a voice whispered, *Do not be afraid*, and when you looked back, the muggers had turned away."

She paused for breath, an action that pushed her back into three-dimensional full colour. Swaying a little with the effort of inhalation, she grinned at the astonished woman. "So, basically, what I'm trying to say here is that you totally need a shaman."

Chapter 44

Edna

I joined the Friendlies a long time ago. "Joined" is the wrong word, and so is "worship" while we're here. "Joined" implies a cult, and we're most certainly not that. It would be rather akin to saying, "I worship the London Underground" or "I bow down before the high altar of the dustbin cart." These things are an intrinsic part of our city, our very lives. I ... appreciate them. And I show my appreciation for the Underground by touching in and touching out at the start and finish of every journey, and the appreciation I feel for the dustbin men by always tying the bags securely and tipping at Christmastime.

But the things that lie just below the surface – the shades of the city, formed from time and use and stories and whispers – they are as important to me as all the obvious, material things, and I feel that they too deserve our appreciation. Their works are hard to perceive, for they are as much in the not-things as any visible deed. They are in nightmares that do not visit you in the night, in the monsters that do not crawl out from the cracks between the paving stones, in the cold winds that do not freeze your cheeks, in the sense of terror in a lonely night which does not, in fact, turn out to be a killer waiting in the place between the pools of street light. They are the park that does not wither, the wall that does not crumble, the glass that does not shatter, the roof that does not fall. I suppose the Chinese would call them a form of energy, that same energy that the sorcerers tap for fire and the wizards manipulate with words. They are the product of life, and life is what they sustain.

Tell me that isn't worth a bit of incense.

Chapter 45

If You Cannot Solve a Problem, Work Round It Until You See the Light

Her name was Edna.

"Like the beauty salon?"

Yes, like the sometime beauty salon turned temple.

"My husband left me a fair bit when he popped," she explained. "And when I got to retirement I looked at this place and thought, 'Well, I could sell it' and Starbucks were very keen to buy, but you know Tooting has such a good, independent spirit about it I couldn't bring myself to sell to Starbucks and I knew the Friendlies were always looking for a place and I thought, 'Why not?'"

"What if Friends of the Earth had asked to buy it?" Rhys queried.

"Well, I'd probably be living in Majorca and the Friendlies would have had to go back to that Portakabin in Hammersmith," admitted Edna. "It's all about community responsibility."

They sat in the Tooting Taj Mahal – Finest Indian Restaurant in London – and ate poppadoms with chutney while, just on the edge of hearing, things sizzled and spat in the kitchen. As Finest Indian Restaurants in London went, Rhys had to admit this was definitely in his top ten to make the claim, which was as common in London as Traditional Family Pubs, Authentic Home Cooking and that staple of the retail market, the Final Reduction Closing Down Sale which had lasted for nine months. The chutneys had been brought on a stainless-steel platter, and Sharon was working her way round from pasty-mild colours to vivid scorchers, trying each with the tip of her tongue and waiting thirty seconds to see if her eyes started to water. Rhys kept well clear of them all, sitting back in his chair. Sounds from Bollywood's greatest hits drifted through the air, and on a flat-screen TV in the waiting area for takeaways, girls in yellow saris performed a dance against backgrounds that switched from mountain peaks to the busy streets of Tokyo without either narrative reason or shame.

"It began three years ago," said Edna, cracking a poppadom on her plate with an expert rap of the knuckles. "We're none of us shamans in the Friendlies, but we keep an eye out, of course, just to make sure the spirits of the city are all right. There's been ups and downs – the business with Blackout was really very messy, and the death of cities – but thankfully all that fuss passed by, and it seemed to be under control. The spirits of things have their natural life cycles, as does the city that made them. It's not like a dryad is really going to stick around once her lamp post has been demolished. And the canal wyvern can hardly keep his sheen if the water that spawned him is covered in algae, but these are just part of life's natural flow, and, generally, things find their way.

"It started small. Gargoyles began to vanish from the sides of the churches, tribes of imps from the rubbish grounds; whole neonfly hatching grounds disappeared from the lamps around the substations. The shrieks that sit on the windowsills of newborn babies, the dream catchers and foil-winged pixies that sneak into houses at night and move your front-door keys – I personally never understood why – they ... faded. Diminished. Vanished. We were concerned, of course we were, but we thought ... well, it couldn't be anything, could it? The big spirits were still there, Father Thames and Greydawn, the watchers who divide the night from the day and then ...

"How do you say that a thing you cannot perceive has vanished? Greydawn was not a face or a voice, she was – she *is* – She Who Walks Beside. I don't want to judge, dear, but you seem like a girl who might know what I'm talking about when I say there's a 4 a.m. feeling. It's a sense you have at four o'clock in the morning, in the city, when all the lights are out – even the lights for the tourists, Big Ben and the London

Eye and all those, they're dark too. And you walk down the middle of the street because you can, where during the day there would be traffic, and nothing moves, nothing stirs all around you and you know are you alone, and it is invigorating, it is marvellous, it is wonderful and it is terrifying all at once because you are tiny and squashed beneath this great silence and the city and then you look up and . . . and you know you aren't alone. Not really. Not ever. Not in a city.

"She walks beside you.

"Greydawn. Our Lady of 4 a.m. She walks beside you and puts her hand in yours, and you never hear it, you never see her, but she's the one who whispers in your ear without words, *Don't be afraid. I am with you.* She is the keeper of the city wall, the guardian of the gate, she keeps your fears of what might be from becoming the truth of what simply is.

"And she's . . . *gone.*" Edna almost choked on the word. "She vanished in the night and now the gates are opening and . . . *things* are coming through that should not be crawling out of the night, and the only shaman in London is a goblin. I mean, a goblin! And not just any goblin, a goblin who managed to anger the Seven Sisters *and* the Bag Lady *and* the Beggar King all at once with his ridiculous arguments with Blistering Steve . . . and . . . the Friendlies should do something, but we don't know what to do.

"I'm sorry, dear, I didn't mean to burden you with all this. Shall we talk about you?"

Rhys recognised this question. It was a staple of his disastrous time trying to succeed at online dating, a phrase which politely informed the other person that he knew he'd blown it and hoped she didn't mind. Dating, when you were a druid, was never easy, he liked to tell himself.

"Uh . . . okay. 'I'm Sharon, I work in a coffee shop.' Actually, I guess I should say worked in a coffee shop. I've probably been fired by now."

"Oh no! What happened?"

"Failed to turn up to work."

"Why?"

Sharon stared at Edna and wondered exactly what it was about her own demeanour that appeared so un-shamany. "Um . . . saving the city?" she prompted.

"Oh yes, of course! That does make sense. And forgive me asking, but how long have you been a shaman?"

Sharon hesitated, a mouthful of chutney halfway to her lips. She put her piece of poppadom back down on the plate, wiped her mouth with her napkin and said, "Are we talking, like, how long I've been walking through walls, or how long I've been getting the training?"

"You need training to be a shaman?" asked Edna. "I thought shamans just . . . knew."

Sharon groaned. "Why do people always say that? Everywhere I go they say that, and I am having it up to here with this whole 'Sharon knows shit' shit. Sorry, no offence there."

"None taken, dear. But you *are* meant to see the truth of things, aren't you? Isn't that what it's about?"

"But what does that *mean*?"

"I think, Ms Li," put in Rhys, "that when you are in touch with the spirit world, as I'm sure you are, then maybe you're supposed to see things that no one else sees. See?"

Sharon hesitated. "Does, uh, does a guy called Dez count?"

"Um . . . is Dez transparent?" asked Rhys.

"Kinda. He's my spirit guide."

"Your spirit guide is called Dez?" There wasn't shock or condemnation in Rhys's voice, but rather the careful tones of a man who really, *really* wanted to make sure he'd understood a difficult concept.

"Look," exclaimed Sharon, "this isn't about Dez. We're talking about Greydawn vanishing and that, so please can we just move on from my knowing shit, or not knowing shit, or whatever the shit is I'm supposed to do?"

There was a silence in which eyes examined napkins and fingers fidgeted around the edge of plates. Sharon shuffled in her chair, then added, "Sorry. I'm getting a little stressed. I read a book which said you should try breathing really slow, but that just gets me breathless. Can I ask, how'd you go about 'vanishing' spirits anyway?"

"Depends on the spirit, dear," said Edna. "Your local household protector, your little guardian spirit – you could steal its nest, smoke it out, summon it, without too much effort – most wizards would know how. But Greydawn . . . she's one of the powers of the city, and she's not defenceless. She has a dog."

Sharon's lifted her head, on her face were the beginnings of suspicion. "Mr Roding mentioned ... What dog?"

"It's how she's symbolically represented. A woman with a dog. It might just be a romantic ideal, but there was always a certain ... darker side, shall we say, to Greydawn's nature. She doesn't keep the nightmares at bay by being just a harmless zephyr. There has been blood associated with her. We don't talk about it in the Friendlies of course, dear, it's rather unpleasant for our tastes. But if our Lady of 4 a.m. is a protector of the lonely in the night, then Dog is the stick with which she might be said to do her beating. Not that it really should affect us, as Dog, like most creatures she protects us from, lives in the shadows, in the places where only the shamans go. So really it's not worth getting worked up about."

"Lived," corrected Sharon.

"Pardon, dearest?"

"Lived," she repeated. "*Lived* in the shadows, the places where the shamans go. But now Greydawn is gone, you said yourself. So ... things can start getting through, yeah? Things that shouldn't be, coming out of the dark. Like Dog."

Edna didn't speak, thinking it through. Rhys leaned forward, for all the world like a fascinated child about to hear something forbidden and possibly gross.

"Perhaps," conceded Edna at last, "it is ... possible."

"Don't look back. It wants you to look back."

"What's that, dear?"

Sharon's head jerked up from her contemplation of the table. She was surprised to find Rhys and Edna both staring at her with an expression of tight concentration. "What?"

"You said, 'Don't look back. It wants you to look back,' Ms Li," offered Rhys.

"Did I?"

"Yes, and it was very shaman-like," he added, turning to Edna for reassurance. "Didn't you think it was very shaman-like? I mean, this glassy look you had on your face was really spiritual, and I'm not saying you usually look glassy because you don't, you look really nice. I mean, not nice, I mean of course *nice*, but nice doesn't really imply what aaaahh ... aaahhh ..."

Sharon and Edna leaned away as Rhys's face began to contract.

"You know, sweetie, I hate to suggest the obvious," said Edna. "But anti-histamines really are wonderful things."

"They ... they make me ... make me dr ... drow—"

"They make him drowsy," said Sharon. "This dog of Greydawn's – if it was here, I mean, if it really had, like, come out of the shadows or whatever, what do you think it'd do?"

"I imagine he'd look for his mistress," mused Edna as Rhys buried his face in his napkin. "That would be my first response, if I was a living spirit of rage and blood tasked with protecting the guardian of the wall."

"Rage and blood?" squeaked Sharon.

"Why yes, dear. Of course."

"No one said nothing about rage and blood!"

"Well, what did you expect? It's all very well having a spirit who walks beside lonely travellers in the dead hours of the night, a guardian who protects her flock, but this is London. There has to be some blood somewhere. There was a rumour—"

"What about candy floss and teddy bears?" demanded Sharon, banging her fist on the table. "Why couldn't this Dog be a nice kind of terrier or something? Or rabbits – I was distinctly promised rabbits would come up in all this."

"There was a rumour," Edna went on, "that Greydawn was once a spirit of sacrifice, not protection. In the old days, when the Temple of Mithras was still standing, a gift of blood was rather more appreciated. Naturally we've grown more civilised since then, but blood has always been potent. Derek would know more about this, of course."

"Who's Derek?"

Edna's fingers flexed uneasily in her lap. Her face turned down and aside, as if deflecting an invisible blow. "He's ... well, he's the high priest," she confessed. "Well, we don't like to say 'priest', so he was appointed high social secretary of the Friendlies, but everyone knows he's the high priest really. He knows about all of this business."

"Hold on ... I thought you were the high priestess."

Edna shifted uncomfortably in her seat. "I am, dear, but only really on an ... acting basis, if you see what I mean."

"I'm not sure I do."

"Well—"

"Whoa there, gonna stop you right now. I know that 'well'. That was the 'well' my careers adviser used when I asked her why I couldn't be a biomechanical engineer in space. Besides, I know what it means when people go 'well' like that. It means 'I've got this really nasty problem, like maybe it's so nasty I don't want to tell you about it, so just leave it alone even though I know you ain't gonna leave it alone.' Well, lady –" Sharon's finger was out, the trembling finger of pure indignation, the pointing finger of a thwarted general who can't believe her troops won't Go Get That Cannon "– screw your 'well' because, like you said, it's all gone to crap, hasn't it, with Greydawn missing and spirits missing and buildings dying and cities withering. So don't you give me this 'well', and you just tell me about Derek."

Chapter 46

Dog

Howl
Howl
Howl
Howl
HOWL!
HOWL!!
HOWL!!!

Chapter 47

The Truth Is Just Beneath the Surface

She said, "He's gone. Derek's gone."

Sharon said, "What do you mean, gone? Have you told the police?"

She said, "We were at the temple and I went out to get some Blutack and when I came back he was gone. But his bag was still there and his coat and his keys were in his coat and he's ... I'm worried about him. That's all. I'm worried about him."

One lamb bhuna, chicken korai and prawn madras later, Edna, Rhys and Sharon stood in the gloomy interior of the Friendlies' temple (CUT + BLOW DRY £35 WOMEN'S HAIR), and Edna wrung her hands. Rhys tried not to stare. He'd heard of people wringing their hands, of course – it was something women possessed of a certain frailty were expected to do in difficult circumstances. He'd just never seen anyone go for it with such panache, such muscular vigour. Edna stood in the middle of the concrete floor and exclaimed, "Derek was such a lovely man, I can't believe he'd just pack up and leave!"

Rhys met Sharon's eyes. Neither of them could believe it either.

Rhys, realising he didn't have much to contribute to the conversation, did some wall leaning and hoped he looked okay. Sharon puffed her cheeks and said, "So ... spirits vanish, Greydawn vanishes, and now the high priest—"

"Social secretary," corrected Edna.

Sharon gave her a look that could have withered brick. "Also disappears, and you're like, 'Wow, that's strange, look how screwed up things are, but I'm sure it'll be okay in the end.'"

"We are not like that!" fumed Edna. "The Friendlies are just . . . we're friendly, do you see? We don't deal in all this high drama."

"Excuse me?" hazarded Rhys. "Do we – I mean, I don't want to interrupt, see, but does Magicals Anonymous deal in high drama? Only, we've only met once and I thought we weren't big on drama, but I still got this sort of swelling under my arms—"

Sharon opened her mouth to speak, but too late.

"Magicals Anonymous?" Edna cut in. "What's that?"

"It's a support group," said Rhys. "It's for everyone who has issues with their mystical state. Miss Li founded it."

A look of grudging respect came over Edna's face. "That's actually an interesting idea, dear. It can be difficult dabbling in the mystical in this day and age. Which isn't to say it wasn't difficult when you were burned at the stake either. But do you know how hard it is to find someone to represent your southern pole during a pepper dance? In Tooting?"

To Sharon's surprise, Rhys leapt into the conversation. "Oh I know!" he exclaimed. "And getting ritual stains out of white robes is a nightmare too. I've tried all the brands but nothing quite does it."

"White wine vinegar," offered Edna. "I've heard people swear by white wine vinegar."

"Does that work on linen?"

"I don't know, I've never tried it. But I used to get this hideous sticky stuff under my nails every time I—"

"Hey!" blurted Sharon. "Missing people? Spirits? Fate of the city? Priorities, people, please?" Somewhat abashed, Edna and Rhys fell silent.

"This Derek," Sharon was slightly breathless with the effort of controlling the moment, "would he know how to . . . I don't know, how to trap or vanish or do whatever has been done to this Greydawn chick?"

"Well," murmured Edna, "I suppose he might, but do you feel that 'Greydawn chick' is very reverent?"

"Okay, how do we find him?"

"Well, you're the shaman. Shouldn't you . . ." The words trailed away in the face of Sharon's glare. "How about scrying?" asked Edna.

"Sounds good. How the hell do we do that?"

"Well, we'd need something personal of Derek's . . ."

"You said he left his bag here."

" . . . and we'd need someone who knows how to scry. Derek did hire a couple of very nice wizards to try and scry for Greydawn when she . . . but they didn't find anything. Which I thought was quite odd, as you'd have expected *some* sort of mystical residue or glow or something like that; but it's really as if she's just vanished into some part of the city. But you're thinking about Derek, aren't you, and I'm sure it wasn't the wizards' fault; they seemed very nice. That said, I don't know if they'll do call-outs at this time of night."

"How about Mr Roding?" demanded Sharon. "He's gonna break down wards and that. Could he do scrying?"

"Who is this Mr Roding gentleman?" asked Edna.

"He's a necromancer, but he seems okay."

"Oh, I say! Is he one of your . . . Magicals Anonymous too?"

"Wouldn't be very anonymous if I answered that, would it?" replied Sharon primly.

"But Mr Roding was going to the pub with the Society of Morticians, Taxidermists and Necromancers tonight," pointed out Rhys. "They're doing a quiz on the theme Great Footballers of the 1990s." Then he snapped his fingers in triumph. "It's all right! I know who! I've got just the guy!"

Chapter 48

Kevin

Oh my *God* it's hard work being a vampire. I mean, so totally not-cool.

I know what everyone says. They're all like, "Wow, the black leather, the chic hair, the eternal youth, the sexy fangs," and I'm like, "Darling, do you know what that jacket is made from, and babe, do you think I'm putting *that* gunk in my hair, and sweetheart, these fangs, they ain't just for fashion." You know what I'm saying?

And you get these freaky people! These freaky people who are all like, "Bite me, sexy," and I'm like, "Hello? Your breath stinks, your skin is covered in other dudes' saliva, your blood-alcohol content is way over the legal limit for driving, and I don't want to wake up with your hangover in the morning, and besides, I don't know where your blood has been! You could be shooting up with stuff, you could be infectious, you could have a fungal disease or something, and I am not going there. Eternity is a really long time to be a vampire, and I've gotta look after myself, you know what I'm saying? Sure, maybe once I've got a full medical history and the test has come back from the lab on a reasonable sample, maybe then I'll have a little nip but, Jesus, you gotta let me sterilise first!"

The others say I'm letting the side down. They're like, "We've got an image problem," and I'm like, "Hell, yeah, of course we've got an image problem; when was the last time *you* flossed after you ate?"

Chapter 49

The Truth Is Buried Beneath

He said, "I love what you've done with your hair."

Edna beamed. 'Thank you, dear, and may I say I'm loving your look. Do you use herbal conditioner or is it merely fragrant?"

Kevin flashed a brilliant, slightly fangy smile at Edna before turning to inspect the Friendlies' temple. He was still wearing the same skinny blue jeans that Sharon felt sure she'd seen him in at Magicals Anonymous. But his T-shirt had been swapped for a dowdy tartan shirt and a thermal jumper on which an old peeling sticker which read SAVE A LIFE – GIVE BLOOD had been proudly placed like a target over the heart. His black sports bag – his very large black sports bag – lay by the door, the zip partially open to reveal a huge array of toothpastes, sterile wipes and latex gloves. Kevin turned one more time through the room, examining its every feature, before concluding his wander and fixing Sharon with a questioning stare.

"You said you could like, put me in touch with a good lawyer? This doesn't look like a solicitor's office."

"A lawyer?" murmured Rhys.

"Kevin wants to sue his dentist," explained Sharon, her smile once more locked in the attack position.

"Really?" breathed the druid. "Well, that's ... that's, uh ... that's very ..." His words dissolved into hopeful gestures and a desperate grin.

Convincing the vampire to come to Tooting hadn't been as hard as Sharon had expected. Certainly she'd lied a tiny bit, offering up promises of lawyers yet to come, and dentists whose practices would be ruined, and quite right too, for their discriminatory behaviour – but Kevin, it turned out, lived in Earlsfield anyway. And, as she suspected, like many in that part of town, he was so pleased and surprised to discover something happening *nearby* as compared to *on the other side of the river*, that far-flung place of wonders, he'd picked up his box of sterile wipes and come almost immediately. The revelation that actually there weren't so many midnight-opening solicitors in Tooting had only slightly dampened his spirits.

"Edna here runs a group called the Friendlies," Sharon hastened to say. "They're very ... uh ... friendly, aren't you?"

"Oh yes, dear, we're definitely that."

"And they can help me sue that gargling bastard?"

Sharon looked at Edna in an emphatic "Help me" manner.

"Um ... I'm sure we can try, dear," suggested Edna. "Tell me, is it nice being a vampire?"

"Nice? It is hard bloody work, pardon my language, that's what it is. Everyone is always judging, which is so twelfth century."

"On a different note," Sharon tried desperately, "how are you at, like, tracking your prey and that?"

Kevin hesitated, suspicion blooming behind the indignation natural to his features. "What kind of prey? Is it NHS-certified?"

"We're looking for a man called Derek," offered Rhys. "He's vanished. And so have half the spirits of the city. And so has Greydawn, She Who Divides the Night From the Day. And there's this office called Burns and Stoke and the walls say, *Help me.*"

"What's this got to do with my dentist?" asked Kevin.

"Um ... well, see, uh ..."

"I can't be handling untested blood! No idea where it's been."

"This is more sort of the fate of the city we're talking about here."

"Do I look like I'm a fate-of-the-city kinda guy?" demanded Kevin. "You're a shaman," he added, waggling a hand in Sharon's direction. "You know what to do; you fix it!"

"It doesn't quite—"

"Aren't you supposed to be a leader of your tribe?"

"Well, the thing is—"

"And actually, babe, I wasn't going to say anything, but I was like, expecting way more feathers in your hair, and this whole, like, 'approachable but ditsy' thing you've got going on, while kinda cute, isn't really very shaman-like – just saying."

There was a moment.

A long, quiet moment.

Not just Rhys, but even Edna looked afraid.

The world held its breath.

Kevin began, "Um—"

Then Sharon Li had seized his tartan-pattern shirt with both hands and was pulling so hard his tongue began to flop against his teeth. His feet arched up off the floor until he balanced precariously on tiptoe as she pushed her face towards his and snarled, "Stop. Telling. Me. What. I. Should. Know! Because if I don't fucking know something it's because you bastards, you moaning 'Sharon do this,' 'Sharon do that' wankers, haven't fucking told me! Do you get that? No one tells me anything, it's just 'Sharon save the city.' I mean, Christ! Burns and Stoke have been buying up buildings which have the souls sucked out of them, a mystery creature howls in the night, the city walls crumble and Our Lady of 4 a.m. vanishes, and you just freak out about your dentist and feathers in my hair! Pull yourself together and get vampiric on this shit!"

It was five minutes later.

Edna held open the bag of Derek, social secretary/high priest of the Friendlies, and said, "Do you think you can find him with this?"

Kevin sniffed. He wore latex gloves over his boney white hands and prodded the contents of the bag with the end of a pristine sharp pencil. "Multitools and greasy bits of tissue – do you know how much bacteria there is in here?" he whined as Edna rattled the bag hopefully.

"Focus," barked Sharon.

Kevin's sniff was both literal and pointed.

"Oh, this is so rank," he exclaimed. "Do you realise that when you smell something, you're basically just inhaling the thing itself? This Derek did keep clean, didn't he? No fungal infections, no thrush?"

"He was – is – a very nice man!" retorted Edna.

"Have you got his scent?" demanded Sharon.

"Darling, I am not some yappy barking dog."

"I thought vampires were all supposed to be brooding and cool and shit."

"Babe, I thought shamans were supposed to know everything and look how wrong we both are."

Sharon glowered but didn't reply. Kevin pushed Derek's old bag away with a curling lip of distaste. He pulled off the latex gloves with a loud snap and dropped them carefully into a yellow plastic bag stamped with a biohazard sign which was stowed neatly in the front pouch of his own large, black bag for future sanitary disposal.

His nose twitched.

He sniffed and sniffed again.

"Well," he said at last, "I don't want to crash your party or pop your balloon or anything like that, but I gotta tell you I'm getting a lot of death."

Edna gave a short sharp cry, immediately stifled beneath her hand.

Kevin sniffed again. "Yep. Once you get through the tasteless incense and the frankly pungent body odours of all assembled – no offence, darlings – your Derek bloke's scent is coming over distinctly ex."

"Can you track it?" demanded Sharon.

"Babes, that's what I'm trying to tell you. There's nothing to track. I'm getting, like, death right here, right in this room, and it's a bit . . . uch, it's very last week's roadkill actually. I mean, Jesus." He fumbled again for his bag and pulled out a pack of white face masks, each in its own sterile wrapping. "Want one?" he asked, slipping the elastic band over his head.

"What the hell are you doing?" demanded Sharon. "You're supposed to be tracking Derek!"

"Babes, there's like, serious death in this room and I can't be doing with that! Do you know what happens to bodies once they start to decay? It's like, hello, plague and rot and – God, *airborne contaminates.*"

"But, um, excuse me?" hazarded Rhys. "There isn't anyone dead here. I mean, not to question you, Mr Kevin sir, but there's just not."

"Darling, you got the vampire in to do the vampire thing and now you're like, questioning the expert!" retorted Kevin, hands flapping indignantly. "You asked me to sniff this Derek's stuff – I've sniffed this Derek's stuff and, based on the sniffing, I'm telling you he is one dead chicken."

Edna suppressed a wail. Rhys edged towards her nervously, wondering how best to offer comfort. Sharon looked round Edna's salon and wondered what Sammy the Elbow would do . . . When had a goblin become her role model?

"You just hold that thought," she said and, turning away from Kevin, she walked.

It was easier now, and took only a few paces to find that thin point in reality where she became invisible, and invisible things became clear. Evidently practice was good for something. She slipped into that grey place where the shadows began to move and heard, a long way off, the sound of Kevin's voice:

"Uh, did anyone else just see her disappear?"

"She does that," offered Rhys. "It's a shaman thing."

Sharon turned, still slowly moving because she couldn't yet pull off invisibility while immobile. She drifted round the room, sensing that place where she was at one with the city, and the city was at one with her, and thus no one would bother to notice her.

Rhys, looked at from this side of perception, seemed a little brighter to her eye. She circled round him as he vainly tried to comfort Edna; and saw threads of light running through his skin and in his blood, a faint tangled mass just beneath the surface like glowing circuitry. Kevin, on the other hand, was even more obviously vampire than in daily life. The gauntness of his face, the pallor of his skin, the redness in his eye, the protrusion of his teeth, all were enhanced; and as she circled him there was the faintest taste of blood and the overwhelming smell of sterile swabs.

She turned towards the altar, and it was a bright glowing heart in the gloom of the shadow walk. Echoes of the men and women who'd made their offerings to a now-vanished goddess were still drifting round it like eddies in incense. The votive trinkets held memories strong enough to be still faintly visible, and as Sharon's fingers rolled over them they were

the rolled up newspaper I had in my hand when the man tried to mug me and I hit him over the head at 5.15 on a winter's morning the sandwich packet that held the last bit of bread in the machine at 3.54 a.m. when I hadn't eaten for a day and a night

the batteries that powered the torch that kept me safe when the power failed

the shard of glass from the broken window of the bus shelter that protected me from the rain as I waited for a night bus in the pouring dark.

They were the memories of the night workers and the dead-hour shifts, of the lonely travellers who'd waited by themselves and, in that time, known that they were not alone.

"That's what Greydawn is," said a voice behind her, and she didn't need to look to know it was Dez. "That's what they mean when they say she walks beside."

"Go on then, spirit guide," sighed Sharon. "Guide me."

"Watch where you step," he replied, and she looked down.

The floor beneath her feet was gleaming with an unnatural sheen. She backed away from the centre of the glow, and her feet slopped and slipped as they moved. The concrete by the altar was turning to liquid, a spreading patch of grey thickness, bubbles popping to the surface from beneath her feet. She scrambled back as the surface of the floor began to shift and wobble, and there was something moving beneath it, something round and smooth, something that was covered once with human hair.

She caught her breath and retreated further, bumping into a wall and slamming back into reality hard enough to bring tears to her eyes. Rhys was by her side instantly, the quiet distress of Edna forgotten as Sharon reappeared on the floor – the now solid, mundane floor.

"You all right, Miss Li? You okay?"

"He . . . down *there*," Sharon rasped, pointing at the solid floor. "I'm sorry. He's been buried beneath us."

Four pairs of eyes examined the undisturbed-looking floor. Kevin said, "That is totally gross."

"He can't be," stammered Edna. "We haven't had any work done to this place for years. I'd know about it! And who'd want to hurt Derek? I don't see why—"

"Maybe the same people," suggested Sharon, "who'd want to own all those places where the spirits have vanished. The same guys who buy up shops and factories and homes which then fall dead and rot. Maybe it's—"

"Burns and Stoke!"

The voice came, not from Sharon nor Rhys nor any of the four assembled there, but rather from a new figure, a man framed in the door of the salon, a man in a badly tailored black suit and white shirt, who smiled radiantly at them all and proclaimed, "But of course yes, and why not? In these difficult times people do require someone to blame. I understand, naturally I understand. These complex human emotions you struggle with – envy, resentment, jealousy – I think I am in the area, yes? They become so . . . confused in your little minds that we should not be surprised that you –" a finger uncurled, pointing towards Sharon " – you would look at men like us, Burns and Stoke, and say, 'I do not understand that thing, so why don't I simply call it evil?'" Mr Ruislip smiled, adjusting his tie as he stepped further into the room. "If 'evil' is the word we are looking for, of course."

Chapter 50

4 Ninja Builders

Thing about being the greatest killers the world has ever known
  You know
  Tits!
  No one can ever know.
  Arseholes.
  That's the point, yeah
  Yeah
  Of being the greatest ever killers
  No one
  Ever knows
  Who we
  Are.
  No one looks at us.
  No one remembers us.
  No one asks us any questions.
  No one suspects us when the
  Wanker!
  Blood has dried.
  We're discreet
  Considerate
  Considerate of our environment

Caring

Community contract community fucking contract bollocks!

How do you know the greatest ever killers the world has ever known?

Lovely pair of

Knockers

On her

Babe!

You know 'em because you never seen them

Before

During

After

And no one can remember what the hell they looked like anyway.

Chapter 51

The Only Thing We Need Fear Is Fear Itself

He's tall.

"Skinny" doesn't handle it. "Skinny" could imply anything, from vegetarian who hasn't quite got hold of the protein situation, through to well-exercised young gentleman with a penchant for soup. "Skeletal" might be closer, but that implies bones protruding under flesh, and he has not much flesh for anything to protrude from; and the skin that would do the bulging were there any bulging to be done is so thin you can see the indigo blood pulse through the capillaries beneath it.

He wears a suit.

His hair is thin and pale, his eyes have a fish-like quality suggesting that even in death their gaze would settle on you, personally, through the mortal mists.

He smiles, perfect baby-teeth in a pencil-thin mouth. The smile is the smile of a man who wishes you to know that he has practised the expression long and hard in an attempt to put you at your ease, and if you cannot appreciate it, well then that's your own damn fault.

And he's not alone.

This is something of a problem, because the four gentlemen who he is not alone with are . . .

. . . difficult to focus on.

Rhys tries and feels something prickly on his forehead, and stops trying. Then he wonders what he's stopped trying to do and why it seemed so important at the time. He tries again and thinks for a moment he can see four men in yellow fluorescent jackets, but why do the yellow fluorescent jackets make it so hard to see them? And they are smiling, four different faces . . .

. . . but all the same smile.

Then the man in the suit steps forward. As if his body has decided to make the decisions his mind is too rational to manage, Rhys feels a deadly itching at the back of his throat and a chill in the pit of his stomach.

"You must be the Friendlies!" exclaims the man in the suit. "Tell me, is it one of those concepts you people have? *Irony*, is that the one, or is it sarcasm? I never can keep track. Are you friendly in an ironic manner, or do you genuinely take it upon yourselves to emit this one quality above all others?"

Rhys looked to Edna for an answer. Edna looked to Kevin. Kevin shrugged and, inevitably, all eyes turned to Sharon.

Sharon's face was crimped in concentration. Her eyes ran from the man in the suit to the four – was it four? – who stood behind him. Or possibly around him. Or who maybe weren't there at all, it was hard to tell.

"And why friendly?" continued the man in the same easy-going tone. "Why are you friendly and not, for example, nice or charitable or generous, or whatever else fits into the 'morally white' –" his fingers mimed a pair of quote marks "– aspirations that you so clearly strive for? What is the quality of 'friend' that is so appealing to you?"

Edna coughed, cleared her throat and rasped, "Would you like a cup of tea?"

All eyes turned to her. Kevin demanded, "You what?"

"I'm just wondering if the gentleman would like some tea."

"Uh, darling, he's like, walked into here and done this whole creepy rant thing and is like, so not human it's amazing, and I've got like this headache coming on and there's a corpse, I mean a *corpse*, which is just so *uch*, beneath you, and you want to have tea?"

"Maybe she's avoiding escalating the situation?" suggested Rhys.

"Escalating?" queried the man in the suit. "Is that what this is – is this an escalation of the situation? That's very interesting, isn't it? This implies all sorts of curious sensations yet to come. Tell me," stepping towards Rhys, who retreated fast, "when things are 'escalating', do you know where they will go? Will we escalate to new levels of friendliness – is that the word? – or did you have in mind an alternative emotional journey?"

A meek "Um" was all that made it out of Rhys's mouth, but that seemed at last to stir Sharon to action. She stepped sharply forward, putting herself between the man in the suit and the cowering druid.

"Hey," she snapped. "I don't know who you are but you are giving off these seriously negative vibes. And my friend Rhys here, he can't be having negative vibes because he's got a very weak . . . most things . . . and I'm a shaman, which means good vibes are really important to me too, maybe with some chanting and nasal breathing and that."

A rather bewildered silence followed. "Is nasal breathing important to the creation of these . . . 'good vibes'?" queried the man in the suit.

"It's a technique," she retorted. "Who are you and what do you want?"

The man's face split into a well-practised grin. "How delightful!" he exclaimed. "Well, I am Mr Ruislip – hello –" a hand was thrust towards Sharon for inspection "– and I have the honour and the privilege of being the CEO of Burns and Stoke Enterprises. Is it Enterprises or is it Limited? Is there a difference? I really don't know, but isn't this friendly?"

Sharon stared at the offered hand, grey skin threaded with blue. She reached out, fighting down a sense of revulsion, and as her fingers closed around the boney offering there was a taste of

blood blood blood blood blood blood blood blood BLOOD BLOOD BLOOD

and she snatched her hand away before the world could turn crimson and the taste of it in her mouth could make her puke across the bare concrete floor. Mr Ruislip was staring at her, smile locked in place, head on one side. "Is that . . . fear?" he asked as Sharon tried to swallow down the taste of blood. "Or is there a better word, a more refined concept we should work towards? How about revulsion, was that revulsion? Revulsion, fear, revulsion, fear . . . maybe it was both? Oh, how complicated. Well!" The hands briskly clapped together. "I leave these questions for you to work on, perhaps to deliver a focus group report in the next fiscal quarter. In the meantime I'm afraid I'm here for two special reasons. Firstly . . ."

His hand moved too fast for Sharon to see. Its fingers were round her throat before she could know that was what they were. As she gagged and tugged at his arm, his smile stretched. "Trespass is naughty, little girl," he breathed. "You come back to Burns and Stoke, I'll tear you to pieces."

"Hey! You don't talk to Ms Li like that!" To everyone's surprise, especially his own, Rhys leapt forward. He tried to grab the hand that circled Sharon's throat but another hand fell on his shoulder. It was large and pink, with oversized fingers stained white by mortar dust, and it lifted him up with a snap of distressed bones colliding beneath his skin. He saw a smiling ruddy face, hair shaved along the side of the scalp and grown across the top to a small lawn. There was a suggestion of fluorescent yellow jacket, sensible steel boots, blue jeans, bad breath and a voice that said:

"Do you want us to bury 'em, Mr Ruislip sir?"

"Foundations," agreed another voice, male, full of gravel and mugs of cold tea, and while it was different, it was also the same.

"Scrawny git," added a third.

"Carrot-top!" concluded the fourth. And for a moment Rhys could see them all, four builders in yellow fluorescent jackets. If he strained with every gram of will he had, he could make their forms solidify, just briefly, into actual shapes, and force his mind to remember that they were real, and they were there.

"No," murmured Mr Ruislip. "Keep them alive. You could shake him a little, though."

Obediently, the hand that held Rhys almost off the ground shook him. His teeth crashed together, biting his tongue; his legs flapped. He tried to mumble words, tried to find magic and fight back, but the shock, like the shame of it, overwhelmed his senses.

And here it came, the tingling at the back of his throat, the overwhelming urge to . . .

"Aaatchoo!"

The shaking paused. Rhys was aware of the four builders in their yellow jackets staring in surprise. Momentarily he realised that their faces all wore the same – the exact same – expression.

Sharon was gagging, her face turning blue. Mr Ruislip's hand was still around her throat, as if he'd forgotten about it.

"Does that ... happen?" marvelled Mr Ruislip, looking at Rhys. "Is that a fear response, something biological? Do people sneeze under stress?"

"Never seen that before," admitted one builder.

"Load of wet panties!" concurred another.

"Tits," offered the third.

"Wanker," concluded the fourth. A moment of mutual appreciation passed, each of them satisfied that the argument had been pushed to its limit.

"Oh my God, you guys are so uncivilised!" exclaimed Kevin. Five pairs of eyes turned towards him. He backed off.

Mr Ruislip let go of Sharon. She flopped to the floor, heaving in breath with the sound of a defective steam engine. Rhys dangled from the hand of one of the builders. Edna was trying not to cower with too much indignity, and Kevin was doing his best not to get involved.

"What were we discussing before this little exploration of sentiment?" asked Mr Ruislip. A snap of his fingers, bone on bone. "Of course! If you come back to Burns and Stoke again you will be killed. Of course, you," indicating Rhys, "are sacked. And the company that hired you has been liquidated, because in successful corporate enterprises," swelling with rehearsed wisdom, "Commitment Is Everything."

Rhys was shaken again until the hand that shook lost interest and he was deposited on the floor with the grace of a splattered ice cream.

"Now ..." Mr Ruislip's gaze slid to where Edna was clutching at the altar of knick-knacks like a sailor to the side of a capsized lifeboat. "What was the other thing?" He stepped neatly past Sharon, who was trying without much success to get to her feet, until, without seeming to move much at all, he filled Edna's world. A face of blue-grey, hands of bone, eyes with the sheen of a gutted fish. His breath was heavy with peppermint, but that didn't disguise the stench of rotting meat at its core.

"Where is Greydawn?"

"Greydawn?" stammered Edna. "She's uh ... She's in the ... the air, isn't she? I mean she's a, she's ..."

Gently, Mr Ruislip reached out and ran the back of two long fingers down the curve of Edna's cheek, pausing to tilt her head up so that her eyes were forced to meet his as he repeated, "Where. Is. Greydawn?"

"Gone!" squeaked Edna. "She vanished!"

"But you are the Friendlies," murmured Mr Ruislip. "You are friendly with her, isn't that the point? You must know where to find her, otherwise what is the point of you?"

"You'd think that, wouldn't you, dear?" Edna stammered. "But actually it's a big mystery we're all terribly worked up about – aren't we terribly worked up? In fact the man you should probably ask is Derek but he's . . . he's gone. He's gone and you . . ." Her eyes swerved to the four men in fluorescent jackets and steel-capped boots. A tiny "Oh" escaped her even as she put her hands over her mouth as if to hold back the sound. She looked from Mr Ruislip to the four builders and back again, and she *knew*.

Mr Ruislip smiled. In a dreamy tone he remarked, "I think I've heard of this 'Derek' character. He was your high priest, yes? I asked my colleagues here – one must say colleagues even when one is innately superior, to encourage teamwork in the workplace – to talk to this Derek concerning the question I now put to you. Apparently, he was most uncooperative, and negotiations grew hostile. Is that the word, hostile? Hostile, aggressive, offensive, terminal – frankly, they all sound apt to me. But now . . ." he ran a nail down a line in Edna's skin, fascinated by it as a kitten might be enthralled by a pigeon's severed foot " . . . a shaman breaks into my office, and a druid works on my servers, and the Midnight Mayor vanishes – indeed, vanishes! – and unprofessionally neglects meanwhile to set up an email auto-reply. So I conclude that the personal touch might be the way to expedite matters. You see, I won't hurt her. Greydawn will be my friend. That's good, isn't it? You like it when people are friendly."

The movement of his fingers froze, and Edna became aware that the sharp points of his nails were resting just below her eye sockets. They began to push, curving in and down, and her hands seemed frozen to the altar at her back and her tears welled up as Mr Ruislip calmly demanded, "Are you friendly now?"

Rhys tried to get to his feet, but a kick from a steel boot sent him falling forward like a man in prayer. Kevin said, "Hey, now that's not . . ." only to find that one of the four other men had produced from a half-concealed tool belt a hammer, which he laid, claw inwards, across Kevin's throat with a murmur of:

"Fucking vampires, bloodsucking sponges on the fucking state."

"Get back to Transylvania!" agreed another.

"Come over here . . ."

" . . . drinking our blood."

"Disgraceful."

"I'm from Liverpool, actually," Kevin said, and the hammer pressed harder. If there'd been much blood left to rise in Kevin's body, it would have risen; as it was, his only reaction was a gagging sound.

A tear dribbled from the corner of Edna's eye. Mr Ruislip scrutinised it, then wiped it away with his fingers and tasted it, flicking his tongue like a lizard. His eyes closed in satisfaction, and a slow contented breath seemed to leave his frame diminished. "Marvellous," he murmured.

Then a voice said from the empty air, "Oi! Respect the aged!"

Something heavy, fast and quite possibly bag-shaped slammed out of the nothingness at Mr Ruislip's back and into the place where spine met skull. There was a sharp, satisfying snap and the suited man staggered forward, his weight knocking Edna down into the altar of little trophies and gifts, which collapsed beneath the two of them with a crash of splintering plastic. As the four men in fluorescent jackets reached for their tools, the same unseen force slammed into the jaw of the one who stood over Rhys. The man staggered back, briefly registering surprise, then scowled and pulled a spanner out of his belt. "Let's get the bitch!" he roared.

Rhys felt something firm close around his arm and before he could so much as sneeze, he was hauled to his feet and into . . .

. . . a grey place. It was still the temple of the Friendlies, still the world he knew and generally feared, but the echoes of things that were, and things that weren't, and things that might have been, swelled and ebbed from the walls around, and as he turned to look he saw . . .

the truth of things.

There stood Kevin the vampire. In this grey place his teeth were fangs, no denying, and his hair was grey and his skin seemed to suck in the light. And there were the four men in yellow fluorescent jackets, but they weren't fluorescent now; here they were seen for what they were – great billowing coats of invisibility, a flowing wizard's cloak that engulfed each wearer so that only eyes and hands and the occasional flash of a foot were visible. The faces of the men who wore them were all the same, the same featureless nothing: eyes in smoothed-over skin pressed flat by an angry potter in a moment of frustration, ears mere holes cut into the head, bodies made of slabs of flesh tacked together at the joins with no sympathy for skeletal structure or nervous system. Lines of power joined the men together, their fluorescent cloaks billowing in and out of each other, so that briefly it seemed as if the four were one.

Then Rhys turned and a sound caught in the back of his throat.

Mr Ruislip was there, right *there*, staring straight at him, or perhaps through him. His eyes were searching the space where Rhys had been, and in this grey place Mr Ruislip's eyes were sodium-pink and -yellow, and his teeth were black glass-grinders, and his skin was flaking off him in great white banners that coiled and snapped in the air around him, and he had claws for nails and blood for spit, and he was a being that Rhys had only heard mentioned a couple of times, an idea whispered nervously in the dark, but he knew it as sure as he knew that pollen was no good for a histamine-primed endocrine system. Mr Ruislip was a wendigo.

A hand fell on Rhys's shoulder and he yelped. Clearly the sound was audible in the real world, whatever that was, for the heads of the four builders snapped round and one of them made a swipe with his spanner that nearly brained Rhys where he stood. Then the hand on his shoulder dragged him back and he half-saw Sharon standing there, the only bright thing in this shadow world, a blaze of purple and orange amid the gloom. She had her bag wrapped around her wrist and was swinging it like a slingshot ready to fire – until Mr Ruislip's distant voice, full of a bile that Rhys had only imagined in the mortal world, but which was here real, announced:

"I will eat the old one's eyes."

Edna was picking herself up from the ruins of the altar, a silent "Oh" of horror forming on her lips as she saw the shattered remains of

the umbrella I found abandoned at the bus stop when the rain began to fall

the receipt for the £1.90 Underground fare bought with the exact change that was the last money I had in my hand to get me home

packet of salted peanuts what was the only food I could find in the night

before Mr Ruislip picked her up by the back of the neck and turned her to face the room. "I will count to ten," he intoned. "Or perhaps I shall count backwards from ten; which would you find more appropriate? Let's see. Ten."

Rhys stared at Sharon. His mouth shaped a soundless "What now?" of terror.

Sharon looked past him at Edna, whose fingers clutched at Mr Ruislip's arm. She couldn't see the way the flesh billowed off him like sails in a gale or she might not even have tried to fight free.

"Nine."

Sharon's fists were bunched tight, the strap of her bag curled around her wrist, but she stood frozen in doubt.

"Eight."

Kevin suddenly dropped the weight of his body, slipping free from the hammer across his throat. As the builder threatening him tried to slam his weapon into Kevin's skull the vampire leapt back, curling animal-like onto all fours, and snarled. His fangs were now clearly visible, and as the four builders surged towards him he hissed, "I warn you! You get really nasty infections from puncture wounds!"

Mr Ruislip looked exasperated, and tugged hard enough on the back of Edna's head for the old woman to cry out in pain.

"Seven!"

Kevin leapt at the nearest builder, who threw up his arm. There was a burst of blood, brilliant and scarlet in that grey place, and the builder seemed to shimmer. He shook Kevin, just once, gently, from side to side, and this little gesture seemed enough, more than enough, to dislodge Kevin, to toss him up in the air and away, slamming him shoulder first into the wall. The vampire collapsed to the floor, eyes wide with astonishment, his mouth stained with blood.

"Six," sighed Mr Ruislip. "You know, you'd really better come out now."

The builder Kevin had bitten was staring at his arm with mild surprise. "You tosser," he exclaimed. To Rhys, the words sounded far off.

"Wanker!" announced another. Rhys saw a hint of red on this man's arm, a faint puncture mark to match his colleague's injury, though Kevin's teeth had come nowhere near him. Yet even while Rhys watched, the mark began to heal, the blood drying and turning black before his eyes, flaking off as a remnant of decaying scab.

Kevin spat crimson onto the floor and whimpered, pawing blood from his mouth with the back of his hand, "Oh God, that's so disgusting ..."

Another cry of pain sounded from Edna as Mr Ruislip jerked her head further back, his fingers pressing against her eyes.

"Five!" he declared. "Goodness, but these friendly people are anti-social, aren't they? Is that the antithesis here? Friendly and anti-social? Or does one merely say 'unfriendly' as in 'willing to let a friend suffer and die' – is that a more appropriate usage?"

Rhys turned back to Sharon, whose shoulders were shaking, but not, he realised, from tears or even dread, but with an anger that stood out on her face so hard and bright, she seemed almost to glow in the darkness. She took a step towards Mr Ruislip and for a moment Rhys wondered if this was it, if she was going to try and fight, to rip the skin off the already skinless monster stood before them.

"Four."

For a moment the world hung in the balance. Kevin tried to pick himself up, but a foot slammed into the back of his neck, pinning him to the floor. Edna tried to close her eyes, but the pressure of Mr Ruislip's fingers against her lids pulled them back to stare madly at their impending end. The four builders in their invisible cloaks tutted and waited, tools in hand – and was it just Rhys's imagination that caked the end of every tool with a crust of aged blood?

"Three!"

Rhys looked at Sharon, and saw her deflate.

Her shoulders sagged, her head bowed, a sigh passed her lips, the bag dropped to her side, no longer a weapon. Rhys swallowed hard against a rising nausea and a hideous itching that made his eyes and nose stream as Mr Ruislip announced:

"Two!"

And Sharon began to slip out of the shadows, taking Rhys with her, sliding back into the world where to be seen was also to be perceived. At the sight of her, Mr Ruislip beamed, though his fingers didn't move from Edna's inflamed face. "How nice of you to join us again!" he chortled. "But we were so close to one."

His fingers slipped up and pressed, very lightly, against the whites of Edna's eyes. She opened her mouth to scream, feet scrabbling at the floor, hands scratching in vain against Mr Ruislip's face and

Sharon's phone rang.

The cheery, chipper rhythm of the ringtone filled the room like the buzz of a bumble bee in an ice palace. Mr Ruislip hesitated. The four builders shifted uneasily.

Ring ring, went the phone.

Ring ring.

They stood there, ten seconds becoming twenty, twenty becoming thirty, and still the call did not pass, and still no one moved.

"Aren't you going to pick it up?" demanded Mr Ruislip at last.

Moving slowly despite herself, Sharon reached into her pocket and pulled out her mobile. The number was "Unknown". She thumbed it on and held it to her ear.

"Yeah?" she asked.

"Hi there!" The voice was cheerful, male and familiar. It was the voice that had spoken to her from the shadows in Clerkenwell, and whispered "Run" at the howling of a distant dog in the night. It brought to mind a couple of words she'd heard uttered by so many people as something that should have mattered – Midnight Mayor.

"Would you mind putting me on speakerphone?"

"What?"

"Speakerphone – your phone *does* have a speaker, doesn't it? I know that phones these days aren't really about talking to people any more, it's all apps and that, but come on."

Sharon looked at Mr Ruislip and saw nothing but curiosity in that strange, animal face. "Okay," she said. She held the phone away from her ear and turned on the speaker.

"Brilliant!" The voice was tiny and far off, but still somehow carried and filled the room through sheer force of enthusiasm.

"Hello, there!" it sang out. "My name's Matthew. How are you all doing? And may I take this opportunity to say that you all suck. I mean really, you're useless, the lot of you. I give you my blessing, I get you free classes in shamaning, I send you clues, I give you pointers, I give you all sorts of really useful advice and what do you do? You just faff around in Tooting. Bloody hell!"

"Who is this?" demanded Mr Ruislip.

There was an audible huff of breath on the other end, which might have been irritation. "You must be the wendigo. Has anyone told you that's a really bad suit? Everyone assume the brace position, please."

So saying, the voice on the other end of the line hung up.

Sharon looked at Rhys; Rhys looked at Sharon.

There was a honking of angry horns on the street outside.

Mr Ruislip's face was a mass of confusion. The four builders shrugged, and it was all the same shrug.

There was a squeal of tyres and the bump of dodgy suspension doing unwise things.

Behind Sharon a flash of headlights through the window.

A scream of tyres, a screech of brakes as cars swerved in the street outside.

Sharon threw herself onto the ground and assumed the brace position.

Chapter 52

To Disrespect Others Is to Demean Yourself

There's a lot of bad driving around Tooting Broadway.

It's not that the local drivers are inherently bad; it's just that all the laws of geography conspire against them. Inhabiting that strange zone where London Transport hands the baton to mainline trains, it is neither a suburban place of quiet tree-lined streets for the casual driver, nor a clearly planned well-thought-through inner-city zone where every traffic light is scrupulously regulated and every driver knows, to the second, how long it takes to get past the bus lane at rush hour. Busy enough to have a continual flow of shoppers, yet residential enough that no one has considered how best to make deliveries to the shops, Tooting Broadway features a continual parp of angry horns, the red lights of stuck trucks pulled onto a narrow pavement, the smell of petrol and thwarted drivers in search of the South Circular Road, who can't believe they're still not there. Averaging a hundred yards every four minutes at the main crossroads, even the most phlegmatic drivers find themselves getting frustrated.

So, when a single-decker red bus to St Andrew's Church, Streatham decided spontaneously to lurch out of the bus lane, shove its way through the opposing traffic with the crunch of wing mirrors and a screech of torn metal, before ploughing nose first through the glass front of Edna's Tanning and Beauty Salon and into the backs of the builders standing inside, the initial reaction of Tooting Broadway was one of rage and disbelief at the selfishness of the bastard who'd gone so wildly out of his way to make a difficult journey that much worse. Just how the bus got itself through the window of Edna's when its driver was standing arguing on the kerbside with a black-clad auburn-haired woman about acceptable levels of hygiene within his vehicle was a question to be asked only some considerable time later.

Glass flew.

The glass was of two kinds. The first was in deadly little pieces, a razored snowfall as the plate glass of the shopfront embedded itself in floor, ceiling, walls – anything, hard or soft, that got in its way. The second comprised the finely coated sheets that exploded out from the windscreen and side windows of the vehicle as it ploughed through the front of the building, the top of the red bus collapsing in on itself and forcing the metal struts that supported it to bulge and shear outwards. Sharon was on the floor, her hands wrapped over her head, knees up to her chin, and it was probably this, she reflected later, that prevented the railings from the pavement outside, torn up by the bus as it swung into its final charge, from ripping her head off as they flew into the room.

As the glass stopped falling, black smoke poured from the grille of the crippled bus and a little engine noise went

whumph
whumph
whumph

inside the remnants of the bus, something trying to turn against cogs that were no longer there.

Sharon raised her head, very slowly, feeling glass tumble from her back like gravel, clattering where it fell.

whumph
whumph
whumph

She looked up a little further and a pair of eyes stared back at her. They were pale blue, set in a great round face topped with pale blond hair: one of the four builders, in his torn fluorescent jacket, had been hit directly by the bus. His back had been snapped in two, his legs bent into triangles, his neck twisted so that now his face was turned fully backwards at her. Splinters of glass were embedded in the skin of his face like the vengeance of a roadkill hedgehog. His lips moved, trying to form a word.

"Ah . . . ahh . . . arses," he whispered.

For a second nothing happened. Then the builder half-closed his eyes, gave a little grunt and turned his head, snapping his own neck back into alignment. There was the sharp snicker-snack of vertebrae scraping against each other, the click of cartilage. Then the glass that had embedded itself in his face began to slip out, pushed away by the flesh knitting back together, thin lines of blood running down his skin as fibres joined and muscle thickened, reconnecting together without even the white trace of a scar.

Sharon felt a sound pass up from her throat that might, under different circumstances, have been a curse. Then a flash of white moved on the edge of her vision. Glancing round, she thought she saw Dez standing by the door, microphone in hand, making furious gestures that might, perhaps, be an exhortation to run.

She groaned, and crawled onto her hands and knees even as the builder in front of her gave another grunt and swung his left leg up and round, the joint snapping loudly back into place beneath his thigh. Two others were on the floor, healing from their injuries at the same speed as their companion; a fourth had been flung through the windscreen of the bus, and was folded round a bent rail inside it like a towel on a drying rack. Edna lay across the broken altar, largely untouched by the debris of the impact. She had frozen in panic like a rabbit, one foot no more than three inches from the nose of the bus itself. Sharon scrambled to where Edna lay, grabbed her by the shoulder and hissed, "Time to go!"

Edna responded with the empty stare of a woman whose mind no longer wanted anything to do with her own senses.

Sharon shook her. "Oi! Time to bloody go!" She hauled Edna to her feet and shoved her towards the door. Edna staggered a few paces, looked down, saw the builders, looked up and ran. Sharon turned and saw Kevin struggling to his feet, shaking glass from his hair, then staring at his hands with a gaping look of horror.

"Oh, my *God*!" he wailed, observing a neat tear through the palm of his left hand. "I need a sterile wipe!"

"Not now," hissed Sharon, shoving him towards the shattered wall behind the bus.

"But *infection!*" he moaned.

"Or death?" Sharon gestured back at the room. One of the four builders was halfway onto his feet, rolling his shoulder back into place and turning to focus, for the first time, on Sharon. His face twisted with hatred and contempt; and even Kevin, holding his bloody hand aloft like a rescued puppy in a flood, gave a whimper and scrambled for the broken wall.

Sharon paused. Fumbling in the debris, she found her bag, half-buried beneath the remnants of a porcelain sink ripped from the wall. Water gushed from the pipe into the dust-filled petrol-stinking gloom. She wrapped the strap round her fist and even as the first builder reached out at her, she swung the bag with all her might, hitting him in the face. He staggered back, surprised.

"N-not . . ." he stammered.

". . . how . . ." whimpered another from the floor.

". . . babes . . ." croaked the one still struggling to snap his spine back into alignment from where he'd wrapped it round a rail inside the bus.

". . . fight," offered the last, this one right by Sharon's feet.

"Screw that!" she retorted and drove her heel as hard as she could into the belly of the builder at her feet. "Rhys! Where the bloody hell are you?"

A feeble groan, a suggestion of dusty ginger hair. Rhys had ended up submerged in an ocean of debris. Torn cushions, shattered furniture and broken glass had fallen around him and over him, so now, as he tried to free himself, his legs slipped and his arms flailed in vain. Sharon hissed with frustration, stumbled towards him, grabbed Rhys by his wrist and hauled, and shifted.

The grey shimmer of invisibility fell over them, sounds deforming, shadows stretching. The change was fast, much faster than Sharon had done it before. A cold weight settled in her belly, and bile rose at the back of her throat. This time she didn't even know what she was doing, nor how she was doing it, only that it had to be done. Rhys's mouth was quivering, but he struggled up obediently as she pulled.

She shoved him towards the smashed remains of the exit, glanced back and saw the claws.

Sharon hadn't known anyone could move so fast. But there he was, Mr Ruislip, skin billowing off him like a warrior's banner, eyes burning and bloody, fingers turned to claws, claws turned to black. He rose up from the shattered remains of the Friendlies' altar like a vortex from a raging sea and lashed out, his face twisted in rage and hate. Sharon recoiled and heard a sharp tearing, then a little, bewildered "Oh."

Blood spangled the grey world like fireworks in a darkened night. She looked down at herself in panic, saw Mr Ruislip's face leer with satisfaction as he examined his crimson-stained claws, and then realised she wasn't actually bleeding.

Rhys swayed.

"I . . . " he began, and Mr Ruislip lashed out again. Sharon grabbed Rhys by the shoulders and dragged him away even as she fell back, the claws tearing the air overhead. Mr Ruislip's mouth parted in a wide O of laughter; but the sound in that shadow place was a hunting cry, a piercing animal call that deformed the air and made the ghosts of things unseen crawl away. Sharon could hear her phone ringing again somewhere in the concrete dust and torn-up metal. She dragged Rhys with one hand and scooped up the phone with the other, dropping deep and fast into the spirit walk, so that the walls bled the whispers of old memories, and the ghosts of the Friendlies gathered round the flickering lights that hovered above the shattered altar. The bus was sticky with dirt and oil, faces moving impossibly under its internal light, two-dimensional shadows pressing against the scarred glass. Beneath her feet the floor was sticky; she could feel things move in the wet concrete, heard a *pop-pop-pop* that might, just might, have been the sound of air leaving Derek's lungs as the floor swallowed him up.

She reached the street door, and Dez was there, gesticulating and shrieking, "Oh my God oh my God oh my God!"

When, she wondered, but when did spirit guides get so useless?

The floor shuddered, sudden and hard. It wasn't the ghost-shudder of things unseen, but real, a jerk in reality. Sharon reached towards the nearest solid object – as it happened, the side of the still-ticking bus – for support. She felt the ground crack beneath her, heard Rhys cry out in alarm, and leapt aside as a spike of metal, rusted and shedding dust, stabbed upwards where she'd just been.

She looked back; three of the builders were on their feet and the fourth was staggering up. Their faces were furious – the same furious expression on four furious faces. They raised their hands as one and, as they did, the floor cracked and split open. Foundation spikes of metal and twists of torn black piping lashed up into the air around them. In the street outside, car alarms wailed as the road began to crack, mains water fountained up, sparks snapped from cables overhead, and dark fault lines opened between gaps in the paving stones. Kevin, trying to support Edna without unnecessary physical contact, ducked instinctively as security alarms began wailing in response to cracks surging through the walls of nearby buildings.

Another lurch: the concrete beneath Sharon's feet was beginning to liquefy, acquiring the texture now of a mattress, now of a swamp, sucking at her and pulling her in. Rhys was pale and shaking and too frightened to scream, and as she looked over her shoulder through the grey half-light of the spirit walk, she saw the four builders wearing their cloaks of nothingness, and Mr Ruislip the wendigo whose laugh was a hunting cry and whose face was split in a fanged grin of ecstasy.

The phone in her hand stopped ringing. She groaned and tried to pull herself up as the floor became grey quicksand, tried to spread her weight without letting go of Rhys, tried to heave herself up by the twisted remains of the single-decker bus, but it too was shrinking, its tyres popping loudly as the growing pressure of the wet concrete caused them to burst. The phone rang again in merry insistence as the pavement outside spat sudden blue flame at the rupturing of a gas pipe and drivers stalled in the middle of the street began to abandon their vehicles, racing for safety, wherever that might be.

Somehow her thumb found the answer button. And there it was again, the bright brisk voice of the man called Matthew, the Midnight Mayor. "Hi there!" it exclaimed. "I have a question for you. When you walk through walls, are *you* the ethereal one, or is it the architecture? Something to consider."

So saying, he hung up, perhaps sensing the torrent of abuse about to head his way.

Sharon was up to her knees in concrete now and gasped as something soft brushed against her ankle inside the liquid floor. How long, she wondered, did it take human flesh to decay in such conditions? Was Derek still down there, or had he become just a bone-filled hole? She bit back on an exclamation as another shudder of the building pulled her lower, submerged to her thighs. Next to her, Rhys was clutching at his side, already up to his hips in cement, blood seeping through his fingers from a tear in his flesh. The four builders were laughing now, four killers in invisible fluorescent jackets and one wendigo, laughing at the remains of the Friendlies' temple, at the shattered altar and broken glass, at the place where Derek the Friendly had been sucked down to die, at where Sharon and Rhys would be sucked down to die; and they were enjoying it, the bastards were *enjoying* it and . . .

"Actually, it is something to think about, isn't it?" mused Dez.

Sharon looked up, and Dez, her panicking spirit guide in his immaculate white suit, was standing exactly in the place where the wall had been, one foot in the street, one in the self-collapsing, imploding remains of the Friendlies' temple. Half in this world, half in the next. The concrete slipped up to her waist, and she looked and saw Rhys struggling to breathe against the weight of it pressing on his ribs, his features rigid with the effort of staying brave, and her face tightened. Her fingers grasped harder around his arm, and she looked back at Dez and the world beyond and this . . . place—

This temple.

It wasn't like the dead places where the spirits had gone. Sure, Edna's Tanning and Beauty Salon hadn't been much to write home about, but the Friendlies had come here and made it their own, and now the walls were watching, the air hummed with voices and memories, the floor was pressed flat with a thousand footsteps, and though the altar had been smashed, the echoes of everything it had been remained, were still real and bright and defiant.

When you walk through walls, are *you* the ethereal one, or is it the architecture?

She could hear them, even now, the prayers of the Friendlies, sent up from this shattered room. *Let me find . . . Grant me strength . . . Give me peace . . . Be not alone . . .*

She bent forward over the collapsing wet floor, turned her face towards Rhys and smiled. He tried to smile back, shaking with the effort. Her fingers tightened on his arm until she could feel the bone beneath the skin, and, half-closing her eyes, she found the voices were louder, tumbling like dust from the walls.

She pulled and barely moved an inch, but it was enough – it was motion – and she pulled again and the world moved with her, darkening as the shadows grew deeper, as the memories thickened and reality seemed thin and far away. Beyond the shattered window of the shop, the past flickered over the street, mingling with the present. Trees sprouted and grew and were felled; cobbles were laid and tarmacked over; shop signs melted in and out of each other as old owners moved on and heralded new; and it was real, it was all real, all here, just waiting to be seen, half-hidden. Somewhere, somewhen, the floor beneath her feet was solid, and she pushed against it and it was real, pushing right back. She heaved herself up as around her the shop was destroyed and rebuilt and destroyed again a dozen times, and reality was far, far away. Her breath fizzled on the air and there was Derek of the Friendlies laying candles on the altar and Edna trimming hair, a long time ago and far, far away. Her arms seemed vast, hands belonging to someone else, skin icy; and as she dragged Rhys onto his feet she saw Dez again, beckoning from somewhere far, far away; and she tried to move towards him, and the world bloomed and shrunk, opened and closed around her, past and present competing for attention all at once. She tried to draw down breath and the air was thin, as if the entire atmosphere was composed of someone else's exhalations. Rhys's lips were turning blue, and as she tugged him she could feel the itching in his throat, the burning in his eyes, the pain in his nose, the sickness in his belly, the shame in his mind, and the blood seeping down his side and staining the top of his trousers sticky-black.

Another step, and in some place, some time, there was a broken bus between her and the way out, but not *this* here, not *this* now. Another step and Rhys tried to cry out and couldn't. The sound was snatched away before it could even form, sucked into the whirlwind. A flash of white, Dez calling from beyond the glass; a howling somewhere far off as Mr Ruislip stretched his claws; the slow bubbling of Derek's breath as it was squeezed from his lungs; a burning in Sharon's palm where somehow the Midnight Mayor had left his mark without bothering to ask her permission, and her face deepened into a scowl and she pulled Rhys harder, dragging him through the shattered place where once there had been a window and now there was broken glass, and into the street beyond.

It was a step too far. The roaring of the shadows and the weight of air slammed into her and knocked her nearly to her knees, smacking the pair of them back into the wailing, cracking, spinning real world. Dropping Rhys as she fell, she landed on paving stones where dust danced like oil in a pan, sand in an earthquake. She looked back and heard the hunting cry of Mr Ruislip, saw the ceiling of Edna's salon begin to sag as its walls gave out, saw the flash of a yellow fluorescent jacket as the builders tore a passage through the walls. Groaning with the effort, she caught Rhys by the scruff of the neck, pulled him up and ran.

Chapter 53

Matthew

So I think I might be dead.

That's not the problem though. I mean, okay, it's not great but actually we're dealing with it, you know? We're dealing with it and it could have been much, much worse. There could have been hair loss, there could have been skin disease, biological decay, bad breath – I know how lucky I got.

The thing is, the issue – I think we're supposed to say it's an issue these days – the issue is, I'm not sure I'm human any more. I'm not sure I can remember what being human means. If it's two arms, two legs, a head and all sorts of bits in between, then that's okay: so far so good. Is it a feeling? Is there an easy formula for humanity – is it loss, or hope, or guilt, or grief, or joy, or pain? Is it hunger or thirst? Is it a longing, a desiring, an imagining of things which could be desired, a wondering of what is to come? Is that it? There was a time before, when these things seemed simple. And now . . . we are become so much more. We are sorcerer, we are Midnight Mayor, we are electric angel, we are greater than the world around us and for all this we are . . .

Unique.

Special.

Alone.

Is that what it means to be human?

Chapter 54

Healthy Body, Healthy Mind

Sharon ran.

She ran until the ground stopped splitting, the wires stopped spitting, the water stopped flowing up from beneath her feet, the car alarms stopped wailing, the windows stopped cracking and the world was at last a solid thing of neat little houses, empty bus stops and the distant wailing of sirens.

Somehow Rhys had managed to run with her, stumbling through the night-time streets of Tooting, all tidy little rows of tidy little houses largely inhabited by people with an appreciation of patios. She hadn't attempted the spirit walk, much less a spirit run, but a stagger through the solid reality of London, no shadows in the walls nor whisperings in the street, just the racing of her own heart as she and Rhys fled the wrecked remnants of the Friendlies' temple. Kevin had scampered after them with a cry of "Don't forget me!" pausing on each street corner to hop up and down with urgency as Edna, wheezing and holding her sides, brought up the rear.

The four of them had united, too breathless to speak, on the edge of a crooked green park with inexplicable apparatus for children to have fun on, if they could solve the intellectual challenge of how.

Kevin, though the least winded, swayed with incredulity and indignation for a good three minutes while the others gasped their way towards normality, before he threw up his hands and wailed, "What the fuck?!" He sagged against the iron railings of the park, his face as morose as his body language.

Edna managed to say, "Are . . . Are they . . . Are they going to . . . follow?"

"I guess we'd know by now," panted Sharon. "Bloody hell, I need to do a sport or something."

Rhys didn't speak. His face was ash-grey and, as Sharon turned to look at him, his gaze drifted down to where his hand was still pressed against his side, fingers red with blood.

"Oh," he whimpered. Then added "Sorry," and fell, slowly and gently, to the ground.

Sharon caught his shoulders before his head could slam into the pavement. "Oh, my God!" wailed Kevin. "There's dirt everywhere and he's bleeding!"

"I'll call an ambulance," stammered Edna. But Sharon interrupted before the older woman could move.

"How are we going to explain this to anyone?"

"But what if there's digestive fluids in the blood?" demanded Kevin. "That's so gross."

Sharon looked into Rhys' face. His eyes were half-open, staring at a distant nothing; his lips tried to move but produced no words. She peeled away the shirt around his side and there were two marks gouged in his skin, the marks of animal claws, the blood too thick and black for her to see anything clearly.

Edna didn't move; Kevin wavered, eyes transfixed by the blood seeping through Sharon's hands. "Rhys?" she whispered. His eyes flickered. "Oi! Rhys!" Louder, more urgent. "Hey, hay-fever-nut druid!" she shouted, loud enough to send his eyelids quivering back up, whites rolling beneath. "Oi, you!" she repeated, shaking him by the shoulder. "You don't bloody go nowhere, you hear? You stay with me."

She turned to the others. "There's a number on my phone," she said, pressing down gingerly against the wound in Rhys's side. "Sammy the Elbow. Call him."

Chapter 55

Dr Seah

Hi there. So yeah, I'm Dr Seah. You'd think I'd get bored saying that but, actually, it took like, seven years to get the Doctor part, so really I'm kinda cool with it. Thankfully I don't want to be a surgeon, because then I'd be a Mister, only obviously I'm a Miss; but you don't really hear about Miss Surgeon Seah, do you, so I'd probably still be a Mister anyway, which would cause a lot of confusion and just not be groovy. But yeah, I guess the point is I'm a doctor and that's pretty fucking awesome.

I don't have any problems, really. I mean, not so you'd notice. I do a lot of baking. I mean, some people say that's because of the rage – like I get pretty annoyed when you're like, "Could you do this, please?" and the nurse is all like, "It's a rabid banshee, no way am I taking swabs" and I'm like, "It's a nice rabid banshee" and then nothing gets done. So yeah, I guess you could say that gets me a bit frustrated. Or when I go out for an evening with my mates and then they're all "So, I've got this curse on me" and I'm like, "Have you tried aqueous cream" and they're like, "Can I show you?" and I'm like, "Guys, this is my only night off, and I get that your curse is like, a problem and that, but, seriously, I'm trying to enjoy a mojito and there are other people here, and then there are these guys and . . ."

Anyway. Like I said. Sometimes I get annoyed. It's not easy working for the NHS, and I guess you could say that baking just helps keep things in perspective.

I'm going to get a piping bag for Christmas.

I really think it'll help with the cupcakes.

Chapter 56

A Journey of a Thousand Miles Begins With a Single Step

Sammy came in a van.

The quickness with which he arrived suggested he hadn't been far away to begin with.

The van was driven by a familiar face.

Sharon said, "Ms . . . Somchit?"

Five foot two, black hair, black jacket, black trousers, black shoes, Ms Somchit exuded friendly unstoppability as she clambered out of the blue Transit van and inspected Rhys. They'd dragged him up onto a park bench, where he lay, head in Edna's lap, Kevin keeping a hygienic distance.

Ms Somchit, who had attended the first meeting of Magicals Anonymous and offered advice on Council Tax, beamed.

"Hello, dear," she exclaimed, easing back the sodden mess of shirt pressed to Rhys's side. "Sammy said you might need a lift."

Sammy the Elbow hopped down from the passenger side of the van, unimpressed by the distance he had to go from vehicle to earth comparative with the length of his knobbly grey legs. He waddled over to Rhys, peered at the bloody mess, sniffed and exclaimed, "Wendigos. Amateurs."

"He needs a hospital," whispered Edna.

"He needs a sterile controlled environment staffed by qualified professionals!" added Kevin, his voice a fraught almost-shriek.

"*We* need help," corrected Sharon, "and you," a finger stabbed towards Sammy's face, "are gonna give it right bloody now."

The back of the Transit van smelt of rubber and wet dog.

Kevin exclaimed "Oh, God, that is so—"

"Can it, vampy," snapped Sammy, "or I'll go garlic on you."

Edna, Kevin and Rhys rode in the back, with Rhys held steady by Edna at his head and Kevin, after two pairs of latex gloves and a sterile scrub, at his feet. Ms Somchit drove the van with the grace of a runaway train, cheerfully unaware of lesser beings that might get in the way.

Sammy and Sharon sat beside her, and Sharon seethed.

She seethed through the backstreets of Tooting and onto the main road to Balham.

She seethed past Wandsworth Common and beneath the railway lines that congregated round Clapham Junction. She seethed towards Battersea, until at last Sammy exploded:

"Bloody hell, can you sulk or what?"

Sharon's fist slammed into the dashboard, hard enough to make its dials jump. "I," she declared, each word falling hard and slow, "have been used."

An embarrassed silence.

"All this . . . all this teaching me to be a shaman, Midnight Mayor, fate of the city crap – you're just using me. The Midnight Mayor potters around in the background and I get to deal with the shit. And you know what? All that'd be okay – I mean crap but okay – because it's not like I had much of a clue what to do with a homework assignment which was 'Save the city', but!" Her fist slammed into the dashboard again, making even Ms Somchit wince. "But now Rhys is bloody bleeding back there and there's a guy who's been buried alive and we could've bloody died so you –" Sammy had the good grace to shy away from Sharon " – you are gonna tell me what the hell is going on, right bloody now! And no cryptic shit, because I've had it up to here with cryptic shit. And no calling me soggy-brains, because you're basically five parts nasal hair to one part mug, and I won't be having it any more!"

Sammy looked at Ms Somchit. Ms Somchit found herself very interested in the middle of the road. Sammy rolled his eyes – an impressive
deed considering the eye-to-skull ratio the little goblin could achieve.

"Okay," he grumbled. "So maybe we've been a little . . . you know . . .
thin on some stuff, okay? But that's only because we thought you'd be
bright enough to work it out."

"Who's 'we'?" demanded Sharon.

"The Midnight Mayor, course!" exclaimed Sammy. "The protector
of the city and all that. Ms Somchit here is an Alderman what works
for him."

"Hello there," sang out Ms Somchit from behind the wheel.

"So you what . . . you came to Magicals Anonymous to spy on us, is
that it?"

"No!" Ms Somchit insisted. "I mean of course I did, *naturally* I did,
because no one in the office could believe anyone would do something
quite as . . . remarkable as organise a society for the magically confused.
And you know, I really do think it's an excellent thing you're doing, Ms
Li, and if the entire welfare of the city wasn't under direct and immediate threat, I would be applauding your efforts and possibly providing
fragrant herbal tea."

"What about you?" said Sharon, glowering at Sammy. "Why'd you
come to the coffee shop? Why'd you decide to teach me?"

Sammy suppressed a groan with the infinite patience of the learned
dealing with the naive. "Because," he said, "you're a shaman and they're
bloody hard to find. And I'm bored with there being so many amateurs
out there who think they can do it 'in their spare time', because that is
shit and it leads to shoddy work and I can't be having that, no thank
you. Also," he added, "because the Midnight Mayor asked me and I'm
just a sucker for toothpaste."

Chapter 57

If at First You Don't Succeed . . .

A moment to consider the fate of Constable Hurst.

A fairly affable policeman by the standards of the area, he was one of the few local bobbies who believed, in the face of all evidence to the contrary, that good policing really did begin with the community. He gave directions to lost visitors, helped old ladies struggling with their shopping, was always firm but polite to the young vandals loitering outside Burger King and, whenever pursing a criminal in the execution of nefarious deeds, always attempted to maintain a calm composure and polite language when nicking the arsehole.

It was therefore unfortunate that he, that day, happened to be the first policeman to arrive at the scene of what had been Edna's Tanning and Beauty Salon in Tooting, in time to find the pavements thronging with a mixture of horrified and gleefully fascinated onlookers, traffic piled up, cars swerved and, to cap it all off, a bus rammed through the front windows of the now shattered temple. Quite how the bus had achieved this was a mystery, since no one remembered seeing a driver either behind the wheel or leaving the vehicle after the event. But this was surely a question that CID would answer, whereas a junior officer like himself was merely there to keep things under control.

"Is anyone in there?" he demanded of the assembled crowd. "Is anyone left inside the building?"

The crowd responded with shrugs and grunts. Then the owner of the jewellery shop across the street stepped forward with a cry of, "I think I saw a man go inside and . . ." But he hesitated. His mouth had wanted to say, "and some builders." However, as he thought it over and tried to pin down the memory of four figures clad in fluorescent jackets, he drew a blank. It wasn't that he lacked some kind of recollection, but rather as if his thoughts slid over the memory like spilt liquid over marble. His eyes had seen, but his brain had failed to perceive.

" . . . I think I saw some people come out," he concluded.

"All of them?"

"I don't know."

Constable Hurst puffed in frustration, gestured at the crowd to stay back and, with a cry of "I'm going in!", plunged through the torn-up window. He hopped over twisted metal and a shattered sink, and edged along the side of the bus, rapping against the still-hot metal and calling out, "Anyone here? Anyone alive?" He felt a mixture of foolishness and immense professional pride as he went, before the sheered edge of a wheel of the bus caught his trouser leg and tore a great ragged slice out of his best uniform from the ankle to the knee. He swore, reaching down to inspect the damage, and as he did felt something move by his ear. His head snapped up, breath drawn in sharply, torn trousers forgotten and for a moment thought he'd seen . . .

. . . but no.

The idea was absurd.

What would a builder, bum hanging out of his trousers, fluorescent jacket torn and grubby, face like a flattened breeze block, be doing here? Why had the idea even occurred to him?

"Arses," whispered a voice, and he jumped, and felt a fool for jumping at nothing.

"Tits," concurred another, and Constable Hurst half-closed his eyes and reflected that this was not how he had imagined he'd behave when tested, not at all, not by imagining things or by seeing . . .

"Is this rage?"

His eyes flew open. The voice was real, it had to be real, and there was the speaker: a man, thin hair, pale skin, unnaturally pale, a clean suit – how could clothes be so clean in this place of shattered concrete and dust? Constable Hurst opened his dry mouth to stammer, "Are you okay, sir?" but the words didn't come; a mumble of not-noises passed his lips and he realised he was afraid, and didn't know why.

"I am experiencing," explained the man in the perfect suit, brushing the thinnest veil of powder from his sleeve, and there was something wrong with his hands, Constable Hurst noticed, something wrong with the man's hands – fingers too long, too bent, too . . .

. . . clawed?

"I am experiencing," repeated the man, as one examining his own feelings with extreme caution, "a peculiar physiological heat which I must assume to be a reaction to some external trigger. How novel. Is it correct to say that one emotion may lead to another? May frustration, for example, be a trigger for anger, and anger of itself then escalate, as though feeding on its own situation, to fury? What an evolutionarily unsound feedback system, and yet I," he smiled and his teeth were too small, shark points in his thin mouth, "appear to have – why yes, I would say it is so! – appear to have all the features that one might classify as rage. To whit, the urge to tear. The urge to fight. The urge to drink blood and gouge the bodies of my enemies in two – or shall I say twain? Twain has an old-fashioned ring about it, though whether that implies a linguistic superiority I cannot say."

His eyes drifted up from his sleeve and met those of Constable Hurst, and for a moment the unfortunate policeman saw not merely what was there to be seen, but also what was beneath, and his mouth opened to shout a warning, and his fingers fumbled at the pouches on his belt for a weapon, his baton, his radio, anything, anything at all to stop the gaze of this man in a suit, the not-man in his disguise of a suit.

Too late.

Teeth parted.

Fingers stretched.

There was a moment of uncertainty as what was seen to be and what was actually the case met and clashed. For just a moment fingers were claws, and teeth were fangs, and Mr Ruislip's suit was no more and no less than the thin illusionary disguise that covered his flayed form as he leapt, tongue flicking at the air, straight for the hot pulsing veins of Constable Hurst's throat.

Some few minutes later someone said:

"Nasty cut, that."

"PC Plod."

"Pigs!"

"Cozzer."

A hand wipes away blood.

A tie is straightened.

A handkerchief mops away the remnant of flesh clinging to a pair of thin grey lips.

"Gentlemen," murmurs Mr Ruislip, "I do apologise for my deviation into emotionally-led behaviour. It will not happen again. In the meantime ..." the handkerchief, stained scarlet, is folded away " ... find the shaman and her friends, and kill them for me, if you would be so kind? If you would also dispatch the Midnight Mayor, preferably tearing him limb from limb, and possibly torching any remaining temples of the Friendlies, ideally with their members inside, it would be of great benefit to my composure."

Chapter 58

A Friend In Need Is a Friend Indeed

A moment to consider the Midnight Mayor.

He has not, contrary to popular opinion, vanished.

He did, he must admit, fail to set up an email auto-reply on his system. But he has other things on his mind.

"Hello, are you Sally?"

Good evening, that is correct. May I help you?

"My name's Matthew Swift, I'm the Midnight Mayor. May I say I love what you've done with this place."

Thank you. It took me a while to find an appropriate paint that would stick to the internal tiling, but I now believe I have achieved the perfect mix.

"Is this one . . . ?"

I call it "Homage to an abandoned gasworks, in the style of Monet".

"It's nice."

I'm glad you think so. Forgive my bluntness, but was there something you needed?

"You know, it's funny you should say that."

I merely ask, as not many people come to see banshees for social purposes.

"But you seem charming!"

Thank you. Are you interested in modern art?

"I'm sure I would be if I had the time. As it is, I do have this little problem ..."

Chapter 59

Of Wise Men and Healers

The van stopped in Battersea, just south of the river.

A place where men who dreamed of apartments with glass balconies overlooking the waters of the Thames had competed with others who pictured white-tiled shopping estates and soft-seated cinema complexes, who had in turn fallen foul of the environmentalists who in turn had waged bitter war on the local council officers who saw in this empty patch of nothing a golden opportunity to build their latest recycling centre. Between all these competing forces, the net result had been nothing. Nothing had been done, and nothing had changed.

A hoarding of blue plywood fenced off a stretch of the river from joggers, dog walkers and tourists. To the west, Battersea Power Station was a monument to architectural insecurity; on the far bank, young trees sat beneath new lights framed by towering apartments for wealthy young couples who knew that there was yet more wealth to come. Trains spat blue-white sparks into the night as they rattled across the bridge to Victoria; empty freight containers huddled beneath silent cranes whose wires hadn't shifted more than a few inches in a strong wind for many years. The water of the river was silent against the embankment, the padlocks were rusted; the wind was beaten off by the plywood walls.

Only one light glowed, shining tungsten-yellow behind the half-open door of an ancient white freight container with the words OFFICE SUPPLIES EXPRESS stencilled on the side.

Ms Somchit parked the van with its rear doors facing this light, then she, Edna and Kevin manoeuvred Rhys towards it. His eyes were closed, his body a sack to be dragged by its dangling parts. Sammy hopped from foot to foot muttering, "Come on, come on, put some backbone into it!" while the three of them sweated and strained.

Sharon opened the door to the glowing container as they approached and heard a voice exclaim, "You know, I was in the middle of making a cake?"

She looked inside.

A metal wheeled stretcher, a bright bulb hanging from the ceiling, a white locked filing cabinet, a white locked cupboard. A high wooden stool and, perched on top of it like a proud parrot on its stand, a woman. Her skin was tea-coloured after a respectable dose of milk; her hair was black, cut to a short bob; her legs dangled from a smart black skirt, and as she swung them to and fro her sturdy-heeled black shoes flapped and flopped against her heels. Only a white coat with a row of coloured biros in its pocket suggested that this woman might be what she was – a doctor.

Rhys was manhandled onto the stretcher trolley. The woman tutted, shooed his sweating companions away, leaned over and said, "Now, who's been playing silly buggers with a wendigo?"

Kevin raised one gloved and bloody hand. "Excuse me," he ventured, "but I have been in like, contact with all sorts of bodily fluids this evening and *none* of them have been screened and I was wondering if you could like, test me?"

"Test you? For what?" asked the doctor.

"Um ... everything?"

The doctor lowered her head and looked up into Kevin's eyes. "Sweetie," she said, "I don't want to sound dismissive or anything here, but you're the walking dead. Deal with it." She paused, and added, "Wow! That was a bit dismissive wasn't it? I surprised myself – was anyone else surprised by that?"

Sharon felt a tug on her sleeve. "Oi," said Sammy. "Soggy-brains. Wanna talk?"

Chapter 60

Honesty Is the Best Path to Friendship

They walked along the river. Neither Sammy nor Sharon felt the urge to move in the shadows, so they simply walked along the waterfront, goblin and shaman, side by side through the night.

"Dr Seah's okay," said Sammy. "Lotsa stupid doctors out there, but she's good. Your druid mate will be fine."

"I don't get this." Sharon's voice wasn't angry or frightened, just the dead flat of fact. "I don't get what this is about."

Sammy sighed, louder than he needed.

"Politics," he explained. "Humans and their politics – why they just can't disembowel each other with the sharpened teeth of the varg like civilised people, I will never suss."

"Tell me," snapped Sharon, "about the politics."

"It's the Midnight Mayor." Sammy kicked a stone as they walked, watched it bounce into the water with a heavy plop. "He's got all this politics on his hands. So, a while back – months back – things start happening. Nasties start crawling out of places where nasties shouldn't have been. Signs have been there a while – spectres in the street, Blackout possessing the walking dead, death of cities summoned by some big-mouthed kid – these things happen, but lately they've happened too easy.

"And the Mayor, he's thinks all this looks bad, which is obvious to anyone with even minor skills, so he starts investigating. He talks to wizards and witches, seers and alchemists what stink of rotting eggs, and finally gets the brains on him to come talk to a shaman – talk to me. And I put him straight. It's the spirits of the city, I say, those shadows on the wall and voices in the stone – them you don't see because you're too thick to see but which you know are always there.

"Only they ain't there, are they? Because they're vanishing. Being pulled out of the buildings, and where they were, now there's gaps. Hollowness, emptiness, and things are . . . coming through. Getting in through the place where these voices oughtta have been. And Greydawn's gone, our Lady of 4 a.m., she who guards the wall. And with her gone, who knows what shit is gonna start coming through the holes in the city walls?"

Sharon remembered City Road, heard the howling of a dog, saw the claws of a dragon.

"There's a dog," she breathed. "It has blood in its fur, and its footsteps burn the earth."

"Not a dog, not *a* dog!" declared Sammy. "*The* Dog! Greydawn's pet, her companion! He's only meant to exist in the shadows, in nightmares and memories. But Greydawn's gone and the gates are open, so now he comes here, he hunts in the city at night, looking for his mistress. And Matthew Swift is a sorcerer, which makes him great at blowing things up but shit at dealing with the stuff of dreams, and Dog *is* the stuff of dreams. He's shadows and blood, and the Midnight Mayor ain't gonna fix that. You need a shaman, someone who can walk the spirit walk, deal with this sorta shit."

"So why can't you?" demanded Sharon. "Why do you need me?"

"Racist bastards," spat Sammy. "I may be the second greatest shaman ever, but the wankers don't talk to me. They shout 'Goblin' and they hide, and sure, I can dream-walk the brains out of a baboon, but that don't mean shit when all you want is a good lawyer and a pack of toothpaste. He needed someone human, someone who could get into places, no history or baggage or that. Swift was like 'Come on, Sammy, help me out' and I was like 'You can't force this stuff; if there's a shaman out there then he's gotta find his own way.' And then look at you! You bloody turn up doing the shaman thing. And Swift is impressed, but I say, 'Have you seen her?' and he has, but seems to think this is a good thing – a good thing that the new shaman is a girl-thing with stupid hair."

"Don't you even *think* about dissing my hair," growled Sharon. "You look like a used vacuum-cleaner bag; don't you *ever* comment on my style."

Sammy grunted, possibly in acquiescence.

"Anyway, it's clear we need a shaman, and someone who's not got ... stuff behind her, so yeah, I teach you. Because you're a shaman and you need to be taught. And because the walls are down and you gotta fix it. So lump it, okay?"

Sharon bowed her head, staring at the ground. Grass was trying to poke up between cracks in the concrete. A small pyre of broken bottles and crumpled cans marked the place where kids sometimes came to smoke, and drink forbidden drinks.

She said, "What do you mean I was 'doing the shaman thing'? Everyone keeps saying that, but what does it mean?"

"You were leading your tribe!" exclaimed Sammy impatiently. "That's what shamans do!"

"That's bollocks. I don't have a tribe; I wasn't leading nothing. It's not ..." Her voice trailed off. "Oh my God," she breathed. "You don't mean ... But that's not how it was meant to work!"

"Magicals Anonymous is a bloody stupid idea," declared Sammy. "But you started it and you brought people together and you became the leader of the tribe. With Facebook," he added in disgust. "You used Facebook to lead your tribe, which I think is just bad kudos, but okay. So the Midnight Mayor goes 'Hey hey, this looks kinda weird' and he sends Ms Somchit down to keep an eye on it and Ms Somchit is all 'Whatcha know, there's a shaman there' and he's all 'Great, maybe she can find the missing spirits!' and next thing you know you've got running and shouting and all this bloody drama. In *Tooting*."

"Yes, but w-wait ..." Sharon stuttered, gesturing. "If the Midnight Mayor – if this Swift guy – wanted my help, why didn't he just ask? Why all this cryptic 'There's bad shit' shit? Because I gotta tell you that's rubbish and I can't be having it."

"Politics, I said, innit! The Midnight Mayor is a powerful guy. But you been to Burns and Stoke, right? You seen what they got? Their head honcho is a wendigo, which for you soggy ignorant thing makes him serious bad news! They've hired the four deadliest assassins the world has ever see—"

"The builders?"

"Yeah, the builders! Them against whom no lock can hold, the unseen ones, the forgotten faces, them!"

"They're the deadliest assassins ever?"

"You never find the corpses of them that they kill, and people never remember them. Cos you don't, do you? You never remember the guys in the fluorescent jackets. They'll turn the walls against you, the floor you stand on. Even the Midnight Mayor thinks twice before fighting them."

"But I still don't get—"

"He needed help. The Aldermen are meant to serve him, they're meant to be on his side, but he's got a dodgy history with them, and even magical protectors gotta eat. They gotta have cash, and offices, and paper clips and all that crap. And Burns and Stoke got themselves into the Aldermen's good books years before Swift came along. They bankroll the Aldermen. They're partners in everything the Aldermen do."

Sharon paused as the words sunk in. "You are bloody kidding me."

"You getting it yet, potato-head?"

"But that's stupid! If Burns and Stoke are run by a wendigo—"

"Racist?" suggested Sammy.

"It's not racism if he's a blood-obsessed torturing murderer!" she retorted. "I mean, I'm sure there are lots of very nice wendigos out there—"

"Hah!"

"—but the fact is that he wasn't very nice, and him being a blood-soaked monster of the night may be a contributing factor. I mean, I'm sorry, I know it's not politically correct to say that, but that's how I feel."

"You see why Swift had a few issues, right? He can't trust no one in his own office. Ms Somchit is one of *two* Aldermen he actually likes to talk to, and the other one is his PA or whatever the human job is what should be called the Hand. And the Midnight Mayor . . . It's not just one guy, it's an inheritance thingy. The Aldermen could turn on Swift and say he's not doing it right and kill him – well, try to kill him. I think it'd be even for the first few corpses, and I don't usually say that about people what take on the Aldermen. Anyway, and the power of the Midnight Mayor would just pass on to the next thick shit and he'd be dead. And it wouldn't be the first time the Aldermen had tried. Going against Burns and Stoke was a stupid idea, and he needed them that weren't part of the Aldermen to make it work. Needed another tribe, you see? He needed—"

"Magicals Anonymous," breathed Sharon. "They're my tribe."

No response.

"Well," she said at last.

And stopped.

"Okay," she added.

The river lapped against the embankment.

Then, "This shamaning thing isn't all how I thought it'd be."

Sammy grinned. "Don't give up the day job."

"It might be too late for that. Kinda think I got myself fired."

"Oh. Well, it was a stupid bloody job and you weren't no good at it anyway."

Sharon looked thoughtful.

Then she said, "No, wait, hold on! You said the Midnight Mayor couldn't go around obviously pissing people off! But he called me, back in Tooting! He called me and said 'Adopt the brace position' and then there was this bus which could have bloody killed me anyway. And I'm no Sherlock Holmes, but it was obvious it was him, and the wendigo guy was there and the four builders and . . ."

"He did screw up the discretion thing there, didn't he? Always thought he was crap at it."

"So what happens now?"

"I guess the Christmas bonus is out."

"Screw him," snapped Sharon. "If he was serious about this whole saving-the-city shit, then he'd have talked to me properly and skipped this politics stuff and . . . I dunno, bought me a posh meal and a bus pass or something. I mean, what happens to us now? The wendigo knows who I am. He must've seen me at the office, at Burns and Stoke; and the walls were screaming there, they were screaming, and I was gonna go in and do the shaman thing, whatever that is. But now . . ."

Sammy's too-large eyes glinted in the light off the river.

"There's this thing," he said, "what Greydawn says. Maybe 'says' ain't right. 'Says' is words and things – and she's not big on words. But there's this . . . notion, I s'pose you'd call it, that in the little hours of the night, when you're cold and lost and afraid and that, it's Greydawn what comes to you and puts her fingers through yours and says – only again, not so much with words – 'Do not be afraid. I am with you.' She's the one who tells us that we ain't alone. No one ain't never alone in a city."

"That's nice, isn't it?" said Sharon. "But it doesn't help me."

"Sure it does. Look at you! You got –" he ticked the points off on his fingertips "– druid—"

"An unconscious wounded druid!"

"—what'll be fine, for what he's worth! You got a high priestess of the Friendlies."

"Former owner of a beauty salon in Tooting," grumbled Sharon.

"Says the girl what can't make coffee for crap," the goblin retorted. "You got a vampire."

"An OCD vampire."

"A necromancer."

"With skincare issues."

"A banshee."

"With a fondness for modern art."

"The second greatest shaman who ever lived!"

"Yeah, who's got this thing for toothpaste and calls everyone 'soggy-brains'."

"You got – you *got*," declared Sammy, stamping a foot for emphasis, "you've got a *troll*."

"Gretel? Yeah, but Gretel is like . . . she's . . ." Sharon paused as thoughts slipped into the place where speech might have been unwise. "She's a kind of seven-foot wall of moving muscle, isn't she?"

Sammy beamed. "See? Told you it'd be all right."

Chapter 61

Gretel

I got a chameleon spell.

A witch from East Grinstead made it for me. She was very friendly; her name is Tabby. She lives in this bungalow off the A22, with furniture for all different sizes: little chairs for imps and big ones for me, which I thought was really nice of her. She said, "How can I help you today?" and I said, "I don't want people to see me," and she tutted and said, "Invisibility isn't all it's cracked up to be. You'll be lonely if you're invisible, and that's the longest way to a death that I know. How about more like a fashion rethink?" So she made me this chameleon spell, and now people see me, but not the real me. And that's lonely sometimes. But lots of times it's the best thing that ever happened.

I used to work at the Dartford Crossing – my whole clan; we try to keep the traditions alive, living under bridges and stuff. There's lots of different clans of troll; mine is the big kind. I got paid twelve pounds a night to scare the bad drivers – the ones who cut up the others or pushed in at the queues, because there's always queues at the Dartford Crossing. We'd hide under the bridge and then when they came along, the men in white vans and the speeding guys in little red sports cars, we'd leap out and we'd go "RAAARRRRGGGGHHHH!" and I think it was a public service we were doing. It was a living, at least.

But then, when there was really bad congestion, all the traffic would stop and we'd hide in the service tunnels – because there's the bridge at Dartford, and there's the tunnel. And I liked the bridge, but you know how it is, people get worried by trolls leaping out of the toll booths and that – but sometimes the traffic would get so bad that all the cars would turn off their engines and just sit there, windows open because it was hot. And there were these families, with kids in the back shouting. The mums would give their kids food to make them stop talking, and the smell was . . . It was . . .

My clan said it wasn't right to be interested in food, that a baked rat served on tyre rubber was all a sensible troll needed for good living. But I've got this good sense of smell. And the kids, they were eating . . . chocolate and crisps and apples and jam sandwiches, and jam-and-peanut-butter sandwiches, and sometimes there'd be salsa with the crisps, and Scotch eggs and pork pies, and hummus! Hummus with oil and hummus with chickpeas or onion, lemon and coriander, cumin on top, and these smells . . . There came a time when I couldn't eat rat any more. I just wanted . . . I wanted something more.

My clan said that getting the chameleon spell, trying to find a way to live with humans, learn how they lived, that was selling out. Betraying who I was, giving up my family, my traditions, my identity and everything. That I was becoming something else – something not wanted by anyone or anything, stuck in the middle.

They were wrong.

I was becoming me.

Chapter 62

Hell Is Other People

Rhys opened his eyes.

"Hi there! Do you know what the elastic limit is of the small intestine, for application to Hooke's law?"

Rhys closed his eyes again.

This was hell.

He'd always suspected he'd go to hell. As a child he'd spent time visiting his uncle's farm, and on the wall of the bathroom there'd been posters charting the virtuous way to heaven and the easy way to hell. Happy children holding the hands of their righteous parents had attended Sunday school, learned to sing together, prayed regularly, eaten well and eventually risen up a steep and thorny hill into glorious sunlight; while scruffy wretched children had travelled through licentiousness and vice, in plush railway carriages and over shining tracks, into the damned pit. As a seven-year-old boy sat on the toilet in the clean white bathroom, he hadn't know what licentiousness was, but he couldn't shake the feeling that, somehow, it meant him.

"How about the death of the female pope?" the voice went on. "Hell, you gotta know this one. What is the name of the old workhorse in George Orwell's *Animal Farm*?"

Rhys opened one gummy eyelid to double-check how his

presumably fiery surroundings could have manifested the cheerful voice that would ask such a question.

The gatekeeper of hell appeared to be an Asian woman. Straight black hair cut into a bob of subtle angles and infinite bounce, a long white coat, sensible black trousers and boots that occupied the fine line where sensible became silly. And, as if you might not get the idea without it, a stethoscope hanging round her neck. The gatekeeper of hell was a doctor, and this doctor was—

"Stuck on page seventy-three of *A Thousand and One Wacky Facts You Ought to Know*." She added, "I don't usually ask these questions. Usually, when I'm on night shift, I catch up with the clerking or chat to the nurses. But since everyone here was all 'He's been clawed by a wendigo' I figured I'd do the personal touch."

Rhys raised one hand, which seemed a very long way away, and made a gesture that was at once *Hold that thought* and *Water please*.

Water was provided, in a blue plastic mug.

He drank a little at a time, shuddering with relief.

Hell, it turned out, was a spare bedroom with a poster on the wall proclaiming STEEL GREEN ELECTRONICS – THE ONLY PLACE FOR THINGS WHICH GLOW, BEEP, FIZZ OR FLICKER!!! *Get your special introductory offer today – free pencil with every order of over £200!!!!!*

Beneath it, a picture of a reassuringly chunky nerd, screwdriver in one hand, spanner in the other, gave him a look that was all technical heroism and chin. Rhys slunk further into the bed, between *Thunderbirds* sheets that could only be infernal.

"Now, I gotta ask you some questions," went on the doctor, laying her damned quiz book aside and reaching for a clipboard.

As her pen skidded across the page, each word was intoned carefully.

"Question 1: Do You Know Who You Are?"

"Um . . . Rhys?"

"Well done!" exclaimed the doctor. "I'm Dr Seah, lovely to meet you – in a totally professional way, or whatever. Next question: Do you have a history of substance abuse?"

"What?"

"Come on, come on, don't be shy. Everyone's been there."

"Is this hell?" he croaked.

Dr Seah hesitated. "Interesting question," she conceded. "Your devil dude said something like 'For this is hell nor am I outta it' and then there's all this BS about how anywhere that wasn't in God's sight was like, hell. But then again, if this is as bad as things get, then you're sorted. That said," she flicked her hair away from her face with the chewed end of her biro, "it depends on how you feel about Kentish Town."

Rhys had a feeling that the world was a long way off and anything it wished to say to him would take a long time to reach its cognitive destination. This being so, he lost no time moving onto his next question:

"Am I dead?"

"Oh God, are you? Because if you are, you should *totally* declare that."

There was a creak by the bedroom door. He turned his head – itself an exercise worthy of mechanical aid – and there she was: black hair streaked with blue, purple boots and a sheepish expression.

"Hi, Rhys."

"Ms Li?" he rasped.

She perched on the end of the bed, gingerly. "How's, uh . . . how are you coping with being stabbed and everything?"

"Lacerated," corrected Dr Seah. "Stabbed is more kind of pokey pokey; our druid here got *lacerated*."

"I thought I was dead," he ventured in the tone of a man hoping to be persuaded otherwise.

Sharon hesitated. Compassion and efficiency briefly fought across her features. Then, "Don't be daft, it was only a bloody wendigo!"

"'Only' a wendigo?" Rhys squeaked.

"Four whole days you've spent tucked up in here," said Dr Seah. "Do you know how much nutmeg you need to expel the contagion of a wendigo's claws?"

"I think I need a tissue."

"Poor chicken! Sharon said you get allergies."

"It's fine," he whimpered as a tissue was dabbed against his reddening nose. "I can . . . can handle the . . . aaahh . . . aacchh . . . acchhii . . ."

'You thought about anti-histamines?" offered Dr Seah.

'They make me dro . . . drow . . ."

"What, even the ones with caffeine in?"

"I think it's a brain thing," Sharon explained, tapping her skull with the subtlety of a cruise missile in an oil refinery.

"How can you be a druid and have allergies?" exclaimed the diminutive doctor as Rhys's face contorted with the effort of trying not to sneeze.

"He's an urban druid."

"What do they do?"

"They ... Okay, so I don't really know what they do, yeah, because of how Rhys gets these allergies whenever he tries to do a spell. But I'm sure if he wasn't like, dribbling snot all the time, he'd do amazing things."

"I'm right here!" he wailed in protest.

"You're busy," retorted Dr Seah. "Now, I'm going to leave some antihistamines in your pocket. I mean, I *know* they're not your thing and you don't want to take them but, seriously, drugs are cool – I mean, like medicinal drugs – they're awesome."

Rhys opened his mouth to explain that, look, no, he understood that, physiologically speaking, anti-histamines would probably work and he appreciated from a rational perspective that there was possibly a psychosomatic element to his physical reactions, but really, the problem wasn't going to be solved overnight and actually he needed space to deal with it in his own way ...

"He's giving me this look of like, 'Oh what the fuck,'" whispered Dr Seah to Sharon. "See the way his left eyebrow twitches? There's thirteen muscles doing just that one nervous tic."

"Are there?" exclaimed Sharon, peering down to study Rhys's face. "That's kind of cool."

Dr Seah patted Rhys on the hand. "Also," she explained, reverting to her professional voice for the ignorant, "there's some stitches in you which you Must Not Pull, yes? Drink Lots of Fluids. Don't Pick Fights With Wendigos. Anything else? Just Say No. I guess that covers most of it. You gonna be okay with him?" she asked Sharon, scooping up an oversized medical bag which, Rhys couldn't help but notice, was adorned with rubber flowers and a badge proclaiming I ♥ THE BRITISH MUSEUM.

"Yeah," sighed Sharon. "It'll be fine."

"Coolio! Bye then, till next time. Try not to get anything nasty!" sang out Dr Seah. "And stay clear of curses!" The door clunked shut behind her.

Rhys looked at Sharon.

Sharon smiled uneasily.

He realised he was staring so looked away.

Then he realised he was deliberately not looking at her. After a moment of confusion he fixed his gaze on her left ear, hoping to give an impression of interest but without causing discomfort.

Sharon's smile faltered. "Okay," she said. "I think you gotta know something important. While I am up for like, bringing you chicken soup and putting the telly in here and that, there is no way – no *way* – I'm doing the brow-mopping thing."

"The—"

"It's not because I'm not feeling bad about what happened to you. It's just that there's feeling bad and then there's compromising your principles."

"Does brow-mopping compromise principles?"

This was something Sharon had thought through. "You know that thing where the guy gets injured, heroically fighting off monsters and that? And then he gets all romantically feverish and kind of sexily sweaty and stuff? And then there's this girl who sits by him and mops his brow with cold water? I can't be having any of that. I just don't see how it makes any sense, because you know how the girl is usually 'Do I care?' at the start, and by the end is 'Wow I love this guy, he's needy'? And I've never got why I should come over all vapid for needy. Or, in fact, why sweaty is sexy. Sweaty smells. Anyway . . ." She paused to consider what she'd just said, then added, "Anyway, I've got spirits to free, dogs to banish, wendigos to kick and cities to save and that. And while, like I said, I'm there with the tins of soup business, you're okay now, and you're gonna stay okay. Okay?"

Rhys found himself distracted by a new thought.

Up till now part of his mind had been experiencing a delay between receipt of a signal and the actual processing of information attached. Now, it groaned, shuddered, and hit "Reset". Thoughts tumbled into his brain, and words tumbled straight back out.

"Ms Li," he said, "where am I and what is going on?"

Chapter 63

United We Stand

The flat was in Kentish Town.

It was owned by a woman called Frances (Hello, Frances) who had "the most *amazing* story about this alchemist called Bill who used to manufacture these enchanted bracelets in Hunan province and then the gnomes got wind of it and we had to flee via Kuala Lumpur to collect on the insurance and I've still got some of them here but obviously the actual master bracelet was sold for £1.99 in Brixton Market and now we're not quite sure where it's got to but we think a girl called Alice has it and that's kind of a problem because no one knows where Alice is, so actually I guess the story isn't that amazing because if we don't get them back then that's the mid-Atlantic rift gone for starters . . ."

– and her more taciturn boyfriend, Raymond.

In the decor of the flat two competing wills had met, fought and ground each other to a draw. In the living room, with its view of a communal garden containing one swing and a broken trampoline, someone with a love of everyone and everything had laid down soft carpets, purple pillows, padded chairs and scented candles. Meanwhile in a former cupboard, now labelled STEEL GREEN ELECTRONICS, a less sociable character had made it a life mission not only to collect hammers, but different types of hammer for very different types of nail. Because you may not think it's important now. But just you wait for when you need to fix the kitchen in a hurry, then we'll see who's laughing ...

The kitchen was barely large enough to hold the grey fridge and greasy hob, above which someone had stuck a sign demanding TURN THE GAS OFF IDIOT!

It was most definitely not large enough to hold the four people who currently occupied it, none of whom were actually the owners of the property. Rhys, in blue dressing gown and borrowed pyjamas, leaned on Sharon's arm in the doorway and tried not to gape.

A goblin sat cross-legged on the kitchen table; he was licking the end of a tube of toothpaste with a foul grey tongue. The fridge door hung open, and a troll, in fact the most troll-like troll Rhys had ever seen, was considering which cheese would serve best as the topping to her five-cheese lasagne. By the kitchen sink Kevin the vampire was unloading a fresh bag of anti-bacterial handcreams, while, from a pipe on the ceiling, Sally dangled, head buried in an copy of *Van Gogh – Life and Times*. A thump from the bathroom and an unmistakable smell heralded the arrival of a fifth – Mr Roding, who greeted Rhys as he swanned into the living room, trailing the odour of lavender and decaying flesh. Over the sound of the TV Rhys heard Edna exclaiming, "Good grief, and what did the gnome do next?" As his gaze returned to the kitchen, the certainty came to him that he wasn't dead, and this couldn't be hell, because even Lucifer couldn't have thought of it.

To Sharon, he said at last, "There's um ... there's a goblin on the kitchen table."

"Oh yeah! You haven't met Sammy, have you?" Sharon waved at the goblin, who exhaled a fluoride-laden grunt of discontent. "Sammy, this is Rhys!"

"Runny-nosed Welshie!" replied the goblin.

"Hello, Rhys," offered Gretel, holding out one fingertip for Rhys to not so much shake, as pat in greeting. "I am glad to hear you are feeling better."

He felt the pull of stitches somewhere under his bandages and managed to respond with "Uh-huh."

"You *totally* need to get yourself checked out," offered Kevin. "I mean, I know the doctor was all like, 'I've handled it,' but you got torn up by *claws*. They hadn't even been *washed* first. There could have been wendigo spit on those claws; those could be the claws he eats with and . . . does the other stuff too." The vampire leaned forward and whispered, "Sometimes it's okay not to put your faith in the NHS."

"Bloodsucker," sang out Sammy.

"So, yeah," muttered Sharon in Rhys's ear. "So, like uh, Magicals Anonymous is getting all, you know, ready . . . on this shit."

The words landed one at a time in the tender places of Rhys's conscience and settled like bricks. "We're what?"

Sharon was trying not to cringe. The druid had never seen her cringe; but now her whole body was twisting, as if attempting to curl into somewhere behind her spine. "Thing is," she said, "it turns out that like, the whole city really is threatened, yeah, and spirits are disappearing. And that is like, a major thing, yeah, and actually like, most of Magicals Anonymous have issues with that, because there's, you know, witches and druids and Tuatha Dé Danaan and all that joining us. And the Aldermen can't do shit because of politics, but the Midnight Mayor said someone had to do something. So basically . . ." she drew in a breath, forced her shoulders back and proclaimed " . . . we're gonna save the day."

Silence.

"Do I have to?" asked one voice. "Only I've got this appointment with the Citizens Advice Bureau about suing my dentist."

Sharon glared. Kevin cowered.

"I think it's an excellent and noble cause," intoned Gretel. "Together we shall rid the city of evil and then we shall have a celebratory feast with aperitifs."

I personally think that this is in the finest spirit of the community, wrote Sally, from her position hanging off the ceiling. It is appropriate that we give something back to our society.

"Ms Li?" asked Rhys. "Can I have a word?"

He hurried her out into the hall. "So, uh, Ms Li," he said, his voice urgent and low, "it's not that I'm not happy to see everyone, see, but are you, I mean . . . are you really thinking we should, maybe, pick a fight with a wendigo and his minion hordes? We just met the men who could turn the ground beneath your feet to liquid sucking concrete and it didn't go well last time with just four of them, and did I mention the minion hordes?"

"They work in finance – how bad can it be?"

"Exactly! It's like bankers, but with claws! And, with the greatest respect, Magicals Anonymous is a wonderful thing, but we're not fighters. We're … well, we're …" he gasped down air, seeding the words, "we're only good in support!"

Chapter 64

There Are No Secrets Between Friends

Something rather remarkable is happening.
It begins here:

Posted at 13.13 on Magicals Anonymous by Rhys Ellis:
Amazing meeting everyone, tell all your friends – Magicals
Anonymous is here to stay!

Posted 14.28 on Magicals Anonymous by Sally:
I would like to say thank you to everyone at Magicals Anonymous
for all their support, and a very big thank you to Jess in particular
for recommending the Kandinsky; once the security guard had
passed out, I found the exhibition very stimulating.

**Posted at 21.38 on Magicals Anonymous by MS (Protector of
the City, Defender of the Night, etc. etc. etc.):**
Hi everybody! So, someone's sucking the soul of the city and I
was wondering if any of you guys felt like doing something about
it? Drop me a line if you do! Cheers!

sted at 21.48 on Magicals Anonymous by S.Rafaat:
o! Is the city going to be all right? I'll bring snacks if anyone
em.

Posted at 23.41 on Magicals Anonymous by Burns & Stoke Ltd:
If you wish to live another night, you will give her to us. We will not
warn you twice.

This last post was censored by admin within half an hour of being
placed. But half an hour was more than enough.

The word spread.

It began with the techno-literates: young summoners who
couldn't quite get their containment circles right and who had fallen
back on Facebook to keep themselves occupied while the sacred
incense was cooked in their mum's microwaves; eager diviners who
scoured the internet for clues as to the future of tomorrow, and who
read the truth of things in the static at the corners of the screen;
bored vampires who knew that it was too early to go out and hunt,
too late still to be in the coffin. The message was tweeted and texted
onwards, sent out through the busy wires of the city, from laptop to
PC, PC to Mac, from mobile phones the size of old breeze blocks
through to palm-held devices that not only received your mail, but
regarded it as their privilege to sort it into colour-coordinated cat-
egories for your consideration. The word was whispered between the
statues that sat on the imperial buildings of Kingsway, carried in the
scuttling of the rats beneath the city streets, flashed from TV screen
to TV screen in the flickering windows of the shuttered electronics
stores, watched over by beggars and security cameras, and the
message said:

We are Magicals Anonymous.

We are going to save the city.

Later, scholars would detect more than a little digital technology in
how quickly the word was transmitted. They would study the emails
that spurted forth, examine the text messages and consider the stories
of those lonely ghouls in their cellars who, in the dead of night,
received phone calls with no voices but which seemed to impart
through static alone a sense of urgency and fear.

Some might question why the Midnight Mayor, usually to be found
on such nights prowling the streets of the city, was sighted sneaking
into a telephone exchange a few minutes before the word began to spill
across the streets, spreading outwards from the website of Magicals

Anonymous. Some might wonder why one or two computers, having received their messages, exploded three minutes after. But, as the Midnight Mayor was the first to point out, all this was speculation. Nothing could be blamed on him.

Chapter 65

A Puppy Is For Life, Not Just For Christmas

It paws the earth.

Paces.

Its snout is longer than a child's arm, its fangs – and let us make no mistake, for they are fangs – are ancient bone flecked with spittle and blood. Its lips curl back from its mouth in a great growl that sends vibrations pulsing through its flesh like ripples over muddy water. By day it is still too weak to break through the city gates, the ancient, unseen gates of London which stand guard against the nightmares. There's thousands of years of magic in those old black stones, too strong to penetrate while the sun shines. But by night ... by night when the minds of the city are sleeping, and the barriers between what is and what is perceived grow thin, by night there is nothing to hold it back.

It growls at the setting sun, willing it to sink faster, and as it paces the shadow lands beneath the veil of what is seen, its footsteps burn the earth.

The scholars call it – or possibly him, although no one has got close enough to speculate – the Lady's Companion, for whereas Greydawn is a comfort in the night, her companion is the terror of the dark. The goblins call him Great Growling and hide their spawn from him as he goes out to hunt. To the White City Clan his are the mad eyes that they paint on the columns beneath the city bypasses; to the Neon Court he is Blackpaw, the footstep in the dark from which there is no hiding.

To everyone else, to the Friendlies who dare not whisper his name, to the shamans and the sorcerers of this city who know enough to fear the rumours, he is simply known as Dog, the companion of Greydawn, loyal and unstoppable.

Dog has lost his mistress.

Time to get her back.

Chapter 66

He Is Perverse, You Are Stubborn, I Am Determined

Magicals Anonymous, assembled again at St Christopher's Hall in Exmouth Market.

Some came because it was that time of the week – meeting day – and because they'd heard about how positive the last meeting was.

Some came because friends recommended the biscuits and said it was a nice place to chill.

At least one came because she was looking for a hot date who didn't mind the occasional lump of lava between the bedsheets.

But many came because of the message, blasted out via emails and telephones: the city is in danger, and now so are you.

Rhys came in a wheelchair. He didn't really need a wheelchair, but once the idea had been suggested everyone was very much in favour. Sally the banshee said he shouldn't take risks with his health after a wendigo attack and explained that banshees had never like wendigos to begin with, though she was sure that wasn't a species thing. Kevin pointed out that you couldn't be too careful with stitches. Gretel said she didn't mind pushing, and, actually, with seven foot of troll at his back Rhys did feel rather more safe.

Sharon hadn't really approved of the wheelchair, but then Sharon had a lot on her mind. Rhys had seen her talking, in corners, voice lowered, with the goblin about what he could only assume were Shaman Things.

Mr Roding the necromancer had decided to attend because, "The Midnight Mayor gave me this spiel about the fate of the city and said he needed a necromancer. I told him how poorly I thought of that idea, but then someone firebombed the local Friendlies shrine, which left a very bad impression on me."

The Midnight Mayor visited me too! wrote Sally as chairs for the guests were laid out beneath her in the church hall. He is a little ignorant of modern art, but I think we had a breakthrough with some of the bolder sculptures. Also, four angry men attacked an ambassador from the Beggar King, proclaiming that none would survive unless they showed them where Greydawn was, which I think is very bad manners.

"Firebombing is a very unpleasant reaction," confirmed Gretel. The plastic chairs were warping beneath her fingertips as she gingerly placed them in a ragged circle around the centre of the room.

There were more attendees this week, Rhys noticed. He'd heard the clattering of laptops as he recuperated in Frances's flat but hadn't appreciated just how far the word had spread. As Junior Judo cleared out and Magicals Anonymous filed in, he spotted a family of imps wriggling out of an air vent at the side of the hall ("Is there more to life than landfills?"), felt the wash of cold air as a grubby ice demon wafted by, spawned from the back reaches of catering freezers ("Global Warming really concerns me"), heard the snicker-snack of tiny claws on the polished floor as a gremlin spider ("You just can't get the recycling"), its plastic head spinning above its articulated body, tried to climb up a plastic chair and into a splayed sitting position. Kevin had retreated to a corner, a white face mask pressed over his mouth and nose.

"Do you know how many germs imps have?" he quavered.

"What disappoints me," offered Chris ("Exorcism doesn't have to be exciting!"), "is how low the turnout of the living dead is."

Before long all the chairs were occupied, albeit with Gretel taking two, and those members of Magicals Anonymous with limbs best suited to the floor were folding themselves up inside the circle.

In the true spirit of the occasion, Sharon had bought biscuits. Gretel had clearly consulted on the purchase for, to the standard fare of

Jammie Dodgers and custard creams someone had added a Deluxe Mixed Family Pack and an Authentic Shortbread.

The time came for Sharon to climb onto one of the chairs and bring the meeting to order.

"Hello!" she called out, and was ignored. "Hello!" she tried again, a little louder. From his corner by the neglected dusty piano, Sammy slurped toothpaste; plastic seats creaked beneath Gretel; and a couple of witches wearing T-shirts proclaiming FREE SANITARY TOWELS FOR ALL! furtively leaned away from Mr Roding's body odour.

"Oi, you lot!" yelled Sharon, and the meeting turned to look. "Um, hello," she added. Dozens of pairs of eyes, only some of which were in the usual blue–brown spectrum, flickered, blinked or bulged at her. "So, my name's Sharon ..."

"Hello, Sharon!" chorused the room.

" ... and I'd like to talk to you tonight about the fate of the city."

Chapter 67

Jess

It started when I was nineteen.

I was at college studying Gothic literature – which was awesome –
but then my sister, she got ill and needed a donor and I was a perfect
match. And that was all cool, you know. I mean, it's not like you get to
save your sister's life every day, is it? So that went fine and she's okay
now and I had the surgery and I was fine too. But they'd put me on
these meds for my blood pressure and then these blood thinners too.
And so, two weeks after we'd both come out of hospital I was writing
my dissertation when I stood up and was all like, "Whoa," and my dad
said, "Are you okay?" and I was going to say "I feel kinda odd" and then
it just . . . happened.

As polymorphic instabilities go, it's kind of awesome. Though I do
know these guys who turn into rats or squirrels, and then bits of them
get eaten by the local cats and they turn back and they're missing toes
or . . . other bits, which is just not cool. Or guys who don't even turn
all the way, but just become bits of other things, like the head of a dog
and the claw of a cat and the fur of a fox and all that. At least I'm not
doing any of that. And pigeons are actually okay, once you get used to
them.

The problem, I guess, is the fact that it is *pigeons*, plural. Lots of
them. It's a mass-energy thing – if I weigh sixty kilograms and all we're

really doing is rearranging the weight, then either I need to turn into sixty pigeons or we are talking one mother-scary bird, and no one wants that. And I think I've got better at keeping it together. I mean, even when the flock divides and there are bits of me flying off all over the place, it's still all me, but like I'm thin, stretched out, if you know what I mean?

My husband – Jeff – he's really understanding.

He even puts down breadcrumbs now, to help guide me home.

Chapter 68

All (Man)Kind Are My Kin

There was a babble of voices. Sharon, still on her chair, shouted, "Oi! Oi, you lot!" but it had little effect. The assembled members of Magicals Anonymous just gossiped and flustered and gave indignant cries of "But why must *we* save the city?" mixed with such as "I've got this terrible cramp in my talon."

"Oi!" yelled Sharon again, stamping her foot. "You lot bloody, shut up!"

There was the crunch of metal on wood – the sound of a chair leg gouging floorboards. All eyes turned. Gretel had pushed back both her seats hard enough almost to destroy part of the floor.

There's something about seven foot of belligerent troll – it catches even the most occupied of attentions.

"Ms Li," grumbled Gretel in a voice like an ancient engine winding up, "has something to say."

Silence fell. Trolls have that effect.

Sharon beamed. "Thank you, Gretel. Now, I know that not everyone here is pleased by the notion that we are the defenders of the city against unstoppable evils. Rhys over there, for example, got torn up by a wendigo, while Edna over *there* has had her shop smashed into lots of bits. And I guess that doesn't encourage the team. But –" she clapped her hands together to show her enthusiasm "– the fact is that this same wendigo has declared war on the Friendlies, who I think we can all agree are really positive people with a really good mental attitude. So, by association, the wendigo and his creatures have declared war on all of us, who they blame for standing between them and Greydawn, which I know sounds like a problem, but I think is more of an issue ... or maybe an opportunity ... or like, one of those.

"Anyway ..." She took a deep breath, aware of the words struggling to escape her. "I really think that if we like, work together as a team, we can kick that wendigo arse and find Greydawn and restore the city wall and send Dog packing and shut down Burns and Stoke and all that, without like, missing any TV or major social events.

"And since we can't exactly go to the police on this, I think that, as a community, we should really try and take the situation in hand and give something back to, you know, people. Because that's what we'd like people to do for us. Whatcha say?"

In the silence a hand went up at the back of the room. The hand belonged to Jess I-turn-into-pigeons. "Excuse me? Can I ask a stupid question?"

"Of course."

"Is there going to be death happening? Only, I've just got a mortgage and I don't think I can be doing death at the moment. I know it's really selfish. Sorry."

"Speaking of death, you can't be killing wendigos anyway," said Mr Roding. "They're like Dog – they just come crawling back out of the shadows, spun together from dust and shed skin. Best thing you can do with a wendigo is slow it down."

"What if we seal the breach in the city wall?" asked Mrs Rafaat I'm-sure-it'll-be-okay. "Won't that keep him out?"

"He's already inside, isn't he!" Mr Roding exclaimed. "Besides, there's no sealing the wall without finding Greydawn."

"Which is what Burns and Stoke want to do," added Rhys. "And I don't know much about Greydawn and that, but it seems like if a wendigo is killing people to find her, then he's probably not going to be very nice."

"We cannot," agreed Edna, "let that ... *individual* find Our Lady of 4 a.m., wherever she is! Greydawn has ... *inclinations* that must never be exploited."

"Inclinations?" echoed Sharon. "Is this like ... when you have an inclination for fried bread even though you know it's wrong? Or is this more like an inclination to inflict a magical doom?"

Edna writhed beneath the gaze of the room. "I told you," she breathed. "I told you Greydawn came originally from blood. In the time of the Temple of Mithras there were ... sacrifices to her in this city. Some accounts suggest she could grant your deepest desires, but there had to be ... blood. Obviously we're not into that now," she added, her voice rising against the sound of general disapproval, "but that isn't to say that others, less ethically inclined, might not be interested in exploiting the legend."

"Oh God," moaned Kevin. "More arseholes wanting to shed blood without proper surgical protection. Have you ever once, ever, seen someone sterilise a sacrificial knife before use? I don't think so!"

"Maybe we could talk to them?" suggested Chris the psychoanalytical exorcist. "Maybe if we just explained the situation patiently ..."

"What about the claws?" wailed Rhys.

"'S all bollocks, innit?" hollered Sammy. "Who cares why the wendigo wants Greydawn? He wouldn't be here if she hadn't gone and vanished, neither would Dog. And things are gonna keep on going all to shit until we get Greydawn back. So you –" a finger stabbed towards Jess "– stop thinking about your mortgage, and you –" pointing at Mr Roding "– get some deodorant, and you –" swerving round towards Edna "– cut out the soppy spirit-hugging shite, okay!"

If Gretel's sheer size had commanded silence, now there was something in the sight of a goblin in a green hoodie bouncing up and down like a deranged jack-in-the-box that required, if not respect, then intense consideration. The room considered.

Sharon cleared her throat, and in a calmer voice concluded, "The thing is, we're all in the shit if the city wall doesn't get sealed again. So it seems we need to find Greydawn, get her back doing her stuff, whatever that is, release all the spirits what have been stolen by Burns and Stoke, however they did that, and get this wendigo dude to leave town, however we're gonna do that."

"Don't forget the builders," Rhys put in. "I don't think they're very nice either."

"And if they're coming for the Friendlies," added Edna, "they'll probably come for us."

"Yeah, and we've got a Facebook group!" offered Jess. "I mean, they could look at that and find us! What if they damage the upholstery?"

"It's a private Facebook group though," said Rhys. "I'm sure there's nothing to be alarmed about."

All eyes turned to Sharon, just to make sure of that.

"Well . . . thing is . . . when you say *private* . . . "

Rhys felt his heart sink.

This time the silence was absolute as her words settled over the room like a glacier. Then Sharon beamed. It was a surprising accompaniment, Rhys felt, to an announcement that should properly have come from a qualified undertaker.

"Now," she went on, "before everyone gets worked up, I just gotta say that we're probably okay! I mean, I know there's these four killer builders what have been murdering their way across London and that. But they've still got a job to do, and that job is all about finding Greydawn. And, let's face it, they're gonna need a shaman, and maybe the Friendlies, to do it, because they're not getting nowhere by themselves. So, really, killing us seems dead thick.

"Also, it seems to me that the whole thing with these killer builders and that is that people don't notice them because they're dressed in these yellow fluorescent jackets and that, and let's face it, no one ever notices *anyone* what's wearing a yellow fluorescent jacket. And –" she took a deep breath as she reached the pinnacle of her argument "– if I was like, a killer builder and I didn't want to be seen, the last place I'd want to be is in a meeting full of vampires, trolls, goblins, witches, wizards and shamans."

She finished speaking.

Eyes flickered, but otherwise the meeting was motionless. It was as if the assembled members were afraid that the slightest motion might attracted attention from unseen sources.

Then:

"Arseholes," exclaimed a voice.

"Wank," offered another.

"Total . . . "

" . . . balls," concluded the fourth.

It occurred to Rhys, as he turned to see the four men who'd spoken, that they'd been there all along, but somehow he'd failed to notice.

Chapter 69

Be Loving to Your Pets

The Midnight Mayor is hunting.

This is something he's got quite good at, learning to read the signs in the streets. A smear of paint on the wall, a single mitten left on the spike of a fence, a cigarette butt stubbed out on the side of a bus shelter, a plastic bag shoved into the paper slot of a recycling bin. Sometimes it's just people mucking about; sometimes it's a sign of something truer, hidden just beneath the surface.

Tonight he hunts a hunter.

His phone rings.

"Help me!" the voice wails. "For God's sake, help me!"

"It's okay," he says. "I know you're scared, and quite right too, but you're doing fine. Don't look back – he wants you to look back. Come to Exmouth Market."

"He's going to kill me!"

"Don't look – he wants you to look. Come to me."

He hangs up and waits. This too is something he's got very good at – mastering the art of being a grey silence in the moving night.

"Come on," he whispers to the empty air. "Walkies."

Chapter 70

Family Is Everything

Rhys wanted to say that they "shimmered into existence". But, thinking about it, the four killer builders in their fluorescent jackets had been so much a part of the room's furniture that not only he, but everyone else, had failed to notice them.

Except perhaps the goblin shaman and his apprentice, who were, after all, seers of the hidden truths and thus should probably get these things right?

One said, "Uh . . ."

One said, "Bloody hell!"

One said, "Tits."

One said, "Here to fix your radiator!"

Sharon said, "Hi there! Welcome to Magicals Anonymous! I'm Sharon . . ."

"Hello, Sharon," offered Jess instinctively. Eyes turned to her in disbelief. She shrugged. "What?"

" . . . and I'm wondering if you gentlemen have any issues you wish to discuss?"

A stumped silence. Then:

"Issues?"

"What . . ."

" . . . fucking . . ."

" . . . issues?"

"Tits!"

"Balls!"

"Pigs!"

"Wank?"

"We're the . . ."

" . . . greatest killers . . ."

" . . . the world has ever known!"

"Why the fuck would we . . ."

" . . . have fucking issues?"

"Babe."

"Chick."

"Darlin'."

"Sweetheart."

Magicals Anonymous was now in the nearest thing to chaos that a well-mannered self-help group could achieve. People were trying to scurry out of the way, their chairs knocked back, or they were staring with the frozen fear of a hedgehog considering a cement truck heading its way. It was also a remarkably quiet chaos, as no one wanted to draw too much attention to themself.

This left Sharon clear to face the builders. And to tell them, "Well, I'm just saying that sometimes it's about offering redemption as well as retribution, and that, I mean, like, being open-minded and saying, you guys may be total psychopaths and that may be what you do, but perhaps you had a difficult upbringing? Then again, you did kill Derek, high priest of the Friendlies, and bury him alive in concrete, which some people would say is kind of beyond the realms of counselling."

"Yeah, but . . ."

" . . . he wasn't telling us what we . . ."

" . . . wanted to know, yeah?"

"We had to . . ."

" . . . get our answers . . ."

"Arses!"

" . . . and our answers . . ."

" . . . led us to you."

"Really?" Somehow, in all the turmoil, Sharon was still standing on her plastic chair, and now, as she digested this information, she radiated warmth and general encouragement. "And why, specifically, do you think we're connected to Greydawn? Why Magicals Anonymous?"

The builders shrugged: one gave a great shoulder-lift of a gesture, another a crooked lurch of his shoulders, a third rolled his arms slightly back, the last stuck his elbows out. But there was no mistaking the unity of purpose, thought and meaning in their movements.

"Cos you gave shelter to the Friendlies," one said, indicating Edna.

"Cos you broke into Burns and Stoke," one added, tugging at his trousers, which had sagged to reveal his bum crack.

"Cos you got conspiring with the Midnight Mayor."

"Cos you're the only shaman in town ..."

"Bitch."

"Slut."

"Babes."

" ... and that makes you Greydawn's friend ..."

" ... but our enemy."

"So, yeah, you see ..."

" ... it's nothing personal."

"Though you got a *great* arse."

"It's cash ..."

"Taxman bastards!"

" ... in hand."

"Job done."

Sally shuffled in the rafters overhead; Sammy the goblin's eyes glowed with malicious glee at unpleasant imaginings only he could see. Sharon nodded, considering everything the builders had said.

"So," she concluded, "is your beef just with me or with all of Magicals Anonymous?"

Another shrug rippled through the four men.

"Know what," one said.

"End of the day," another concluded.

"You gotta be thorough ..."

" ... to get the job done."

Sharon beamed.

"Fantastic," she murmured. "Thank you, gentlemen. I think that was all we wanted to hear. We appreciate your free and frank testimony, and may I say on behalf of everyone at Magicals Anonymous ..." there was a gleam in Sharon's eye, a tension in her body and a weight in her voice that Rhys had never heard before " ... hello, murderers."

It occurred to the builders, perhaps for the first time, that the inhabitants of the room were staring at them, and not all of the eyes doing the staring were quite human. Sally shifted her whiteboard and pen to one side, and as her wings flexed beneath her robes, there was a definite impression of talon, not finger, hanging above their heads. Kevin bit his bottom lip and there were fangs doing the biting; the sound of Gretel scratching her head was of trollish bone rubbing on trollish bone, and the builders realised, as one (for was there any other way?), that Gretel the troll was not a nice hamburger-munching member of the species, but rather a bridge lurker bred in Dartford to haunt the Crossing, battle-scarred by victorious conflict with toll-jumping lorries and speeding trucks.

The four builders looked at her, looked at each other and, as one, moved. One grabbed the mousy-haired woman called Jess by the throat and dragged her over the back of her chair; it thumped to the floor beneath her tangled kicking feet. Another caught Mrs Rafaat by the arm as the old woman tried to escape, and pulled her in front of himself like a human shield. The other two fell into line behind them. Beneath their feet the floor was already warping, the boards creaking and cracking as the building began to hum around them.

"Now, see here."

"We're only doing ... "

" ... what we're fucking paid to."

"Fuck it!"

"So you don't come in here ... "

" ... talking rules and regs ... "

" ... until you've ... "

"Arses!"

" ... learned a little respect."

"Babes."

"Darlin'."

"Sweetheart."

"Yeah?"

They were edging towards the door, the floor splintering beneath them, thin cracks spreading through every pane of window glass. Four builders who knew how to destroy the buildings they were in, pulling their two hostages with them.

Sharon said, "Did you just call me 'sweetheart'?"

"Oh G-God I don't feel s-so . . ." stammered Jess.

"It's not like I called you 'rosebud' or 'pretty-pants'!" the shaman raged, arms folded, still standing on her wobbly plastic chair.

"Yeah, but . . ."

" . . . you're a girl!"

"There's differences, innit?"

"Gender differences and that."

"So don't go all like . . ."

" . . . indignant."

"Girls like different things!"

Jess was visibly shaking now, her fingers clutching at the arm across her throat. "I'm really not . . ." she gabbled. "Oh G-God, I think I'm going to . . ."

"Don't give me that!" exploded Sharon. She hopped off the chair and marched towards the retreating builders. "I mean, patronising shite is patronising shite."

"I really think I'm g-going t-to . . ." stammered Jess.

"It's not like I called you 'dandelion' or 'my little cauliflower' or anything like that. And just because I'm a shaman, and Jess there she turns into . . ."

There was a moment of polymorphic uncertainty.

A certain chilliness bit the air.

Where Jess had cringed, pulled back against the heaving mass of a builder's chest, now there were pigeons.

A lot of pigeons.

About the same mass of pigeons, in fact, as, an instant before, there'd been the mass of Jess.

The birds flocked up and out across the room, great clouds of white and grey feathers spinning down to the floor, beaks stabbing and yellow eyes flashing, a whirlwind of beaten air and puffy flashing chests. The builder who'd been holding Jess yelped and covered his eyes with his hands as the great mess of airborne vermin spilt out around him. And as his companion tightened his arm across Mrs Rafaat's throat, something dropped from the rafters. Like the pigeons, it was mostly grey and possessed wings, but there the resemblance ended.

Sally drew back her lips to reveal that beneath an affable smile there glinted the silver-white teeth of a banshee. She dropped teeth first from the roof, her wings tucked back into her body and the long talons of her legs swinging down and out to grapple with the builder. Great gouts of blood spurted from the arm that held Mrs Rafaat, even as Mr Roding, with more presence of mind than most, grabbed the startled woman by the arm and pulled her free. She gave a little "Oh!" before stumbling over the outstretched leg of a cowering exorcist and falling, palms first, on top of Mr Roding.

There was a blur of talon and claw, a beating of great leathery wings and a wail as Sally's mouth came up from the top of the builder's head, bringing with it a mess of blood and scalp. This time, as the builder screamed, so did the other three, every head going back, every mouth contorting in an expression of pain – all the same expression, all the same pain.

One staggered against the wall, which warped and buckled at his touch; he recovered just enough to pull out from his jacket an impossible crowbar rusted with more than water, flecked with a blackness that stank of salt and meat. With a roar he slammed it down into the floor of the hall. Where the crowbar hit, the floor cracked, a great rushing gape that shattered the floorboards and split the poured concrete beneath, delving a chasm clean across the room as the members of Magicals Anonymous shrieked, screamed and clattered out of the way.

Sharon saw Sammy vanish into the grey place of the spirit walk. Then a pop-fizz caught her attention. Turning, she saw Ms Somchit, the diminutive black-clad Alderman, rising from her chair; scarlet fire was flicking from her fingertips and a metallic silver sheen spreading over her skin, and there was a depth to her eyes and a spikiness along her back that hadn't been there before. The pigeons – what Sharon guessed she still had to think of as Jess – were circling wildly in the rafters, while the builder who'd held Jess coughed and spluttered, spitting feather and dust onto the floor. Sally was still clinging gamely on to her builder, while the one with the crowbar was drawing it back for another earth-splitting smash. He raised it, his face twisted in fury, and as it reached the very height of its swing something blond flashed in front of him, too fast to perceive, and for a moment the builder froze. A bright red line spread across his throat. He swayed as the blood began to spill from the tear across his neck, the crowbar still held aloft, ready to strike. His eyes swivelled to the source of his distress, which exclaimed:

"Oh my *God*, there's blood *everywhere*. That is so *gross!*"

Kevin hopped from foot to foot, staring at his own hands in an ecstasy of hygienic distress. This gave the fourth builder the opportunity to come up behind him, draw his arm back and drive the sharpened end of his crowbar through to the centre of the vampire's chest.

Kevin's mouth fell open. He looked down, saw the bloody point of the metal sticking out from his sternum, put his hands to his face and screamed.

"Oh my God! I need sterile wipes!"

Behind him the builder's face twitched with satisfaction until a very large, very round, rather furry fingertip tapped him on the shoulder. He looked round, and then up, and then up a little further.

"You're not very well mannered," grumbled Gretel. And, with the casual momentum no creature but a troll can muster, much like the easy-going inevitability of a double-decker bus, she pushed her fist into the builder's face.

Rhys dived for the ground as the builder sailed through the air with an expression of surprise and confusion on his face, before he slammed into the wall with a crack of breaking bones.

In the stunned silence that followed, Rhys heard a voice proclaim:

"Oi, runny-nose! We need to get 'em separated, okay?"

He couldn't see Sammy the Elbow, but he doubted that, even in these heightened emotional circumstances, anyone else would address him as "runny-nose".

"Everyone!" shouted Sharon. "The builders are the same individual, the same thing! We need to separate them. Everyone move!"

No one did.

Then Gretel, with a shrug of "Okay then," reached out and picked up the still-startled form of the nearest builder. Blood had run down his fluorescent jacket from the tear in his throat, but the wound itself was already beginning to heal. She shuffled over to the door, found it too small for both herself and her burden, then, with another shrug, walked through anyway, taking with her a significant piece of wall.

Others followed suit. Sally leapt clear of the builder she'd seized in time for a blast of flame from Ms Somchit to land squarely on his chest and knock him off his feet. As he landed, Sally was there again, digging her talons into his wrists, while Ms Somchit took hold of his feet, reluctantly joined by Chris the exorcist and Mr Roding the necromancer. With Sally flapping vigorously and Ms Somchit pushing from the other end, they dragged him out into the night. Gretel was already striding away towards Farringdon Road so, with a cry of "To the public park!" from Ms Somchit, the four and their stunned charge turned in the opposite direction, heaving their burden down the sleeping street.

"Oh dear, strong man, please?" quavered Mrs Rafaat back in the hall, looking down at the builder to whom Gretel had so pointedly explained the rules of polite social interaction. His limbs were splayed at strange angles, but even as Rhys watched, they began to creak and click, snapping back into place with the sound of bone-on-bone.

"Hurry up!" barked Sammy. "We gotta get 'em far enough away from each other that they ain't themselves no more!"

Rhys realised, with a shudder of reluctance, that both the glare of Sammy and the hopeful stare of Mrs Rafaat were locked on him. Gingerly he crawled over to the builder, whose head still wouldn't turn but whose furious eyes swerved towards him. Rhys thought he could see vertebrae locking and unlocking in his neck as they tried to reassemble in some human – or at least humanesque – form. Weakened by revulsion, Rhys nonetheless grabbed the builder under the arms as Mrs Rafaat took hold of his feet. The two tried lifting him; the two failed.

"Bloody hell," whined the goblin, and then he was there, by Rhys's side. For a naive moment the druid thought the goblin intended to help; instead Sammy clapped his hands together and exclaimed, "All right, team! On a count of three! One ... two ... heave!"

They heaved; the builder shifted a few inches.

Something cold settled on the air next to Rhys. He looked up. It was the freezer elemental, the air falling in white clouds around him, a greenish tint to the ice on his face, the thin pipes of his veins visible beneath the frost on his skin and, just audible, the gentle whirr of his compressor-heart. He leaned down and slipped a pair of frozen hands under the builder's arm. Rhys took the other arm even as the builder's eyes started wide at the touch of the elemental. Ice crystals began to form on the underside of the man's arm, then spread, blooming like petals in spring. There was a final cry from Sammy of "Come on, you soggy-blankets!" and the three of them hauled the builder out through the door.

That left one.

One, Sharon realised, who was already climbing to his feet, wiping pigeon feathers from his hair. His face was wild with rage, his fluorescent jacket torn by pigeon claws, bits of feather were hanging off his clothes, and his boots were stained with dubious white streaks. His eyes found Sharon, and he snarled:

"You're gonna . . ."

And stopped.

Halfway down the Farringdon Road, a builder carried across the back of an ambling troll whispered:

" . . . fucking die . . ."

On the leafy edge of Spa Fields, another, clutched in the claws of a banshee, whimpered:

" . . . you stupid . . ."

And in the backstreets of Islington, beneath the branches of a weeping willow in Wilmington Square, a third murmured:

" . . . bitch," before the ice from an elemental's touch turned his lips grey-blue and smothered all sound.

In St Christopher's Hall the remaining builder hesitated. He was surprised, alarmed even, not to hear the usual call of his kin, the synergy of voices completing his own words. For a second longer his mouth worked in astonishment.

"You can't . . ."

Was there a whisper from another mouth, on Farringdon Road?

A murmured reply from Wilmington Square?

A half-hushed response from the edge of Spa Fields, where even now a banshee was turning her head to the sky and opening her mouth to howl the impossible howl of her kin?

The builder listened and heard nothing.

"Babes," he tried.

Nothing.

"Arseholes."

Sharon stepped closer, picking her way past overturned chairs and fallen pigeon feathers. She fixed her eyes on the builder.

"Call that driving?" he spluttered. "I didn't ... more than my ... Wanker!"

She stopped an arm's-reach in front of him. He didn't seem to notice. Though his head didn't turn, his eyes wandered, and his lips were working, albeit in response to sounds he couldn't hear.

"You must be what they call a composite personality," murmured Sharon. "I saw that when I was in the shadows back there in Tooting, where you killed that Friendly. I looked at you, and you were all the same. You're all the same thing, at the end, but in four bodies. I wondered what you'd be like if you were ever pulled apart. I guess now we know."

For a moment the builder's eyes locked on hers. "Bacon sarnie!" he exclaimed, then flinched as if surprised by his own words. "Cuppa tea," he blurted and shook his head as if to release true meaning from his addled mind. "Tits!"

And where Farringdon Road met Clerkenwell Road, it seemed to Gretel the troll that the struggling of the builder on her back had grown weaker. She hesitated beneath the red glow of the traffic lights and examined her burden. Anyone who bothered to look may have briefly seen ...

... but then no, because what they saw was not something they cared to perceive.

And in Wilmington Square, beneath the hanging branches of the willow tree where for a hundred years young lovers had felt classically romantic, Rhys the druid sat back on his haunches and panted and sweated and wondered why the builder, his bones nearly healed, didn't leap up and try to kill them all. Or why Sammy the Elbow, usually so vocal in his opinions, was silent. Why was everything about them so silent?

A breath is released. In the shattered hall on Exmouth Market a man in a fluorescent jacket sways, sweat standing out on his forehead, and whispers:

"I ..."

In Spa Fields, a voice picks up the cry: " . . . can't . . ."

On Farringdon Road, a whisper beneath the traffic lights: " . . . be . . ."

In Wilmington Square, on the leaf-strewn grass: " . . . alone."

And they die.

Not a death of blood or bone.

Not even a death of falling and decay.

It is an exhalation.

Four builders breathe out at last, and with their breath go their lives, their strengths, their shapes, their weights, their colour, their mass, their solidity, and their everything, until, for each of them, only a yellow fluorescent jacket and a pair of steel-capped safety boots remain.

Four bodies, but only one breath.

Chapter 71

When the Going Gets Tough ...

Kevin was saying, "You can't have too much antiseptic ..."

He stood in the wrecked remains of the hall surrounded by a largely curious gathering of Magicals Anonymous. The crowbar was still lodged firmly in his chest but, from the fact he was still on his feet, this didn't seem cause him nearly as much physical distress as hygenic.

Two witches, their hands covered by latex gloves, their faces by white masks, were tentatively slathering the crowbar with bright pink antiseptic fluid from a bottle found in the copious depths of Kevin's bag. Sharon approached gingerly, and at the sight of her Kevin shrieked, "Face mask, face mask! Oh my God, haven't you people heard of germs?"

A face mask was proffered, by Chris the exorcist, whose eyes were locked on the crowbar protruding from the vampire's chest.

Holding the mask over her nose and mouth, Sharon mumbled, "You okay, Kevin?"

"God no!" he replied. "They completely missed my heart, but have you seen this?" He gestured at the crowbar, all the while dripping a mixture of blood and medication onto the floor. "It just screams tetanus!"

"It's a *magical* crowbar through your chest, stupid!" corrected Sammy.

"That's worse!" wailed Kevin. "What if it carries magical tetanus?"

Nearby, Rhys sat, a cup of tea pressed into his hands by the concerned Mrs Rafaat. Every aspect of his body language suggested that here was a druid who had been pushed to the edge and whose survival could only be attributed to luck.

"Is that it?" he murmured as Sharon came over and sat next to him. "Have we won?"

"Uh ... yeah. But kind of no."

"Oh," he said. "But at least it's progress?"

"I think it's all terribly sad," put in Mrs Rafaat. "I mean, those poor psychopathic builders probably had no choice about being a composite destructive murderous personality. I blame their upbringing."

Sharon turned to stare at the older woman. There was something about this lady, a certain ... normality that, in this place, made no sense. Mrs Rafaat smiled, fidgeting with the long embroidered scarf around her neck. "Well, that's just what I think," she offered.

Sharon thought she saw the white-suited shape of Dez flit across the wall behind Mrs Rafaat. "You ... get weird dreams, right?" she asked carefully. "I mean, you're not like ... magical or unstable or explosive or anything like that; it's just that you get, you know, weird stuff happening, yeah?"

"I wouldn't want to exaggerate things," ventured Mrs Rafaat. "There are so many people in this world who are far worse off than me."

"Out of interest," Sharon heard her own voice, as if from a long way off, "when did these weird dreams start happening?"

"A few years ago, but really shouldn't we be focusing on this nice vampire with the impaling problem?"

Turning on the spot, a full 360 degrees, Sharon looked slowly round the room. As she did she saw, with a shaman's eye, all the truths behind the shapes – of Kevin

so gross so gross so gross

of Chris the exorcist, who wondered:

will the builders haunt this place I don't know it looked like a peaceful way to go, in a violent sense, but then with mystic forces such as these there are always deeper issues at work ...

Her gaze wandered up to the rafters, where in the clouds of pigeons still flapping around she could see another shape, drawn out of the falling feathers, which swirled and drifted round each other and

which formed, for a very brief moment, the shape of a human arm
curling round the verminous flock, or a hint of a human face twisting
up. Look a little deeper, and there were the shadows of the things
which had taken place in this hall – kids in judo uniforms tumbling on
old stuffed mats; actors prancing round the room doing whatever exer-
cises actors did as preparation for emoting; the Sunday prayer seminar
for singles concerned about their love lives. Can't find a boyfriend?
Can't sustain a relationship? Monstrous sounds or manifestations while
having sex? Come to our singles prayer seminar, and all shall be
explained.

And there was Dez, white suit and fake tan, big red microphone
held up as he exclaimed, "And now a message from our sponsor! Do
you have problems seeing the truth of things? Is the journey down the
hidden path just a little too hard-going? Not convinced you've got the
right aura of shamanly wisdom? Try doing it better, the ultimate solution for a difficult situation!"

Sharon glared at him, and her spirit guide had the good grace to
fade unobtrusively into the grey realms of psychological discord from
which he had sprung. Finally Sharon turned back to Mrs Rafaat: there
she stood, a nice old lady with curling grey hair, one of Wembley's
finest saris modestly sparing her ankles from the gaze of lewd
observers, and she was ... normal. Utterly and entirely 100 per cent
Mrs Rafaat, not a hint of power, not a shadow of a doubt, not a glimmer of magic, not a—

What had Edna said?

"Derek did hire a couple of very nice wizards to try and scry for
Greydawn, but they didn't find anything. Which was odd, as you'd
have expected some sort of mystical residue or glow, but it's really as
if she's just vanished into the city."

And being a shaman wasn't, Sharon recalled, about being invisible.
It was about being so much a part of your environment that no one
even bothered to look.

"Excuse me?" Mrs Rafaat was staring politely at Sharon's left shoulder. "Um ... Ms Li? Are you still there? Only you do appear to have
vanished into thin air."

For a second the two of them stood there, shaman and smiling old
lady, trying to puzzle each other out. Then Sharon turned around,

snapping back into the world of perceived reality, her mouth already opening to shout, "Sammy! Get your arse here now!"

The goblin shimmered out of nowhere to appear where he'd always been, just behind Sharon. "No need to shout," he grumbled. "Drama drama drama, that's all humans ever – *ow!*" Sharon's fingers had closed round one of his ears and she dragged him towards the troll-sized remains of the door. "You can't! It's my . . . This is not dignified!" shrilled the goblin as he was pulled out into the night.

She dragged him into the alley down the side of the hall, let go of his ear and hissed, "At one with the bloody city!"

Sammy paused, just in case he'd missed a deeper meaning to this sentiment. "I know you've got potato brains," he concluded, "and you're gonna have to talk me down to your intellectual level."

She hissed with frustration, turning on the spot like a caged animal. "At one with the city! That's how you vanish, that's what being invisible means – being at one with the bloody city!"

"Yeah, and—"

"And why would anyone care about us lot anyway, really? I mean, I know that like, Chris is looking to get more business and Rhys has these allergy issues, but no one cares about Magicals Anonymous."

"I'm with you there."

"But Mrs Rafaat isn't magical, isn't special, isn't powerful, isn't dangerous, isn't angry, isn't anything really that you'd think would make seeking help important; but you know what? She's so much not all of these things it's like she's nothing else, do you see?"

"No. What are you talking about?"

"That's all she is! Mrs Rafaat is too human!"

"Too—"

"Too human," insisted Sharon, "to be bloody true."

"Oh." Then silence. "*Oh!*" repeated Sammy, struggling with this syllable as being something not present in regular vocabulary. Then, raising his voice a little, "You may look thick as a brick wall, but maybe you're not so dumb after all."

"Thanks."

"Which isn't to say you're right, cos you probably ain't . . ."

"That's fine."

"... but if you are, then well ... yeah. That's something, innit?" mused Sammy. Then, as if the desire to say it had been welling up until it became unstoppable, he exclaimed, "If it was so bloody obvious all this bloody time, why the bloody hell couldn't the Midnight Mayor arsehole figure it out for himself? Incompetent wanker!"

There was a polite cough from the end of the alley.

Sharon turned with the shuffle of one who has seen a lot of disaster but can't believe she's seen the last of it.

A man stood at the end of the alley, a disruption of the dark.

"Excuse me?" he said. "Would you be talking about me?"

Chapter 72

Mrs Rafaat

I really feel very embarrassed bothering you like this.

I have this ... dream.

Again and again, it comes to me in the night.

I am ...

... air. Or not air; I am a cloud within the air. No, that's not right. Not a cloud; that's far too like the weather.

I am breath.

That's what I am. My body is breath, my thoughts are wind, my fingers are the warm curling whispers from air vents, my toes are the rattling of old papers along the ground, my hair is the swaying of leaves and the singing of glass in the high towers.

I dream of the night, of the city at night, when everything is sleeping, that beautiful hour before the sun comes up when the roads are empty of all traffic except for the street cleaner and the late-night painter of lines; when the lights burn in empty offices where only the woman in rubber gloves moves between silent stations.

I sweep above the goods train creaking along empty railway lines; I dance through the tunnels where the engineers walk with grubby faces; I spin round the TV set of the lonely security guard in the too-quiet car park. I am everywhere they are, these people lost in the dark; and sometimes, to delight them, I tangle a plastic bag in my arms and a newspaper round my ankle and let it spin round me so that they may look up and see, in the detritus of the day, that I am there, walking beside them. That they are not alone.

And when the moon is hidden and the street lamps are flickering, I walk along the city wall, and it is as real to me as any paving stone in London. And outside the demons of the night howl and hammer and scream for admittance, all the nightmares that mankind has tried to lock away – the spectres and the ghouls, the ghasts and the ghosts, the devils with pointed faces and the wendigos clad in the skins of the fallen – and my dog is beside me, and he howls and growls, and they cower and are afraid, and I feel pity for them, and my dog does not.

That's my dream.

Every night it comes to me, and sometimes even when I am not sleeping I think I hear him, my dog, howling, calling to me, trying to find me.

Then I wake and remember what I really am.

I am a cleaning woman from Wembley, widow of a loving husband, and I cook an excellent prawn madras.

All the rest is just . . . longing, I suppose. Longing, and wishing for something more.

Nothing I can't live without.

Chapter 73

... The Tough Rise to the Occasion

He stood at the end of the alley, bright blue eyes beneath dark brown hair, fingerless black gloves at the end of a dirty beige coat, second-hand jeans and second-hand T-shirt. The T-shirt proclaimed:

SAVE OUR NHS

Sharon walked up to him, staring into his too-blue eyes, and said, very quietly and fast, "I think I should slap you but I'm not going to slap you because that would give off a negative energy and we're working really hard on doing positive stuff here but if it wasn't deeply immature and not at all socially responsible, I wouldn't just slap you now, I'd put a knee through your testicles, just so you know."

To her surprise, Matthew Swift, sorcerer, Midnight Mayor and all-purpose destroyer of anything flammable that got in his path, flinched. "What've I done?" he demanded. "I've been helpful without being crushing, useful without being obnoxious, handy in a corner—"

"Patronising without being informative," she corrected. "Cryptic without being directional and, *and* —" and there it was, the pointing finger of accusation before which all who knew her quailed "— and you drove a bus at me! That was bloody you, in bloody Tooting, wasn't it?"

Was it dignified for the protector of the city to fiddle so with the ragged end of his sleeve, whether or not beneath the baleful gaze of an angry barista-turned-shaman? "I drove a bus at the wendigo," he insisted. "At the *wendigo*. And I sent Ms Somchit to look after you, didn't I? And got Sammy to give you shamaning lessons—"

"A *goblin!*" Sharon felt nothing more needed to be said.

"Frickin' brilliant goblin!" corrected Sammy.

"And what I want you to really appreciate," Swift went on, gathering pace beneath Sharon's red-hot glower, "what I think is very important for you to understand is that, actually, while you've been dealing with these minor inconveniences, I've been offering a distraction. Serving, in fact, my role as a walking target."

"Minor inconveniences?! Wendigo! Killer builders! Blood! Claws! Liquid concrete! Howling in the night! Did I mention how calm I'm being here because of my self-control and responsible attitude, because I don't think I made it clear just how my positive attitude stands in such magnificent contrast to you, being an oily little shite! You tell me –" the finger quivered with rage beneath Swift's nose, his eyes nearly crossing in an effort to focus on it "– everything you know right now, no cryptic bollocks or I swear I'll start losing control of my more modest nature and go testicular on you!"

Swift breathed in long and slow, and on the exhalation said, "Uh, okay." He ticked the points off on his fingers.

"I knew that the city wall was down and Greydawn was gone, and therefore that nasty things were getting in, including her dog.

"I knew that a few years ago Burns and Stoke attempted to summon, bind and compel Greydawn and something went wrong.

"I know that in the last two months every member of the summoning team who attempted to bind Greydawn has been killed by what looked like an animal attack – although where in London you can hide a twenty-stone animal with teeth the size of my fist and whose footsteps burn the earth I have no idea.

"And I suspected – *suspected*," he added, "that the new CEO of Burns and Stoke might well be more than he seemed." He hesitated before the sustained ferocity of Sharon's gaze. "Honest, that's kind of it from me."

"He's probably telling the truth," admitted Sammy, "seeing as how he's just an arsehole sorcerer with as much spiritual sense as a cucumber."

"Did I mention the politics?" complained Swift. "Did I mention that the Midnight Mayor's office needs cash to run it? I mean, good intentions are all very well, but how far are you going to get on an empty stomach?"

"What politics?" Sharon's voice dripped suspicion.

"Burns and Stoke is heavily invested in Harlun and Phelps ..."

"And I care because ...?"

" ... and Harlun and Phelps," he explained, hastening to address the smoking gun disguised as Sharon's indignation, "is the company that finances the Aldermen. And the Aldermen, like Ms Somchit, are the people I rely on to do my job. But the thing is, if Harlun and Phelps goes down, there'll be a lot of people who don't get their Christmas bonus. And I'm just saying, while I don't know much about managerial technique, I imagine that might dent company morale? And when company morale has a company armoury and that company armoury includes at least one bazooka, as a good boss I get concerned, yes?"

Sharon considered all these points. "Okay," she said, "so I don't have much management experience or anything like that, but I did do business studies at school and I'm just wondering why they couldn't hide the bazooka."

"I must admit, that never crossed my mind."

"There are books, you know? I mean, on how to do management?"

Now it was Swift's turn to scowl. "Books?"

"There are –" a nasty grin formed in the corner of Sharon's mouth "– *evening classes.*"

For a moment shaman and sorcerer locked gaze and wills. The Midnight Mayor's eyes were unnatural in colour and a little inhuman in their intensity. Not many people could look steadily into their bright blue depths. But Sharon hadn't spent long hours learning to meet her own gaze in the mirror and long, long hours riding the Underground and practising the art of making and breaking eye contact while whispering to herself the secret of all things that concerned her: "I am beautiful, I am wonderful, I have a secret, the secret is ..."

... just so that she could flinch now.

Sammy stared, doing his best to disguise his un-shaman-like expression of surprise.

Swift looked away. He couldn't remember the last time he'd done that.

Still glaring, Sharon carefully put her hands in her pockets as if to contain the righteous fury that might yet erupt.

"We've got a problem," she said.

"Actually, we've got two," muttered the Midnight Mayor, but as Sharon's eyes flashed bright again, he raised his hands defensively and said, "But why don't you go first?"

"The problem," declared Sharon, "is that Mrs Rafaat is human."

Swift and Sammy both considered this. "No," Swift admitted. "That's not what I was expecting at all."

"Why, what's your problem?" Her eyes narrowed sharply when Swift cringed. "And how much am I not gonna like it?"

"The thing is," muttered Swift, "the circle of wizards who tried to summon Greydawn for Burns and Stoke . . . they've been dying, yes? I mean, Gavin McGafferty was . . . and then Scott Hidsley was mowed down while running for the old city boundary, and Christian Ardle was disembowelled on Fleet Street, and half of Camilla Long was found floating under Blackfriars, and . . ." he became aware of the looks on his audience's faces so hastily moved on to " . . . and the only member of Burns and Stoke's summoning team left alive, Eddie, has been hearing the howling in the dark for a couple of nights and so a few hours ago he broke cover and turned king's evidence, or maybe queen's evidence, or whatever that evidence is you turn when you try to use it to escape prosecution or being disembowelled by an angry dog spawned of the nether reaches of nightmare and time looking for his mistress, and he is rather running for his life and I did perhaps tell him to come here."

Silence in the alley.

"You pillock," said Sammy.

"It seemed like a good idea at the time."

"You incompetent arsehole!"

"I figured, save Eddie's life, maybe get a couple of shamans to have a look at Dog—"

"You undead wanker nit!"

"Hey, that's a bit much really."

Sharon said nothing.

In the stillness she became slowly aware of the ever-present gentle smell of urine which was a required feature of all such passages between dark places. She could smell the beer-soaked breath of the man who'd left his mark in this place, hear the footsteps of the beggar looking for a place from the cold, the laughter of children playing hide and seek in the park at the end of the alley, smell the coal smoke that had once burned in the chimney stacks of Clerkenwell, see the footsteps that stretched out impossibly behind Sammy, a great long journey at his back, still not complete, and she thought she saw a flash of brilliance as Dez flickered across the surface of her mind, her spirit guide winking lewdly as he passed, and when she looked at the man called Matthew Swift she saw . . .

feet shuffle lonely on cold street too far too far too far
splash! bus tyres through the puddle sheet of water drenching the passer-by
    help us
aerial hum with TV signal
        window rustle with feedback noise
we be light we be life we be fire!
        hoooooowwwwllllll!
come be we and be free
        blood in the stones
. . . everything.

"I'll just go and combat Dog with all the primal forces of fire and magic at my command, shall I, while you have a mull," Swift was proclaiming.

"Bloody hell," she said, and didn't realise she'd spoken until the words were already out, "you're, like, an angel."

Swift started. The words came from so far from beyond his field of expectation, he didn't know how to respond.

"Which isn't like, to say, divine or pretty or sweet or any good at playing the trombone," she asserted, "because there's blood on your hands and fire under your skin, and where you walk the shadows turn. But I'm just saying . . . holy shit, and that."

Sammy nudged Swift in the kneecaps. "Told you I was a bloody amazing bloody teacher," he murmured. "Less than a week and she's already doing the truth-of-things shit. Just you wait till we get on to the walking-of-the-path stuff, it's gonna be immense."

"You left your tribe." Sharon knew she was speaking but couldn't connect the knowledge with the power to stop. The words happened around her, through her, with the absolute certainty of fact, and as she spoke she saw Sammy's eyes widen and felt the dirt beneath his feet and the dryness in his mouth. "You were their shaman and you left. Why would you do that?"

"Then again," offered Sammy, "there's being a decent student and being an insufferable swot."

"Sharon?" Swift's voice was lined with cautious concern. "You okay?"

"I . . . Yes. I'm fine. I can see . . . and I can *hear*." She swayed, the sweat beginning to stand out on her face. "He's close. His feet are silent, but his footsteps burn the earth. He can smell his mistress – he knows she's here – but the scent is confusing. He's frightened, Dog is frightened. So he grows angry. That's how he lives with being afraid. He wants his mistress back."

Swift gave an uneasy thumbs up. "Fantastic!" he exclaimed. "Full marks on channelling the raging essence of an unleashed primal monster. Minus several hundred for freaking me out while doing it."

"Oi! I give the grades for shamaning round here," snapped Sammy. "And while I'm with you on the high marks for sensing the stones of the city and that, I got a few technical niggles with technique. There weren't no chanting or ceremonial drums or *nothing*, and that's just gonna let down the punters."

"Ceremonial drums?" demanded Swift. "What the hell?"

"You gotta think what your audience wants. It's all very well being wise and shit, but if people don't buy into the spiel then what's the point?"

"Chanting? I thought more of you."

"Like you haven't added a few pyrotechnics when you wanna—"

"Hey, if I do that, to convince people that throwing spells at me is a stupid idea, it's showmanship where *death* is on the line, rather than this whole dancing, drumming, feathers shit."

"Did I say anything about *feathers*, did you hear me say anything about feathers?"

"He's here." Sharon was leaning on the wall for support and there was a ghostly greyness about her face, eyes focused on nothing much and everything in particular.

Howl!

And there it was, all around, not so much a sound as a pressure, a shaking, a street-depth wall of fury that rose up from the stones beneath their feet, split the air, tinkled the drifts of broken glass and sent birds flapping for safety.

HOWL!!

Sammy looked at Swift, Swift looked at Sammy. In a moment of immediate resolution they each took Sharon by an elbow and guided her back down the alley and into the wreckage of St Christopher's Hall. The ragtag remains of Magicals Anonymous were still gathered round Kevin, who, minus one crowbar to the chest, was now sitting back on a broken plastic chair being fanned by Chris with his copy of *Psychoexorcism Monthly*. Pigeons still fluttered in the rafters while beneath, Jess's partner, the long-suffering Jeff, struggled to lure them down with biscuit crumbs strewn on the splintered floorboards.

Mrs Rafaat was staring up through the shattered windows at the gloomy night beyond. "Did anyone hear something?"

A second later, Edna, red-faced and breathless, was by Sharon's side. "Did you hear it? It's—"

"Dog, yeah, we know," said Sammy. "Oi, Sharon!" He shook her, but, having only an elbow within shaking distance, the effect was rather feeble. "Oi!" he shouted. "Soggy-brains!"

Sharon blinked dreamily down at him. "Hello, Sammy," she replied with an empty smile. "I think I need an early night."

"Who's that?" demanded Rhys on seeing Swift. It came out more defensively than he'd intended.

Swift beamed at the ginger druid and held out a gloved hand. "Hi. Matthew Swift, Defender of the City, Guardian of the Night, Keeper of the Gate and so on and so forth, nice to meet you. You wouldn't be, by any chance, an extremely competent battle mage ready for a fight?"

"I'm a druid, see," blundered Rhys, too numb to shake the hand that was offered.

"A potent and angry druid?" suggested Swift hopefully.

His only answer was a profound and sudden sneeze.

HOWL!!

There were no doubts this time, no illusions; the whole hall looked up at the sound, felt it ripple through the earth, bend the walls.

Mrs Rafaat drifted towards the door before Edna grabbed her and exclaimed, "Dearie, I'm not sure you'll like it out there."

An inane grin was still stuck to Sharon's face. "Actually," she offered, "I think she'll be okay."

Edna detached herself from Mrs Rafaat. "Maybe," she said quickly, "I haven't told you everything you need to know about Greydawn's dog."

"No, we got the gist," said Sharon with a cheerfulness that Rhys was beginning to recognise as near-hysteria. "Partner of Greydawn, does the darkness, does the violence, killing all those who tried to trap her, roaming the night, looking for its mistress. Am I missing anything?"

Edna looked taken aback. "I heard a howling . . ."

"Dog's coming here."

"Why?"

"Uh . . . fiendishly brilliant luring?" suggested Swift.

"This one," Sharon pointed at Swift and giggled, "thought it would be a good idea!"

"But he can't! Without his mistress there's nothing to hold him back. He'll—"

Another howl broke the night, closer now. The battered building creaked.

"We ought to close the door," whispered Edna.

Sharon pointed at the place where the door had been, a troll-sized tear in the wall, and giggled again.

"Is Ms Li all right?" queried Rhys.

"She's fine," retorted Sammy, patting his apprentice on the knee. "She's at one with the city, is all. Happens like that – stress, tension, that sort of thing – but she'll snap out of it."

"Now the thing is," tried Swift. "I don't want to put any pressure on people here, but the thing is—"

"Help me!"

The voice came from the door, a shrill, faint wail. All eyes turned. The source of the wail didn't look as faint as his voice. He was a squat well-muscled man with a body tone suggesting that here was a gentleman who enjoyed the gym. He wore a pale blue suit and a red tie tangled from running; buttons popped from the strain of his breath, and as he staggered through the door his eyes showed a breathless delirium from more-than-strenuous exercise.

"Help me," he pleaded again and, without another sound, collapsed.

"Oh. My. God." Kevin's voice broke the silence. "He could be like, diseased!"

Swift ignored this and stepped towards the unconscious body. "Ladies and gentlemen," he exclaimed, "please meet Eddie 'Magners' Parks, hedge-fund manager, captain of the South Harrow five-a-side football champions, sometime summoner and employee of Burns and Stoke. Most of his colleagues have passed away over the past few weeks, their bodies torn limb from limb by the rampaging monster known as Dog, but Eddie here –" Swift gave him a not-too-fond prod in the ribs with his toe "– was bright enough to appreciate that, and so came to me for help. And whatcha know!"

Another howl split the night, so close it seemed to come from inside the room. It was a sound with no physical properties, but went straight to the brain.

"I figured he'd be perfect bait to bring Dog running. Cool, huh?"

The assembled Magicals responded with dumb incredulity.

"You what?" asked Kevin.

"No, no, because think about it – it's perfect," insisted the sorcerer. "The last surviving summoner of Burns and Stoke, his colleagues murdered, comes running to us, and of course, but of course Dog is going to follow and—"

"And what? And we all get rabies?" shrieked Kevin.

"Perhaps if we all just sat down and talked about it," offered Chris.

"Does he like stewed rabbit?" contributed Gretel.

"I spent thirty years getting reasonable blood flow to my right arm, I cannot be having it detached now," fumed Mr Roding.

"Oh, dear, but I'm really not sure any of these will work," whimpered Edna.

Do you think we can distract this Dog with some coloured sheeting?

"I get this terrible itching from dog hair," Rhys said. "On the other hand the anti-histamines do make me drows—"

"Look!" cut in Swift before the babble of voices could become a storm of inaction. "I understand that everyone is very concerned here, but really … Where'd Sharon go?"

Eyes looked, but Sharon was nowhere to be seen.

As it were.

"Outside!" barked Sammy.

The street was sleeping. The pub had closed its doors, the sports café had turned off its TVs, the Spanish restaurant had pulled down the shutter over the chorizo and legs of ham in its window, the lights had gone out above the pharmacy. The city slumbered in the still, cold sleep where dream walkers wandered.

Mrs Rafaat stood in the middle of the street, with its black iron bollards and occasional long-dead bicycle, and stared. Her mouth was open, her head raised, her fingers stretched out though her arms hung at her side. Her orange sari looked mud-brown beneath the street lights, her hair, pulled back, revealed the grey at her temples. She stared down the street, past the bookshop and DIY stores and sandwich shops. And, not thirty yards away, Dog stared back.

His fur was matted and oily, his jaw hanging low and huge; a black tongue lolled between his fangs; his red eyes were wide with exertion and madness, his ribs puffed and swelled like a blacksmith's bellows and, as his feet padded over a layer of drizzle on the street, it steamed and hissed beneath his claws.

Sammy stopped, a few yards behind Mrs Rafaat, so fast that Swift piled straight into the goblin, knocking him off his feet. Edna bumped into Swift, and Rhys just about managed to avoid them all by pivoting around Gretel – only to stare straight at the great black head of Dog.

Rhys sneezed.

Dog growled, a low rumble that rippled all along his body. On the back of his neck the fur stood up, blood and brown-black oil parting as the knotted mess stiffened for a fight.

Mrs Rafaat took a step towards Dog. The monster's attention snapped towards her. Two great nostrils puffed and flared, oozing a trail of exhaust smoke. He didn't strike, didn't attack. But he stared at the approaching old lady, legs hunched, ready to pounce.

Edna whispered, "Oh God, stop her."

"Lady, I'm good," asserted Sammy, "but a goblin's gotta learn when to be modest about these things."

Twenty yards; ten. Dog was still crouched, soft steam rising beneath his paws where the rainwater burned. He examined Mrs Rafaat.

Five yards; three. If Dog had stood up like a man, he would have been taller than the fiercest basketball player, wider than a sumo wrestler who'd let himself go. But as the old woman approached, Dog seemed to curl into himself, limbs folding in, head turning this way and that, nostrils sampling great whiffs of air. Rhys could see the ribs moving in Dog's chest, each longer than his own arm, thicker than his wrist; an opening of Dog's jaws could have encompassed Mrs Rafaat's head right down to her neck.

The old lady didn't care.

She was squatting down in front of the creature, reaching out a hand and laying it on Dog's snout. Her fingers became smeared with oil and blood as she ran them over his fur. Dog leaned in and sniffed, first with one gaping nostril, then the other, as if to confirm the data imparted to his brain.

"There, there," murmured Mrs Rafaat, as Dog shifted uneasily from side to side before her. "Who's a good boy?"

From Dog's throat there came the strangest sound. It started high, and grew thinner and fainter as it stretched, and stretched, an impossible, agonised, pathetic, hopeful whine. Dog pushed his muzzle closer to Mrs Rafaat and buried it in the crook of her arm.

"There, there," she repeated. "There, there."

"That's not ..." whispered Edna. "That's not what ..."

"Bugger me," muttered Swift. "She actually bloody is."

Edna was a woman trying to understand a concept outside the remit of all comprehension. "But she's ... She can't be. I mean, it's not possible."

Dog whined again, shuffled closer so that one great paw was against Mrs Rafaat's knee. Beneath his claw he'd caught a corner of her sari, which began to blacken and smoke, but Mrs Rafaat, unregarding, held Dog's head in her arms and murmured, "Who's a pretty boy, hmm? Who's a pretty boy?"

"Um." Rhys raised a hand requesting permission to speak. Seeing the expressions of everyone around him, he tried speaking instead. "Where's Ms Li?"

Sammy pointed at a patch of empty air behind Mrs Rafaat, and Rhys looked. As he did so, it occurred to him that Sharon had been stood there a long time.

The shaman knelt down beside Mrs Rafaat as she held Dog's head in her arms. Dog turned to stare at Sharon, but didn't roar, didn't pounce, just rolled a little in the old woman's arms to inspect this new, interesting phenomenon.

"Hello," said Sharon softly. Then, in concession to the blood on Dog's coat and the sharpness of his fangs, she added, "Good doggy."

"He's beautiful, isn't he?" sighed Mrs Rafaat.

"He's uh ... he's definitely special," replied Sharon. "Do you mind if I just ... ?" She reached down and eased the smouldering end of Mrs Rafaat's sari out from under Dog's great black paw, hastily smothering some embers. "Oh," she added, seeing the claw-sized scorch mark. "I don't think that's coming out."

"Oh well," said Mrs Rafaat, "it only came from a shop in Euston."

Something deep rumbled with contentment inside the great pumping void of Dog's lungs. In other creatures it might have been a croon. Mrs Rafaat scratched Dog under the chin and murmured, "I didn't think the colour suited me anyway."

"It did! It does."

"I was thinking green?"

"Green is tricky," said Sharon. She shifted into a sitting position and patted Dog on his great, sticky side, hardly aware of what she did. "So, I guess I gotta ask you ... about the dog."

"Isn't he a cutie?" exclaimed Mrs Rafaat, rubbing her nose up against Dog's great black snout. "Yes, you are; yes, you are!"

"I'm sure he's lovely," confirmed Sharon, "but the thing is, he is also an eight-foot-long mystical killing machine. Which is totally cool, but, you know, it does raise some questions."

"Killing machine? My little puppy wouldn't hurt a fly."

"So he is your little puppy, is he? I mean, you don't just have a knack for animals?"

"Oh no, I don't think so. I leave out biscuits for the neighbourhood cats, but they never eat them, and sometimes I open the curtain at the back of my flat and there's foxes there, just staring at me, but they never eat the biscuits either, and I have always wanted a little doggy, yes I have, yes I have!" The sentence dissolved back into a croon. "And he's such a good little boy, isn't he?"

"He's lovely," Sharon hastened to agree. "But like I said, he is a kinda killing machine, and he is sorta here to kill that Eddie guy. And, you know, some people might question all that. If you don't mind me saying."

"I'm sure my little puppy doesn't mean anything naughty, do you?" To Sharon's surprise, as Mrs Rafaat nuzzled up against Dog's great snout, Dog nuzzled right back.

"Even if you were in danger?" Sharon ventured. "What if he was lost and afraid and with nowhere left to go?"

Mrs Rafaat hesitated, pursing her lips.

"Also, yeah, I don't want to say nothing, but isn't it a little kinda . . . you know . . . weird to have a pet who's quite so, uh . . . *grrargh?*"

"People keep snakes!" retorted Mrs Rafaat.

"Yes . . ."

"I don't see why people should have any problems with my little puppy," she declared. "He's got a heart of gold."

"It's not really a problem with your dog," Sharon ventured. "That's not what I'm trying to say here."

"Then what?"

Sharon looked into the open, innocent face of Mrs Rafaat as she cradled her pet monster's head with the affection of a child for a fondly kept teddy bear.

"I think, basically, what I'm getting at here is that . . . uh . . . it's not common for people to keep, like, mystical guardian monsters as pets, yeah. And actually Dog here is probably not so big on tasty treats as he is on like, grinding the bones of his enemies, or Greydawn's enemies or . . . your enemies. If you see what I'm saying."

Innocence, hopeful of enlightenment, stared back.

"You know how you have weird dreams?" Sharon tried one last time. "And you think that something's wrong, but you don't know what it is?"

"Yes!" agreed Mrs Rafaat. "It's very frustrating, but I don't want to make a fuss . . ."

"Thing is," murmured Sharon, "I think I might know what the problem is. I think . . . you may . . . sorta be . . . Greydawn."

Mrs Rafaat recoiled as if stung, blinking hard. Then she puffed out her cheeks, drew back her shoulders and barked, "That is the most ridiculous thing I've ever heard!"

Chapter 74

To Prosper and Grow Is Only Human

A moment to pause and consider.

Consider an office.

It is big, white, glass down one wall, abstract images of ...

... well, art ...

... down another. Fluorescent lamps burn above the long table, where during working hours important meetings for important men are held, complete with bottled mineral water to encourage important thoughts to flow. But now, here, in the dead of night, the lights are off, and the room is silent.

A man stands by the window.

Only ...

... not quite a man.

Look at him, and you will see a stick-thin figure with wrists of bone made to snap at the lightest touch, pale hair and skin barely thick enough for the blood to pass, standing with his hands clasped behind his back, surveying all beneath him. The lights of Canada Water, steel and glass, concrete and iron, planned, perfect, cold.

But turn your head to one side and for a second, just a second, you might perceive what is truly there, your mind bursting apart as his skin floats from his back; and there he will stand, wendigo in all his glory, claws for fingers, bones of iron, flesh flying loose around him like banners in a breeze and even as you perceive ...

... you will forget, your mind unable to accept what it has just beheld.

A knock on the door.

His head doesn't turn as the door is opened. A woman, dressed in a grey trouser suit, makes her way in.

"Yes?" His voice barely an exhalation. The glass in front of him shows no sign of steam as his breath plays over its surface.

"M-M-Mr Ruislip sir?" Her knuckles are white, her skin pale as the silk that covers her body.

"Have they found her yet?" he murmurs, his eyes fixed on the lights of the city below. "Have they found Greydawn?"

"There's been a problem, Mr Ruislip sir. The builders you sent to Magicals Anonymous, they're ... gone."

"Gone?" A flicker of an eyebrow above a watery eye, a bare twitch in the corner of his mouth. "How 'gone'?"

"Vanished, sir. Uh ... dissolved, sir, the scryers say."

"But I was assured that they were indestructible," breathes Mr Ruislip. "I was assured that no lock could hold them, nor no magic bar their path."

"Y-y-yes, sir."

"I am disappointed by this turn of events. It seems to me that I have, at every step, made great efforts to guarantee the survival of this company. I have given it prosperity, which is a source of happiness to men; I have given it success, which causes pride; and yet the one favour I ask in return, the one ... *desire* I express, has not been achieved. Why is this?"

"Ed-Eddie Parks fled."

"Redundant. The summoning circle failed to bind and compel Greydawn, and I removed their Christmas bonuses. If Eddie wishes to seek employment elsewhere, then that is an acceptable reallocation of human resources."

"The summoners are dead. They're all dead. Dog is in the streets. The Midnight Mayor—"

He moves so fast she can hardly see, but he's there by her side in a second, and, God, it's fingers he runs over her cheek, fingers not claws, *fingers* ...

"Tell me about your fear," he breathes, so soft now, curious and quiet. "It is a feeling but it causes a physical change, yes? Your heart – it beats faster. Your face is red. Your breath comes quickly. This is a hormonal response to feeling? Your mind tells you that you are in danger and so your blood moves faster in preparation for a fight? Tell me, if you experience joy, how does your body alter?"

The woman half-closed her eyes, ran a leather tongue over sandy lips. "We can still find her," she pleaded. "We'll find Greydawn. The Friendlies . . . the shamans . . ."

"The Friendlies and the shamans are united!" roars Mr Ruislip, his anger a too-hot wave of breath in her face. "The Midnight Mayor has joined them, the builders are slain, and now they will come, and when they are all dead I will be no closer to my objective! All I ask is a very simple thing and yet you fail again!"

His fingers move.

It is a tiny gesture, a flick that might swat away a fly.

The woman sways.

She feels the blood from her neck run down and seep into her shirt. Feels the hot pulse of it draining away from her veins, the lightness in her skull as gravity takes over where the heart can no longer reach. She tries to speak, but air cannot pass through what is left of her throat. She falls, her blood a scarlet spray up the nearest wall.

Claws, not fingers, then.

Mr Ruislip turns away.

There is a phrase he has heard, uttered by humans in seeming jest, but meant to disguise some other feeling. How he despises it when mortals do that – layer one sentiment beneath the hollowness of another.

What was it?

"If you want something done, do it yourself," he murmurs. It's said so often in jest, but what it really means, what it so often disguises, is rage.

Chapter 75

A Dog Is a Man's Best Friend

They had persuaded Mrs Rafaat back inside the hall.

Dog had padded quietly after her, and now sat, a shaggy, panting monster at his small mistress's feet, examining the members of Magicals Anonymous with a beady, bloody stare. Whenever his gaze turned to the barely conscious form of Eddie Parks, his lips curled back in rage, and only a gentle pat on the head and a cajoling "Who's a naughty doggy?" from Mrs Rafaat appeared to quell Dog's otherwise unrestrained loathing. Eddie Parks quaked at Dog's stare, and turned away only to find a clipboard and a biro hovering in front of his nose.

"Hi," exclaimed Kevin. "So, I just lost like, disgusting amounts of blood tonight, and I was wondering . . . what's your rhesus type?"

Rhys passed Mrs Rafaat another cup of tea, his hand shaking as Dog's great head turned to examine the brew. The druid had always worried that animals never liked him, and now his anxiety made him feel quite faint.

"Thank you, dear," murmured Mrs Rafaat. "It's been a very stressful night."

Sharon was examining the wreckage of the hall, aghast. Whatever heightened state of non-drumming-based spiritual enlightenment she'd reached a few minutes before, it was fading fast against the onslaught of practical considerations. "Oh shit," she muttered. "Am I gonna have to pay for all this?"

"I'm sure they've got insurance," offered Ms Somchit. The black-clad

Alderman was cradling her mug of herbal tea like someone whose happiness is proportional to their share of tannin.

"Yeah, but I haven't!" wailed the shaman. "And where are we gonna have meetings now?"

I know a lovely gasometer – spacious, warm, fascinating acoustics? suggested Sally from her perch.

Edna, meanwhile, couldn't stop looking with horrified fascination at Dog and Mrs Rafaat. Kevin nudged her conspiratorially. While Eddie Parks's hand trembled its way down a health questionnaire, the vampire had tried to disguise the bloody hole in his shirt with a tactfully draped tea cloth, albeit in vain.

"Uh, babes?" he murmured. "You're kind of staring at the nice lady with the giant monstrous killing machine, and that's like, not really polite."

Edna forced her features into something more composed and shuffled uneasily towards Mrs Rafaat. Dog sniffed as she approached but, at a pat on the head from Mrs Rafaat, sank back down on his haunches.

"Um . . . my lady?" hazarded Edna. "Ma'am? I'm Edna. I'm uh . . . I'm your high priestess."

"Are you?" snuffled Mrs Rafaat, whom the evening's events had now made rather teary. "That's very nice of you, dear, but I'm afraid I really don't know what you're talking about."

"You *are* Greydawn, aren't you?" demanded Chris the exorcist. "I mean, you're who all this fuss is about?"

"That's what people tell me," she sighed. "But really, I don't know. Everyone seems to think my little puppy here –" she fondled behind Dog's ear, provoking a potent whine of appreciation "– is somehow mystical and . . . well . . . anti-social. But I keep explaining he's just my little diddums."

Edna's gaze turned to the bloodied face of Mrs Rafaat's little diddums. She took a step back, her throat pulsing as she swallowed. "Uh . . . well, I just wanted to say what an honour it is, ma'am, and I, uh . . . Thanks for all your hard work." She retreated, desperate to take her eyes off Dog but not quite able to do so.

In a corner of the wrecked hall, Sammy, Swift and Sharon were huddled in urgent conference on the problem of Greydawn – namely, that Mrs Rafaat didn't seem to realise she *was* Greydawn.

"She's human," murmured Sharon. "I mean, isn't that it? She's human *and* she's Greydawn. But mostly she's just human. Like, I look at you," pointing at Swift, "and I can see you're a sorcerer and other shit too. And I look at Rhys over there, and I can see he's got like, these major psychological issues with his allergies and stuff, but is also a druid . . . but I look at Mrs Rafaat and she's just . . . Mrs Rafaat."

"On the other hand," Sharon mused, "I kind of doubt Dog would let anyone other than Greydawn give his tummy a rub. And if Burns and Stoke tried to capture Greydawn, and if Dog has been killing the summoning team involved in that, then I guess it's not a huge leap to say that something clearly went crappy last time Burns and Stoke tried to bind and compel Our Lady of 4 a.m., and so . . . and *so* . . ." Sharon spoke with the care of someone double-checking every logical twist before even thinking of uttering her thoughts out loud ". . . maybe Mrs Rafaat is the side effect of what went wrong?"

"What, you think the Lady's mortal form is some Indian bird from Wembley?" demanded Sammy.

For once Swift's face was not a picture of discontent. "Speaking as someone who has been at the centre of many mystical cock-ups, I can think of several ways in which—"

"But why Mrs Rafaat?" interjected Sharon. "Why'd she become *this* woman?"

Swift hesitated, then grumbled, "I have no idea." His eyes surveyed the room and fixed on the cowering shape of Eddie Parks. "Why don't we ask?"

Chapter 76

Eddie

Hi, I'm Eddie ...

(Hello, Eddie)

... please don't let the monster hurt me.

I got into magic at uni when I puked up in my hall of residence's cabal. They were well secret, but I was well pissed and I thought it was my door I was opening, but it was theirs and they were in the middle of this ritual thing and I'd had a few, and I guess you could say ...

Anyway, they said they could curse me, or I could join, and I figured yeah, looks cool, I'll do it! I'm not very good at magic – I get the words muddled and forget if I'm moving the sigil from left to right or right to left, but I do okay, you know? But it doesn't really pay, and I've always wanted money. I mean, not just for the sake of having money, but because it's there, someone's gotta have it, and if I have a choice between being the guy who's happy and the guy who's not, I'll take happy any day. And so thank you, yes, very much, for a Christmas bonus, you know? People talk about greed like it's a bad thing, but it's not – there's always gonna be rich people and there's always gonna be poor, and all greed is a conscious decision of which end of the ladder you're gonna fall. I think that's admirable, actually; I think that's something to make you proud.

I joined Burns and Stoke seven years back. They were good times on the market, and I'd forgotten most of the magic stuff anyway because it wasn't worth shit next to knowing where the derivatives market was gonna go. I knew there were a few others in the department who dabbled, you know, but it was all regulated and we had this deal with Harlun and Phelps, who everyone knew was *seriously* into the magic shit – no major financial gain through mystical means unless it was run by the Bank of England first. And getting anything by those tossers is practically impossible, so we just ignored it. Didn't need it, you know?

Then it all kicked off – Lehmans, Northern Rock, the Eurozone debt crisis, Greece, Spain, Italy – and we hadn't been too stupid, you know, we'd spread our bets and taken our positions carefully. But in that climate it didn't matter where you were at because everything, all of it, stank. And it's fucking stupid, yeah, because the government will bail out the banks when it's like, little people's money and that, but they won't raise a finger when the real fat cats, the guys who drive everything, when they're gonna burn. And so there we were, and we were all eyeing up our favourite pencils and the knick-knacks on our desks and wondering how much stationery we could sneak out of the cupboard before the entire thing went down, when *he* turned up.

Mr Ruislip.

I don't know where he came from, but one day I was called into a meeting and he was just there, sat at the head of the table. And he said:

"Good afternoon, Mr Parks. I hear you have some mild skills with magic. Kindly remain in the office after work today. I will see you at 8.45 p.m. precisely."

And that was it.

I turned up at 8.45 like the guy said, and there were like, a dozen other guys there including my boss, Gavin McGafferty, who even I thought was an arse, and I work in finance. And Mr Ruislip walked in just as the second hand hit the button and said:

"Gentlemen, you have been requested to remain behind as you have some moderate skill with summoning magics. I am not expecting wonders from you, yet, but from now on please consider your Tuesday and Thursday evenings to be within office working hours. And if you could each see to purchasing a box of latex gloves, that would be appreciated."

And he got us . . . doing things.

Spells I'd never heard of.

Big spells too, like . . . proper bindings, and compelling. We'd go to buildings all across the city, every Tuesday and Thursday night, and we'd make the summoning circle and we'd pull these . . . creatures out of the walls and floors. I guess you had to call them spirits, but they were all twisted shapes on the air, or odd bends of light, or shrieks with no bodies.

I was kind of freaked out at first. We were pulling out the souls of a place, but we always bought the building we were gonna perform the spell in, because that made it easier, because Mr Ruislip said if you held the deed of ownership in your hands then the binding would sit better on the stones. And he was right.

I got really good at it, in fact; though I didn't see why we were bothering until, one day, McGafferty said,

"You're a fucking stupid little arse, Parks, and I'm only gonna fucking show you this once so you can piss off and shut up, okay?"

And he took me downstairs, I mean right downstairs, lower than the lift went, to the basement of the building, past locks and doors and men with fucking guns – I mean, *guns*, can you believe it? – and into this giant vault thing. And at the bottom of this vault there was this great black hole, this spinning, whirling black pit. And I'm not much good at magic, but I could taste it, hear it on the air, and I looked into this thing and thought, shit, that's it, they've opened up a portal into hell. But it wasn't like that, it was a . . . a prison. They'd made a prison in a pit under the building and in it they trapped all the spirits we'd been summoning from the buildings, hurled them all together. And McGafferty said:

"These fucking ghouly-ghosts are old, old as the fucking streets. And they've changed with the times and they've become powerful with the times, and even the smallest little shit-rag spirit sucked from a fucking stupid laundrette has power. And we've got them now; we've got 'em and we can make 'em work for us, the way nature should be."

He told me that they had spells to suck the power out of the spirits, and spells to make them dance and obey, spells of summoning and control; that he himself had sent the soul of an Internet café flying round the world to steal data from a Hong Kong computer and made

two point three million that day. Or the spirit of an abandoned fire station which he'd dispatched to burn the warehouse of a company he'd
bet against. Or the soul of a nursery school which he'd sent to sing
lullabies into a trader's brain so he bid up, up, up, when he should have
just sold.

"Usually these beasties just sit around in the city and do shit," he
explained, "like the 'soul' isn't a fucking commodity! Fuck that, I say to
you, fuck that! This is the twenty-first century! Time for the fucking
soul to earn its way."

That's what we did.

We made magic a commodity. That's kind of what we do, I guess.

And I was okay with it. Jesus, I know you're gonna hate me now, but
I was okay with it because I was selling high and buying low, and it
didn't matter what the real value of the product was because if it went
too high I could just wave my fingers and tweak it back, and if it went
too low, no worries! Click my heels and problem solved. It was great,
I mean really, really great – it was what magic should've been, no sweat,
no consequences. So when Mr Ruislip called us into his office I was on
top of the world. I was like, "Yeah, screw you!" and "Rock on, universe!"
– only not to his face, of course – but that's how it felt, you know?

"Gentlemen," he said, "I am moderately satisfied with your efforts so
far. Stocks are recovering and there shall be Christmas bonuses for us
all."

He liked to talk about bonuses a lot, even when it was only spring,
did Mr Ruislip.

"I now feel confident enough in your endeavours to propose a far
more ambitious project. There is a spirit known to the sentimental as
Our Lady of 4 a.m. To date we have only attempted to bind petty
souls, little dabbling shadows, but Our Lady is a different creature
entirely. She can command life and death itself and grant the wish of
any standing before her willing to pay the price. I have produced a mission statement and business strategy for our next steps in capturing,
binding and compelling her; you will all find your tasks inside."

We did it – I mean, of course we did. Our heads were spinning with
money, with the taste of it, especially since so many other firms were
struggling, but we – we were the smart ones, we were frickin' gods! I
was tasked with finding appropriate sacrifices to compel this spirit –

which took fucking weeks I may add – and then we all assembled at
11 p.m. sharp – Mr Ruislip always meant sharp when he said sharp –
nine of us, to perform the summoning. McGafferty was leading it, and
as it got under way Mr Ruislip came in with a woman.

She was a cleaner.

She was shaking.

Crying.

Scared.

And you know how you know something, you know it but you can't
quite believe it? I didn't believe it, I didn't think we could, but then they
put her in the middle of the circle and she was sobbing, this Indian
woman with greying hair in a blue cleaner's overall, and she was beg-
ging and McGafferty had a knife and I thought no, he's not gonna, it's
a trick, he's not really gonna, but I knew he was, he had to, but I
couldn't say anything because no one else was saying anything and
fuck knows I wasn't gonna be the prat who asked a stupid bloody question or blew everything now, and besides she'd seen my face! I didn't
know ... I mean, I couldn't ...

... so I guess I didn't. Because no one else did. And looking back
now, I suppose everyone else there was kind of thinking the same
thing. But fuck me, why did I have to be the guy to speak? Why did I
have to do it, why couldn't someone else?

We got to the height of the spell, and I could feel the power, feel the
moving, and it was 4 a.m., bang on 4 a.m., and I thought, here we go,
and McGafferty stepped into the circle and raised the knife and just ...
he just did it. We were all swaying and chanting and there was this
power in the air, this incredible pressure, and I was burning hot from
it and felt like I was about to be snapped in two and McGafferty stuck
the knife in, wham, and I nearly laughed. Jesus, I nearly fucking
laughed because when the blood came out of the cleaner's chest you
could feel it, the power of it, the weight of it. I could taste it in my
mouth, boom! She fell to the floor and we all waited but ...

... nothing happened. McGafferty just stood there, blood dripping
off the blade, shaking, this stupid fucking grin on his face, but nothing happened. The spell was fucking working, we knew it was working,
but Greydawn wasn't there. We must have stood there for five minutes,
waiting for something to happen, until suddenly McGafferty dropped

the knife like he'd only just realised he was holding it, and the stupid grin vanished from his face and he just stood there, still trembling all over, muttering, "Fuck fuck fuck fuck . . ."

Then someone was sick. Someone else went to the door and puked outside. Other guys just sat down where they stood. I felt dizzy, confused, the blood still spreading across the floor. I went to the window and pressed my head against it, and Mr Ruislip was standing there, silent, hands folded behind his back, and I thought, he's gonna kill us, he's actually gonna kill us.

"Gentlemen," he said when the last of us had found some sort of composure, "shall we adjourn to the boardroom?"

And we would have adjourned to that fucking boardroom, blood still on McGafferty's hands, but someone said, "Where's the woman?" and we all looked round and she was gone. There was this trail of blood, not footsteps, just a great wide dragged-along streak of red, heading through the side door to the emergency stairs, and we all followed in a panic, fighting with each other, and I knew then, if she was still alive, I'd kill her, not to finish the spell but because she'd seen my face and had to die. She'd pulled herself all the way to the office below and collapsed on the floor. There was paper everywhere, like a whirlwind had been through the room, like a tornado had torn it apart, and she was already dead, staring up at nothing, and the lights were on and there was no fucking blood in her left to bleed and I felt relief, so much I nearly cried, to know that she was dead. But I thought I heard someone running down the hall, and I was too frightened to follow.

Only after, when Dog started hunting, did we begin to realise what had gone wrong with our spell.

It takes all your blood, every last drop, to summon and compel Greydawn.

But by the time the cleaner died, she wasn't in our summoning circle any more. The magic was good and true, but it was the dead woman who got her wish, not us. I just hope she wished for something good.

We didn't try that spell any more. All of us, we were too shaken. I knew Mr Ruislip was angry about it, but when we tried to scry for Greydawn, see where she was at, we got nothing. Like she wasn't even in the city any more.

Then things started to happen.

Rumours at first, odd warnings of things breaking out into the night which shouldn't have been there. Then one night Christian said he thought he'd heard howling, and Gavin said that was the stupidest thing he'd ever heard, and Scott said he thought there'd be consequences. And the next day Gavin was dead, torn apart in the dead of night, and there was no sign of his killer, except these footprints that had burned the earth. Then Christian heard the howling again, and he was dead two days after that, and Scott said, "We have to run we have to tell someone," and Mr Ruislip said, "You are entirely overreacting. Please, consider your bonus," and Scott, I think, did try to run, and did try to get help, but he didn't make it in time and the police asked me to identify the body, and I knew, Jesus, I knew it was gonna come for me too. There are nine of us in the summoning circle; now only three are left. I said:

"We gotta go to the Midnight Mayor! We have to get help!"

But Mr Ruislip replied, "Should you be so foolish as to refer to this gentleman for assistance, I shall be forced to refer you to that clause in your contract regarding premature termination." And by now I wasn't standing still for shit, I wasn't gonna do that stupid fucking thing of going "Does he mean it?" Because I fucking *knew* he meant it, he meant every word.

Then last night I heard the howling.

And I rang this guy at Harlun and Phelps and said, "I know everything. I know about Greydawn. I know why she's missing. It was us, we did it," and then the Midnight Mayor got on the line and he said:

"You're a shifty stupid little shit, but you're the best I've got to work with, so run."

And I ran.

I ran so hard, and so fast, and so far . . .

. . . and it brought me here.

Chapter 77

Listen Well and You Shall Learn

Eddie Parks was sitting, a wretched bundle of twisted suit and tie, in the centre of a wide circle of Magicals Anonymous. Members stared at him, mouths, or perhaps jaws, agape.

"Well," said Sharon at length. "So," she added when no one stirred. "Usually I'd offer you a cup of tea and ask you about your issues and that. But actually I think you're gonna crash and burn, and I'd kind of like to point and laugh while you do."

Hearing herself, she flinched. "Did I say that out loud? Sorry, that's really unprofessional of me, I mean . . . sorry. But yeah."

This wasn't the sympathetic reception Eddie might have hoped for. But any urge to come back with a sharp reply was discouraged by a low grumbling from the pit of Dog's belly. It seemed unlikely that the animal understood much English, but he did seem to have got the gist.

"The cleaner," ventured Sharon, "was Mrs Rafaat?"

As he talked, Eddie had gone to great lengths not to look at Mrs Rafaat. But now there seemed no choice.

"Yes," he admitted. "It was . . . it was . . ." He gestured feebly towards the old woman, who couldn't quite prevent herself from touching a hand to her chest and raising her eyebrows in a "No, me?" manner.

"But I'm not dead!" she exclaimed. "And I certainly don't remember being used as a human sacrifice."

"Ever worked as a cleaner?" asked Sharon with forced brightness.

"Well, yes . . . but that was years ago!"

"Maybe . . . two years, for example?"

Mrs Rafaat rubbed uneasily at Dog's back, a comfort gesture she didn't notice herself making. "But surely I'd remember being stabbed?" she suggested. "I don't want to disappoint anyone here, but really this all seems very unlikely."

"Blood," said a voice so soft that at first no one believed it had spoken. Sharon peered around to look at the speaker.

"Blood," she said again, and there was Edna, high priestess of the Friendlies, very still on a broken plastic chair, staring at Dog and his mistress.

"Uh . . . blood in a nice way?" hazarded Sharon.

"In the old days, in the darker days," murmured Edna, "Greydawn was . . . more complicated. Before street lighting, when the smog was in the streets, when the rats brought the plague and traitors' heads were put on spikes on London Bridge . . . she was still the protector of the wall, she guarded the lonely travellers in the night. But her touch was . . . more than just protection against the coldness and the nightmares. Her favours could be bought, with blood."

Several pairs of eyes tried their best not to stare too hard at Mrs Rafaat, who'd just become distracted by an earnest conversation with Sally the banshee about whether green was really such a bad colour for a sari.

"What kind of favours?" asked Sharon. "Though I really think I'm not gonna like the answer."

"It was said that for a prick of blood on the end of your finger, she could guard your path against all ill. But that for the blood of life, for a dying breath, there was no power that could stand before her."

There would have been silence, except that Rhys sneezed.

"Okay . . ." said Sharon. "I guess that kind of explains the whole Burns-and-Stoke-hunting-her-down thing."

"But why?" demanded Swift, scowling with frustration. "I mean, put me on the spot and ask me what I'd do with unimaginable power and I'd have . . . well, a failure of imagination."

"Lots of toothpaste," replied Sammy with a malignant glow in his eye. "And I'd make sure everyone got the truth about stupid bloody Blistering Steve and his stupid bloody spontaneous combustion."

"I need a new job," admitted Sharon. "I mean, I'm okay with working nine to five, but I'd kind of rather do ten to five, or maybe even ten to four, and I'd have a short lunch break and work really hard, and uninstall solitaire from my computer and that . . ."

"People!" cried Swift. "We're talking about she who divides the night from the day, Our Lady of 4 a.m., Greydawn herself, being paid for with the lifeblood of mortals! I think we're a bit past a supply of toothpaste and reasonable working hours!"

"Yeah, but *you* didn't graduate into a recession," grumbled Sharon. She raised her voice. "Hands up everyone here who wants infinite power."

One hand was cautiously raised from the far end of the room, before someone swatted it back down.

"And hands up everyone here who wants an annual income of around £35,000 after tax and a reasonably sized one-bedroom flat within Zones 1 or 2 and easy walking distance of an Underground station?" Nearly every hand shot up, including one or two which bore talons. Sharon turned to Swift, grinning with satisfaction. "This," she explained, "is why I'm a shaman, with people skills and that, and you're just some git in a tatty coat."

Swift threw his hands up in exasperation. "Okay. But the fact remains that Mrs Rafaat – the *first* Mrs Rafaat – was stabbed and died and made a wish, and now this Mrs Rafaat, *our* Mrs Rafaat, is sitting here alive and very not dead. Can you explain that, shaman?"

Sharon looked at Mrs Rafaat, who shrugged. "I'm so sorry, dear. I rather feel like I'm having something of an existential crisis. Might I have another cup of tea?" Rhys was at the kettle before Mrs Rafaat had completed her request. This was something he did know how to accomplish. In the confusion of recent hours, replete with human sacrifice, blood-soaked monsters and a CEO with an ambitious and unusual business model, tea was a lighthouse of certainty in a stormy sea.

"You said –" Sharon resisted the urge to kick Eddie as she spoke "– that Mrs Rafaat – the other Mrs Rafaat – died on the floor of the office. That by dying she completed your spell. What if she made a wish with her dying breath? What if Greydawn granted it?"

"What on earth could she have wished for that would lead to all this confusion?" demanded Mrs Rafaat.

"'Oh God, let me live'?" murmured Sharon.

Breaking the silence that followed, Swift admitted, "It does make a certain sense. I know that's what I'd be thinking."

"Maybe she made this wish," Sharon pressed. "And maybe Greydawn heard it, but maybe she didn't quite understand. The blood had been spilt; the spell had been cast; they'd summoned Greydawn. But it was Mrs Rafaat's blood on the floor and Mrs Rafaat who whispered her desires – and Greydawn tried to fulfil them? Only, she couldn't bring back the dead, couldn't undo the blood, so she tried the next best thing. She tried to make Mrs Rafaat live."

All eyes turned inexorably towards Mrs Rafaat.

"No," murmured the older woman. "That's just not ..."

Dog crooned at her feet, turning all attention back to him. He'd rolled onto his back and now lay, stretched out with his paws in the air, tail beating like a piston. Mrs Rafaat hesitated. Her gaze roamed from Dog to Eddie to the eyes fixed on her from all round the room, then up to the cracked walls and shattered windows.

"No," she repeated, shaking her head. "No, it's not ..."

Words failed her, and she stood up. Dog rolled onto his feet and followed her as she turned away and hurried towards the door.

Swift moved to go after her, but Sharon got there first.

"You're still an arsehole. I'll do this."

Outside, the old woman stood leaning against an iron bollard. Dog sat by her side, the street scorching lightly beneath his feet. The evening's drizzle had turned into night-time rain, thick cold splats falling with a busy static buzz.

"You okay?" asked Sharon.

"I remember ... I remember everything," Mrs Rafaat insisted. "My whole life. Where I was born, where I grew up, my husband, my work – I remember being me! That is who I am."

Sharon said nothing, but waited as Mrs Rafaat turned on the spot, looking this way and that like a startled cat.

"Even if I am ... even if there is any truth to this," she declared, "I don't know how not to be me! I don't know what they did to ... to me."

"It's okay." Sharon shuffled closer, soaking up the worst of Dog's glare as she did so. "We'll work that bit out."

"I don't think I want to be Greydawn," snuffled Mrs Rafaat, dabbing at her eyes. "I don't know what it means."

Sharon hesitated. Then, "Mrs Rafaat? Can I tell you something I haven't really told anyone? I mean, seeing as how you're probably the living essence of an immortal spirit, I figure ... Can I tell you?"

"Of course, dear – I mean, if you don't mind that I might *not* be a living essence."

"That's cool," said Sharon. "That's fine. Only, the thing is ..." She took a slow, deep breath. "The thing is ... five days ago I had a job, kind of crappy but still a job, and a flatshare I could just about afford as long as we didn't leave the central heating running, and I was gonna try and apply for this temping agency, and life wasn't great, but it was okay.

"But now ... *now* ... I'm on the wrong side of a wendigo; I've got this howling monster thing sat here, by the wreck of a community hall I might be responsible for, along with a bleeding druid, a wailing vampire, a toothpaste-addicted goblin, a gourmet troll and a socially inhibited banshee, not to mention there's this confused sorcerer who's not as much use as he should be, plus there's a hundred pigeons to round up. And as if that wasn't enough, my social life is a mess, my job prospects are nil, and I haven't got a boyfriend."

Mrs Rafaat's face was a picture of trying-to-help-despite-herself.

"And I know," insisted Sharon, "that not having a boyfriend is, compared to finding you're probably not who you think you are but maybe the walking essence of an ancient power, pretty low on the 'Oh, shit' scale of things. But it matters to me, because it's not like you can just go up to your friends and say 'Everything's crap. Please hold me unconditionally.'

"So, basically –" Sharon gestured in frustration as she tried to seize control of what she was saying "– what I mean is ... I think my life might not be going where I thought it was gonna go. And I'm not sure what the hell I'm meant to do about it, but ..." She was breathless with the force of her own oratorical conclusions. "But! If there's one thing I do know, it's that a shaman's gotta have a tribe. And that lot in there," indicating the remnants of the hall, "are *my* tribe. It's like that thing they told us about in school – social identity and that. We're all brought together by a shared-identity thing, and it's not black, or white, or Christian, or atheist, or good at knitting or anything like that, it's . . ."

She considered, then declared with sudden relish, "It's totally screwed up! We are the tribe of guys who are screwed up, each in our own different screwed-up way. And the best bit about it is, that's kind of what makes us human. That's what makes us ourselves. So yeah." Suddenly grinning at Mrs Rafaat. "You're screwed up, basically. And, more than any other crap, that's what makes you human. So come inside and have a cup of tea, and we'll work something out, yeah?"

Mrs Rafaat smiled despite herself and blew her nose. "You're very nice, dear," she said "even if you are a little strange."

"Come inside," repeated Sharon. "We're here to help, aren't we?"

Chapter 78

Sharon

Lonely.

I didn't mean it to come out like that. I mean, it's not like I sit down with total strangers and go, "Hi, I'm Sharon, I'm lonely." It's just that . . . this is about being honest, saying the things that are true. And the things that are true underneath. I didn't use to know what that meant, but now I think I start to get it – I mean like, true is true, yeah? There are the true things on the surface, and on the surface it's true that I'm okay. I really am. My parents aren't like, tyrants or divorced or dead or anything, and my friends are all okay. I've got a roof over my head and stuff – although I did kind of get sacked from my job two days ago, seeing as how I just didn't turn up to work, what with this saving-of-the-city thing – but it was a crap job anyway, so that's not so bad. You know, if we're just looking at big-picture stuff, then I'm fine.

And I'm lonely. That's true too. It's the truth that's underneath all the other stuff that's true. It's what is but what no one, not even me, wants to perceive. That's what being a shaman means – it's not about knowing the truth, it's about seeing all the other truths underneath.

There was a moment – this great big terrifying moment – when I looked up and I knew . . . everything. I was still me, but I was everything else: I was the paving stones and the wind and the water in the pipes and the words in the wires and the lights fizzing above garden doors and the grass growing and the iron rusting and the fences cracking. And I was ... I was the city, and I was still me, and I was everywhere and everything and knew all that there was to know and then ...

I lost it. I mean, not all of it. That was the day I started walking through walls, turning invisible. But even "invisible" is wrong; it's not "invisible" that I become, it's ... part of the furniture. It's something everyone sees but no one notices, kinda like parking meters, only more glamorous than that, if you see what I'm saying.

I was the city.

The city was me.

And now – now that I'm a shaman, wanderer of the hidden path and all that – I'm lonely.

Time to get myself a tribe.

Chapter 79

Have a Little Sour With Your Sweet

It was five minutes later.

Rhys was boiling another kettle for yet more tea. Tea for everyone, he realised, was an ongoing project. But he didn't mind; it was something he felt comfortable with.

Mrs Rafaat sat between Chris and Gretel, explaining to the fascinated exorcist that the only way to handle dogs was to show them that you were firm because you cared.

Eddie Parks, comforted perhaps by the sight of a troll eating custard creams, was on the verge of almost relaxing when –

"Oi oi, slime-shitter,"

– a goblin, a sorcerer and the girl-shaman were standing right behind him.

He'd never realised how threatening a pencil could be. But the way the goblin held it – perfectly upright, tip pointing at the ceiling, combined with a maniacal grin – invoked in Eddie's imagination all sorts of unwelcome things.

"You've screwed up the city big time and you're gonna pay, shrivel-brains," added the goblin. "Back in my tribe, if shits like you stepped out of line, we'd get two buses and a length of chain, and drive *really* slowly while—"

"Tell us how to break the spell," interrupted Sharon.

"Really?" said the sorcerer. "I was interested in hearing how Sammy's story ended."

Eddie's eyes flashed from one to the other, in search of the Good Cop among this wall of unimpressed features. Failing, he looked instead for the Least Bad Cop and, in a moment of naive desperation, focused on Sharon.

"Y-y-y-y-you need blood!" he stuttered. "I don't know how it was done before, but I know you need blood!"

"Can we see if he has any?" asked the goblin. "I hear that if you nick the femoral artery just right—"

"Let's say we haven't got blood," interrupted Sharon again. "How else do we fix it?"

"Uh . . . you need the sacrifices."

"What sacrifices?"

"The s-s-sacrifices we used to summon and compel. They're part of the spell."

"Okay, how do we get them?"

"Burns and Stoke kept them," he said hurriedly. "They're in the office vault."

"Your office has a vault?" demanded Swift. "My office doesn't have a vault – why do you get a vault?"

"We could hang 'im upside down," suggested the goblin, "and collect the blood in a really big bucket! Though I s'pose we'd need a lid for it, to get it across the city. And maybe ice. People never think about the temperature of bodily fluids when casting magics like this. Incompetent bastards."

"What about the spell?" demanded Sharon. "How do we get Greydawn back?"

"There's a c-counter spell," he stammered, "to release all bindings! You need the sacrifices to perform—"

"Any special preparations? Ritual baths, ceremonial massages, that kind of crap?"

Eddie shook his head. Moisture clung to his skin as his body suffered a sweaty, adrenaline-fuelled overdrive.

"Excellent!" Swift slapped his hands together, business-like and brisk. "Get sacrifices. Say spell. Job done. Early night. I'm on board with this."

"You . . . need a shaman!"

The way Eddie said it seemed to suggest that this would be the final straw which broke the camel's back. But Swift grinned, patting the quaking wizard on the knee. "Way ahead of you there, sunshine."

"Blood. You still need blood."

Sammy looked at Swift; Swift looked at Sharon; Sharon shrugged. "I got nothing," she said. "Can it be from the donor banks?"

"Uh, babes," Kevin chimed in from across the room, "I don't want to be the voice of civic responsibility here or anything, but there is like, a serious stock crisis going on right now across all major blood groups."

A glare from the assembled room induced some polite cowering. "Then again," Kevin grumbled, "maybe saving the city is an okay use of limited NHS resources."

"But it's not about haemoglobins!" exclaimed Sammy. "Else we'd all be using rump bloody steak and chips in our magics! It's about life – blood as life. What peanut-balls is saying –" here, a firm kick connected with Eddie's shins "– is not 'You need some sticky red stuff' but 'You need life and death.'"

"Whoa!" Sharon gestured defensively. "When I signed up for this, I had this big thing about no feathers, no dancing and no blood."

"Dancing?" queried Swift.

"And no blood! My mum would have a fit if I got piercings, especially if it was feathers. And can I just add, cos I think it's important, no blood!"

There was a embarrassed pause while Swift patted her on the shoulder with the lightness of a man toying with nitroglycerine.

"Well," he said at last, "maybe we could try three sheep and a—"

He was interrupted by a ringing sound.

Ringing wasn't quite the word; ringing implied a bell. This was an electronic pumping sound, an eight-beat intro followed by a little tinny chant. The chant proclaimed:

"I'm so cool, I'm so cool, I'm so cool, *yeah!*"

All eyes turned to the source of the sound, and Eddie Parks cringed. Through the material of his trousers, the bright white screen of a mobile phone was visible. Mr Roding said, "Will someone please stop that ghastly noise?"

Eddie levered the phone out of his pocket, handling it like lit matches in a sea of oil. He passed it to Sharon without a word. She looked down and saw that the number was "Unavailable".

The phone kept ringing.

"I'm guessing this isn't your mum, calling at 2 a.m., to check up on whether you're going to the dentist?" she hazarded. At the ripple of surprised expressions she added, "Come on, like I'm the only one that happens to."

"I-I-I-I-I-I ..." Eddie's attempt at responding dissolved into a wheeze of despair.

"Fine," grumbled Sharon and, before anyone could stop her, she thumbed the phone on and put it to her ear. "Hello, Magicals Anonymous, self-help for the mystically traumatised. Sharon speaking, can I help you?"

A stunned silence on the end of the line. Then, "Please hold."

A pre-recorded assault on a Chopin theme began. Sharon put her hand over the mouthpiece and whispered loudly at the room, "I think it might be a sales pitch."

Then, "Is Eddie Parks dead?"

The voice was soft, cold and smooth, male inasmuch as it wasn't overtly female. It sounded detached, and was entirely recognisable. It was the voice of Mr Ruislip, the wendigo.

"Uh ..." The sound just came out, a default filler in the empty air.

"What is 'Uh'?" asked the voice on the other end of the line, keen and curious. "I've heard people make these noises as though they have meaning – uh and ah and um and aaaggh – and I did investigate them in the dictionary but found it unsatisfactory. Do they imply an emotional state? Or have they a meaning in the human mind that language does not have the capacity to fulfil?"

Sharon hesitated. The entire room was staring at her, dozens of faces contorted with the doubt and fear of people who knew, who just *knew*, who and, perhaps more importantly, what, was on the end of the line, but really didn't want that knowledge confirmed. In the silence, Sharon took in the upside-down face of Sally, dangling from the rafters, the puckered frown of Kevin, the disgruntled query of Mr Roding, the hopeful, open eyes of Rhys as he seemed to say, without twitching a muscle in his flushed face, *Go on, go on, go on* ...

And it occurred to Sharon, with an almost physical shock, that someone in this room, for reasons beyond her comprehension, believed in her. She tried to remember if anyone had believed in her before. Certainly the careers officer hadn't, nor had her boss Mike Pentlace. Indeed, throughout her whole life ...

"Kind of both, actually." She was amazed to hear the words pass her lips, amazed at how confident they sounded. "Uh is a kinda filler sound, sorta like going 'Fuck me, I don't know what to say to that, but shit, I'd better make this kinda noise to make it clear that I'm still paying attention.' So I guess you could say it's rude, because it's like going 'Please hold' only without saying it. But I think it's actually okay, because it's like saying 'Please hold while I come up with a sensible and groovy response to you.' And we're always told, aren't we, that you should stop and think about your replies, and I guess life would be better if more people did that, you know?"

It was Mr Ruislip's turn to be silent. Sharon ploughed straight on, warming to her theme, provoking a dangle of astonishment in the corner of Rhys's mouth, and filling with an energy she hadn't known she possessed.

"But the great thing about uh is it's so context-specific, you know? I mean, like, when you just called now, and I went 'Uh,' it wasn't so much 'Please hold' as a kind of 'Bugger me, I'm talking to a wendigo.' So there was, I guess, fear and surprise and a bit of curiosity, but mostly terror in it, as well as the 'Please hold' meaning. So you see, actually, uh is this really flexible sound; I mean, it gave you all of that, didn't it, so didn't really need me to say it."

Eventually he said, "I see."

"See!" she went on, almost hysterical now with enthusiasm for her theme. "'I see' is another example of those filler things. Because, when you said that, it was totally obvious that you don't see, that you haven't, in fact, got a frickin' clue what I'm talking about. But you felt this need to fill the space, didn't you?

"So your 'I see' didn't mean 'Yes, I comprehend.' What it actually meant was 'Bloody hell, this isn't going where I thought it would and what is this woman talking about I really don't get this crap but I wish I did.' And, Mr Ruislip, I was thinking about this, because it seems to me that you've got serious issues, with like, language and death and stuff, and I was wondering if you'd considered talking to someone about them."

Rhys's mouth was now hanging all the way open. So, for that matter, was Swift's. "Recognising the problem," she hissed down the phone, almost conspiratorially, "is the first step to recovery."

This time she let the silence linger.

"Is Eddie Parks dead?" The question sounded to Sharon's ear like a retreat to familiar territory.

"Why, should he be?" she asked.

"Apparently Mr Parks heard a howling," sighed the wendigo, "which is usually indicative of an imminent demise. However, my office informs me that a few hours ago the professional gentlemen I hired to conduct some private research for this company vanished. And though Dog howled, it seems there is not as much blood being spilt as I would have predicted from this event. And so, I wished to enquire of Mr Parks directly whether he was, in fact, deceased."

"Uh . . . no, he's not. Sorry."

"In that case, may I speak to him?"

Sharon glanced at Eddie, who shook his head, hands shaking in his lap.

"I think Eddie here has got some issues he needs to work on in a private way," sang out Sharon down the line. "Maybe another time?"

"In that case, would you kindly inform Mr Parks that, in the light of his attempting to run away and contact the Midnight Mayor for assistance, his contract has been terminated, and his blood, muscle, bones and all other associated vital bodily fluids are now mine for the taking?"

Sharon raised her eyebrows. "Wow," she said. "That's like, one hell of a contract."

"In matters of private enterprise, penalties must be equal to rewards," replied Mr Ruislip primly. "We are not running . . . a *public-sector* enterprise." The words dripped off his lips like venom. "On a similar theme," he went on, "I must inform you that, should you and your ilk fail to hand over the spirit known as Greydawn, I will most reluctantly be forced to hunt you all down and kill you one at a time. Is reluctantly the word? Was its usage correct?"

"I dunno," murmured Sharon. "Depends whether you're going for literally 'I'll be really sorry to do it and it'll be a right pain in the arse,' or more kind of 'Whoopee, I'll kill everything that moves and bathe in its blood, but let's be all polite while telling people about it in order to freak out my prey.'"

"Oh, the latter, absolutely."

"Then, yeah, I guess you could go with 'reluctantly'."

"Thank you, Ms ... Sharon, was it?"

"That's right."

"Sharon, thank you. It's so refreshing to meet someone willing to clarify these finer points. Tell me, if I were to inform you that I shall take great satisfaction in ripping you apart limb by limb, tearing your body asunder to the smart pop of bones pulling out of their sockets, the gentle tear of tendons ripping under a slow but inexorable pressure, would that add to the sense of growing terror and imminent destruction that I am attempting to imbue?"

"It's pretty good," she admitted. "I like the way you said 'satisfaction' there – kinda like it was more 'I'm a professional, controlled psychopath and therefore you should be afraid' vibe than if you'd gone with 'glee' or 'delight' or anything like that, which would've implied you're a wacky out-there psychopath and therefore kinda easier to deal with."

"How marvellous!" exclaimed Mr Ruislip. "Satisfaction it shall be, then."

"Excuse me?" The speaker was Swift, one hand raised. "I'm sorry to butt in like this, but as the Midnight Mayor I really feel I should be threatening to rain hellfire down upon the wendigo's head, if that's okay."

Sharon turned to listen, then added down the phone, "Mr Ruislip sir, I hope you don't mind but the Midnight Mayor wishes to inform you that he shall rain hellfire down upon your head. How'd you feel about that?"

"Kindly inform the Midnight Mayor," murmured Mr Ruislip, "that I have long relished the opportunity to hunt one worthy of my skills. And when we two at last meet in the heat of bloody battle, and the stones turn black beneath our feet, and the sky cracks at the screams torn from our throats, I shall experience an immense ... *satisfaction* ... in the experience of the moment, quite regardless of who is destroyed at the end of it."

Sharon covered the mouthpiece and muttered at Swift, "The wendigo says he's groovy with that."

"Oh. Okay."

"As it is," went on Mr Ruislip, "I believe the Midnight Mayor right now should be more concerned by the fact that Burns and Stoke will be withdrawing all its finances from Harlun and Phelps, thus seriously undermining the stability of the company and depriving a large number of Aldermen of their Christmas bonus."

Sharon covered the mouthpiece again. "He's gonna use finance on you," she hissed.

Swift scowled but made no reply.

"As for yourself and all the other members of Magical Anonymous ... May I call your organisation quaint? Quaint ... curious ... unexpected ... really, what adjective would best describe it? Anyway, would 'annihilate' do or is that rather jumping the gun? What is the origin of the phrase jumping the gun, do you know? I understand its usage but not its—"

"Let's stick with quaint," interrupted Sharon.

"Oh, very well. As for yourself and the members of your *quaint* organisation, if you hand Greydawn over to me right this second, I may spare the majority of you. If you refuse to cooperate, I will be forced to take aggressive action, namely to *annihilate* you and all your kind. I hope these terms are agreeable to you?"

Sharon considered long and hard. "You know how you have language concerns," she said. "Have you considered evening classes?"

"What?"

"Evening classes," she repeated. "I mean, I know it's kind of a middle-class thing, because, like, everyone who really needs extra education is probably too poor to pay for it and the government is totally trashing public services. But you sound like a rich guy, and money buys you time and time buys you opportunity, and I seriously think you're the kind of limb-rending psychopath who'd do really well with a few evening classes, a bit of counselling, maybe a course in ethical philosophy and cookery or something. Maybe Italian food or that, because that's quite relaxing."

"I'm sorry, is this your fear reaction?" asked Mr Ruislip. "I do find the telephone makes it so much harder to judge, as I cannot actually smell the terror dripping off your skin like blood from a butcher's blade. So I am forced to enquire: do you in fact manifest these words as a result of a deep horror and dread of who and what I am?"

"Uh ... I guess a bit," she admitted. "But actually I really think the world would be a better place if people just sat down and looked at their lives. I keep lists of things I've gotta do before I'm thirty, and I practise breathing out slowly while counting to ten. But I'm guessing you're not into that sorta thing, which is really sad. And I like completely see how you're probably not gonna get past the rending-limb-from-limb thing, which you're stuck on, any time soon. So I guess all that's left to say is . . . well . . . uh . . . bring it on?"

Even as the words passed her lips, she flinched.

"Bring . . . it . . . on?" Mr Ruislip echoed each word with dull astonishment.

"Uh, yeah. Kinda. I mean, in that if you *do* try and hurt me or anyone here, then I guess we'll have to like, get all aggressive with you, which is really sad. But you know, sometimes a girl's gotta do what a girl's gotta do. So, uh. Yeah. Sorry about that. I just want you to know how embarrassed I feel to have to resort to mystical violence like this. But so it goes. Was there anything else?"

Mr Ruislip was silent save for the slow in-out of his breath between clenched teeth. Sharon found herself grinning at nothing much and no one in particular.

"Okay then!" she sang out. "Well, it's been great talking to you. Hope you're okay with this and are moving on to a new and groovy place, and see you on the other side of the bloodbath! Bye!"

She hung up, and nearly dropped the phone in her haste to pass it back to Eddie. Eddie whimpered as it fell into his hands and threw it to Rhys, who just about caught it and looked around for guidance as to what to do with it. The nearest person who could help with that turned out to be Gretel, who very carefully picked up the phone between her thumb and index finger and crushed it to a handful of electronic debris.

Throughout the room every eye was on Sharon, mostly in aston-ishment. Sammy and Swift were looking at her open-mouthed, and there was a glow in the goblin's eye that could have been disbelief at the foolishness of his apprentice but also pride in her work. Rhys was looking at her with a strange dreamy grin plastered on his face. He was, Sharon thought, a man lost in thoughts that she didn't particularly want to divine.

As she turned, the flash of Dez's white suit was visible as he flickered in and out of existence between the crowd, and she half-imagined his tanned-orange thumbs were raised at her from behind Kevin's head.

"Now you've done it," whispered Dez in a corner of her mind, but was he laughing?

"Right," she said, sensing that something profound was expected.

"Well," she added.

Then, "Okay."

After the rush of talking to the wendigo, she evidently wasn't handling her audience well.

"So," she concluded, "we're screwed, aren't we?"

Chapter 80

To Go to the Heart of the Matter

The walls are singing.

This is what they say:

Help us, help us, help us, help us!

Help us, help us, help us!

HELP US!

HELP US, SHAMAN!

They've been singing for a long time now, calling out from the dark.

Except, perhaps, singing isn't the right word.

Perhaps what it's been, all this time, is a scream.

Chapter 81

I Am Beautiful, I Am Wonderful...

Rhys woke with a start.

It was something he'd been doing a lot lately, in fact ever since he'd encountered Sharon at Burns and Stoke and learned of captured spirits and angry wendigos.

For a moment he didn't know where he was, and then something large – no, not large – huge – turned over on the floor beside him.

Oh yes.

He was on the floor of Sally the banshee's gasometer, sleeping in a borrowed blanket on a piece of card next to a troll, a vampire and a goblin.

"Consider all homes, flats, houses, dens and lairs dangerous!" the man called the Midnight Mayor had proclaimed. "Burns and Stoke are clearly on to you lot as being guys in the know, so stick together and don't be arseholes!"

Motivational speaking, Rhys had decided, was not one of the Midnight Mayor's job requirements.

My gasometer really is very roomy, Sally had suggested, and I find the touch of moonlight to be rather stimulating if you need a nocturnal guard ...

Rhys looked up and, yes, there she was, her wings folded in tight around her body, head dangling and mouth open wide to reveal in full, tongue-dangling glory the sheer black depths of a banshee's throat. Somewhere behind those deadly fangs was a set of vocal cords that could freeze the blood of man. As Sally slept, her body swayed, the whiteboard she used for communication dangled from her neck, with a washable marker pen Sellotaped to its top.

Rhys felt at the bandages round his middle. They, and he, were intact despite the exertions of the night before. Somehow Magicals Anonymous hadn't left the shattered remnants of St Christopher's Hall until four in the morning, when Sharon had posted a note on the splintered front door: *Bomb fell – sorry for the inconvenience.* He looked at his watch; it was 2.30 in the afternoon, and the rest of the society was still mostly asleep.

Moving with a vain attempt at stealth he crawled out from under his blanket and stepped around the others' unconscious forms. They included Chris the exorcist, Edna the Friendly and Jess I-turn-into-pigeons. She'd finally turned back into a human, while the long-suffering Jeff shouted, "I'll black the eyes of anyone who peeks!" before producing clean clothes and a towel kept packed for the occasion. Kevin lay sleeping with a note taped to his shirt warning, *Do not wake until sundown or else.* Underneath, someone had written, *Or else what?*

The door to the gasometer was a rusted iron affair, which shrieked as he eased it back before wriggling through the narrowest gap he could and out into the sunlight.

The air was mild, the day brisk and clear. The gasometer stood in a wasteland of buddleia, brambles and tall Japanese knotweed, where piles of toppled brick were stained orange–green by lichen, and the inevitable broken shopping trolley lay upside down with the remnants of soiled plastic bags dribbling out.

Ms Somchit sat on a small pile of breeze blocks by the door, reading a novel. Its cover featured women in romantic floppy hats and a title promising exotic adventure and love ever after. Without glancing up the tiny Alderman informed Rhys that there was a greasy spoon up the road that served breakfast all day.

"No worries, my lovely," she said as he thanked her. He began to walk, then a thought struck him.

"Where's . . . Dog?" He tried to frame the question, shoulders back, as if it concerned a small family pet.

"Walked off at the dawn light," replied Ms Somchit, turning another page. "Looked east and walked away, and where he had been before, there he suddenly was not. I wouldn't worry about it; mystical manifestations are like that. Light of day and the incorporeal nature of their beings, all that kind of thing. I'm sure he'll be found when we need him."

"Oh . . . good."

Le Café Delight stood on a nearby street between a laundrette and a newsagent whose window advertised lessons in Arabic, massages, tango classes (beginner–intermediate) and finest Polish delicacies. The sound of sizzling and the smell of bacon dragged Rhys, zombie-like, through the door, past the early-afternoon clientele of steel-capped construction crew and retired gentlemen reading the naughty pages of the tabloids.

"Can I have . . . everything?" he said at the counter, reaching into his pocket.

"Full English?" asked the woman.

"With extra tomatoes?" he hazarded and froze. His pockets were empty. Somehow, in all the excitement of the night before, he'd put his wallet down, and he wasn't quite sure where. "Uh . . . "

The woman behind the counter put on the universal expression of kindly matrons everywhere who've had their kindliness taken for a ride. "You okay, luv?"

"How much is it?" asked a voice behind Rhys.

He couldn't turn. Relief and shame fought for control of his features and settled for an all-purpose blush.

Sharon leaned past him and pushed a banknote over the counter. "It's okay," she added as change was handed back. "He's had a bad couple of days."

Rhys swayed with gratitude as Sharon guided him to a plastic bench by a red plastic table shimmering with rubbed-in grease. He realised he'd never been so hungry in his life. As a fresh set of slightly grubby cutlery was placed before him in a crumpled paper napkin, he recalled what must have happened.

"I, uh, think I lost my wallet back in Exmouth Market while dragging a murderer far enough away from his friends so that they all dissolved . . . you know, into the nether mist. Oh," he added with a flush of relief, "but I left my credit card in Frances's flat. Only, seeing as how I'd already been stabbed and it had blood on it, I took it out with my library cards and cycling club card and left them all behind in case something bad happened . . ."

"It's the shock," said Sharon, settling opposite him to resume her breakfast of scrambled eggs, bacon and toast. "Apparently scented candles are very good for this sort of situation."

His almost-teatime breakfast was put in front of him, and he attacked like it was personal. Some time passed before he felt free to pause and look up. Sharon was wearing a frown of concentration. She said, "You know, there's no point denying it. Things are crappy, I mean like, generally. And we may as well say so, because that is the only way in which we shall Overcome Our Issues." She intoned the words carefully, as one making sure she had them right and hoping others would share in her appreciation.

"Acutally," she went on, "I've been thinking this through . . . I've got no job, no degree, no experience, and I'm what the accountants call financially fucked, *and* I'm registered to vote in a safe seat, so when the elections come round it's not even like I can help get these wankers out of government . . . and I've got to save the city and that. And I feel . . . okay." The word slipped out, slow and considered.

She tried it again, just to make sure it was right. "O-kay. Yeah! I actually feel . . . all right about it all. I mean, I can kiss goodbye to new shoes or anything like that, but for the first time since . . . well, for ever . . . I feel like I've got . . . something that's for me. Something I'm meant to do."

There was a clatter as her fork hit the plate.

She jerked upright, eyes wide. "Oh shit," she muttered. "*That's* what I am. I'm a bum. I'm a self-help shaman and a spirit-walking bum. *Jesus.*"

Rhys felt he should say something significant. Before he could utter a word, Sharon cut him off anyway.

"We gotta go back to Burns and Stoke. We gotta free the spirits they've been pulling from the city. We gotta find these sacrifices they talked about. Undo the spell. Get Greydawn back. Problem is —" her face twisted into a scowl "— it's the only thing we *can* do and the wendigo is gonna know it. And it could go really, really bad."

Her eyes widened at a further thought.

"This must be how heroic stuff happens!" she exclaimed. "I always wondered why people would go running towards the fire, but I guess I get it now – because there's a bigger fire somewhere else! Wow." She sank back against her chair. 'This has been a learning experience, hasn't it?"

"Um ... Ms Li?"

Sharon's eyes drifted towards Rhys's gaze, and he managed to hold her look without flinch, dribble or snot getting in the way.

"I know I'm not very good at the magic thing," he confessed. "And I know I haven't been very helpful so far, except in bringing biscuits to meetings. But I *was* nearly the chosen leader of the sacred circle and I *did* almost pass my exams. And if I can help, I'd like to."

Sharon smiled at him.

"Actually," she said, "I've been wondering ... What is it that druids do?"

Chapter 82

I Have A Secret...

Matthew Swift, Midnight Mayor, sorcerer extraordinaire, guardian of the night, etcetera, etcetera, sat on the highest part of Sally the banshee's home gasometer and ate a cheese and pickle sandwich.

"Wotcha," he said to a particular place in the empty air.

Sammy grudgingly shimmered into existence beside him.

"I always meant to ask," the sorcerer said, through a mouthful of grated cheese and heavily spiced onion, "why I can't see you when you're invisible, but I can smell you. Surely invisibility should affect all the senses?"

"It does," grumbled the goblin. "You can't smell Sharon, yeah? It's just I've got a more magnificent odour than the mind can ignore. Lifetime's work, smelling like me."

Swift swung his legs out over the drop and went on eating. In the distance a long freight train snaked into a tunnel; its engine, just audible, throbbed deeper as it picked up speed. The Golden Mile was a stubble of silver-grey towers, Canada Water a more distant clump of spikes in the flatlands of inner London, far out to the east.

Below, Rhys and Sharon wandered back through the overgrown wasteland. They were, Swift realised, picking flowers: fistfuls of buddleia, rubbery webs of crawling ivy, the white fluff from seeding thistles; all of it being shoved into a large cloth bag. And more – flakes of rusty iron scraped from old foundations, crumbling shards of mortar, great armfuls of green algae from the nearby canal and finally dirty old water from foul settled puddles.

Swift half-thought he could also hear voices, rising up from far, far below.

"This is very kind of you – *atchoo!* – Ms Li."

"Not a problem."

"I'm sure once we've got it in the summoning circle it'll be – *atchoo!* – it'll be all right."

"Got every confidence, Rhys."

"Looks like dribbly-nose is making potions," commented Sammy, who'd also been watching them. "You wouldn't know about that shit because you're all about the elemental power and stuff. But some people, *some* people have to actually study, and work, and pay attention to their craft."

"Is that what urban druids do? Make potions?"

"Nah, it's what baby druids do," replied Sammy. "It's what druids do what fail their exams because they get sneezing fits during the sacred intonations."

"An embassy from the Sacred Circle of Muswell Hill tried to explain it to me once. But they'd just accidentally awakened a slumbering ent in Highgate Cemetery who managed to damage Karl Marx's grave before tripping over a telephone line. So we got a bit disrupted."

"Lotta amateur pillocks doing crappy magic," agreed Sammy.

The two sat in silence a while longer, watching the city bustle beneath them.

Swift sighed, his chin sinking deeper into the shapeless stained mass of his coat. "I can't – and this is a novel experience for me – I can't fix this alone. We are not used to these ways, to the hidden things. Our strength is only potent against tangible evils, whereas this ... this world of spirits and shadows and things unseen, is beyond our ... beyond my usual remit. Ever since the business with the Tower, with Bakker, I've tried to cut myself off from much of the world. The lessons I learned were that friends leave you, or they die, or they are damaged by the life you lead. I lie to the ones I love to keep them away when, to be honest, I probably need them the most. And now this ... It is not our world."

Sammy considered this for a long while. Then he reached out and patted Swift on the knee. "Can I give you some advice?" he asked, "as a shaman and spiritual guide, and that?"

"Sure."

The goblin sucked in air through his mighty teeth, considering his next few words.

"Live with it," he announced at last. "Lump it," he added. "And deal with it."

The sorcerer reflected on this advice.

Beneath him he half-thought he heard the druid mumble:

"Now, the secret to being a good druid, Miss Li, is always to have a fresh pack of facial wipes."

Swift groaned. "Yup," he admitted, "fair enough."

Chapter 83

The Secret Is ...

The sun was setting over London.

Sharon sat on the edge of a rusted iron staircase curling up the outside of the gasometer, and watched it. The sun was watery orange-yellow, sinking towards a horizon obscured by rolling grey cloud. A pair of angry blackbirds were shrieking at a cat that was stalking through the bushes on their territory. Somehow the best part of the afternoon had vanished, spent offering Rhys tissues from a box of Man-Sized Economy Deluxe, while he intoned between allergic symptoms and wrapped up various potions and powders in fragments of rag, labelling them with a felt tip pen and a piece of masking tape.

The names used by the druid seemed a little disappointing. But if nothing else they helped the inexperienced user. A small pack of powder was marked "Sleep"; another, "Hysteria". At one point Gretel, intrigued by the smells, had wandered into their improvised shelter, made of buddleia branches and plastic sheeting, only for Rhys to shoo her out with a cry of "We can't let Hysteria near a troll!" Thereafter the mere possibility had provoked a great, watery fit of coughing.

Now, Sharon knotted her fingers together between her knees and whispered under her breath:

"I am beautiful, I am wonderful, I have a secret ..."

The first time she'd walked through a wall by mistake, it hadn't been psychological counselling she'd required, since the fact of her turning invisible and being able to pass through solid surfaces was undeniable. What troubled her was more a question mark over whether any of these truths could be *healthy*. What effect, for example, did invisibility have on blood pressure?

Shamanism, it turned out, didn't come with a manual.

She'd read a lot of self-help books. Not as a conscious decision; it was just that titles such as *It's Okay, It's Not You* and *Working Through Your Problems Without Working Yourself Up* had seemed at that time to chime with her very essence. And in one of them, on page one, there it had been – the mantra to be uttered whenever doubts assailed and confidence fled:

"I am beautiful, I am wonderful, I have a secret, the secret is . . . "

"Oi oi, scrawny!"

The voice of Sammy the Elbow.

"You got your battle paint ready?" demanded the goblin. " 'S okay!" he cackled, seeing the look on her face. "Only stupid-git kinds of shaman do the battle-paint shit."

"Sammy," Sharon's voice had the rising edge of someone testing a difficult hypothesis, "I've always wondered . . . do you *enjoy* watching people suffer?"

The goblin thought about it, then clapped his hands with glee. "Love it!" he exclaimed. "Arseholes everywhere, may as well stick . . . "

"Never mind."

He hesitated, waiting for Sharon to move. Her face was turned towards the sunset, as if waiting for the last of the light.

"Uh . . . squelchy brains?"

She didn't answer.

"It's your tribe," he said. "You're their shaman. You're the one has gotta lead 'em."

"I know," she murmured. "I think I always knew. But that's . . . I think it's gonna be okay."

For once in his life, Sammy said nothing.

Sharon smiled, turning away from the setting sun.

"Right," she said. "Let's go fix this, shall we?"

Chapter 84

Anonymous, Assemble!

Later, when the history of Magicals Anonymous was assembled and compiled by one B. Cartiledge, scholar, wizard and sometime player of bagpipes, the rally cry of Sharon Li would be recorded in the following manner:

"Friends! Colleagues! Comrades! We here gathered today are the latest, greatest assembly of magical might ever to walk the stones of the city! I look at you and I see scions of the darkness, masters of the decaying flesh, queens of the sky, guardians of the bridge and the chosen druid of his circle, and I know, as the city's soul stands in the balance and the very fate of our friends and loved ones resides in our hands, that we, together, can achieve a magnificent victory for truth, for brotherhood, for life!"

In the bibliographical reference for this section a small footnote suggests that, in the author's humble opinion, the quality of this speech, given to Magicals Anonymous before they went off to do battle with the forces of the dark, may in fact have been exaggerated.

An alternative wording was offered which, while lacking some of the glamour of the standard accepted version, had, it was felt, an indefinable tang of authenticity, and it went like this:

"So, yeah, guys. Basically, we're in so much shit until we sort this shit out, so I know it's not really your problem, but it kind of is, which is cool, because it's also everyone's problem, but kind of groovy that we're the guys standing up to deal with it, so I guess you can all feel proud and that.

"But I figure we'll be okay, yeah, because we've got a troll and a druid and a vampire and a necromancer and a sorcerer and a high priestess and a dog and shit on our side, whereas Burns and Stoke are only like this mega-evil banking corporation led by a psychopathic wendigo and all his forces of darkness, so we'll be totally fine. Oh, and Gretel's made sandwiches, so if we can all thank Gretel that'd be great, and if you could keep any receipts for travel expenses, then the Midnight Mayor's gonna see if he can reclaim them. Cheers for that."

And with those inspiring words, the combined forces of Magicals Anonymous went forth to do battle for the city.

Chapter 85

The Dark Is Merely Light Unseen

He's waiting.

He smooths the silk of his suit and the thinness of his hair, and watches, and waits.

Mr Ruislip, the blood cleared from the walls, knows they're coming.

The four builders are gone.

The Friendlies are fled.

Magicals Anonymous turned around and, for a bunch of self-indulgent whiners, revealed itself to have claws.

They're coming to free the spirits of the city, to find the truth about Greydawn, to take revenge against him and his darkness.

They're coming to fight.

He smiles.

At last, something Mr Ruislip understands.

Chapter 86

The End of Today Is Merely the Dawn of Tomorrow

The sun sets over the city.

It disappears prematurely at the end behind a bank of thick cloud, spilling great bursts of golden light into the sky above as the darkness encroaches.

Gold fades to orange, to pink, to red, to purple, and purple turns at last to the light-stained blue-black of an urban night.

Two figures and a body odour stand in the shadows of the Barbican, that great maze of towers, fountains and walkways on the edge of the City of London.

One says, "This is really very kind of you, Mr Swift. But as I said, I'm sure my little puppy won't do any harm."

Another says, "I have every confidence, Mrs Rafaat. But as you have such a natural touch with him, I was thinking maybe, all things considered, we should just double-check on his well-being."

The body odour says from the empty air, "Oi oi. You two are thick as cold syrup and can't see nothing. But I'm looking at the city wall right now and I gotta tell you the gate is *well* down. Someone's been mauling and tearing at these city walls, and if I wasn't such an amazing shaman I'd be really worried by the thought of what could be getting in."

"I do hope this isn't my fault," wailed Mrs Rafaat. "I know that you think this ... Greydawn character ... is somehow responsible for these ... city walls you say you can see. But I really don't remember any of this, and actually I'm very concerned that you may have made a terrible mistake."

"Ma'am," said Swift, "shall we recap the manner in which a primal monster covered in gore rolls over at your feet and wags his tail at your touch? Or can we take that particular conversation as read?"

"Maybe I've just got a knack?" suggested Mrs Rafaat.

"'Sides," whispered the odour of Sammy the Elbow, "you can't be talking to Greydawn like that, cos she's Our Lady of 4 a.m. and you don't wanna piss her off, stupid."

"Oh, I could never be annoyed with you gentlemen!" exclaimed Mrs Rafaat. "I can see that you're only concerned for my well-being."

"Yeah, *that's* why we're stood on the edge of the city wall waiting for an angry dog to come barking," grumbled the goblin. "Concerned is what we is."

"Sammy, may I, as Midnight Mayor, just say you demonstrate a shocking lack of civic—" Swift stopped abruptly. "Anyone hear ...?" he murmured. And there it was, rising in low, mournful greeting from the dark, a swelling round of animal pain and longing:

hhhhhhoooooooooooooooowwwwwwwwwwwwwwllllllllll!!!!!

Chapter 87

Man's Greatest Gift Is Reason

Anyone passing through Canada Water Underground station at 11.15 p.m. that night might have been a little disturbed at the following events:

A train pulled up, heading north, its carriages disgorging a small number of people, most of whom, at this hour, were only here to change trains. Any of them, stepping onto the rising escalator, might have overheard the following conversation drift from the empty air:

"Don't shove will you. Bloody hell . . ."

"This is interesting, isn't it?"

"Excuse me, we need to keep moving. I can't keep everyone invisible if we stand still; it's all about walking speed."

"Why walking speed?"

"Gotta blend in with the city, that's what it's about, see?"

"How do you know?"

"Well I've already been into the spirit realm with Ms Li, while we were being beaten up in Tooting."

"There is no such thing as real invisibility! Merely tricks of the eye."

"Thank you. Coming through . . ."

Maybe passers-by managed to ignore these noises, filing them away in that corner of the brain entitled, *Don't look, shan't look, don't want to know.*

There was, though, no denying the minor pile-up at the ticket barrier, as the gates opened and gates closed a half-dozen times around . . .

. . . nothing.

Vacancy.

Or rather, not vacancy, because there was something there: there were people, or not people, figures moving. But then there couldn't be, there simply couldn't be; and if there couldn't be . . .

. . . it was all right, because there weren't.

Such is the power of the rational mind.

Chapter 88

Victory Is in the Preparation

Mr Ruislip was excited.

He was excited because the scryers reported that Dog was prowling the city that night, and Dog was an enemy with fangs, and Mr Ruislip loved it when his enemies had fangs.

He was excited because his contact in the Aldermen had rung to say that the Midnight Mayor had vanished, and Mr Ruislip had said, "Is he dead?" and the contact had replied, "No, because whenever Swift vanishes it's because he's about to do something stupid." And Mr Ruislip knew that today Matthew Swift's stupid thing had to be him.

He was excited because every witch, warlock and wizard in the office had been ordered to stay late and prepare to fight, and because when they looked at him he could smell their sweat and hear the pounding of their hearts; and they were scared, scared of what was coming but mostly scared of him, and that tasted so *good*!

He was excited because battle was coming, and battle was something that, at last, he understood.

He knew that his adversaries were coming to steal the spirits back. "They will try to find a way to the hole," he declared. "They may attack from above, so we shall watch the ceilings. They may try to come in from below, so we shall watch the floors. They may try teleporting, so we ward the offices. They may try invisibility, so we shall guard the stairs.

"The Midnight Mayor likes fire, so we shall answer with ice; the shamans like shadows, so we shall answer with light. The fate of this corporation hangs on defeating these people tonight and on finding Greydawn – at last! I have every confidence that you shall put up a good fight. I shall kill any who run. Thank you for your hard work and bonuses to all!"

This last phrase, this great, potent phrase was, to Mr Ruislip, a magic spell in itself. In the years since he had managed to worm out of the shadows, to slip through the mystical walls that guarded the city from the night, he had learned much about humans. He had discovered that not all of them embraced battle as he did, and some of them were even afraid of things that should have been wondrous.

He had also learned that power stemmed from little numbers on screens, which in turn represented the perceived value of some good somewhere, or maybe just an idea somewhere else, and which little numbers, if they were bought, could make more little numbers, which made bigger numbers, which caused whoops of delight and glee in mortal men. And if he could only convince people that bigger numbers were just a simple deed away . . .

. . . or a simple spell . . .

. . . or a simple murder . . .

. . . he could control all that he surveyed.

Chapter 89

To Fail to Plan Is to Plan to Fail

Silence in Canada Water.

Lights still burned within the great glass towers and on the streets; their reflections wavered in the water lapping against the quayside.

In Burns and Stoke the lights shone brightest of all. In another life Sharon had stared skywards at these shining glass walls and watched the tiny people move about, each in their office, unseen by their colleagues but on display to the world, like a life lived in a computer game. Now no one up there was visible. But she knew they were waiting.

Sharon turned to her motley crew, huddled on a bench and perched on the concrete rocks of the little strip of garden between the bus stops.

"Right," she said. "It's very simple. Me, Rhys and Mr Roding, we're gonna find all the spirits that Burns and Stoke have trapped, and set 'em free. Gretel, Kevin and Edna, you're gonna try and find these sacrifice thingies that Eddie was talking about. Sally is gonna be air support in case of shit going down – have you got your mobile phone?"

Yes, Sharon. It is fully charged and I have set its ringtone to "Urgent klaxon".

"Cool. Chris, Jess and Jeff are gonna stay out here in case something shitty happens, in which case you phone someone or call the police or something. Jeff has got sandwiches and a first-aid kit. Jess is also possible air support."

"You make it all sound very simple," fumed Mr Roding, "but I really don't think 'We're gonna find all the spirits' is a sound tactical plan. When I was speaking to the corpses in Vietnam, I learned a lot about—"

"Excuse me," offered Gretel, cutting through Mr Roding before he could reach his oratorical climax. "Do you think we're going to have to hurt people? Only trolls have a very bad reputation and I don't want to sully my community's name."

"Uh ... try *not* to hurt people," offered Sharon. "But if you must, maybe apologise and leave them a number they can call afterwards?"

"Where's the Midnight Mayor and Mrs Rafaat in all this?" demanded Mr Roding. "I don't see *them* trying to break out the trapped spirits of the city, do you?"

Sharon fixed Mr Roding with the stare of all good officers faced with irredeemable troops. Mr Roding, to her surprise, cowered a little.

"Swift, Sammy and Mrs Rafaat are in the centre of town waiting for Dog to reappear. Since he only does this in the dead of night, he might be a little while. But as soon as he *does* turn up, the Midnight Mayor, protector of ... stuff ... along with the third – second! – greatest shaman the world has ever seen, are gonna power on over here with the mortal form of Greydawn and a furry killing machine. Questions?"

"Shouldn't we wait for the furry killing machine?" offered Rhys.

"You want to wait for a monster that only Mrs Rafaat can control," grumbled Mr Roding, "which has killed half a dozen men in a month, and get it to do the hard work while its mistress, who has been hunted by killer builders and angry claws for the last two years, sits around with a sign stamped on her forehead saying ENSORCEL ME NOW – is that your suggestion?"

"Mr Roding is right," said Sharon, doing her best not to glare at anyone. "The longer the city goes without Mrs Rafaat, the worse things will be and the better Mr Ruislip's chance of working out who she really is. Now I figure that Burns and Stoke know we've gotta be coming. So, we're gonna use the element of surprise."

"Uh, babes, how exactly are we going to do that?" asked Kevin.

"I figured we'd ask the way at Reception."

Chapter 90

A Fond Reunion Is a Form of Rebirth

"Who's my little doggy, who's my little doggy? Yes you are, yes you *are*!"

"Mrs Rafaat, thrilled though I am that we've found your pet again—"

"Good boy, good *boy*! Yes, you're so good, aren't you? Yes, you're so *good*!"

"—if we could perhaps take this opportunity to head for the nearest public transport . . . ."

"Fetch boy, fetch! That's it, that's it! Good boy! Mummy's got a treaty-weaty for you."

If Matthew Swift was unnerved by the sight of an old woman in a sari lovingly stroking behind the ears of an eight-foot killing machine, he did his best not to show it. His manful stride up to the flanks of Dog may have turned, at the last moment, to a cautious creep, but he felt that his cry of "Now, Mrs Rafaat, please, there are people depending on us!" had an undeniably heroic ring.

"I'm sorry, Mr Swift," she sighed. "It's just I did miss my little diddums."

"And you can have all the time in the world with him," replied the sorcerer, "just as soon as we get to Canada Water."

"But Mr Swift! Will they let my little puppy on the train?"

"Tell you what. Just this once let's get a cab."

Chapter 91

Our Staff Are Here to Help

The foyer of Burns and Stoke.

Everything is open, airy, light and planned. Welcome, all who enter here, this building proclaims, for here you shall see all that can be seen and, through your seeing, become a better, brighter part of the team. Playing solitaire and wasting time on Facebook are out; cooperation and the go get 'em work ethic are in.

There were four men on guard plus a receptionist.

"On guard" wasn't quite the phrase; "on guard" implied bayonets and patrols and maybe steel helmets, whereas the guards were ex-hirelings of the sometime security firm Amiltech, trained enforcers and sometimes dabblers in the mystical arts. They wore clean white gloves and smart black suits with a badge on the shoulder proclaiming the name of each employee, their licence number and, on a flap on the back, their next of kin, should the worst come to pass.

A sign tucked away behind the reception desk declared enigmatically that the building security level was BLUE HIGH. Not many people knew what BLUE HIGH meant, and settled for the uncomfortable supposition that BLUE was better than RED but HIGH was bad news for everyone.

Of the four men – and they were men, very much men, men who

liked to demonstrate their masculinity through weightlifting more than alcohol – two stood outside like hotel doormen, ready to scrutinise any and all who headed within. It was these two who had the dubious privilege of being the first to perceive that Burns and Stoke was under attack.

"Uh . . . Ian?" said one.

"Yeah?"

"Um . . . there's a troll coming towards us."

The guard called Ian considered this self-evident truth. He reached for the radio at his side but then noticed that the approaching wall of troll was in no hurry. It wasn't charging, or shouting, or baring its teeth; in fact it was shambling – yes, that was the word, *shambling* – towards him with an amiable air, accompanied by a ginger man and a dark-haired girl in purple boots.

Nevertheless, they were at BLUE HIGH alert, having been hired with the purpose of securing the building against unlicensed access, any seven-foot troll probably not excepted. Also, Ian the security guard couldn't quite accept that this obvious member of the magical community thought it okay to walk around unhidden by a chameleon spell.

He reached for his radio.

Before he could seize it, a hand fell on his.

No – not a hand – a talon. He looked down to see curled black claws pressing delicately against his skin. The lightness of their touch suggested that their owner was going to extraordinary lengths to avoid causing permanent damage. A small whiteboard was pushed under his nose. On it, in careful green letters, someone had written,

We apologise for the inconvenience.

He looked up to see the man with the ginger hair step in front of him holding what looked like a perfume bottle and spray it directly in his face. Ian opened his mouth to protest and passed out.

His companion guard, an unfortunate gentleman by the name of Louis who didn't really deserve the fate about to befall him, pulled his radio off his belt, tried to operate it and was, for his troubles, also sprayed in the face from a perfume bottle, this time by the dark-haired girl.

He swayed, then gave a mute giggle.

The girl stared in surprise at him, then at the bottle.

"What did you use?" wailed Rhys, as Louis pressed his hands over his mouth to prevent himself laughing.

"Says 'Distraction'."

Louis shrieked with laughter, his head rolled back and his shoulders shook.

"I don't think it's meant to do that," muttered Rhys. "Sorry, maybe I got something wrong when measuring it out."

"For goodness' sake," barked Mr Roding, striding forward. He reached up, pressed one hand against Louis's forehead and murmured, "Slumber with the damned."

The guard's eyes closed, his head rolled. Mr Roding caught him in the small of the back as he toppled, easing him to the floor and pulling the radio off him.

"Oh my God!" shrilled Edna. "You didn't *kill* him, did you?"

"Of course not!" barked Mr Roding. "I merely put him to sleep until dawn! He'll wake completely rested, entirely rejuvenated and only marginally more prone to zombie attack."

Sharon put back the bottle marked "Distraction" into her badge-strewn shoulder bag and pulled out another instead. "This one says 'Peaceful' – is that good?"

Rhys hesitated. "Um, I'm not sure we should be using Peaceful yet. It's a little, uh, advanced, is Peaceful. I'm sure it'll work, but maybe Mr Roding can put people to sleep instead?"

"I'm a necromancer, not a wizard," retorted Mr Roding, flicking away a decaying fingernail. "If I do magic, I do it using flesh and blood. And if there's no flesh and blood to hand, I'm forced to use my own. And I would like to leave this experience with my own head of hair at least, thank you very much."

"I do hope we're doing the right thing," quavered Edna as they stepped over the unconscious security men and into the foyer. Sharon picked up the first guard's radio as they passed, slipping it into her bag. She was disappointed that there didn't seem to be any magical wards or glowing wands they could appropriate.

Maybe the staff down here weren't those kind of people. Of the three people inside the main foyer, one was a receptionist, sat behind her desk with a look of disbelief as the alliance of troll, vampire, necromancer, druid, priestess, exorcist and shaman stepped through the

door. The two others were security guards. One of them was bran-
dishing a police baton, its end dented from an impact with something
firm but probably organic. Sharon could taste the anger, and violence,
and blood that clung about it – but no magic.

"Stand still or we will be forced to take action!" barked the guard
holding the baton. As defiant challenges went, it had a reluctant quality.

Sharon looked at Rhys, who shrugged. She looked at Mr Roding,
who was irritably looking through the old receipts among the depths
of his pockets for a plaster to cover the finger with the missing nail.
Kevin reached into his great black sports bag and handed him a plastic box containing an eclectic range of plasters.

"I mean it!" the guard shouted. "Come closer and we'll be forced to
take action!"

Sharon stepped forward. "Excuse me," she said. "Can I ask you a
question?"

"*What?*"

"Well, it seems to me that you're looking at us as if we're somehow
here with hostile intent. You've got this sort of tension about you. And
I'm wondering if it's because you've noticed Kevin's fangs, or the fact
that Gretel could crush you like Blu-tack between her thumbs, or
because Mr Roding is smelling his age and that. Because if you are, I
really think that's discriminatory of you. I mean, you're like, judging
based on appearance rather than on who we are, and I actually think
there's some government legislation about that. Just because a seven-
foot wall of muscle, a blood-sucking fiend from the nether reaches of
the night and a living immortal whose blood flows black with the souls
of his enemies come walking through the door, it doesn't mean we can't
have a conversation."

"A . . ."

"Yeah. Like, don't you guys feel that it's really bad of your employ-
ers to just *leave* you here. I mean, just the two of you, guarding this
place against possible attack – which isn't to say we *are* attacking,
because I don't think we are, are we?"

A chorus of "No, us?" went up from the gathered Magicals
Anonymous members.

"The point being, if we were attacking, then you two, for all your training, would be smeared across the floor in big bloody splats before you could go 'Oh shit.' And I think it's really irresponsible of your boss or manager or whoever, to put you in this position. What do you think?"

Whatever they wanted to say, they didn't seem able to turn thought to speech. To ease things along, Sharon kept on talking.

"Now, I run this group for people who have issues with magic. We meet in ... Actually, we probably don't meet in Exmouth Market any more, but we've got this Facebook page and you'd be welcome to join. Because I really think that it's important to share the debate on stuff like this, rather than just stand by your position of 'What the fuck is that?' yeah?"

"Our job—"

Sharon interrupted. "You seem like decent guys. I mean, like you want to do the best by your employer and that. But you gotta ask yourself, will it serve any purpose at all if you get, say, crushed or savaged or mauled or bitten or fried or enchanted or beaten to death? I'd say no, because there's like, insurance costs to consider there and medical bills and stuff if you have private – do you have private care? Seems very poor to tell you guys to 'Stop that troll' and not provide private medical care."

"It's just a freelance job," declared one.

"Gotta think of the mortgage," insisted the other.

"A mortgage?" exclaimed Sharon. "Jesus, I so understand where you're coming from – I mean, not me personally, I don't have a mortgage. But every month I go online and look at my bank statements and I'm like, where did it all go? I mean, the rent, Council Tax, the service charge, gas, electricity, water, medical costs ... Not my medical costs, I go NHS, but I imagine you guys won't be able to if you need treatment for magically induced necrotic decay or vampire bites."

"Babes, I am *not* biting the fat one," offered Kevin from his corner. "*Hello*, can't you smell the bad dietary habits?"

In silence the guards exchanged a look. Without a word, the one who'd threatened them with a baton turned and walked towards the door.

"Fuck it." After a second's hesitation, his colleague followed him. Passing Sharon, one stopped to reach out and offer her his hand.

"You seem nice enough," he said. "You could just be one of those whacked-out hippy types who plants bombs against animal testing, but you seem okay. Good luck to you."

"Thanks," said Sharon, blushing a little. "You guys seem cool – hope the mortgage works out."

Each of them shook hands and departed.

Magicals Anonymous watched them go.

Rhys turned to Sharon.

"Can I buy you a drink some time?" said a dreamy-toned voice, possibly his own.

"Uh . . . sure."

The receptionist was still frozen in an attitude of astonishment behind her high counter. Sharon walked up, leaned against it and rested her chin on her folded arms.

"Hi there," she said. "We're looking for this wendigo."

Chapter 92

Look Your Fate in the Eye

He sits, and stares, and smiles.

"Oh look," he says, "they came in the front way."

This is something of a surprise to Mr Ruislip. He has come to assume that anyone foolish enough to take him on will try to do so through as furtive a means as possible, in the naive hope that this will prolong their life expectancy by a few minutes. Observing a gaggle of mystically challenged individuals getting into a lift in Reception, he feels his surprise is perhaps good. This particular emotion is one he always finds interesting.

"Let them come in," he says. "Let's see how far they get."

Chapter 93

Expect the Unexpected

A door opened in a darkened office.

Feet padded on hard thin carpet.

The quiet and darkness of the office were broken by the scraped-metal sounds of the Docklands Light Railway passing outside the windows, and electric sparks outlining figures that moved between the desks.

"Are we even in the right place?" whispered Edna.

"The nice lady at Reception said that Magical Affairs were through Human Resources, and first left past Development," Gretel intoned. She added, "Are humans resources?"

"*God*, yes," sighed Kevin. "But like everything else on the planet, they're a resource that's been screwed up."

There was a thump in the dark. It was Gretel bumping into a computer-laden desk, which shuddered under the force of the impact.

"I'm so sorry," she whispered in a voice like a gale through a cheese grater.

"I'm surprised we haven't seen more security," said Edna. "Surely if this wendigo character knew we were coming, he'd be trying harder to stop us?"

"Oh my God," moaned Kevin. "Have you guys been living in like, the twelfth century? Never invite the wrath of God by wondering why things are going well!"

"Are you always this pessimistic?" asked Edna, ruffling within her purple cardigan.

"Uh . . . undead, duh?"

A pair of double doors swung back before Gretel's cautious touch, revealing a long white corridor. It was lit by fluorescent tubing and bore such motivational notices as THE FUTURE IS STABLE GROWTH and IS YOUR DATA SOUND? At the far end stood another pair of doors. Kevin sniffed the air, then flung out a hand to stop Gretel advancing.

"Uh, guys, I don't want to fulfil the pessimistic undead cliché," he declared. "But I'm like, smelling major-league magic down here. And I'm no wizard, so I don't want to be like, cleaning up from that shit."

Edna peered round the vampire. "What does major-league magic smell like?"

"You know eucalyptus?"

"Really? Is that what it smells like?"

"No, I was just hoping I could get you to stop asking annoying questions."

"You really are a very difficult young man, aren't you?"

Gretel, perhaps with a more sensible grasp of the situation, picked up a heavy red fire extinguisher by the door. She tossed it thoughtfully from hand to hand like a juggling ball.

"Uh, you're not thinking of—" began Kevin as Gretel drew her arm back and, with the ease of a fast bowler throwing an orange, lobbed the extinguisher down the hall. It travelled ten yards through the air, struck an invisible barrier and exploded with a great ringing bang that sent white foam spilling up the walls.

"You are correct, Kevin," mused the troll as the cowering Kevin and Edna waited for the last of the shrapnel to fall. "The corridor does appear to be warded."

"But we need to go this way to find the sacrifices!" wailed Edna.

"See, I'm pessimistic," muttered Kevin, "but at least I can handle stress."

Gretel looked thoughtfully down the corridor, then up at the ceiling.

"I'm not very good at numbers," she said. "But if one of you would be prepared to count footsteps, I may have an idea."

At the far end of the corridor the double doors swung back. A security guard, hand on his radio, hurried through. He gawped at the foam splattered everywhere and the red metal shards buried in the walls.

"Backup, backup, third floor," he babbled.

"Okay, now," muttered Kevin, "let's try going with Plan B, shall we?" They ran.

Chapter 94

If Life Throws You Lemons...

Eleven floors above the events in Human Resources, a lift door went *ping*.

Glass swished back to reveal more glass inside.

The lift was empty.

This was a source of some surprise to the two waiting security guards, who'd been phoned by Reception with the information that three burglars were on their way upstairs. They stood either side of the lift, batons out, and in one case shimmering with a sickly red runic magic, and waited for trouble that failed to come.

One said, "Uh . . ."

Another barked, "Wait!"

They waited.

"Can you smell that?"

"Jesus, yes. What is that?"

"Smells like . . . God, it smells like something rotting. Something . . ." The guard stopped. He thought he'd heard, just on the edge of hearing, the tiniest huff of indignation. He strained. Footsteps?

Were those footsteps moving on the carpet behind him?

He turned very slowly. For a second he thought he saw . . .

. . . but no, it couldn't be . . .

. . . but then . . .

"Oh, screw it," said a voice. "Just use the sodding potion."

And where there hadn't been a ginger druid in front of the guard, suddenly there was. In one hand he held a perfume bottle; in the other a large grubby tissue was being applied to the druid's inflamed red nose. The guard had just enough time to notice this before a cool spray trickled down his face, his thoughts and his dreams, and sent all to darkness.

Ten busy seconds later on the lift landing, there were two unconscious guards and three people who were no longer invisible. Music tinkled from the still-open door of the lift, on a theme of abusing the greatest hits of the Beatles. Rhys shook his bottles of potions aloft and proclaimed, "Take that, Birmingham exam board!"

Sharon looked around her, trying to work out which way to go.

"This week Sharon takes the road less travelled," whispered the voice of Dez in her ear. Briefly she thought she saw the white-suited spirit guide flicker through a door to her right, waving for the camera as he passed.

"This way," she barked.

"Are you sure?" asked Mr Roding, a schoolmaster judging a precocious child's work.

Being a shaman, Sharon had decided, was as much about seeming right as being right. "Yup!" She grabbed the still-exultant Rhys by the sleeve and pulled him after her.

More offices, half-familiar from the last time she'd been here, but silent now. It was the silence of the stopped engine, the place where noise should have been. As she strode between the desks with a confidence she did not feel, Sharon realised it had only been people that made this space seem small, and busy, and exciting. Now, with the dead tables and empty chairs, the open-plan place was too cold, too still, too big. The great panes of glass let in enough night-time light to reveal the depth of the shadows without driving any of it away.

And there they were, whispering on the edge of perception, just on the other side of invisibility, things moving, ghosts of workdays past. There the shadow of the place where a hundred workers had grouped and muttered after a bad meeting; here the slow swirl of paper through the air, dancing like mating birds just in the corner of her eye; on the computer screens the burning after-images of dancing numbers; here

too the whisper of changing minds in the telephone wires, the crackle
of energy and salty taste of wealth, the sick tug of doubt and the creak
of sensible shoes beneath uncomfortable chairs ... All here, all just out
of reach, and there, *there*

Help us ...

... help us help us help us ...

She'd felt it before, fear coming out of the walls, but last time she'd
thought it was merely the babbling voices of things not understood,
the whisper of trapped souls behind locked doors. But now she walked
and listened, and felt fear in the mouths of the people who worked
here, too scared to ask their neighbours if they too were afraid, and
therefore living alone in their fears.

She looked, and saw the shadow of the wendigo move across the
walls. Paint that had peeled looked, to a shaman's eyes, more like skin
flaking away from the office walls. Paper was leather, the stains on a
coffee cup too dark, too thick. The wendigo had walked these halls,
and where his foot fell, the building itself seemed to cringe, as if stone
as well as flesh was afraid of challenging him.

"Ms Li?" Rhys hovered behind her, and at his back stretched away
the shadows of things seen and dreams broken, his whole history written in a language of lines and crinkles on his face and in his voice. "You
all right?"

"I can hear them," breathed Sharon. "I can hear ... This way."

She moved fast through the office, past posters showing the positive growth trend sought in futures and dividends, round the
waste-paper baskets clogged with biscuit wrappers and old cigarette
packets, past the cleaning cupboard locked up for the night against any
and all who dared steal its industrial-strength blue toilet tissue, and
round to the anonymous white door where the voices whispered the
loudest and where not even a spirit walker could pass.

Mr Roding sniffed the air, running his hands down the heavy lam-
inated wood. "Warded all right," he grumbled. "Fairly good work too,
not too shoddy."

"Can you open it?"

Mr Roding thoughtfully scraped an orange fingernail of wax out of
the hollow of his ear and flicked it away. "Yeah," he said. "I can open
it. But I won't be much good to you for a while after."

"They're in there," murmured Sharon. "All the spirits Burns and Stoke have stolen – I can hear them."

The necromancer grunted. "You'd better stand back."

Rhys ducked behind a desk, peeping over the edge like a child playing hide-and-seek. Sharon moved more slowly to join him, thinking how bad could bad really be?

Mr Roding put his palms against the door and closed his eyes. She thought she saw his lips move, heard a slow, rattling breath across the dry surface of his tongue. She looked, for a moment, as only a shaman could look, and saw Mr Roding as he did not want to be seen: a skeleton clad in patchwork flesh, skin grey-white, draped over protruding bones, hands pressed to the shimmering surface of the door pulsing with blood-red power.

She shuddered and looked away, but even in the normal world, the real world of only three dimensions, the air around Mr Roding was thick, spiky hot, a rotting jungle stench in the cold dryness of the room. His face wrinkled with effort and, as the magic passed through him, Sharon saw the thin white surface of his skin begin to peel. It rolled back from his face like liquid glue, revealing soft untouched tissue beneath. It peeled and cracked off his lips, like a time-lapse sequence of decay. His teeth began to yellow; his hair shrivelled and thinned, drifting down around him; his nails turned brown and split; capillaries pulsed vivid red against the whites of his eyes. The necromancer groaned, and his voice was older and cracked and his back violently bent as, with one last, great push, he slammed his palms against the door.

Something hot and white snapped, a camera-flash burst of intensity right in Sharon's eyes. The door clicked open, pushed back by Mr Roding's weight, and with a little grunt the necromancer fell forward.

Sharon rushed to grab him, and was surprised by how light he was. His breath nearly knocked her out, and a tooth rolled out of his mouth.

"Damn me," he hissed. "That was one hell of a ward."

"You okay?" asked Sharon.

"Nothing a bit of ghoul tongue in the coffee won't fix," he grunted, "but that took more out of me than I thought and . . ." He paused, noticing the hollow where his tooth should have been, then reached up and casually pulled another yellow gnasher from his gums.

"Great," he grunted. "Took me six months to fit those, thank you very much."

Sharon looked past him through the open door.

She'd expected, at the very least, a spiral staircase or a hall of Gothic horrors, but no. A bland cream-coloured corridor led to a white lift door. Above the lift a sign read, AUTHORISED PERSONNEL ONLY.

If that was all, what *was* the worst that could happen?

"Will you be all right getting out?" asked Sharon. "I mean, if we go on . . ."

"Course I'll be all right," grumbled Mr Roding. "I've cast spells with a body mass index of ten point one, you know. And still had power left for cursing the pension authorities. Just . . . help me up."

Sharon and Rhys eased Mr Roding onto his feet. He leaned heavily against the wall to catch his breath. "Christ, it's been a while since I had to do that," he grumbled. "Being on the side of righteousness is really not my thing. Listen to me, you two."

They looked uneasily at him.

"This building is far too quiet. And I'm sure you don't need me to inform you, being as you are so excited by all this, that it's a trap. But it *is* a trap, and very obviously. Now I'm going to go and chew on some raw flesh, hopefully not mine. Call me if you need some more old-fashioned damnation."

So saying, shaking slightly all over, Mr Roding turned and hobbled away.

Sharon looked at Rhys; Rhys looked at Sharon.

He blurted, "But it's a trap! What are we going to do by ourselves?!"

Sharon shrugged.

"Come on, dribble-nose," she muttered. Seizing hold of him by the sleeve again, she dragged him onwards, through the opened door.

Chapter 95

... Make Some Lemonade

They were being chased.

This was problematic for Edna, Gretel and Kevin, since Edna's maximum speed was barely more than her usual waddle, and Gretel doing corners was a hazard to both her companions and the local architecture.

Kevin stood on the landing of the emergency stairs, haranguing his companions.

"Come on, guys!" he wailed. "Security is like, so close behind us!"

"Now dear ..." panted Edna. "When you're ... like me ... you won't ... be in such a hurry ..."

Kevin groaned with impatience. "This is just brilliant. We're like, being chased by these guys with sticks and wands and shit, and I'm stuck with Mother Teresa and a gourmet troll. Gretel!"

"Yes, Kevin?" rumbled the troll.

"Can you carry Edna?"

"I am not going to be carried!" barked the priestess. "It is simply not dignified!"

Below them, the doors to the staircase slammed back and two men barrelled through. One carried a baton and a radio; the other didn't, but only because his fingers were in the process of growing into long black claws.

"I'm very sorry," rumbled Gretel, scooping up Edna and popping her under one arm. "But I do think this is for the best."

"Stop there!" roared the guard who was still human enough to muster speech. His companion was already dropping to all fours, face breaking out into a snout, ginger-red hair spreading across his flesh; and while he wasn't quite a fox, being larger and more unrestrained, he nonetheless had the fox-like teeth all sorted, and by now the claws and growl.

"Uh, guys," Kevin squeaked at the guards as Gretel lumbered past, "I know you are doing your jobs and whatever. But I am like, so totally a master of the night and spawn of darkness, and you are seriously cramping my style."

"Vampire!" exhorted Gretel from beyond the swinging doors to the next floor.

The man-fox-guard prowled up the stairs, the remnants of his uniform barely clinging to his back, hackles raised, teeth bared. Kevin raised a finger in polite request. "Actually," he said, "hold that thought."

To his surprise, both the man and the not-quite-man hesitated. Kevin felt himself puff up a little with pride.

"Vampire!" yelled Gretel again, in a voice loud enough to make the banister hum. "Are you coming?"

The fox-man's lips curled back. A low growl spread from the base of his belly.

"Tell you what," quavered Kevin. "I'll like, spare you my awful vampiric wrath, just this once. But only because I'm feeling merciful and it'd totally ruin my hair."

The fox-man pounced. Kevin gave a shrill cry and ran, slamming through the double doors to the adjoining office. Claws raked the air behind him. Gretel was waiting with a desk manoeuvred and ready. "Get rid of them get rid of them get rid of them!" shrieked the vampire as he ran.

Calmly Gretel waited for the doors to slam back behind Kevin, then pushed the desk across, jamming them shut. There was a scratching of claws and scrabbling of hands from the other side, but the doors rattled against the heavy desk in vain.

"Oh dear," quavered Edna, propped up in a swivel chair to catch her breath. "Do you think they're going to be terribly upset?"

"Darling, I think we're a little past that."

The scratching at the door abruptly stopped. There was a shuffling of feet and a crackle of radio. Then silence. A deep, expectant silence.

"Uh . . ." murmured Kevin.

The doors blew in off their hinges, taking the big desk with them down the central gangway. Biros, papers and computer fragments spilled across the room as they flew by. Through the smoking wreck of the doorway stepped the fox-man and his companion. And now there were marks visible on the upright guard's skin, runic sigils burning – the line through the circle, the zigzag scar of the railway, the raw red stop sign and the blue and white police wards – and carved into his flesh. Seeing the trio, the man with burning skin grinned and drew his hands back, power flickering between his fingertips, lips moving silently around a new spell.

Gretel lurched towards him, swinging a great fist back. The fox, its body as long as a man and its forelegs still patchy with human skin, leapt on her, fangs bared. Fox and troll crashed down together as heavily as a melting cliff of ice; blood and fur mixed as they battered each other.

The rune-wearer turned, seeking a target, and saw Edna cowering behind a pillar. He flung out his hands towards her, and their palms issued a blast of rippling, scalding air flecked with crimson. Edna yelped and dived for the floor, the back of her hair curling and blackening. Behind her the wall turned dark and sticky under a layer of melting chemical goo. The old priestess crawled over the wreckage of a nearby table, looking for safety, and the rune-wearer advanced, drawing more power out of the signs in his skin. Another blast of airborne force, this one black and garnished with diesel fumes and the roar of a bus. It smashed the desk behind which Edna was hunched, sending its remnants into a bookcase above her. Files and folders tumbled all around the priestess.

Grappling on the floor with Gretel, the fox-man was beginning to have the worst of it. His claws had torn her flesh, leaving vivid grey scars through which viscous yellow-brown blood seeped like engine oil, but no matter how much he bit and scratched, there was simply too much of Gretel between him and any vital internal organs. With a surge of silent energy, the troll gave a heave and rolled, slamming the fox-man against the floor beneath her. Like a bear smothering her prey, she flattened herself on top of him, wrapping one giant hand over his head and knocking it back hard onto the floor. Teeth tore at Gretel's palm, and brown blood began to roll and mat in the spines of the troll's skin, but she slammed down again and again until, with an impotent shriek of fury, the fox grew still beneath her.

Edna crawled out from beneath the mess of files and papers. The rune-wearer was not three paces away, pulling his hands apart for another spell. Dizzy and bewildered, she sat with ears ringing and hair still smoking, a lemming on the cliff top, as his hands moved with inexorable, ritual slowness, drawing up power.

Something moved behind him.

It was dark, fast and very nearly silent.

It said, "Oh God, I am *so* going to regret this," and an instant later seemed to fold itself round the man.

His face changed.

A look of surprise flashed briefly into pain, before his features crumpled, along with the rest of him. His head rolled back, his jaw dropped. A line of blood dribbled down his neck and began to seep into his clothes. His eyes drifted shut. A second later the darkness unfolded from around him, and he slid silently to the floor.

Kevin wiped his mouth with the back of his hand, then stared in horror at the streak of blood across his bone-white skin.

"Oh. My. God," he whispered. "Oh my *God!*"

He fumbled in his sports bag, throwing out handfuls of latex gloves, sterile wipes and plasters. Finally he hoisted aloft a great bottle of blue mouthwash, with which he set to rinsing his mouth like he'd swallowed cyanide.

"Where's my dental floss?" he wailed. "I don't feel well."

"Kevin, dear? Are you . . . quite all right?" Edna asked, as she picked her way past the bloodied body of the guard.

"I didn't do a medical history! Pass me that!"

A finger gestured imperiously at a syringe in a clean plastic package which had fallen from Kevin's bag. Edna handed it over, and with practised professionalism Kevin ripped it from its package, bent down over the unconscious guard, rolled up his sleeve, slapped the soft skin in the crook of the man's arm and pushed in the needle.

"I need a sample," he explained. "For testing!"

"Testing for what?"

"Typhus!"

"Typhus?" echoed Edna. "I'm not sure that's very common any more, dear."

"Chlamydia!"

"Well, yes, I do hear that rates are on the rise."

Kevin withdrew the needle and held it up to the feeble light. "Do you think he's got the right antigens?" he asked. "Or if there's any ice in this office?"

"May I have one of your bandages, please?" asked Gretel quietly.

"Oh no, you poor dear!" cried Edna at the brown blood seeping from a dozen cuts across Gretel's great surface. "Kevin!"

"Help yourself," mumbled the vampire, drawing back hastily as the troll bent down to rifle the bag. A fat wad of cotton was pulled out and Gretel wrapped it round her bloody fist.

To Edna's offer of a safety pin she politely replied, "Thank you, but I think I will be all right."

Kevin was swaying, his face even greyer than usual. "Yeah," he muttered. "I'm not sure I will be."

He removed the last of the blood from his hand and mouth with a sterile wipe, then dropped all his medical detritus into a yellow plastic bag marked BIOHAZARD.

Looking up, he added, "Someone said something about a plan?"

Chapter 96

The Past Is Another Country

There were only two buttons in the small lift.

One was "Up", the other was "Down".

"Up" didn't seem to go anywhere, so Sharon and Rhys rode the lift down.

The lift played more tinkly muzak at them as it descended.

It descended a very, very long way.

When the door opened, it did so with a little *ping*.

The air beyond was noticeably colder, damper.

The corridor was noticeably darker, lit only by bare bulbs hung on the wall.

It was also older.

Brick walls, turned black-grey with a hundred years of lichen and moss. The floor was smooth flagstones, worn down by centuries of footsteps. Water dripped in the distance. The smell of the river was close, the lift a brilliant sparkle of modern brightness in the dark. Its door slid shut behind Sharon and Rhys as they stepped out into the cold wet air, cutting off the muzak.

Dirt had settled on a sign nailed onto the corridor wall. Sharon brushed it off, leaving an orange-brown slime on the palm of her hand. Its ancient scratched letters read, NO FIRE PAST THIS POINT.

"Where are we?" Rhys whispered. His voice bounced down and

down the corridor, into thick darkness. He was staying close to Sharon, so he told himself, in his guise as a manly protector, and not at all a guy who had this problem with the dark. It wasn't a big deal, just . . . dark, see?

Sharon didn't answer. As she moved down the tunnel, her fingers brushed the ancient brickwork, taking away a stain of mould, dust and time. Her head was tilted and, listening, she could hear . . .

creaking of masts swaying above still water

smell of sewage

    oi oi ready to sail!

  out of the way boy

help us

      where's the master?

  lapping of water on stone

      rat claw scurry scuttle scurry fleas in flesh bite of plague and leap!

    Help Us!

  black lumps under the arms

    salt in the skin

  tide turning at midnight

HELP US!!

"This was part of the old quayside," she heard herself say in a distant voice. "Back when this place was a dockyard, they'd keep things down here so they wouldn't spoil. Meats and fish and that. Then when the docks went, they knocked everything down, but this survived. It goes deep."

"What do Burns and Stoke want with it?"

"They use it to trap their stolen souls in. Places that are old, and cold, and dark, and deep – they make good cages."

"Um, that's slightly scary, Miss Li. Not that I'm scared, see, but you know, if I wasn't so not scared, that'd probably freak me out."

"This way," she replied, walking faster.

The corridor curved gently down and, as it did, water began to appear, silt-stained brownish water from the river that had crept in, forming salt crystals on the brick walls, little trickles that flowed up through imperfections in the floor, eating at its stones, grinding them down. Occasionally passages would lead off to the side. Glancing down one, Rhys thought he glimpsed a hall, vast brick surfaces and darkness, pools of black water, fouled walls and the scuttle of rats. Sharon didn't stop, didn't look, but strode forward now with a greyhound determination. Rhys scampered to keep up.

He thought he heard . . .

. . . but no, nothing else was moving down there, nothing living . . .

. . . not that that meant anything dead was moving either, what Rhys meant by *nothing living* was nothing was moving which they needed to be afraid of, nothing but shadows, only shadows, and only little boys were afraid of shadows whereas he was a druid – a very good druid, if only the exam board had realised it and—

"Atchoo!"

The sneezed echoed away down the corridor, vivid and loud.

Atchoo! the walls whispered back.

Rhys froze.

Could he hear . . .

. . . was that . . .

. . . a bicycle?

"Help me here!"

Sharon had reached the end of the corridor, where a great iron door with a wheel for a lock stood shut, almost rusted into the brickwork. Rhys scurried up and, straining against the weight of the wheel, muttered, "Don't you think there should be, maybe, more guards and that?"

"One problem at a time," grunted the shaman. With a lurch, the wheel spun, and the door swung open.

They stepped through into a round chamber, lined with smooth grey stone, a metal walkway stretching across the middle of the room. Beneath the walkway, going down into darkness, was a great black pit. The air stirred in it, twisting and turning. Rhys, through the haze of his fear, thought he could hear . . .

Help us . . .

Sharon was clinging to the rail of the walkway, her face ashen, body swaying.

"They're here," she whispered. "I can hear them – all the souls the wendigo stole, ripped out of their place."

"What is this?" breathed Rhys.

She didn't answer.

"It used to be an ice store!"

The voice had come from behind them, bright and crisp and deafening in the stillness of that place. Rhys felt the pit stir beneath him, shadows twisting more violently in the darkness, writhing like creatures in pain.

And there he was, Mr Ruislip, immaculately dressed as always. He was flanked by three men and one woman, wearing suits. The humans wore the bright ties and shiny shoes of office workers, but signs including grey hairs and ostentatious cufflinks suggested that here were no ordinary servants of money. These were senior management, gathered to witness the triumph of their CEO. Mr Ruislip drifted towards the cold hollow of the pit, savouring the darkness like a connoisseur studying a piece of art. The four members of management, and here was a word that rose unbidden to Rhys's mind – the four *surviving* members of management – followed at a distance, heads bowed, none daring to interrupt their boss's triumph.

"Ice was considered a privilege for the wealthy," explained Mr Ruislip, looking down into the depths of the pit. "A sign of prestige. Prestige makes men feel good. Prestige can only be achieved if other people believe the owner of the prestige to be good. In some way, that is. After all, good is a moral statement as well as a feeling. Can one do bad and feel good? I suppose one can."

He spoke, Rhys realised, as one perpetually trying to solve a puzzle, a child reasoning out loud, faced with concepts whose importance he couldn't quite believe in. Meanwhile there it was, that flicker of something inhuman in his eye, that flash of something ancient, dressed up in someone else's skin.

"Nowadays we use this place to store souls, rather than ice. But the purpose is, I believe, the same. Prestige," he mused. "In the past the idea of prestige was honest, visceral. Power was through blood and the exercise of might; it was a truth embodied in the very acts of life and death. Then it was a thing founded on wealth, the ownership of other men, and symbolised by things including the possession of ice in summer.

"I did struggle at first with this concept, but now I comprehend – the ownership of wealth is, in fact, precisely the same as ownership of blood and death, which was so much simpler in the old days – except, through wealth I may buy the souls of men, as well as their lives. Humans do so complicate things, don't you think?" The wendigo's eyes flashed up to Rhys, who gulped and staggered back a pace. The druid turned to look for Sharon, who'd have something to say – of course she would.

But Sharon was not there.

Chapter 97

A Transport of Delights

"Are we there yet?"

"Not yet."

"Are we nearly near there yet?"

"Not yet, Sammy."

"My puppy doesn't like cabs."

"I'm very sorry to hear that, Mrs Rafaat. But as it is, your puppy is sitting on my left foot, which may yet get gangrene. So really I think we're all suffering here."

"My puppy doesn't like leaving the centre of London. He gets all pensive, don't you? Yes, you do! Yes, you dooooo!"

"Think of this as an exciting adventure."

"Are we there yet?!"

"No, Sammy, shut up!"

"You can't talk to me like that, I'm the second greatest shaman who's ever lived!"

"And we're the blue electric angels, and we're getting really, really annoyed."

"Are you the blue electric angels, Mr Swift?"

"So it would appear."

"That must be very uncomfortable."

"We manage, Mrs Rafaat."

Chapter 98

Form Serves Function

In Burns and Stoke's department of Magical Affairs, something architecturally unsound is about to happen.

Wait for it . . .

Wait for it . . .

KABOOM!

The ceiling thunders, then shakes; dirt drifts down and ceiling panels collapse.

Silence.

KABOOM!

Silence again.

KABOOM!

If a sound engineer had been asked for a precise description of this noise, he might well have described it as that of a large, unathletic troll jumping from the top of a broken, sagging desk onto the floor as hard as she could.

KABOOM!!

On this last great roar of noise, the sound engineer might have been pleased to find his hypothesis, if not confirmed, then heading in the right direction by said troll crashing bum first through the ceiling of the office below in a shower of torn cables, twisted pipes and billowing white dust. Sitting on a debris-strewn floor, she batted ineffectually at the pulverised architecture drifting in the air around her.

Peering down through the troll-sized hole Gretel had made, there appeared the faces of Kevin and Edna.

"Well," said Edna. "That's certainly one way to get past the wards."

"I don't feel well," moaned Kevin. "I think I swallowed the wrong kind of blood."

"How can you swallow the wrong kind of blood? You're a vampire!"

"Antigens!" he wailed. "When you have Seah's syndrome, it's very important to get the right antigens!"

"Are you going to jump?" asked Gretel from the floor below.

By now Kevin was swaying, eyes out of focus. He smiled absently, muttered, "Some damn drinking spree," and stepped forward blindly into the hole.

Gretel scrambled out of the way as the vampire crashed to the floor beside her. Kevin picked himself up slowly, one limb at a time.

"Aren't vampires supposed to be graceful and agile?" enquired Edna.

Kevin's grin was still locked in place. Gretel carefully poked him in the shoulder, and he rocked one way, then the other, like a punchbag.

"I don't think Kevin is quite himself," admitted the troll. Then, "If you jump, ma'am, I'll try to catch you."

"I'm far too old for this, you know," muttered Edna, easing herself feet first to the edge of the sagging hole. "You promise not to peek?" she added with sudden alarm as her skirt began to hang over the edge.

"I promise," said the troll.

With a sigh and a little "Whoops!" Edna pushed herself off. Gretel caught her, carefully cradling the old woman as she set her down.

"Well, yes," the high priestess proclaimed, brushing herself down. "In an odd way, this experience is really rather marvellous, isn't it?" Her gaze settled on Kevin, framed against the sparkling lights of the city through the long windows behind. "My, but he really doesn't look well. Should we do something for him?"

"I'm afraid I don't know much about vampires," admitted Gretel, "other than their powdered fangs make for interesting seasoning in casseroles."

There was an unexpected thump.

It was the sound of Kevin going from vertical to horizontal in a single falling-tree movement. He hiccuped. Blood ran from his nose.

"Oh hell," he whispered. "Why do I never get any of the good stuff?"

Something moved behind them. It rustled along the floor, a thin, crinkling sound. Neither Edna nor Gretel paid it much attention, but Kevin, grinning up at the ceiling, raised a trembling finger.

"Oh look," he said. "Bag."

A plastic bag was billowing in the air behind them, as if caught in an upward draught of heat. As Edna watched, it seemed to expand and contract like a jellyfish, before sinking to the floor, to rustle and roll away.

"Would troll blood be of any assistance?" asked Gretel, still mindful of Kevin's condition.

"Wow, babes, that is like the sweetest offer . . ." groaned Kevin, "but, uch."

"I had jaundice as a baby," stammered Edna. She was half-turned towards the desk behind which the plastic bag had billowed. "So I'm not sure if I'm allowed to donate—"

"Bag," repeated Kevin, pointing again.

The plastic bag was back, drifting up like a balloon on a breeze. This time, however, it had a companion, a crumpled blue bag whose logo said it had at some point contained shoes and which floated up from a waste-paper basket, buoyant as a Chinese lantern. Another joined it, then another, drifting upwards with the delicacy of oceanic squid, from bins and desks around the office, until the air was full of plastic bags, gently billowing.

"Um . . ." began Edna.

As if this were a signal, all the rustling bags snapped to attention. With unerring aim and gathering speed, they spun in the air and accelerated towards the three invaders.

Chapter 99

Actions Have Consequences

Rhys turned frantically on the spot as Mr Ruislip stretched his fingers through the cold air of the pit. But Sharon was not there.

"Are you here to release the spirits?" asked Mr Ruislip. "I like saying that: 'release the spirits'. It's almost as empowering as 'release the lions' or 'unleash the dragon'."

Rhys sneezed, colossally.

"Is . . . nasal phlegm," enquired Mr Ruislip, craning in so close Rhys could feel his breath on his face, "a common fear response?"

"I don't think so," he babbled, "but I can only speak for me, can't I?"

"I remember you," murmured the wendigo. "When my claws went through your flesh, I had to look again to see if any blood had been spilt. Your skin was so soft, I couldn't feel it tear. Why is that?"

"Moisturiser?" gasped the druid. His back was pressed against the railing round the pit and his head bent back over the drop, so much did he want to avoid the wendigo's stare.

"Did you bring Greydawn? I did so hope you would. That's why I let you come so far, travel so deep, bringing the mistress to her master."

"Uh . . . bring who to what?"

"I know you have Greydawn," Mr Ruislip murmured. "I know you've found her, because Dog howls in the night but he does not kill. And we watch him, by the streets burning in his wake. Now he comes here, still submissive to somebody . . . and no one but Greydawn can tame the Dog."

Rhys sought for something manful to say. Nothing came to mind. He was, he realised, grinning inanely in the hope that this might make the problem go away.

"There was a girl with you," murmured Mr Ruislip. One finger absently wrapped some of Rhys's hair about it as if he couldn't comprehend the gingerness of it. "The shaman. But she's run into the shadows, leaving you here. Call for her."

"I . . . don't think I should, see?"

Mr Ruislip's other hand closed gently around Rhys's fingers. "Call her," he breathed, "or I'll break each bone, one at a time."

His grip tightened on Rhys's little finger. Rhys barely managed to bite down on a shriek of pain. "I can't!" he gasped. In response, agony shot through his fingers, his hand, his wrist, up to his elbow and into his shoulder: a great tearing lance that lingered and burned. "Only thing is, Ms Li, she's really nice, see, and —" another burst of fire, and Rhys's words dissolved into a scream that echoed round the hall. Behind Mr Ruislip, senior management cowered, turning their eyes away "— and while I don't want you to hurt me, Mr Wendigo sir, I really don't want you to hurt Ms Li, so —" this time something cracked in Rhys's hand. He shrieked, his knees buckling his and eyes filling with tears "— sooooo," he wailed above the sound of his own gasping, "so please stop hurting me, because, see, nothing you do will make me call for Sharon!"

"I think you're wrong," breathed Mr Ruislip. His fingers danced over the pulsing of Rhys's blazing hand. "I have observed that when females and males of your species are put together in situations of extreme stress, bonds may form which have no bearing on the reality of their various natures. Thus, the shaman-female may regard you, with the rationality of objective thought, as merely a dribbling male of dubious sexuality; yet where danger induces a chemical response, it is more than possible that she, like you, may mistake such a hormonal reaction as, in fact, an inclination towards *affection*," the word was spat with contempt, "and thus act without the intelligence that such a situation demands."

Rhys strove to think beyond the pain shooting up his arm and down the length of his spine. "Eh?" he managed.

Mr Ruislip mimed patience. "Then let me demonstrate. If I hurt you like this . . ."

This time senior management turned their backs as Rhys's body arched and his scream bounced away down the hole.

" . . . then the shaman will react in a manner resembling—"

"This!"

The voice came at the same time as a blow that swung out of nowhere, to connect with the side of Mr Ruislip's head.

Sharon appeared where she had always been. She pulled back her bag for another strike and swung it as hard as she could. The wendigo staggered.

"You!" The bag swung again, with a crack of metal badge on bone. "Do not!" Again, knocking him back off his feet. "Get to tell me!" Smashing into the crown of his skull as he sprawled across the floor. "About my chemical responses!"

Senior management glanced at each other as Sharon knelt on Mr Ruislip's chest and hit him again and again.

Then Mr Ruislip moved.

His hand shot up and, through every obstacle, locked itself round Sharon's throat. Her eyes bulged and the bag slipped from her fingers as she clawed at his stick-wrist and its steely strength.

"Little girl," hissed the wendigo. "Were the grown men too scared to come and play?"

Something spasmed across Sharon's face. As her vision blurred and the blood sang in her ears, she grabbed the wendigo by a thin handful of hair and pulled his head up, even as she smote it with her own.

Her skull, his nose.

Mr Ruislip wailed, an animal keen of distress. His grip loosened and a hand flew to his shattered nose. Blood rolled down, thick and dark, curling over the contours of his mouth. Sharon crawled away, gasping.

But now senior management moved. One staggered forward and grabbed Sharon by the collar, pulling her to her feet. Another caught hold of Rhys and swung him against the wall with a jarring thud. Rhys groaned and sank to the floor, cradling his arm, his chest, his whole body with whatever limbs he could spare.

Mr Ruislip staggered up, swaying from surprise and feeling around his nose. Cartilage clicked as he twitched it this way and that, exploring the depth of the break. His mouth twisted with dissatisfaction and pain.

"I think . . ." he muttered, spitting blood, "that this must be . . . rage."

Sharon tried to close her eyes as the wendigo approached. Shuddering, she pulled away from his stare. One of his hands ran up her arm, and she swallowed bile at its touch. For a second she saw a flash of what he really was: flayed skin flapping beneath a silk-suited surface. His hand tightened on her shoulder. Somewhere in the black hole below shadows moved, though there was nothing there to move them.

Help us, shaman . . .

"Tell me," the wendigo breathed, "does the human body have a fixed resistance above which it may be ripped apart? Or does it vary from one specimen to another?"

"Okay," muttered Sharon. "That's gotta be up there for one of the most whacked-out questions I've ever been asked. Sorry, didn't pay attention in biology."

His fingers dug into her flesh, creaked against bone.

"Shall we find out?"

"Excuse me?"

All eyes turned to see who had spoken.

Rhys was staggering to his feet, leaning against the wall for support. There was something in his hands, something thin and silvery, possibly covered in foil. As Sharon watched, he slipped it back into his pocket, and his neck tightened and stretched with the effort of swallowing what might well have been a couple of Dr Seah's antihistamines.

Aware of all eyes on him, with an effort Rhys straightened and repeated, "Excuse me, I don't want to cause trouble, see. But I think you should let go of Ms Li."

Sharon glanced down at the pit, and heard . . .

> *footstep on stone*
> *wind through old newspaper*
>> *glass shattering in the night*

thump of door
  swish of window pane
Help us, shaman!

"Are you ... attempting to fulfil a gender obligation?" suggested Mr Ruislip, his grip on Sharon not slackening. "I have observed that it's considered apt for the male of your species to defend the female, regardless of whether the effort is appreciated."

"This isn't a bloke thing," asserted Rhys. "This is me asking you, politely, to not rip Miss Li limb from limb, because that would make me very angry."

"Angry? And what form, dare we ask, will your anger take?"

Rhys drew a long breath.

And there it was, that flicker of power about him, that flash of magic which Sharon had glimpsed when she had been in the shadows but which had never got past the hay fever long enough to make itself known. The filaments in the bulbs around the edge of the room flickered and flared; a cold wind, stinking of factory chemicals and ammonia, gently stirred the air. Wires rippled beneath Rhys's feet. It occurred to Sharon that *this* was what a druid was, always had to have been, even in the city – somebody at one with their surroundings.

"I'm a druid nearly of the first circle," he hissed. "I was almost the leader of my peers, practically the chosen one. I didn't quite summon the essence of the waterways from beneath the city streets, nearly brought forth the glory of the heavens, was almost on time for a conversation with the whispering dryads of the thousand and one lamp posts, and was only a few words away from sealing up the nether gate across the rotting railway tracks. You should maybe fear me, perhaps."

A stunned silence greeted this statement.

Mr Ruislip raised his eyebrows at one of the suited members of management who, after a second of hesitation, rounded on Rhys and drew back his fingers in the opening gesture of a ritual spell. Rhys threw out his hand and the bulbs around the room flared, a vivid stream of tungsten light. Thin filament coils, burning cherry-red, burst up from the floor and lashed themselves around the feet of the unfortunate member of management, who turned red, then white, then grey, then finally, trousers smoking and hands twitching in pain, began to scream. The filaments, spider-thin and electric-fast, grew and wound themselves round the wizard like a cocoon, dragging him to the ground and smothering him in a writhing, glowing mass of wire, cutting off all sound from within.

Rhys took a step towards the wendigo, and the three remaining members of management took a step back.

"Interesting," murmured Mr Ruislip. "You appear not to be leaking organic compounds any more from your nostrils."

Another member of management made the mistake of raising his hands into an attacking spell. Rhys turned, eyes flashing fluorescent-white, and the wizard choked, clawing at his throat, his mouth opening and twitching, his cheeks bulging, until with a hacking cough that brought him to his knees, he spat out a great fat mouthful of tar-stained goo that dribbled from his lips and stained his teeth grey.

"The next person who tries that," murmured Rhys in a dream-like voice, "will drown in liquid tar, see?"

Mr Ruislip caught Sharon's eye. She gave a tiny shrug. "Hey," she said, "this is your own crappy fault."

The woman, smartly trouser-suited, turned and ran for the door. Her colleague hesitated, eyes flicking from Rhys to Ruislip and back, then with a little gasp he too ran, bolting out into the dark.

Mr Ruislip, still grasping Sharon by the shoulder, yelled, "Betrayal will be reflected in your Christmas bonuses!"

Footsteps echoed down the corridor, the man and the woman running for the lift.

There was the swish of . . .

. . . a bicycle tyre?

And the footsteps stopped.

Sharon strained and heard . . .

She heard . . .

A child laugh.

Somewhere out there, in the dark.

She turned to stare into Mr Ruislip's pale eyes. "What've you done?" she breathed. "What's out there?"

"The gates are down," replied the wendigo with a tiny-toothed smile. "Did you think I was the only one to come through the wall?"

"Rhys?" Sharon raised her voice, louder than she'd meant. "You feeling druidic enough to blast this guy into lots of sticky bits?"

"I can try, Ms Li."

Mr Ruislip turned abruptly, pulling Sharon across his body, one arm over her throat.

Rhys yawned, then put his hands over his mouth. "Sorry, Ms Li," he exclaimed, "That was really inappropriate."

"It's okay," croaked Sharon, against the pressure of the wendigo's arm. "'These drugs may cause drowsiness.'"

"Yes, but I wouldn't want you to think I was yawning – *yawning* – while you're in danger, Ms Li."

"Rhys, can we concentrate on the wendigo?"

In the darkness beyond the door, where footsteps had run and stopped abruptly, Rhys heard it again – the swish of tyres on stone, moving fast, far too fast for the narrow gloom outside.

"Now," Mr Ruislip said, shuffling closer to the edge of the pit, "the situation is very simple. You are mortals of no significance, whereas *I*—"

"What's in the pit?" Sharon cut in, wheezing with the effort of breathing.

The question caught Mr Ruislip off guard. "What?"

"I can hear ... voices. All the spirits you stole, right? You locked them up down there?"

"You really expect me to ans—"

"Well, the way I reason it is this. You're gonna use me as a human shield, right, against Rhys here until he like, gets mega-drowsy from all the anti-histamines and that. But that's kinda dumb. Because if you do hurt me, then Rhys is so gonna blast you into tiny bits. And, actually, you may have summoned the nether hordes of darkness or whatever shit it is you've got going out in that corridor there. But *me* ... " Her hands tightened suddenly around Mr Ruislip's arm and it occurred to the wendigo, a second too late, that a vice-like grip went both ways. " ... I've got this serious shaman shit going down."

Sharon vanished.

So, for that matter, did Mr Ruislip.

There was a second of confusion.

Mr Ruislip looked round at the shadow world where the shamans walked, and for a second saw all that the shaman could see: walls

encrusted with a hundred years of river salt that sparkled like dia-
monds; the ice that had once been buried here, still visible between the
stones; metal crawling with rust mites that burrowed in and out of the
iron of the walkway; Rhys burning, blazing with anti-histamine-fuelled
magic that spluttered and spat around him like oil in a frying pan.

And, down – a long way down – the pit, a spinning, roaring mass,
a great writhing mess of voices and shadows: there the red-brick soul
of a warehouse plucked from the cracks in the mortar; there the silvery-
glass back of an abandoned church hall, still rippling with the music
that had once played within its embrace; there the soapy guardian of
an old spa house where Victorian gentlemen had perfected their
beards; here the sharp clattering voice of the factory floor, stolen at
night from the hollow quietness of the waiting machines – dozens of
them, *hundreds* of them, the stolen souls of the city whirled beneath
him, screaming, hammering at their prison bars.

And, as Mr Ruislip looked up, he saw for a brief second his own
hands, his own arms, his own skin, the billowing flayed flesh rippling
around him like sails in a storm, and he grinned, and in this place his
grin had fangs, and for a glorious moment he remembered how he had
enjoyed the taste of blood and the thrill of the hunt until . . .

"Yo, saggy-skin!"

Sharon caught him by the waist, charging head first into his middle
and knocking him back against the iron railing of the walkway . . .

. . . or, to put more fine a point on it, *through* the iron railing of the
walkway.

For a second Mr Ruislip clawed at empty air, but there was nothing,
only time and voices, to cling to; and he opened his mouth to scream
as he, and Sharon, fell together into the whirling pit below.

Chapter 100

Recycle Your Household Waste

Several floors above the pit where Sharon and Mr Ruislip had just fallen into endless dark, things were not going well.

They were not going well for a number of reasons.

Firstly, the office Kevin, Edna and Gretel were exploring had suddenly, and unhelpfully, filled with plastic bags. And while this was not, in and of itself, a major problem, the sudden animation of the plastic bags and the seemingly unified decision these items of garbage had taken all at once to come to life and attack the inhabitants of that space was definitely creating a difficult working environment.

"Get it off!" screamed Edna, as a shopping bag proclaiming EVERY DAY IS DISCOUNT DAY! wrapped itself around her arm, pulling her towards the ground.

"Sweetheart, I'm kind of busy!" hissed Kevin, swatting a bag with his sports holdall as it flew directly for his face. Gretel was already half swamped. Plastic bags were clinging to her legs, her belly, her arms, her shoulders, and even as Kevin glanced her way, the troll's great form spun sideways, pushed down by the thickening mass plastering itself to her flesh. A bright orange Sainsbury's bag drifted down and tried to spread itself over the troll's nose and mouth, only for Gretel to roll like a carpet out of its way, crunching and rasping in the swathes of plastic already clinging to her. Even the troll's immense strength didn't seem enough, and Kevin groaned with a foreboding of defeat as something cold and crumpled managed to stick itself across his back, rippling and writhing against his touch as he tried to peel it off.

"There's a trigger spell somewhere in here!" he screamed. "Destroy the trigger!"

Edna was cowering under a desk, a doodle-strewn notebook held up in front of her to bat away the incoming clouds of plastic, which swarmed and circled the room. Gretel roared feebly as a bag wrapped itself around her throat and began to twist and tighten. Kevin tried to get to her, but a bag had got around his foot and didn't want to move, pulling him back down. He flailed at the empty air, then fell, blood running freely from his nose.

He'd taken the wrong blood type, that much was obvious. And now, as Kevin lay on the floor reflecting on all the untoward things that might be happening to his internal organs, he felt the cold pressure of another bag wrap itself around his hand. Another settled across his body, embracing him like a taxidermist's blanket. He saw a white bag settle, so slowly, over Gretel's features. It morphed itself to the troll's nose and mouth, then flared up and down as the troll groaned, choking for breath under the plastic seal.

"Edna," croaked the vampire. "Find the trigger!"

Under the desk, Edna whimpered, swatting away a bag that had attempted to ram itself into her mouth like a sponge. "I can't," she cried.

Gretel's struggles were growing less, her lungs slowing in their battle against the death mask stuck over her face, and even as Edna looked around her in panic, more plastic was encasing the vampire too, pinning him to the floor.

There was . . .

. . . not so much a sound as a *pressure*, a sense of particles moving with a sound just beyond human hearing. The floor-to-ceiling windows hummed; mugs bounced along the surface of the desks; cables buzzed inside their shielding. Something grey, fast and winged was spinning through the air outside the office. Banking tightly, it snapped its wings in close and barrelled towards the building's vibrating glass exterior, which now began to pop, began to splinter, began to crack; and an instant before Sally the banshee burst through into the office, mouth agape and vocal cords singing beyond human powers to hear, the glass walls of Burns and Stoke exploded.

Chapter 101

All Good Things Come to Those Who Wait

"What was that?"

"Did anyone else hear . . . ?"

"Oh my God. Look at that!"

"Dear me, is that something to do with us, Mr Swift?"

"You know, Mrs Rafaat, I think it might be."

"But all that glass! That's going to cost a fortune to replace."

"That's what makes me think it might be something to do with us."

"Do you think everyone is all right?"

"Well, personally I find massive symptoms of architectural destruction a rather positive indication."

"That's because you're incompetent, sorcerer."

"Thank you, Sammy. The next time I'm fighting off unstoppable evils, I'll remember that key piece of feedback and advice."

"Should we do something?"

"You took the words out of my mouth, Mrs Rafaat. Let's . . . do something bloody mythic."

Chapter 102

Regret Never Helped Anyone

In the flickering gloomy pit beneath Burns and Stoke, Rhys gasped and slid to the floor.

He'd just seen Sharon and Mr Ruislip vanish, only to reappear a second later as two shapes tumbling into the black pit. He'd rushed to the edge, and seen ...

... darkness.

He hadn't realised how quickly the dark could swallow light, how easily living things could become small.

Now he sat, dizzy and bewildered, eyes heavy and throat clear, mind fuzzy and thoughts racing.

She'd fallen.

She'd fallen.

She'd fallen.

And he hadn't stopped it.

"Aaa ... aaa ... *atchoo!*"

A child giggled out in the darkness of the corridor.

A bicycle tyre slid on stone.

It occurred to Rhys that these were not the normal sounds of an industrial-era storage pit beneath a financial building in Canary Wharf. Also, that if there was nothing left for him, no purpose, no meaning, no future, there was no further point in fearing things unseen and unknown.

He staggered to his feet, cradling his broken hand against his chest, and pushed back the door to the corridor.

In the distance, tiny and pale, the lift stood waiting to carry any who dared approach back into the light. Rhys fingered the packet of antihistamines in his pocket and wondered what would happen if he combined the pills with coffee. Was that medically allowed?

He raised his head and called out, "There's nothing you can do to me that hasn't been done, so don't even think about trying."

So saying, he stepped into the dark of the corridor.

Swish of a wheel in the dark, splash as it rippled through a puddle on the stone floor, then nothing again.

It occurred to Rhys that these corridors were too narrow for a cyclist, even a lithe and dextrous one, but frankly he no longer cared about such practicalities. He took another step forward and heard a child giggle. Then another step, and another. As he walked down the corridor it seemed that no matter how far he went, the lift door still seemed a very long way off, too far off in fact, but when he looked back, so did the door to the pit.

Something dark and fast moved in the corner of his eye; he turned quickly, raising his hands to strike, but it was gone, as if swallowed by the walls themselves.

Something else blurred behind him: a rattle of chain on gears. He spun again, but it was out of sight, swallowed up by the darkness.

"Atchoo!"

The sound of his sneeze echoed down the corridor. He whispered the words of the druid's guide light, opening his palms to release a sodium-stained creature the size of a small blackbird, its skin glowing with a pervasive pinkish glow. It rose up to circle above his head, spilling its light across the stones around him – and there!

He saw it just for a second, a shadow all in black on a bicycle all in black, as if rider and transport were made of the same stuff, an insubstantial absence of light which wheeled across his vision before vanishing into the wall itself. He heard the laugh again, and there was another figure, a child, a boy in a black hood with black fingers moulded to the handles of his black bicycle. He too rode through the wall, and no sooner was he gone than another appeared, pedalling out of the brickwork itself and circling Rhys; then another, and another, appearing and vanishing into darkness, forming a shoal of childish riders who giggled at their prank. Rhys turned uselessly on the spot as he tried to think of a spell ...

"Atchoo!"

Suddenly one rider swerved and pedalled straight for him. Rhys turned to run, but he had nowhere to go, cut off in the circle of riders. He felt something cold and liquid slam into the small of his back and then pass through him – it passed *through* him and took with it all the warmth in his belly, all the solidity in his bones, knocking him to the ground. As the shadow cyclist giggled and rejoined the circling mass of riders, Rhys thought he could hear them whisper in the dark, *Ride with us, ride with us, ride with us ...*

He crawled onto his hands and knees, gasping for air, and another cyclist pedalled out of the wall and slammed into him, knocking him back to the floor. He gave a faltering gasp of pain as his fingers, now turning blue, scrabbled at the wet stone beneath him. The little circling guide light went out.

Ride with us, ride with us, ride with us ...

He saw one of the riders turn and swerve his bike to a stop down the corridor, lining up the front wheel with the end of Rhys's nose for one last, great charge.

Something glassy rolled in Rhys's pocket. He felt it: a small bottle containing a spray distilled from canal water and slime. He didn't need to see the masking-tape label to know what the label said: "Peaceful".

The shadow cyclist gave a bright "ting-a-ling" on his bell, swung upright into his saddle and charged, standing up on his pedals and leaning forward into his handlebars like a champion jockey as he sped through the darkness towards Rhys. Rhys raised himself onto one arm, pulling the bottle of Peaceful out of his pocket and thrusting it aloft in his shaking, swollen, disfigured hand.

Ride with us, ride with us, roared the bicycle swarm.

"Grow up," grunted the druid, and as the rider burst through the circling darkness and upon him, Rhys smashed the bottle as hard as he could into the ground.

Chapter 103

Destruction Is Merely an Alteration of a State of Being

Sally the banshee burst into the shattered remains of Burns and Stoke through the window, talons outstretched through a billowing cloud of plastic bags and pigeon feathers. Her wings beat at the mass of detritus that spun around her, caught in the turmoil of her passage as she descended on the bags smothering Gretel and began to rip away at them with her claws. The banshee had torn a great gash through the bags covering Gretel's face and scraped off a large swatch from the troll's side before a cloud of plastic, turning in the air as tightly as a flock of starlings, slammed into her, knocking her to the floor with a great *ploomph*.

Gretel was rolling, using her free arm to tug away the rest of the bags holding her down, while Sally kicked and bit and slashed at the rustling clouds that threatened in turn to engulf her. Edna managed to wriggle, snake-like, across the floor to where Kevin lay choking and hacking, his face almost lost beneath a writhing mass of plastic. She struggled to drag a couple of bags away from the vampire's face, then threw them aside, at which they drifted upwards to join the swarm attacking Sally.

As Kevin's mouth and face came free, the vampire looked up, and shrieked, "Stop the spell!"

"I don't know how."

"Find the trigger mechanism!"

"I don't know what that looks like!"

"Smash stuff until you do!"

Faced with this uncouth suggestion, Edna hesitated. Meanwhile a sudden ear-splitting shriek announced that Sally, raining shredded plastic around her, had pulled herself free enough to stagger to her feet and snap her wings open. Hopping clumsily, one foot still tangled in plastic, the banshee struggled to the window and, with the aerodynamic elegance of a sofa, launched herself out into the night. A great billow of plastic bags followed, twisting like live creatures. For a moment, writhing across the sky, the swarming mess of plastic seemed to take on a single dragon-like form.

Then Sally was gone, plummeting towards the earth. The mass of plastic followed, snapping in the sky with the sound of a battle pennant in a storm. The banshee got to within a few feet of an uncomfortable encounter with gravity, then snapped her wings back open and twisted in the air, passing over neat hedges and tidy stone paving with enough speed to send leaves dancing up in her passage. She skimmed over bus shelters, then looped her way above the nearby railway, and still the plastic swarm snaked after her, hissing in her wake.

"Smash things!" hissed the vampire amid the wreckage of the office. Edna, shaking from the ends of her pendant earrings to the toes of her sensible slip-on shoes, grabbed the nearest waste-paper bin and started to break up what remained of the place. Glass flew from computer screens, desks splintered, drawers spilt their contents across the floor, books tumbled from shelves, paper exploded in the air as Edna tore through the office, apologising silently to each and every item that she trashed.

Outside, Sally folded her wings in tight and swerved along the platforms of Heron Quays station, dipping so low her claws nearly scratched the shining metal rails. Behind her, the snake-swarm, lashing wildly in its flight, lost half its tail as it tangled itself on the station announcement board and shed a storm of ripped plastic across the platform and track. Sally swerved again and spread her wings, beating her way across the short distance to Canary Wharf station, whose raised platforms stood overshadowed by two great towers. There she turned once more, swooping almost vertically upwards and away, climbing between walls of steel and glass towards the narrow glimpse of sky far above.

Chapter 104

Just When You Think It Can't Get Worse ...

Rhys opened his eyes.

He coughed.

He coughed mortar dust, phlegm and ...

... canal water?

Broken potion-bottle glass crunched beneath him as he got to his feet.

Something wet slid down his face, pausing at the end of his nose. For a moment of panic he thought it might be blood, but it was too cool and dripped too easily into a puddle on the floor. Rhys ran his one good hand through his hair, and it was soaking. So were his clothes. So, in fact, was a large part of the corridor, whose brickwork now oozed a sheen of canal water into a growing pool on the floor. The thick green algae taken from the canal was embedded in the walls as if it had always been there.

The riders on their bicycles were gone.

So was the light from most of the bulbs that lined the corridor. Their broken globes were now dripping with the same water that had started running from the ceiling and across the floor.

Rhys had a feeling, if nothing more, that the potion known as Peaceful could have some unpredictable effects. But, he told himself, if you ignored the wet and the freezing cold, his spell might well have turned out worse.

He listened, but no sounds of bicycles or riders could he heard.

Rhys turned and began to make his way back towards the great black pit into which Sharon had fallen. He knew there was nothing to be achieved by this. On the other hand, it seemed nothing would be achieved by going anywhere else. He decided to let instinct guide him while the rational part of his mind gratefully relinquished all duties.

The spirit-trap hole seemed quieter now.

He wondered if, in some way, being fed the body of a wendigo and . . .

. . . yes, and that of a shaman . . .

. . . had briefly calmed the ragings of the spirits trapped within. He wondered if anyone other than a shaman knew how to free them, release them back to where they'd come from.

He wondered if he wondered too much, and sank back against a wall to catch his thoughts.

He heard a thump on the other side of the pit.

He looked up to see a pale hand emerge from the darkness below and grasp the edge of the walkway. There was a moment of gravitational doubt, then another hand caught at the metalwork. The two hands, having settled their grasp, gave a great tug, and a body followed them.

The body was . . .

. . . not quite how it should have been.

The suit was now torn, its fine silk sheared into snippets. The tie had been shredded, and a shoe had had its sole almost torn away. More significantly, the fraying of the suit had produced a certain . . . exposure . . . of the man beneath it. It wasn't so much a revelation of flesh and bone, but rather that the skin itself seemed . . . flayed. Banners of ripped fabric and thin white flesh swelled and flapped around the man – or not-man, as the case had to be. And where before his smile had been too neat to be possible, now there were signs of sharpened fangs inside the lipless curling mouth.

Having swung himself up onto the metal walkway, Mr Ruislip paused to gasp for breath. A hint of black claw showed through his disintegrating shoe and a fine rust-coloured dust had settled on his skin.

As he staggered to his feet, the wendigo swayed. His eyes drifted in and out of focus before, finally, they settled on Rhys.

"Right," groaned the druid. He raised his swollen, broken hand in a gesture of conciliation. "Okay," he muttered, leaning against the wall for support as he tried his best to square off against the battered wendigo. "So I think we should now fight a bloody battle to the death, you and me."

Confusion showed on Mr Ruislip's face. His tongue flickered over the place where human lips should have been, and the tongue was too pointed and too yellow for Rhys's comfort. "You ... wish to duel ... with me?"

"Yup."

"But ... I am wendigo. You are human. You will die."

"Maybe," grunted Rhys. "But, and I hope you're taking note of this, because it's an important thing you need to understand, I've thought this through very carefully and decided. To hell with it."

Mr Ruislip blinked at Rhys as if attempting to reconcile the sight of the druid with the words he was saying. Then, having failed to do so, the wendigo scowled. "I do not understand you people," he hissed, "but now I do not care."

So saying, Mr Ruislip took hold of his jacket and peeled it away. As it fell from him, so he seemed to expand beyond the confines of his clothes. The tatty remnants of his shirt warped around him as claw and bone and flesh outgrew his human disguise. Flesh sank back into bone; skin spread out to billow around him like a warrior's flag; fingers stretched into claws, and teeth expanded out of a black, mawing mouth. His eyes turned to boiling red, nose flattened, ears stretched, and as his knees clicked backwards and talons ripped out through the constraint of his leather shoes, Mr Ruislip rolled his neck from side to side and hissed:

"So good to be me!"

Rhys braced himself and wiped a drop of canal water off the end of his nose.

The great red eyes focused on him as a cat might study a scurrying mouse. "Goodbye, druid," the wendigo hissed, raising his claws to strike. "I regret that I shall never come to understand the motives behind your death."

A great black talon swung through the air, taking its time, for it needed no speed to finish its work. Rhys looked up at it and wondered what his motivation for dying was anyway.

Then something fast and hard slammed through the air just above his right eye, punching the talon aside and knocking Rhys to the floor.

"Hey, you! Wendigo!"

The voice came from the pit itself, loud and clear, and carried by more than just human breath, and it had force and weight, and sent concrete dust spinning around the room. Rhys looked down, but there was only darkness and swirling air.

"Don't you dare touch my druid!" said Sharon.

Chapter 105

Let Yourself Go

Edna was . . .

. . . rather enjoying herself.

She'd never smashed things like this before. Now, as she tore through the office of Magical Affairs, ripping out drawers and knocking over desks, she felt a certain sense of liberation.

In the skies outside the office, Sally's marvellous aerodynamics might also have made the banshee glory in the moment's experience, were it not for her suspicion that the plastic-bag snake rippling through the air behind her was catching up. How this could be, the banshee had no time to speculate. But as she swung round the great silver summit of Canada Tower and began a nosedive back down towards the street in a dizzying blur of windows passing at her back, the plastic was undeniably gaining.

Sally turned out of her dive at the last instant and swooped down a silent street which by day thronged with suits and taxis. Swerving beneath a sign proclaiming that the future of futures lay in sensible spread betting, with a talon she snagged a giant awning over an area of empty café tables, which crashed and clattered down behind her. She darted over the low black chain that bordered the quayside and threw up a great wake of spray as she passed over the still surface of the water, soaking the snake at her back. Something rustled close by and lashed out at her feet, dragging her down. She lurched in mid-flight, and her wingtips scraped the water itself before, with an effort of will and a great leathery flap, she pushed up. Banking hard, she tried to escape her pursuer by darting through the masts of the yachts moored beside the Thames.

Behind her a flapping and a burst of feathers caught her attention. Part of the plastic-bag snake had been caught by a dive-bombing mass of pigeons, which now struggled with it and writhed in fury, plummeting towards the surface of the river. The airborne snake-shape wobbled as if deciding what to do, then, with a great swell of bag, it split in two, dropping its pigeon-laden half like a snowstorm towards the ground, while the front half, relieved of this burden, accelerated towards Sally.

Inside the office of Magical Affairs, Edna swung her waste-paper bin with increasing zeal, knocking a calendar off the wall and sending a jar of biros flying across the floor. She turned, seeking something else to smash and, from the corner of her eye, saw a flash of green metal in the wall itself. A safe, until now hidden behind the calendar, sat squat and forbidding and very solid. She went for Gretel, but the troll was still struggling to pull plastic bags off herself as fast as they settled. In vain too she turned to Kevin. The vampire was gasping for breath, blood running freely from his nose, ears and eyes as his body went into full rejection of the blood he'd supped on a few minutes before.

Edna stared at the safe, then reached up for the combination lock. A hand fell on hers.

She swung the waste-paper bin, slamming it into the source of the unwelcome grasp. In response there came an unintimidating cry of "Bloody hell!"

Edna dropped the bin and exclaimed, "Oh, I'm so sorry, I didn't realise it was—"

"I can see that!" exclaimed Swift, batting away a plastic bag trying to settle onto his head. "This is a fine spell you've unleashed ..." Another bag began to wrap itself around Swift's ankle. It was met with a blast of rolling power that propelled plastic, paper and shards of broken furniture across the room from the epicentre of Swift's upraised hand, which was still smarting from Edna's assault with the bin. "The safe's warded," he added, pulling a penny from his pocket. He flicked it at the heavy green door and ducked as the copper rebounded with enough speed to bury it in the far wall. "You touch that and you're crispy."

He approached the safe warily. Edna took a nervous step back as blue sparks flickered briefly around the sorcerer's fingers. She saw him move his lips, fingers twitching at the air. Then she felt a pressure, a great ear-aching pressure, gather, grow, stretch and suddenly snap with an audible collision of metal, magic and will.

The safe went "click".

Swift pulled it open, handling it through the end of his sleeve. "Hot hot hot hot hot."

Edna craned to look past him. Inside she saw . . .

One woman's slipper, old and grubby.

One child's mitten, pink and with a bobble hanging from the wrist.

One broken umbrella, the spokes blown backwards.

One greasy sheet of paper in an empty fried-chicken box.

And one woven hemp bag. The bag was old, worn and torn at the bottom. The lettering on the front, much faded, read, T IS BAG W LL LAST YOU A LIFETI E.

Swift snatched it from the safe, turned to the room, opened it wide.

Edna thought she heard some words slip from the sorcerer's lips. But later, when asked, she couldn't believe that what she'd heard could possibly have been uttered.

"Choose biodegradable," whispered the sorcerer. "Consider your environment."

In the skies above the Isle of Dogs, Sally felt a sudden turn in the movement of the snake at her back. Glancing behind her she saw the great plastic creature twist in midair and begin to fly back towards the silvery lights of Canary Wharf.

In the office of Magical Affairs the still-dancing plastic bags coalesced into great knots of blue, white, orange and grey, and flew all at once, like bats to a cave, towards the opening of the hemp bag. They flooded into it: dozens, then hundreds, more than the one saggy bag could possibly contain. But still they kept filling it, while Swift held the bag open as if it weighed no more than a T-shirt, watching and waiting as the cascade of plastic tumbled and collapsed into its depths. The last piece settled with sullen slowness into the bag, which Swift quickly clamped shut, weighting it down with a desk fan wrenched from its socket.

Throughout the room, nothing stirred.

A flapping of leathery wings announced the arrival of Sally through the shattered windows. Beneath her, the pigeons that were probably Jess circled and cooed in the still night air.

The banshee was already reaching for her whiteboard. Kevin coughed blood, Gretel was lumbering uneasily to her feet.

Is everyone all right? wrote Sally.

Edna looked at Swift; Swift surveyed the room.

"Vampy-boy looks a bit the worse."

"I think Kevin drank the wrong kind of blood," ventured Edna. She was still shaking, though she didn't know why. She could sense every capillary beneath her skin and felt at once more tired, and more alive, than she remembered being in a very long time.

Someone hesitantly opened the door, and Mrs Rafaat stepped through, followed by Dog. Hanging back from his clawed companion came the small shape of Sammy.

"What a drama," grumbled the goblin, hopping over the recumbent form of Kevin. He saw the safe. "Hey – sacrifices! Maybe you lot aren't as totally crap as you look."

Without pausing, Sammy took off his coat and began unloading the single slipper, lost mitten, broken umbrella and empty fried-chicken box into its hood.

"Should we call a doctor for Kevin?" asked Gretel.

"Good idea," murmured Swift. "And maybe for you too?"

"I'll be all right, Mr Mayor sir," replied the troll. "Thank you for your concern."

"Good. That's good. One quick question ... where's Sharon?"

Chapter 106

Embrace the Spirit of the Thing

Mr Ruislip loomed over Rhys, claws out, teeth bared, ready to strike – but didn't.

"It's like, really dark down here," boomed Sharon's disembodied voice.

Rhys slid away from Mr Ruislip's reach and peered into the darkness of the pit.

Shadows stirred, spun, twisted, and it seemed to Rhys that, as they did, something was rising with them, getting closer and closer, very fast.

"I mean, I know you're no magical genius and that," went on Sharon's voice, and it seemed that it too was getting nearer, carried by a rising blast of warmth that shook the water from Rhys' hair and made his eyelids want to flicker tight shut, " but did you seriously think it was a bright idea, throwing a *shaman* into a pit of pissed-off trapped spirits?"

And there was something coming, getting larger very, very fast, something bright and burning and brilliant, with jet-black hair streaked with blue, and purple boots and an orange top and a look on its face – on *her* face of . . .

"You total arsehole," said Sharon.

And up she came from the pit. It seemed to Rhys that the shaman, as she emerged from the darkness, was standing on nothing, being carried by nothing. But when he turned his head he thought he could see in the corner of his eye a great mass of shapes, twisting, writhing, burning, dancing – none human, none even animal, but the flashing souls of streets, of buildings, of memories and time, snatched from their homes and now released, spinning through the air around Sharon. Her hair billowed around her and there was a silver-grey glow to her skin that ebbed and flowed like a thing alive in itself, and when she looked at the wendigo, Mr Ruislip cowered – he *cowered* from her glare – and there was something in her eye, something ancient and vast and old.

"You thought you could imprison us?" she roared. And at her voice the air lurched and danced and spun, and for a second glimpses of red mortar dust, of spinning electricity, of whirling voices, of cut glass, flashed in and out of existence around her.

"You thought you could control the city?" she bellowed, and this time the pit shook, the walls creaked, powdered mortar tumbled down and away into the dark while the pulsing mass of magic around Sharon shimmered and spun, and her voice wasn't human. "You have no idea what we are!"

She didn't move, didn't blink. But a sudden fistful of power slammed into Mr Ruislip and threw him off his feet, knocking him against the wall hard enough to crack the bricks at his back.

"Did you think . . ."

Another wave of power caught Mr Ruislip in its grip and spun him round before he had time to recover himself, slamming him into the floor.

". . . that you could understand the city?"

The wendigo gasped as an unseen fist caught him, wrapped itself around his whole body and lifted him up off the floor, squeezing until his eyes bulged in his face and his feet twitched at the empty air.

"Did you think . . ."

It dropped him again, only to pick him back up like a doll in a giant's paw.

". . . one creature could command us?"

Mr Ruislip gagged and writhed at the unseen force that contained him, black blood pulsing beneath his skin, tongue lolling in his mouth. "P-p-p-please . . ." he rasped. "Please!"

"Ms Li?" Rhys's voice was a bare grasp.

The shaman's snapped her head round to stare at him and Rhys recoiled before the sudden sense of . . .

door slamming in night

feet on stone on stone on stone on stone

running then running now running yet to come stone deep city deep

"No one can command the city," she said.

"Sharon?" For a second a flash of something in the shaman's eye, a flicker of doubt? "Ms Li?" he tried again. "You're um . . . you're sort of floating there a bit."

The grey fires dancing around Sharon faltered, swirled like smoke in a storm. She swallowed and whispered, "Rhys?"

"Um . . . you okay?"

"I'm . . . I'm – we . . . we are . . . The voices are the . . . the . . . I am . . . " She squeezed her eyes shut, fingers clenching and opening at her side, a sound of pure frustration and concentrated rage rising from the back of her throat. "Rhys! They're . . . in my – can't stop us – mind!"

"Please!" wailed the wendigo, and Sharon's head turned back to him, too fast, a flash of something else in her eyes.

"Rhys," she murmured, and her voice wasn't just her voice, there were a thousand other voices dancing behind it too, "I think the city wants to tear this creature limb from limb. Now, that's kind of gross, but I really am feeling it, so if you don't wanna watch I'd suggest you leave now."

"Please, please . . . " groaned the wendigo.

"Um . . . w-when you s-say the city . . . " stammered the druid.

"I am the city and the city is me," she replied, eyes fixed on some unseen point. "For without the city, I am not myself, and without me, the city is not complete. I am shaped by its streets and the journey I take, and it becomes what it is through my footsteps on its stones. I am at one with the city, and it is at one with me, as it always has been, and always will be."

"Okay," mumbled Rhys, "That's kind of cool, but a little bit freaky, see?"

"I know." Sharon's lips trembled, her hands still blazing at her side. "And this floating thing, it's making me feel a bit sick, actually. I mean, I've never been great with sheer drops, and while being held in the embrace of the spirits is all well and good, it's really a long way down, and I don't exactly know what I'm doing here."

There was a clattering of running feet from the corridor behind them, and Rhys staggered out of the way as the door opened to let in the combined shapes of Swift, Sammy, Edna, Mrs Rafaat and Dog. Swift looked up, saw Sharon and stopped so hard that Dog nearly flattened him.

"My servant," breathed Sharon, a smile of hopeful recognition on her lips.

"What?"

"You are the servant of the city," she breathed. "Its stones call and you obey, as you have always obeyed our call."

"Uh ... yeah, I guess that's fair, if a little unexpected," Swift mumbled. Then his bright blue eyes settled on Mr Ruislip, and fury flared in them. "You!" he snarled. "You little wanky pile of wendigo shit, you tell us how to restore Greydawn or we will tear you apart!"

"Actually, the city's already gonna tear him apart," offered Rhys.

"You poor dear, what happened to you?" cried Mrs Rafaat, hurrying over to comfort Rhys and his twisted hand.

"Oh, you know, manful heroic stuff," insisted the druid. "Ow!"

Sammy was staring up at the still-floating Sharon, speechless. Swift nudged the goblin in the skull, that being the highest part available. "Uh ... what's with the floating?"

"She's at one with the city," breathed the goblin. "Actually properly at one with the city." For a moment he just stood there, then raised his head and barked, "Oi, soggy-brains! Your soul been subsumed into the mystic frickin' ether yet?"

Sharon turned her head to peer down at the goblin. "Hello, Sammy," she murmured. "The Seven Sisters are still very angry with you."

"Fat is fat," he contended. "And I'm not gonna pretend it ain't just because the silly cow is attuned to the Wood Green ley lines! You having fun being at one with the city?"

"Not really," whispered Sharon. "It's all a bit ... a bit ... big."

"Wanna stop mucking about then?" barked the goblin.

"I don't think I can."

"Course you can."

"I remember ... everything," she whispered. "I remember when the first stone was laid on my streets. I remember the first bridge across my waters, the first foundation laid into my soil, the first ship to moor at my quay, the first grave dug on my edges, the first coffin laid, the first child born in my arms, the first fire struck. I remember the taste of ashes and the fog that hid the plague, the weight of bombs breaking my bones, the rattle of drills behind my eyes, the rush of steam through my veins. I remember . . . Sammy? Help me?"

"You still clearly remember being you, skinny strange human girl-thing," retorted Sammy. "Else there wouldn't be all this drama. So just focus on that, yeah?"

"I don't think I can."

"Arses!"

"I am . . . I am . . . I . . ." She dragged in a shuddering breath, and the mass of nameless shadows flowed in and out of her lungs as she gasped for the air to speak. "Help me!"

"Help yourself! You're Sharon Li. You're an unemployed, uneducated ex-maker of coffee with no real job prospects and some overdue rent you've gotta worry about – how hard can it be to focus on that?"

Something fiercely human and familiar flickered over Sharon's face, and Sammy warmed to his theme. "You're single, your friends don't really get you, you've been lonely for so frickin' long you've started reading books with crappy titles like *How to Be Loved*, you've got *no* social skills, your shamaning sucks, you run this Facebook group with a stupid name and gotta go apologise to a vicar tomorrow morning for blowing up his hall."

"I did *not* blow up his hall!" she barked, and it seemed to Rhys that the silver-grey fires clinging to Sharon's skin flashed at her indignation, spinning away from her like a corona, growing brighter, whiter, more violent. "Four killer builders blew up his hall; I just happened to be there!"

"Yeah? If you're so innocent, then how come dribble-nose is all swollen and sticky right now?"

"Can I query 'swollen and sticky'?" hazarded Rhys.

"Look," cried Sharon, and now the room was spinning around her, a great voiceless roar in the air, drowning out all but her indignant words. "I've only been doing this shamaning thing for a few weeks, properly, I mean.

"And you," stabbing a finger at Sammy, bringing with it a swirl of still-laden wind, "you're like, the most unsupportive teacher *ever*. I mean, 'soggy-brains'? What kind of crap name is that? You gotta encourage your pupils, you've gotta be supportive, encouraging, flexible. You can't just go around insulting everyone who's taller than you, because that's the whole world and ... Oh."

Rhys dived for cover as the light spinning around Sharon exploded out from her like a sky-borne magnesium flare. Peering from behind his hands, he saw Sharon's fingers open at her side, her eyes widen, her face turn towards the ceiling. There came a rippling in the centre of the room, a cacophony, a cracking, a tearing of the darkness in two, as if nothing could be torn into a deeper nothing yet.

With a roar, a churning mass rose from the pit – the trapped spirits, a great dancing conundrum of them twisting in the air, a vibration of voices that made no sound. They whirled around Sharon like an old friend, tangling their fingers in her hair, whispering their stories in her ears, wrapping round her ankles like a family cat. Dog sat up on his haunches as the spirits tornadoed about the room, raising his head to the ceiling as, screaming or singing, or maybe both, they rose, spread across the ceiling in a wall of silver-grey fire and burst out into the dark.

Dog's howl followed them, a rising farewell to speed them into the night.

Silence fell on the pit.

It was, Rhys reflected, a deeper, truer silence than any that had gone before.

The hole was now ...

... exactly that.

A hole, and a dull and uninteresting one at that.

He looked, and there was Sharon, standing now on solid ground, her fingers still open at her side, her hair standing almost on end, sway-ing a little, eyes closed. The last of the silver-grey fires went out over her skin, and when she opened her eyes, she saw the members of Magicals Anonymous staring at her with a mixture of trepidation and respect.

"Oh," she murmured, "so that's who I am." A pause as she considered this fact. Sammy was grinning, arms folded, one foot tapping a told-you-so rhythm on the floor.

Sharon glared. "So none of this makes anything I said about Sammy actually *wrong*, because you still are a really rude individual, and I think your hiding behind the whole goblin identity thing isn't good enough."

There was a gentle snuffle.

It was the sound of Mrs Rafaat trying not to cry.

"That," she sniffed, "was the nicest thing . . ."

Sharon edged towards Mrs Rafaat, her indignation briefly forgotten. "You, um . . . feeling yourself?"

"Oh yes, I think so, dear. I mean, if this is who I'm meant to feel like."

"She's still not Greydawn," interjected Sammy. "All you done is released the spirits what Burns and Stoke caught. Greydawn was never caught – just changed."

Swift looked impatient and turned to the prone Mr Ruislip. "All right, you little . . ."

Mr Ruislip wasn't there.

All eyes turned to the doorway. Edna stood in it, swaying, a hand pressed to her side.

She whispered, "I think he went . . . that way . . ."

Her hand fell from her side. Down her purple cardigan was a dark stain, which was spreading. Edna crumpled; Swift rushed forward to catch her. He eased her onto the floor, and tried pushing down on the crimson tear spreading across Edna's body. At the end of the corridor, a long, long way off, the lift doors went *ping* and closed on a figure of flayed skin and shadow.

"Oh dear," sighed Edna. "This wasn't meant to happen, was it?"

Sharon looked at Swift, who shook his head very gently. Edna saw the look and swallowed painfully. "Well," she muttered, "at least I won't have to argue with the pension office any more."

"Nonsense," murmured Sharon, squatting down and fumbling the trailing end of Edna's cardigan over the wound. "You'll be losing out on winter fuel credits before you know it."

"Now, Sharon," chided Edna. "That's really very nice of you to say, but I think we both know it's a naughty little fib."

"We'll . . . get an ambulance," exclaimed Rhys. "We'll get a doctor! Has anyone got a mobile phone?"

Silence in the cavern.

Sharon stared down into Edna's face. To her surprise she saw the old woman smile. Edna's hand closed around Sharon's, squeezed it once, tight. "You don't get something for nothing, dear," confided the high priestess. "Sooner or later, someone has to pay the price."

Sharon opened her mouth to say something profound, something like, "Don't be like that. That's really negative; there's always a way, a good middle ground, a . . ."

And found that she couldn't. She stared into the old face beneath her. Edna smiled again and squeezed Sharon's hand tighter, then, still gripping, eased it away from the wound. Sharon's fingers were red with blood, which was welling freely now through the fabric of Edna's clothes.

"Naturally, we like to express our appreciation," whispered the woman, so soft Sharon barely heard it, and barely needed to, already knew the words. "Do not be afraid," breathed the priestess. "She is with us."

Sharon straightened up, looked round the room. Everyone seemed to be waiting for her to do something, their arms limp, their faces bare and grey. Sharon looked from Edna to Swift, from Swift to Mrs Rafaat, then at the open door.

"Oi, sorcerer," she blurted, "you gonna do that fire and lightning thing now?"

Swift hesitated.

His eyes met hers.

"Oh," he breathed, realisation dawning. "Yes, I suppose I should."

Carefully – very carefully – he pressed Edna's hands tight over the seeping blood in her belly. Mrs Rafaat gave a little gasp of distress as Edna flinched, and scampered forward to press her hands over Edna's, murmuring, "You'll be fine, dear. I'm sure you'll be fine."

"Druid," barked Swift. "You're with me."

"But Edna," protested Rhys. "Ms Li—"

"Now."

Pushing the druid out of the door, Swift glanced back at Sharon. She smiled, a brief flicker without any humour, then turned to Sammy. Beside the tiny shape of the goblin stood the great bulk of Dog, his tongue dangling, his tail between his legs.

"I could . . ." ventured the goblin.

"It's fine. I'll do it."

"I mean, I've got nothing better to do with my infinite abilities . . ."

"I'll do it," repeated Sharon firmly. "I know how."

Sammy hesitated, then gave a faint smile with a hint of two great teeth over a dangling lower lip. "Yeah," he declared. "You do, don't you?"

Swift was already closing the door behind him, shutting off the darkness of the corridor. Sammy nodded once at Sharon, patted Dog uneasily on the flank and walked out through the metal as the lock clicked shut.

Chapter 107

Death Is Only the Beginning

"Well," wheezed Edna, "there are worse ways to go."

Mrs Rafaat held Edna's hand tight. "You're not going anywhere, dear," she whispered. "You'll be fine."

"No," sighed the old woman. "I don't think so."

Dog peered down curiously from Mrs Rafaat's side, sniffing at Edna's blood as it pooled on the floor. Sharon wordlessly picked up all the sacrifices Sammy had stolen from the upstairs vault and circled the prone form of Edna, laying them out as she went. The slipper stuck with a faint sound of wetness to the growing pool of blood, which started seeping through it as Sharon placed it at Edna's feet.

"I feel . . . cold."

"I know," whispered Sharon. "I'm sorry."

"W-what are you doing?" stammered Mrs Rafaat. "She needs an ambulance, first aid . . . "

Edna gripped Mrs Rafaat's hand harder, commanding silence. The hem of Mrs Rafaat's sari was lying in the blood, a rising crimson stain spreading through the silk. "Please," breathed Edna. "Stay with me?"

Sharon stepped back from the slowly discolouring slipper. Arms limp at her side, she declared, "This is the slipper of the old woman who has lost her way. She sneaked out of the nursing home in the middle of the night, and wandered in search of a lost love through the silent streets. Her slipper fell off on the way, but she was not afraid, for even in the darkest hours of the night she was not alone."

"Stay with me," repeated Edna as Mrs Rafaat made to pull away. "My lady, stay."

Sharon didn't know where the words were coming from, didn't know what they meant. But as she held up each object, she knew it was true, knew it was right. "This is the child's glove found abandoned on a spike on the fence. The parents called out for their missing infant but could not find her, but though she wandered lonely through the night, hands bitten by the cold, she was not alone. No one is alone in the city."

"I'm not sure I . . . I-I-I don't think . . ." stammered Mrs Rafaat.

"This is the greaseproof paper that held a piece of chicken given to a starving man as the last shop closed. He was told, 'Come back, whenever you want, and I'll give you what you need to live,' and as he walked away he offered his thanks to Our Lady of 4 a.m., who had preserved him through another night." Sharon tore up the greasy piece of chicken paper, scattering the fragments over Edna's body. The priestess was smiling, but her pupils were widening and the blood was coming slower now, too slow, from her wound.

"This is the umbrella that blew inside out while crossing Hungerford Bridge. The woman who carried it was soaked through, her clothes clinging blackly to her skin. But in the quietest hour of the night she took her shoes off and pulled down her hair and laughed at the rain, free from the judgement of men and safe in the city that was her own."

Dog was sitting up straight now, his ears sticking up from his head like antennae. Mrs Rafaat stared into Edna's eyes. "I don't think . . . I-I didn't mean . . ." stuttered Mrs Rafaat.

"It's all right," breathed Edna. "It's for the best."

"This is the bag the beggar man carried his clothes in. Lasts a lifetime. Worn out in a week. Life passed him by, but she did not."

Sharon laid the bag above Edna's head and stood back. Mrs Rafaat's clothes were sticky with blood, her hands crimson with it. She looked down at her feet, at the slow spread of the redness up her sari, then back into Edna's eyes.

Edna Long, sometime hairdresser, beauty parlour owner, high

priestess of the Friendlies, thankful congregation to Our Lady of 4 a.m., smiled at her.

"You're in the presence of She Who Walks Beside," murmured Sharon as Dog dipped a curious paw into the blood on the floor. "And the sacrifice has been made. Tradition says you get to make a wish."

Edna smiled still.

"Greydawn," she breathed, and it seemed to Sharon that the breath kept coming from the furthest depths of Edna's lungs, rolling out between her lips, her bare-whisper sending shimmers through her blood and skin, seeming not to cease even as the last vestiges of sound passed from her body and the smile on her face faded to an empty stare, fixed up at nothing.

Dog whined – a long, slow, animal note.

Mrs Rafaat carefully laid Edna's hand aside, folding it across the high priestess's chest. She stood, the blood shifting beneath her feet, and turned to look at Sharon.

"Oh," she said, and seemed surprised she'd spoken. "Oh," she said again. "Is that what I mean?"

The blood rippled at her feet like a cup of water trembling in an earthquake. Mrs Rafaat looked down at it, curious, then back up at Sharon.

"The thing is . . ." she murmured as the crimson stain spread further, racing upwards faster than nature could accomplish.

"What I think I wanted to say . . ." And the blood passed from the sari she wore and spread over her hands, a wriggling, living thing. It stretched tendrils up and around her neck, wove itself across her face and into her hair.

"What I was trying to say all along, really . . ." Her fingers began to dissolve, falling away into nothingness beneath the sheath of Edna's blood; her sari billowed around her knees and hips as the bones that had supported them shimmered down to no more than raging air.

" . . . was how very much I liked being me." Lips curled into face, face dissolved into air, air contracted, twisted and shrank down, pulling the hollow shroud of the blood-soaked sari to the floor with it, and, without any more fanfare or calamity, Mrs Rafaat was gone.

Chapter 108

A Girl's Gotta Do What a Girl's Gotta Do

They were waiting for her outside the metal door.

Rhys staggered to his feet as Sharon stepped out, her hands stained with Edna's blood.

"Are you . . ." he asked. "Is she . . ."

"Edna's dead." Sharon's voice spoke a hollow fact, no room left for anything else. "Mrs Rafaat is gone."

"But . . . but then . . . are *you* . . ."

As Rhys fought for words, Sammy peered past him. On the floor by the hole lay the body of Edna. Both Mrs Rafaat and Dog were gone.

"Greydawn," he breathed. "She's gonna be pissed off."

Sharon glanced down at the goblin and her face hardened. She turned away and marched towards the lift. Swift scrambled to catch up with her, seizing her by the arm.

"Sharon!"

She turned, but there was something in her face which made him let go. Before the force of her stare, he recoiled.

"I'm . . . sorry for Edna."

"There had to be blood," she snapped. "And you knew it. Come on."

He didn't move. But Sharon wasn't stopping. Rhys ran to join her, followed by Sammy. Reluctantly, Swift came too.

"Where are we going?" asked Rhys as the white door of the lift slid open.

"Gonna end it," Sharon replied. "The way it always had to end."

Chapter 109

You Cannot Outrun Fate

He runs.

He has never run before, but now the city is moving, the streets dancing around him, and he runs.

He is a wendigo of the urban forest, he is the shadow that turns as you pass beneath the lamp post, he is the claw waiting on the other side of the locked ancient door, he is the laughing beyond the gate, he purses his mouth and puffs, and the lights go out; he is ancient and old as nightmare and he is …

… running and afraid.

Is this fear?

It must be.

He has never been afraid before. But now he rounds a corner and the streets seem to turn back, trapping him. Left, here, should have been the path to the gate, the traffic gate lowered across Canada Water, but it is not! How can it not be?

He runs again, runs and runs for the bridge across the water, and he can see it. He can see it, but there is the passage to the shopping subways up ahead, the grille drawn across, and as he looks it seemed to grow and grow and swallow him whole, and when he raises his eyes again the bridge is gone!

It is gone because he is not where he should be, and he looks up and thinks he can see a banshee circling overhead, and he sniffs the air and can smell the decaying flesh of a necromancer, and he looks at his hands and they are no longer human, not even close, not even the shadow of a pretence. Not even the red wash of human blood can disguise the truth that he is wendigo! And wendigos cannot be afraid!

"The city doesn't want you here."

A voice from the shadow. And she's there, of course she's there, stepping out of the night. But even as he screams with fury and lashes out at her, the shaman is gone, vanished back into the gloom.

"You've pissed off the very stones."

He snarls with fury and lashes out at the air, tearing at cold nothingness.

"You've angered the streets themselves."

"Fight me!" he roars. "Fight me!"

"All this time I never stopped to ask ... Why did you do it?"

A glimpse, the girl, *there*, beneath the lamp post, but she is gone again, a flimsy vision sinking back into the spirit walk.

"I don't think it was for wealth, or power, or prestige – so why? What could be so important to a monster that it would tear the fabric of the city itself?"

"Little girl, little girl!" he screams. "If you're so concerned for these streets, then fight me for them!"

"Don't have to. I'm a shaman. I'm part of these streets, and they're a part of me, and when you attack them, you attack me. I'm sure there's a name for it. Something old, and deep, and full of time. I forget the details."

"I'll kill you! I'll kill you and all of yours."

"No, Mr Ruislip. You won't."

And there she is, standing where – but of course! – where she'd always been, outside the shattered glass and burning lights of Burns and Stoke, watching him, waiting.

Mr Ruislip spreads his claws, opens his jaws that can sever a head with a single snap and, with an animal scream that sets the bulbs singing in the street lamps, launches himself at her, flying through the air, trailing shredded flesh and spatters of bile.

He came to within an inch of her. Something cold and hard and unforgiving manifested in his path, knocking him off his feet and sending him crashing back. Groggy, Mr Ruislip stared at the thing that had come between him and the smell of blood.

There was nothing there.

Sharon smiled, seeing his confusion, and exhaled into the empty air.

Her breath struck something cold and unseen, and condensed at once into a shimmering cloud. The cloud spilt out and around, winding itself around the invisible nothing that had barred Mr Ruislip's way, and for a moment, that nothingness had a shape written in steam: it had arms, and legs, and a head, curved and twisting in the air, and it was . . .

"Greydawn," whispered Mr Ruislip. He crawled towards the shape even as Sharon's breath faded. "Greydawn, I have a wish. I'll pay you in blood, so much blood. I'll pay—"

There was the soft sound of crunching glass. Mr Ruislip looked past Sharon to where Dog, blood in his coat and hatred in his eyes, was walking towards him across the pavement.

"I'll pay you. I'll pay blood, anyone you want, as much as you need. I'll give you anything, everything . . ." he babbled. "Greydawn!"

"Sorry, Mr Ruislip," replied Sharon. "The city doesn't want you any more. Time to go."

Muscles bunched in Dog's back. The ground beneath his feet smoked and charred.

"Anything you want, anything you desire," whined the wendigo. "Just grant me my wish!"

Dog leapt.

It seemed to Sharon that Mr Ruislip went on screaming for a very, very long time.

Chapter 110

Mr Ruislip

Is this ... confession?

Confession is the deed, is it not? But it brings with it feelings such as ... cleanliness? Is cleanliness not a state of hygiene? Relief, is that the notion we are struggling towards here? I confess to you, and through the act of expressing my inner secrets I acquire a ... relief? From a burden? Are emotions a burden; do they have a physical weight? Frankly there is so much nonsense surrounding this ridiculous humanity business I find thoroughly distressing. Why can you creatures not find a reasonable means of expressing whatever it is you're feeling without resorting to all these unnecessary physical concepts such as *weight* and *burden* and *cleanse*. Or is it a language problem? Have you not yet developed suitable language to distinguish the physical concept of a burden from this emotional idea you carry, whatever that may be? I would have hoped for better from you, after all this time.

Well, then, my ... confession.

I am wendigo.

My ancestors once roamed the forests, now I roam your streets. I am mighty, unbound, unlimited, unstoppable and ... alone. It isn't merely that my species only mates once every sixty-three years and the rest of the time devours its own kind. It is that I move among you, a shadow in the crowd, and I am, for all my glory, unseen, unregarded, unremarked and alone.

There is no loneliness greater than being the stranger in a crowd, the one who cannot be accepted into the tribe. All I seek – all I ever sought – was to understand what it was that made your tribe, your city, what it seemed to be. What is it, this secret thing that you call humanity? Men have tried to explain it to me, but the words they use have too many meanings. Sorrow, grief, longing, happiness, loss, despair, fury, rage – why can you not apply one simple term to one simple state of being? Why must there be layers beneath layers of all these things? Why must you hide the truth of it from me? Why will you not share your secrets?

So I "confess", if that is the word you wish me to use, to my deeds. It was I who summoned Greydawn. I who ordered the rite. I who have spilt blood and I who have sought this knowledge that your entire species seems determined to deny. I would have asked her to show me the way; I would have asked her to make me human. And for this you would condemn me?

All I ever wanted was to understand.

Chapter 111

All Good Things Come to Those Who Wait

Time passed.

It passed, reflected Rhys, with a certain lethargy, as if, having kept itself busy with adventure for the last few weeks, the universe as a whole was now sitting back and reminiscing like an old man by the fireplace as the night drew in. Through the clouds the sun made a harmless golden stain on the surface of the river as Rhys crossed Southwark Bridge on his way to the evening's meeting of Magicals Anonymous, his hand swathed in a clean bandage, a new pair of shoes on his feet and in his pocket a fresh pack of tissues. He paused in the middle of the bridge to indulge in the traditional pastime of waving at the tourists on a passing boat and wondered exactly *why* Southwark Bridge had been built in the first place, connecting as it did nowhere especially exciting with nothing much in particular. On either side far more glamorous constructions across the busy waterway linked hubs of transport and glorious monuments.

He kept on walking as the sun slipped below the horizon.

The doctor had said:

"Broken fingers? Do I look like I deal in broken fingers? I'm an expert in magical conditions, dammit!"

Dr Seah could be precious about her work when she needed to be.

"But Dr Seah," he'd pleaded, "they *were* broken by a wendigo."

"And you think that affects the quality of the bone?" she barked. "If you *were* a wendigo, maybe we could talk, because you'd have that extra little joint in your hand which is surprisingly hard to set and I wouldn't trust orthopaedics with it for shit, but as it is, you're not a wendigo, you're a druid, and when I last checked, druids' hands were *boring* hands."

Then Sharon, who, to Rhys's surprise, had insisted on accompanying him to the clinic, stepped up to Dr Seah and used her not particularly impressive height to tower over the tiny doctor. Dr Seah glowered up for a second, standing her ground, then saw something in Sharon's eye that reduced the glower to a half-hearted smile of NHS-funded warmth and compassion, only slightly tainted with professional pride.

"Dr Seah," said Sharon, "Rhys here just stood up to a wendigo and all his evil minion hordes. He was stupid when I was in danger and noble when I wasn't, and now his hand hurts and he's only had some paracetamol and the anti-histamines you gave him. And I think that even if his fingers are really, really dull, you should still consider the taxpayer and that, and bloody well fix it, okay?"

Dr Seah bit her lower lip for a second, then shrugged. "Okay," she sighed. "Fuck it."

A few hours later Rhys woke from an anti-histamine-induced drowsiness to find that his fat, plastered hand already bore the message, in felt-tip, Sharon woz 'ere.

"You know," whispered Dr Seah when the druid was sleeping again, "I never really prescribed him anti-histamines."

"Seriously?" said Sharon.

"Totally! Placebo, yeah?"

"But he took the pills down there in the tunnels and went all like, mega-druid."

"Gotta think about the NHS cutbacks," muttered the medic. "'Sides, I can recognise psychosomatic shit when I see it: seven years medical training, yeah?"

When Rhys woke again, several hours later, he had expected to be alone.

Yet, oddly, he was not.

*

Rhys had not been the only visitor to Dr Seah.

"Oh my God, I love what you've done with your trolley! And the colour coding on your files is so to die for."

"Sweetheart, I'm glad you noticed! I'm a little obsessive about my files, in fact, but people don't seem to care. Now, what can I do you for?"

"Well, Dr Seah, I like, totally went and drank the wrong blood type."

"Oh no, poor lamb!"

"I know, but it was like, this mega-mega-emergency, and everyone was like 'Oh Kevin, save us!' and I was like, a vamp's gotta do what a vamp's gotta do, so I stepped up there. And I know it was stupid, but I need to know ... have I got haemophilia?"

"Sweetheart, haemophilia is a genetically transmitted disorder, and you're a vampire, so like, deal with it. We'll do a few transfusions to flush out the wrong blood type from your system ..."

"Okay, babes."

" ... and I'd like to keep you in overday for monitoring."

"Whatever you want, Dr Seah. You're like, such a professional, it's so good to be in capable hands. Tell me – where do you get your sterile wipes?"

Time passed.

A small bell in the doorway of a little French restaurant on the overly-restauranted highway of Upper Street announced the arrival of new customers a few hours before closing time. The waiter scurried to greet them, all white sleeves, only to pause by the door, struggling to make sense of what he saw.

There was a girl – that much was easy. She had black hair streaked with electric blue at the front, and carried a large bag sagging with badges. There was a man with ginger hair and a bandaged hand, and then there was ...

... it was hard to say what it was.

An impression of largeness, a sense of overwhelming mass, and yet when the waiter looked away, he realised that there was nothing to worry about really, of course not, because he *couldn't* have just seen a seven-foot troll come through his door. And frankly, what a ridiculous notion, what an absurd idea; it was just a person . . . a person whose face he couldn't quite remember, that was all.

The three sat at a small table lit by a candle stuck in a bottle, and one of the wicker chairs sagged, beneath the . . . the large individual. The waiter handed out menus and didn't fully understand why his hand shook.

"Tonight's specials," he gabbled, "are on the board for you. May I especially recommend the rabbit on a bed of black cabbage, or the swordfish in white-wine sauce?"

The man and the woman looked at their companion.

Gretel gently laid the menu down on the tabletop, careful not to break anything, and brushed the ends of her knife and fork with the rounded mass of a fingertip.

"Can I have . . . all of it?" she asked.

Time passed.

In the great turbine hall of Tate Modern a security guard wandering late at night, torch in one hand, radio in the other, thought he heard something flap up in the high, dark ceiling. He shone his torch up and for a second imagined he could see great leathery wings and hear the scrape of claw on iron. But as this seemed so unlikely, he shook his head and, cursing pigeons under his breath, continued with his patrol.

Behind him a single crumpled piece of paper drifted, swaying in its descent through the still night air.

THANK YOU FOR VISITING TATE MODERN. YOUR FEEDBACK IS IMPORTANT TO US. PLEASE RANK THE FOLLOWING ASPECTS OF YOUR VISIT FROM ONE TO FIVE, AND WRITE ANY OTHER COMMENTS IN THE SPACE BELOW.

In the "Any other comments" box, a careful, neat hand had written:

I especially enjoyed the current exhibition on street art in the 21st century, although thought that the curator's interpretation of "Two Men, One Stick" was over-laboured. The toilet facilities are clean and pleasant, but the café is, I feel, very overpriced and doesn't sell pigeon. Many apologies for the broken skylight; I have left some money and the number of a very professional glazier trained in safe working at heights by the till. Yours faithfully, Sally.

When the note was found during the morning shift, it was dismissed as something of a joke. Then again, someone *had* broken the skylight above the finance office. Again. And not from the inside.

In Coffee Unlimited, finest coffee within a good five yards, the door opened on an unexpected customer.

"Sharon!" squealed Gina, dropping her tray to run and hug the woman who stepped inside. "Babes, I've been so worried about you when you didn't come in for work, and then when you stopped answering the phone, and there was all this stuff on Facebook and—"

"Sharon?"

She turned. Mike Pentlace, erstwhile employer, iPhone still glued to his hand in a way that made Sharon wonder if, in fact, he'd had an industrial accident, stood there, flushing to the roots of his hair.

"I assume you're here to buy a coffee, yeah?" he asserted. "You can't think you've got a job here any more. Sorry, yeah, but your behaviour has been outrageous – utterly outrageous – and I always said you had a bad attitude, yeah, but now I see just how bad it was, yeah, so don't think you can come in here and just beg for your—"

"Mr Pentlace," Sharon cut in, "let me put your mind at ease. I am not here to ask for a job. In fact, asking for a job from you is probably the last thing I would ever do on the planet ever, after eating boiled cockroaches, learning to juggle a chainsaw and doggy-paddling in an oil slick.

"The thing is, Mr Pentlace sir, your shop sells the worst coffee in north London and you're the worst manager I've ever met, and even if you paid me a million quid I wouldn't wanna work for you, because a million quid isn't enough to buy comfort from all the bloody grief you give, albeit on a habitual rather than personal basis.

"And I can see – course I can see – that you're actually a frail little man with deep-seated self-confidence issues which manifest as a flagrant abuse of power, a bullying aggression and a reflexive sense of righteousness. And I really think, Mr Pentlace sir, that you should look at joining a self-help group in order to learn how to be more at one with yourself, and then maybe you can cope with being more at one with everyone else. Something like t'ai chi, perhaps. Or knitting.

"Either way, I figured you'd wanna know that I officially resign because, at the end of the day, working for you just isn't worth my time. I can do so much more. Goodbye, Mr Pentlace. I hope you can find a group willing to take you on."

So saying, Sharon walked away.

This time she remembered both to open the door and close it behind her.

Night settled over London.

One place where it didn't settle as thoroughly as it might have wanted to was the scaffold-encrusted remains of St Christopher's Hall. Lights burned through the brand-new windows, chairs scraped across the fresh plastic covering on the floor, and the smell of tea was almost as unignorable as the noise of gossiping voices from within its walls.

"So what kind of exorcism do you do, Chris?"

"I believe in the psychological approach. It seems to me that if the souls of the departed aren't moving on, then it's almost certainly because they have issues they need to resolve. The book, bell and candle business is very Middle Ages; I've studied Freud and firmly believe that his essential principles can be extended into the nether realms."

The sound of a teaspoon being rattled against a teacup bought the meeting to order. There was a scraping of chairs, a folding of wings, a relaxing of talons, a hiding of fangs, a lowering of bristles and a diminishing of intense magical auras.

The sound of a throat being cleared.

A chair pushed back.

The owner getting to her feet.

"Hi there." Sharon's voice rang out into the hall. "It's so good to see how many of you there are here tonight. Before we begin, a few quick notices. While rebuilding of the hall is going well, any contributions to the church's restoration fund are greatly appreciated, and we would ask that everyone stacks their chairs under the dust covers at the end of the session.

"If you are attending Yoga for Magicians on Tuesday evenings, can I please remind you that all clothing must be fireproofed before you are allowed to practise; and Friday night's quiz, Mystics, Mythics and

Magic, has been moved to the Ferret and Fishcake on Essex Road, owing to a clash with karaoke night at the original venue.

"Also, the Society of Friendlies will be handing out leaflets tonight. Their temporary temple will be based in the former Roger's Eel Bar until a new tenancy can be agreed elsewhere, and I'm sure we'll all want to attend their first-service drinks and nibbles. There is also a memorial service for Edna the following Friday. I know many of you have expressed a desire to contribute to this occasion, so Rhys here is going to start a kitty, and once we see how much we collect we'll buy some flowers, or if we have more than that, Rhys may look at buying something better, something that Edna would have liked. I'm sure we all miss her and remember her fondly. If there's no other business, then let me all welcome you to this meeting of Magicals Anonymous. My name's Sharon . . ."

"Hello, Sharon!"

". . . and I'm a shaman."

In the streets outside, a shadow moved across a wall and settled down beside the hunched-up shape of a man in a grubby coat sheltering from the drizzle.

"Oi oi," said the shadow.

"Wotcha," said the man.

"You gonna sit outside or you going in?"

"Don't really know what I'd say," admitted the man. "'Hello, my name's Matthew Swift. I've been dead a few years now but actually, I think I'm okay'?"

"But are you okay?" countered Sammy. "Only you look like you've been dragged through a cheese grater, and you're sitting out in the rain. I don't need to be the second greatest shaman what ever walked the bloody earth to draw a few conclusions, you know."

"Sammy . . ."

"Yeah?"

"About your people skills . . ."

"Screw 'em."

"No, but really."

"I'm a frickin' goblin!" Sammy shrieked. "Jesus, if that doesn't buy you a few perks then what's the friggin' point?!"

"Have you ever considered, though," suggested the sorcerer, "how goblins could, in fact, be *cute*?"

"Cute?" Sammy spat the word, which was promptly chased by a ball of greyish spittle.

"Well, you're small, you're occasionally furry, you've got these big eyes and a kinda button nose. If you got over the poor body hygiene and the rending of your enemy's raw flesh with your teeth, you could have serious market potential."

"Up yours, sorcerer!"

"That's what everyone says," he conceded.

They loitered, watching the lights moving within the scaffolded hall.

Swift said, "I'm in serious shit, Sammy."

"Like that's new."

"No, but I mean . . . serious shit. I've been getting lucky for a while, pulling favours, sacrificing . . . sacrificing things I shouldn't have sacrificed, things I didn't have the right to give away. Making compromises. Sooner or later, my luck had to run out."

"Still here, ain't you?"

Swift sighed, pinching the top of his nose. "That's just it," he muttered. "I'm still here by the skin of my teeth. And now . . . there's something coming, Sammy. Something . . . moving beneath the streets. I don't know what it is. I can't . . . I can't name it, can't see it. And if I can't see it I can't fight it, and that scares me.

"But we can feel it moving. There are whispers, shadows at our back, and we look over our shoulder all the time now. All the time we're on guard and we don't know what it is. I think something's coming. Coming for me. And I don't know how to stop it."

Sammy sucked a judicious lungful of air through his crooked teeth.

"Well, then," he said, "in my professional and highly trained opinion, you're kinda stuffed, ain't you?"

"Thanks."

"You gonna sit there moping or you gonna do something about it?"

Swift hesitated. Then a slow grin spread across his face. "Well," he said with a half-hearted shrug, "no harm trying, is there?"

*

Time passes.

Sharon sits in the entrance to an office.

There is a small collection of magazines on the table in front of her. They have tag lines such as:

THE PERFECT FACIAL – WHAT WORKS FOR YOU?

and:

OUR DREAM CYCLING HOLIDAY – *NIGHTMARE*.

The door to the office opens, and a woman dressed all in black, with a high collar and long sleeves, sticks her head out and beams at her.

"Hi there!" she exclaims, and her gaze is a lighthouse on a foggy night, her smile dazzling and white, her hair bright auburn and her handshake warmer than spring after a long winter. "I'm Kelly, I'm Matthew's assistant here at Harlun and Phelps? You must be Sharon, yes? I love your work, just love it, really, everything you've done, it's so marvellous – I hope you haven't been waiting long?"

"I, uh . . . no?"

"So glad, so glad," Kelly sang out, sweeping Sharon through the door and into the office beyond. It was, Sharon briefly noticed, a bombsite. Paper on the floor, paper on the desk, and paper pinned to the walls, on which more paper had been pinned bearing messages such as:

You really have to deal with this Mr Mayor!

Followed by a reply in another hand:

How about carpet-bombing?

Sat amid this scene of destruction, as best he could considering his chair was also covered in paper, was Matthew Swift, with his head buried in a report.

"Kelly!" he barked before realising that his assistant was already back in the room with Sharon herded before her.

"Oh," he added. "Yes, right, of course. This," he waved the report at the woman in black, "is a pile of horse manure and I can't be buggered, okay?"

"Absolutely, Mr Mayor. Shall I file it under M for manure or B for buggered?"

"You!"

Sharon realised that Swift's finger was directed at her. "You desperately want to have coffee, don't you?"

"Actually, I had—"

"Good! Let's get out of here."

They had coffee.

Sharon felt guilty about hers, as it was her second in an hour. But then Swift was buying, and who was she anyway to argue with the Midnight Mayor?

She sat in a padded chair which leaned too far back while being simultaneously too close to the table, and waited for Swift to collect his order from the counter. Men and women in suits flowed around them, busy busy busy at the height of the day. Sharon half-closed her eyes and whispered under her breath,

"I am beautiful, I am wonderful, I have a secret, the secret is—"

"What the hell is that?" demanded Swift, plonking himself down opposite her like a duck onto ice.

"What? What's what?"

"'I am beautiful, I am wonderful, I have a secret.' I've heard it some-where before."

"Oh," mumbled Sharon, flushing crimson. "It's uh . . . it's this secret, the secret to being confident and comfortable in yourself, I mean. It's like a life-coach thing, only you can teach yourself and that. Whenever you're worried or stressed or don't feel confident or anything, then you can say it and you'll feel, you know, better."

"Better?" queried Swift, as if this was a concept he couldn't quite handle.

"Yeah."

"Because you're . . . beautiful, wonderful and have a secret?"

"Uh . . . yeah."

"But . . . but . . . what exactly is your secret?"

"Oh that's easy. The secret is me."

A silence followed, punctuated by the sound of the Midnight Mayor slurping his coffee. "Ah," he said, when it was clear no more was going to be offered. "Well." Then, as if the words could no longer restrain themselves, "But that's total bollocks!"

"Um . . . well, it's, uh . . . it's . . . " Somehow everything Sharon wanted to say wasn't quite happening. She sat up a little straighter, surprise showing on her face. "Actually," she declared, "it really is."

"Oh good."

The Midnight Mayor cleared his throat as if he intended to project an air of authority. "So, Sharon," he ventured, "how are you?"

"What?"

"How are you? It's something polite that people are supposed to ask on this sort of occasion."

"What sort of occasion?"

"Well . . . you know, professional meetings."

"Is that what this is? A professional meeting?"

"Of course it is! I bought coffee! With money! Which I had to sign for and everything!"

A moment of sympathy passed over Sharon's features. "Actually, I've been kinda thinking, what with me being a knower of the truth and that . . . Do you *like* being Midnight Mayor?"

"I think it's a question of options," replied Swift primly. "If you're asking 'Would you rather be Midnight Mayor than, say, a smear of coagulating blood on some street corner?' well then I love it. Somehow, in all the excitement, those two seemed to be the only options. Too late to do anything about it now, anyway. Besides! We're not here to talk about me; we need to discuss Magicals Anonymous."

Sharon gave a shrug. "Okay, so, yeah, I know you've got problems with it. But before you say anything, I think you should know that we've got way more members joining now. And if you do try and shut us down, then I think there'll be letters, and maybe we'll have to get a solicitor and that, and it'd be really shit of you anyway."

"Actually—"

"And don't think you can intimidate me with this 'I'm the Midnight Mayor' crap, because I'm way past the point where that's impressive. And actually, just because you're good at fire and lightning doesn't mean you know shit about where to shoot it, so really . . ."

"What I wanted to say—"

"And Facebook is a useful tool of social media!" she insisted. "I mean, we get like, all these hits there, and so far no one's posted to say 'Whoa, you mean magic's real?' And Rhys is putting in a new spam protection system anyway, to prevent anyone who can't complete a basic TFL ward from accessing the group, and I think that'll make a massive difference and—"

"Sharon!" Swift gestured violently to get her attention. "Ms Li," he corrected himself as the shaman raised her eyebrows expectantly. "While, naturally, I think you and your support group are possibly the most whacked-out thing I've heard in a long while, and while obviously times are hard with the financial crisis being what it is, and while I really think you should consider getting beanbags, not chairs, for Gretel to sit on, because your furniture budget is just gonna soar otherwise, what I meant to say is, all things considered . . . would you like a job?"

The words took a while to sink in.

"What?"

It came out before Sharon could stop it, an involuntary splutter of incomprehension. Swift pushed his coffee aside and leaned towards Sharon. "I'm thinking of a title – something like community support worker. The salary's not great, and the hours are . . . a little unusual, and I can't promise much in the way of expenses or anything like that, though I think I can swing you something reasonably okay from the Aldermen's fund. But you can decide for yourself what it is you want to do, since, I figure, you invented the job anyway."

"I . . . I did?"

"Yup."

"You . . . want to pay me . . . to run Magicals Anonymous?"

"There might," he admitted, "be memos too."

Time passes.

The lights fade across London.

Office lights switching off on a timer; pub shutters pulled down over the last glow of tungsten. Cars parked and headlamps extinguished for the night; the grey dancing of televisions going out behind window panes; the golden glow of bedside lamps snapping out behind curtains. The great tourist lights – the orange lamps of Westminster, the purple circle of the London Eye, the green washes of the Westminster Clock Tower, the silver spires of Canada Water, the spilt colours from the bridges that stain the river washing beneath them – all fade as the night progresses. The streets fall silent, a kingdom where rats and foxes scuttle through the dark.

Here – a lonely security guard paces beside a shuttered multi-storey car park.

There – the cleaning woman in her bright blue gloves runs a vacuum cleaner across the floor of a deserted office.

Below – the railway maintenance man checks there is no power left in the track before stepping into the waiting maw of the Tube's coal-black tunnels.

The dead-shift nurses pace through the silent wards of the hospital, clipboards in hand, and struggle not to sleep.

The duty fireman, left awake in the empty crew room, flicks from quiz show to porno movie in search of something to fight back the drowsiness that no amount of caffeine will prevent.

A lorry rattles across the empty space of Waterloo Bridge.

A woman pulls off the heels that she has worn for eight hours continuously at an utterly worthless party and steps barefoot onto the ground, sighing with relief as her ankles relax and her toes curl against the cool wet paving stones.

A night-bus driver accelerates into fifth gear down Oxford Street, tearing past the empty stops, and whoops in triumph as he jumps the red light and passes forty miles an hour at the top of Dean Street, honking his horn at the sleeping silence.

Sharon Li walks alone.

She walks the ordinary walk, the tired-man's shuffle, the walk of 4 a.m. and a long journey home, of a mind that has thought too long and too hard, and now can't remember how to think at all. Easily – so easily – she could walk the spirit walk and drift through the time and shadows of the city, tangling her toes in the bones of the dead and listening to the stories spat out with the chewing gum stuck to every stone beneath her feet. Easily too she could walk the dream walk, tangling her mind in the thoughts of others, riding the great snore of the sleeping city, the flashing white coat of Dez at her side, her spirit guide, lighting the way. Easy to fade, easy to turn invisible, easy to become a part of the city.

She doesn't.

She walks down the middle of a street where, by day, there would be traffic, hopping from yellow line to yellow line, and stretches out her hands to catch at the cold night air.

She feels the breeze stir against her palm and wonders if it is possible to catch a fistful of it and carry it home like a souvenir from the beach, then shakes her head and realises she is tired – too tired. She thinks she hears something scuttle in the dark, and pauses, one foot poised above the next yellow line.

A snuffle in the dark.

A pumping of lungs.

A scratching of claws.

A grumbling of great, monstrous, blood-washed flesh.

Something cool brushes the palm of her hand. It has no shape, nor weight, nor form, nor visible nature; it cannot be called any thing by the normal rules of reality. But Sharon smiles as it passes by, stirring the leaves in the trees overhead as it moves, tumbling yesterday's rubbish along the surface of the street beside her, rippling across the waters of the puddles.

It speaks, this nothing, as it moves, and though it has no voice to frame the words, it whispers in her ear:

Do not be afraid.

I am with you.

extras

extras

about the author

Kate Griffin is the name under which Carnegie Medal-nominated author Catherine Webb writes fantasy novels for adults. An acclaimed author of young adult books under her own name, Catherine's amazing debut, *Mirror Dreams*, was written when she was only fourteen years old, and garnered comparisons with Terry Pratchett and Philip Pullman. She read History at the London School of Economics, and studied at RADA.

Find out more about Kate Griffin and other Orbit authors by registering for the free monthly newsletter at www.orbitbooks.net

if you enjoyed
STRAY SOULS

look out for

THE TROUPE

by

Robert Jackson Bennett

Chapter 1

A Departure

Friday mornings at Otterman's Vaudeville Theater generally had a very relaxed pace to them, and so far this one was no exception. Four acts in the bill would be moving on to other theaters over the weekend, and four more would be coming in to take their place, among them Gretta Mayfield, minor star of the Chicago opera. The general atmosphere among the musicians was one of carefree satisfaction, as all of the acts had gone well and the next serious rehearsals were an entire weekend away. Which, to the overworked musicians, might as well have been an eternity.

But then Tofty Thresinger, first chair house violinist and unofficial gossip maven of the theater, came sprinting into the orchestra pit with terror in his eyes. He stood there panting for a moment, hands on his knees, and picked his head up to make a ghastly announcement: "George has quit!"

"What?" said Victor, the second chair cellist. "George? *Our* George?"

"George the *pianist*?" asked Catherine, their flautist.

"The very same," said Tofty.

"What kind of quit?" asked Victor. "As in quitting the theater?"

"Yes, of course quitting the theater!" said Tofty. "What other kind of quit is there?"

"There must be some mistake," said Catherine. "Who did you hear it from?"

"From George himself!" said Tofty.

"Well, how did he phrase it?" asked Victor.

"He looked at me," said Tofty, "and he said, 'I quit.'"

Everyone stopped to consider this. There was little room for alternate interpretation in that.

"But why would he quit?" asked Catherine.

"I don't know!" cried Tofty, and he collapsed into his chair, accidentally crushing his rosin and leaving a large white stain on the seat of his pants.

The news spread quickly throughout the theater: George Carole, their most dependable house pianist and veritable wunderkind (or *enfant terrible*, depending on who you asked), was throwing in the towel without even a by-your-leave. Stagehands shook their heads in dismay. Performers immediately launched into complaints. Even the coat-check girls, usually exiled to the very periphery of theater gossip, were made aware of this ominous development.

But not everyone was shaken by this news. "Good riddance," said Chet, their bassist. "I'm tired of tolerating that little lordling, always acting as if he was better than us." But several muttered he *was* better than them. It had been seven months since the sixteen-year-old had walked through their doors on audition day and positively dumbfounded the staff with his playing. Everyone had been astonished to hear that he was not auditioning for an act, but for *house pianist*, a lowly job if ever there was one. Van Hoever, the manager of Otterman's, had questioned him extensively on this point, but George had stood firm: he was there to be house pianist at their little Ohio theater, and nothing more.

"What are we going to do now?" said Archie, their trombonist. "Like it or not, it was George who put us on the map." Which was more or less true. It was the general rule that in vaudeville, a trade filled with indignities of all kinds, no one was shat upon more than the house pianist. He accompanied nearly every act, and every ego that crossed the stage got thoroughly massaged by abusing him. If a joke went sour, it was because the pianist was too late and spoiled the delivery. If a dramatic bit was flat, it was because the pianist was too lively. If an acrobat stumbled, it was because the pianist distracted him.

But in his time at Otterman's George had accomplished the impossible: he'd given them no room for complaints. After playing through the first rehearsal he would know the act better than the actors did, which was saying something as every actor had fine-tuned their performance with almost lapidary attention. He hit every beat, wrung every laugh out of every delivery, and knew when to speed things up or slow them down. He seemed to have the uncanny ability to augment every performance he accompanied. Word spread, and many acts became more amenable to performing at Otterman's, which occupied a rather obscure spot on the Keith-Albee circuit.

Yet now he was leaving, almost as abruptly as he'd arrived. It put them in a pretty tight spot: Gretta Mayfield was coming specifically because she had agreed to have George accompany her, but that was just the start; after a moment's review, the orchestra came to the horrifying conclusion that at least a quarter of the acts of the next week had agreed to visit Otterman's only because George met their high standards.

After Tofty frantically spread the word, wild speculation followed. Did anyone know the reason behind the departure? Could anyone guess? Perhaps, Victor suggested, he was finally going to tour with an act of his own, or maybe he was heading straight to the legitimate (meaning well-respected orchestras and symphonies, rather than lowly vaudeville). But Tofty said he'd heard nothing about George making those sorts of movements, and he would know, wouldn't he?

Maybe he'd been lured away by another theater, someone said. But Van Hoever would definitely ante up to keep George, Catherine pointed out, and the only theaters that could outbid him were very far away, and would never send scouts out here. What could the boy possibly be thinking? They wasted the whole morning debating the subject, yet they never reached an answer.

George did his best to ignore the flurry of gossip as he gathered his belongings, but it was difficult; as he'd not yet made a formal resignation to Van Hoever, everyone tried to find the reason behind his desertion in hopes that they could fix it.

"Is it the money, George?" Tofty asked. "Did Van Hoever turn you down for a raise?"

No, answered George. No, it was not the money.

"Is it the acts, George?" asked Archie. "Did one of the acts insult you? You've got to ignore those bastards, Georgie, they can be so ornery sometimes!"

But George scoffed haughtily, and said that no, it was certainly not any of the acts. The other musicians cursed Archie for such a silly question; of *course* it wasn't any of the performers, as George never gave them reason for objection.

"Is it a girl, George?" asked Victor. "You can tell me. I can keep a secret. It's a girl, isn't it?"

At this George turned a brilliant red, and sputtered angrily for a moment. No, he eventually said. No, thank you very much, it was not a girl.

"Then was it something Tofty said?" asked Catherine. "After

all, he was who you were talking to just before you said you quit."

"What!" cried Tofty. "What a horrendous accusation! We were only talking theater hearsay, I tell you! I simply mentioned how Van Hoever was angry that an act had skipped us on the circuit!"

At that, George's face became strangely still. He stopped gathering up his sheet music and looked away for a minute. But finally he said no, Tofty had nothing to do with it. "And would you all please leave me alone?" he asked. "This decision has nothing to do with you, and furthermore there's nothing that will change it."

The other musicians, seeing how serious he was, grumbled and shuffled away. Once they were gone George scratched his head and tried not to smile. Despite his solemn demeanor, he had enjoyed watching them clamor to please him.

The smile vanished as he returned to his packing and the decision he'd made. The orchestra did not matter, he told himself. Otterman's did not matter anymore. The only thing that mattered now was getting out the door and on the road as soon as possible.

After he'd collected the last of his belongings he headed for his final stop: Van Hoever's office. The theater manager had surely heard the news and was in the midst of composing a fine tirade, but if George left now he'd be denied payment for this week's worth of performances. And though he could not predict the consequences of what he was about to do, he thought it wise to have every penny possible.

But when George arrived at the office hall there was someone seated in the row of chairs before Van Hoever's door: a short, elderly woman who watched him with a sharp eye as if she'd been expecting him. Her wrists and hands were wrapped tight in cloth, and a poorly rolled cigarette was bleeding smoke from between two of her fingers. "Leaving without a goodbye?" she asked him.

George smiled a little. "Ah," he said. "Hello, Irina."

The old woman did not answer, but patted the empty chair next to her. George walked over, but did not sit. The old woman raised her eyebrows at him. "Too good to give me company?"

"This is an ambush, isn't it?" he asked. "You've been waiting for me."

"You assume the whole world waits on you. Come. Sit."

"I'll give you company," he said. "But I won't sit. I know you're looking to delay me, Irina."

"So impatient, child," she said. "I'm just an old woman who wishes to talk."

"To talk about why I'm leaving."

"No. To give you advice."

"I don't need advice. And I'm not changing my mind."

"I'm not telling you to. I just wish to make a suggestion before you go."

George gave her the sort of impatient look that can only be given by the very young to the very old, and raised a fist to knock at Van Hoever's door. But before his knuckles ever made contact, the old woman's cloth-bound hand snatched his fist out of the air. "You will want to listen to me, George," she said. "Because I know *exactly* why you're leaving."

George looked her over. If it had been anyone else, he would not have given them another minute, but Irina was one of the few people at Otterman's who could command George's attention. She was the orchestra's only violist, and like most violists (who after all devoted their lives to an ignored or much-ridiculed instrument) she had acquired a very sour sort of wisdom. It was also rumored she'd witnessed terrible hardships in her home in Russia before fleeing to America, and this, combined with her great age, gave her a mysterious esteem at Otterman's.

"Do you think so?" asked George.

"I do," she said. "And aren't you interested to hear my guess?" She released him and patted the seat next to her once more. George sighed, but reluctantly sat.

"What is it?" he asked.

"Why such a hurry, child?" Irina said. "It seems like it was only yesterday that you arrived."

"It wasn't," said George. "I've spent over half a year here, which is far too long."

"Too long for what?" asked Irina.

George did not answer. Irina smiled, amused by this terribly serious boy in his too-large suit. "Time moves so much slower for the young. To me, it is as a day. I can still remember when you walked through that door, child, and three things struck me about you." She held up three spindly fingers. "First was that you were talented. *Very* talented. But you knew that, didn't you? You probably knew it too well, for such a little boy."

"A *little* boy?" asked George.

"Oh, yes. A naïve little lamb, really."

"Maybe then," said George, his nose high in the air. He reached into his pocket, took out a pouch of tobacco, and began rolling his own cigarette. He made sure to appear as nonchalant as possible, having practiced the motions at home in the mirror.

"If you say so," said Irina. One finger curled down, leaving two standing. "Second was that you were proud, and reckless. This did not surprise me. I've seen it in many young performers. And I've seen many throw careers away as a result. Much like you're probably doing now."

George cocked an eyebrow, and lit his cigarette and puffed at it. His stomach spasmed as he tried to suppress a cough.

Irina wrinkled her nose. "What is that you're smoking?"

"Some of Virginia's finest, of course," he said, though he wheezed a bit.

"That doesn't smell like anything fine at all." She took his pouch and peered into it. "I don't know what that is, but it isn't Virginia's finest."

George looked crestfallen. "It . . . it isn't?" he asked.

"No. What did you do, buy this from someone in the orchestra?"

"Well, yes, but they seemed very trustworthy!"

She shook her head. "You've been snookered, my child. This is trash. Next time go to a tobacconist, like a normal person."

George grumbled something about how it had to be a mistake, but he hurriedly put out his cigarette and began to stow the pouch away.

"Anyway," she said, "I remember one final third thing about you when you first came here." Another trembling blue finger curled down. She used the remaining one to poke him in the arm. "You did not seem all that interested in what you were playing, which was peculiar. No—what you were mostly interested in was a certain act that was traveling the circuit."

George froze where he was, slightly bent as he stuffed the tobacco pouch into his pocket. He slowly turned to look at the old woman.

"Still in a hurry, child?" asked Irina. "Or have I hit upon it?"

He did not answer.

"I see," she said. "Well, I recall you asked about this one act all the time, nearly every day. Did anyone know when this act would play here? It had played here once, hadn't it? Did they think this act would play nearby, at least? I think I can still remember the name of it . . . Ah, yes. It was the Silenus Troupe, wasn't it?"

George's face had gone very closed now. He nodded, very slightly.

"Yes," said the old woman. She began rubbing at her wrists, trying to ease her arthritis. "That was it. You wanted to know nothing but news about Silenus, asking all the time. But we would always say no, no, we don't know nothing about this act. And we didn't. He'd played here once, this Silenus, many, many months ago. The man had terribly angered Van Hoever then with his many demands, but we had not seen him since, and no one knew where he was playing next. Does any of that sound familiar to you, boy?"

George did not nod this time, but he did not need to.

"Yes," said Irina. "I think it does. And then this morning, you know, I hear news that Van Hoever is very angry. He's angry because an act has skipped us on the circuit, and is playing Parma, west of here. And the minute I hear this news about Van Hoever today, I get a second piece of news, but this one is about our young, marvelous pianist. He's *leaving*. Just suddenly decided to go. Isn't that strange? How one piece of news follows the other?"

George was silent. Irina nodded and took a long drag from her cigarette. "I wasn't terribly surprised to find that the act that's skipped us is Silenus," she said. "And unless I'm mistaken, you're going to go chasing him. Am I right?"

George cleared his throat. "Yes," he said hoarsely.

"Yes. In fact, now that I think about it, that act might be the only reason you signed on to be house pianist here. After all, you could've found somewhere better. But Silenus played here once, so perhaps he might do so again, and when he did you wished to be here to see it, no?"

George nodded.

Irina smiled, satisfied with her deductions. "The famous Silenus," she said. "I've heard many rumors about him in my day. I've heard his troupe is full of gypsies, traveled here from abroad. I've heard he tours the circuit at his choosing. That he was touring vaudeville before it was vaudeville."

"Have you heard that every hotel saves a private room for him?" asked George. "That's a popular one."

"No, I'd not heard that one. Why are you so interested in this man, I wonder?"

George thought about it. Then he slowly reached into his front pocket and pulled out a piece of paper. Though its corners were soft and blunt with age, it was very well cared for: it had been cleanly folded into quarters and tied up with string, like a precious message. George plucked at the bow and untied the string, and then, with the gravity of a priest unscrolling a holy document, he unfolded the paper.

It was—or had once been—a theater bill. Judging by the few acts printed on it and the simple, sloppy printing job, it was from a very small-time theater, one even smaller than Otterman's. But half of one page was taken up by a large, impressive illustration: though the ink had cracked and faded in parts, one could see that it depicted a short, stout man in a top hat standing in the middle of a stage, bathed in the clean illumination of the spotlight. His hands were outstretched to the audience in a pose of extreme theatricality, as if he was in the middle of telling them the most enthralling story in the world. Written across the bottom of the illustration, in a curling font that must have passed for fancy for that little theater, were three words: THE SILENUS TROUPE.

George reverently touched the illustration, as if he wished to fall inside it and hear the tale the man was telling. "I got this in my hometown," he said. "He visited there, once. But I didn't get to see." Then he looked at Irina with a strange shine in his eyes, and asked, "What do you remember from when he was here?"

"What do I remember?"

"Yes. You had to have rehearsed with him when he played here, didn't you? You must have seen his show. So what do you remember?"

"Don't you know the act yourself? Why ask me?"

But George did not answer, but only watched her closely.

She grunted. "Well. Let me think. It seems so long ago . . ." She took a contemplative puff from her cigarette. "There were four acts, I remember that. It was odd, no one travels with more than one act these days. That was what angered Van Hoever so much."

George leaned forward. "What else?"

"I remember . . . I remember there was a man with puppets, at the start. But they weren't very funny, these puppets. And then there was a dancer, and a . . . a strongwoman. Wait, no. She was another puppet, wasn't she? I think she might have been. And then there was a fourth act, and it . . . it . . . " She trailed off, confused, and she was not at all used to being confused.

"You don't remember," said George.

"I do!" said Irina. "At least, I *think* I do . . . I can remember every act I've played for, I promise, but this one . . . Maybe I'm wrong. I could've *sworn* I played for this one. But did I?"

"You did," said George.

"Oh? How are you so certain?"

"I've found other people who've seen his show, Irina," he said. "Dozens of them. And they always say the same thing. They remember a bit about the first three acts—the puppets, the dancing girl in white, and the strongwoman—but nothing about the fourth. And when they try and remember it, they always wonder if they ever saw the show at all. It's so strange. Everyone's heard of the show, and many have seen it, but no one can remember what they saw."

Irina rubbed the side of her head as if trying to massage the memory out of some crevice in her skull, but it would not come. "What are you saying?"

"I'm saying that when people go to see Silenus's show ... something happens. I'm not sure what. But they can never remember it. They can hardly describe what they've seen. It's like it happened in a dream."

"That can't be," said Irina. "It seems unlikely that a performance could do that to a person."

"And yet you can't remember it at all," said George. "No one else here can remember, either. They just know Silenus was here, but what he did up on that stage is a mystery to them, even though they played alongside it."

"And you want to witness this for yourself? Is that it?"

George hesitated. "Well. There's a bit more to it than that, of course. But yes. I want to see him."

"But why, child? What you're telling me is very curious, that I admit, but you have a very good thing going on here. You're making money. You are living by yourself, dressing yourself"—she cast a leery eye over his cream-colored suit—"with some success. It is a lot to risk."

"Why do you care? Why are you interested in me at all?"

Irina sighed. "Well. Let me just say that once, I was your age. And I was just about as talented as you were, boy. And some decisions I made were ... unwise. I paid many prices for those decisions. I am still paying them." She trailed off, rubbing the side of her neck. George did not speak; Irina very rarely spoke about her past. Finally she coughed, and said, "I would hate to see the same happen to you. You have been lucky so far, George. To abandon what you have to go chasing Silenus will test what luck you have."

"I don't need luck," said George. "As you said, I can find better places to play. Everyone says so."

"You've been coddled here," she said sternly. "You have lived with constant praise, and it's made you foolish."

George sat up straight, affronted, and carefully refolded the theater bill and put it in his pocket. "Maybe. But I'd risk everything in the world to see him, Irina. You've no idea how far I've come just to get this chance."

"And what do you expect will happen when you see this Silenus?" she asked.

George was quiet as he thought about his answer. But before he could speak, the office door was flung open and Van Hoever came stalking out.

Van Hoever came to a halt when he saw George sitting there. A cold glint came into his eye, and he said, "You."

"Me," said George mildly.

Van Hoever pointed into his office. "Inside. Now."

George stood up, gathered all of his belongings, and walked into Van Hoever's office with one last look back at Irina. She watched him go, and shook her head and said, "Still a boy. Remember that." Then the door closed behind him and she was gone.

Less than a half an hour later George walked out the theater doors and into the hostile February weather. Van Hoever's tirade had been surprisingly short; the man had been desperate to keep George on until they could find a decent replacement, and he'd been willing to pay accordingly, but George would not budge. He'd only just gotten news about Silenus's performance today, on Friday, and the man and his troupe would be leaving Parma tomorrow. This would be his only chance, and it'd be very close, as the train ride to Parma would take nearly all day.

Once he'd been paid for his final week, he returned to his lodgings, packed (which took some time, as George was quite the clotheshorse), paid the remainder of his rent, and took a streetcar to the train station. There he waited for the train, trying not to shiver in the winter air and checking the time every minute. It had been a great while since he'd felt this vulnerable. For too long he'd kept to the cloistered world of the orchestra pit, crouched in the dark before the row of footlights. But now all that was gone, and if anything happened before he made it to Parma, the months at Otterman's would have been in vain.

It wasn't until George was aboard the train and it began pulling away that he started to breathe easy. Then he began to grin in disbelief. It was really happening: after scrounging for news for over half a year, he was finally going to see the legendary Heironomo Silenus, leader of wondrous players, legendary impresario, and the most elusive and mysterious performer to ever tour the circuits. And also, perhaps most unbelievably, the man George Carole suspected to be his father.